DRAGON GIRL

The Secret Valley

Other books by Jeff Weigel

Atomic Ace and the Robot Rampage
Atomic Ace (He's Just My Dad)
Thunder from the Sea: Adventure On Board The HMS Defender

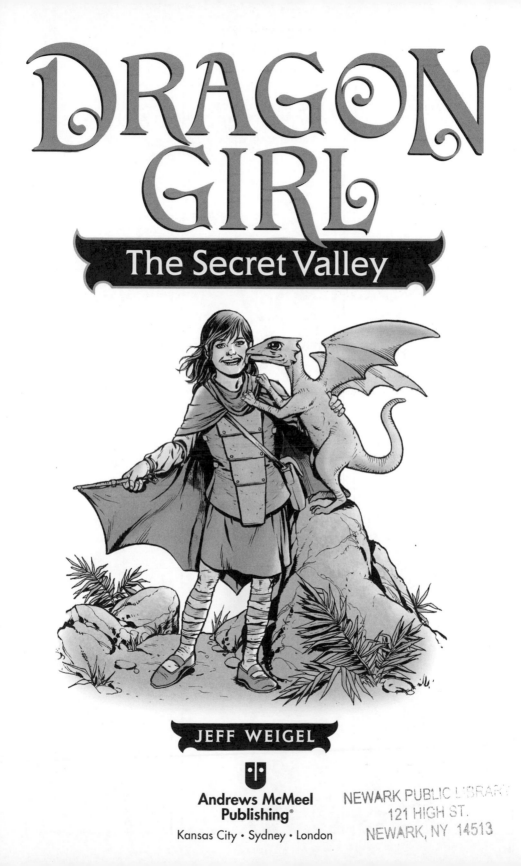

DRAGON GIRL

The Secret Valley

JEFF WEIGEL

Andrews McMeel
Publishing®

Kansas City • Sydney • London

PROLOGUE

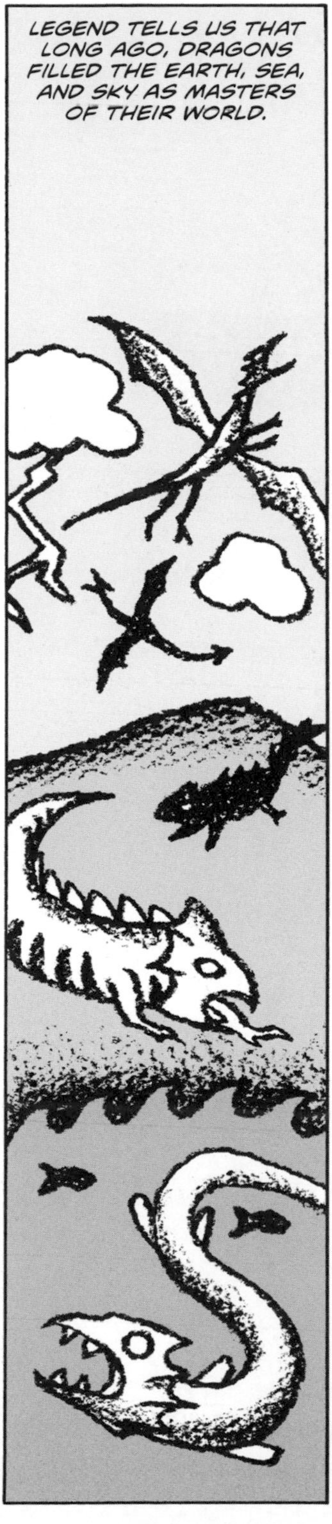
LEGEND TELLS US THAT LONG AGO, DRAGONS FILLED THE EARTH, SEA, AND SKY AS MASTERS OF THEIR WORLD.

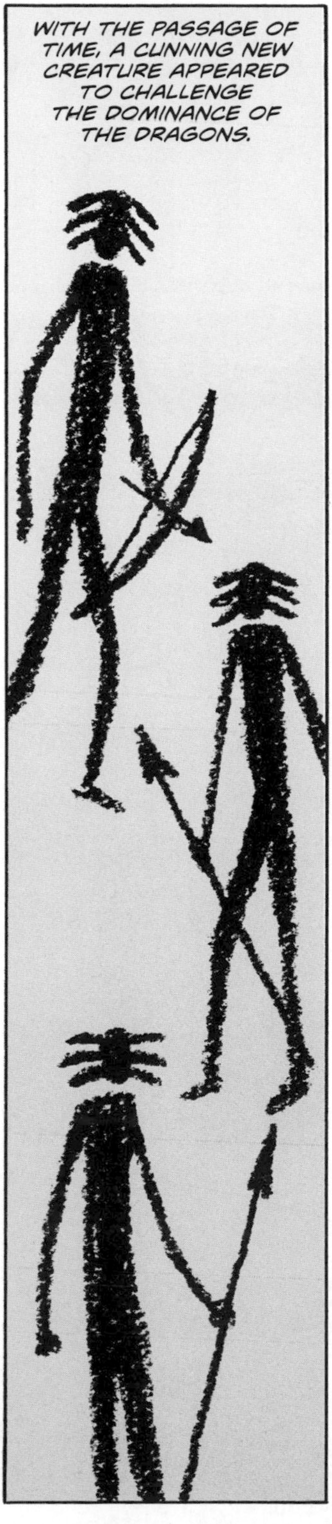
WITH THE PASSAGE OF TIME, A CUNNING NEW CREATURE APPEARED TO CHALLENGE THE DOMINANCE OF THE DRAGONS.

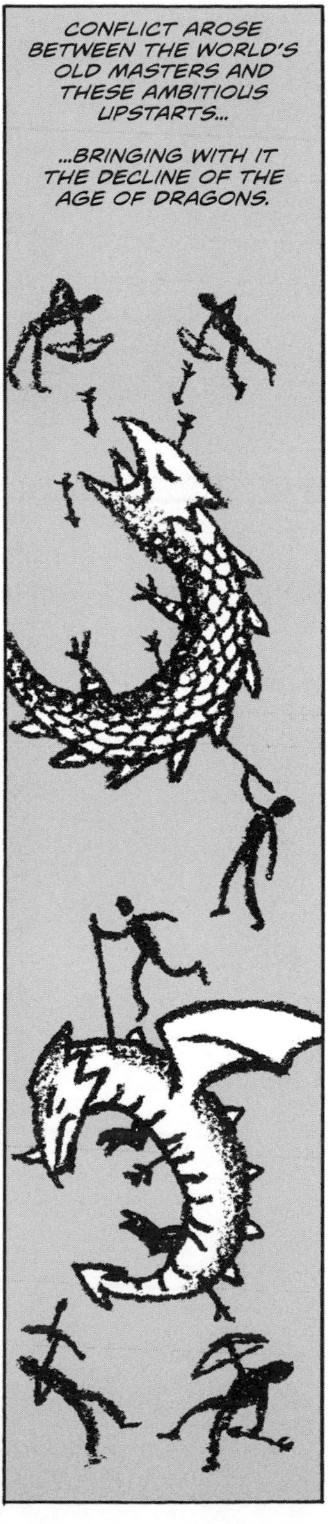
CONFLICT AROSE BETWEEN THE WORLD'S OLD MASTERS AND THESE AMBITIOUS UPSTARTS...
...BRINGING WITH IT THE DECLINE OF THE AGE OF DRAGONS.

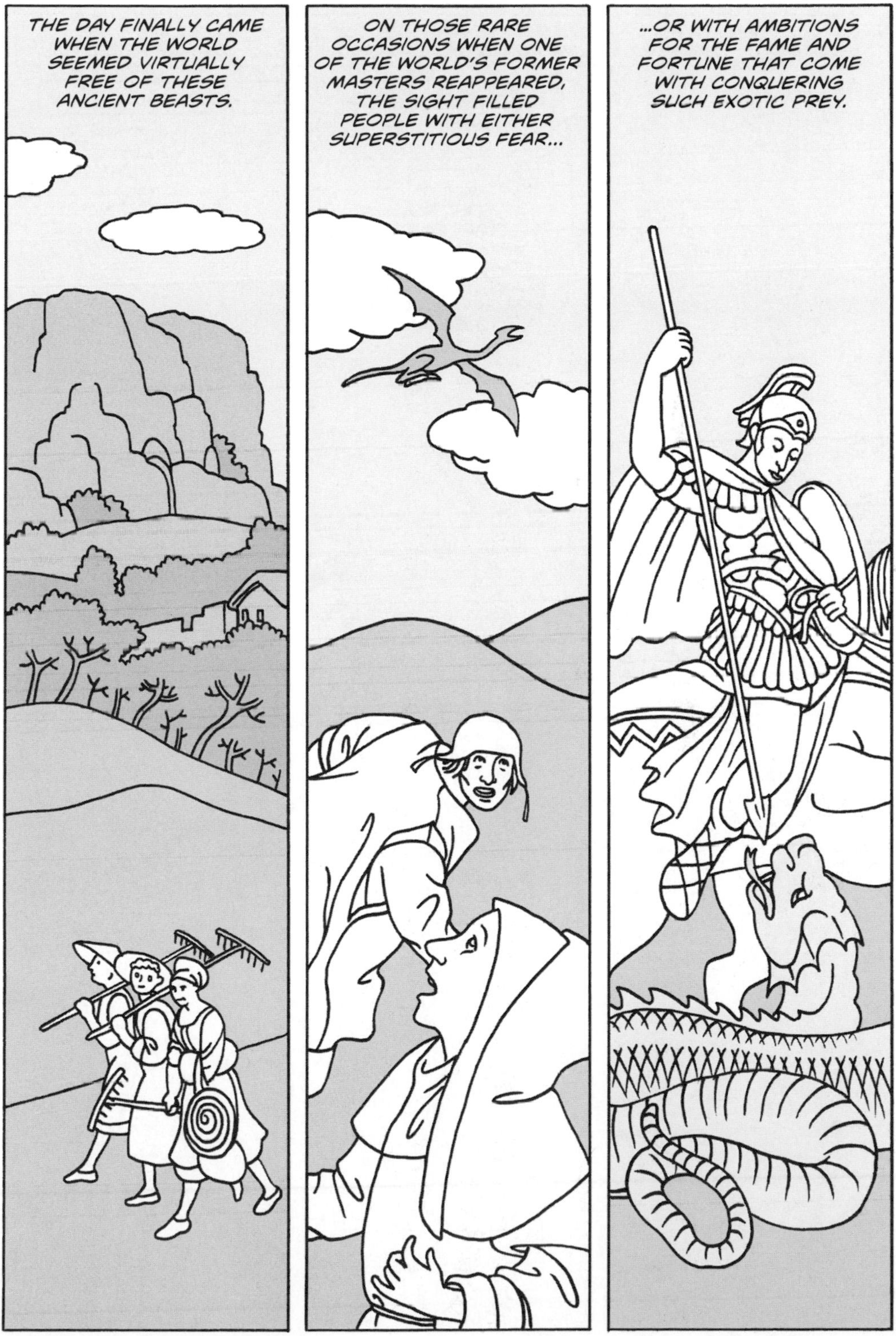
THE DAY FINALLY CAME WHEN THE WORLD SEEMED VIRTUALLY FREE OF THESE ANCIENT BEASTS.
ON THOSE RARE OCCASIONS WHEN ONE OF THE WORLD'S FORMER MASTERS REAPPEARED, THE SIGHT FILLED PEOPLE WITH EITHER SUPERSTITIOUS FEAR...
...OR WITH AMBITIONS FOR THE FAME AND FORTUNE THAT COME WITH CONQUERING SUCH EXOTIC PREY.

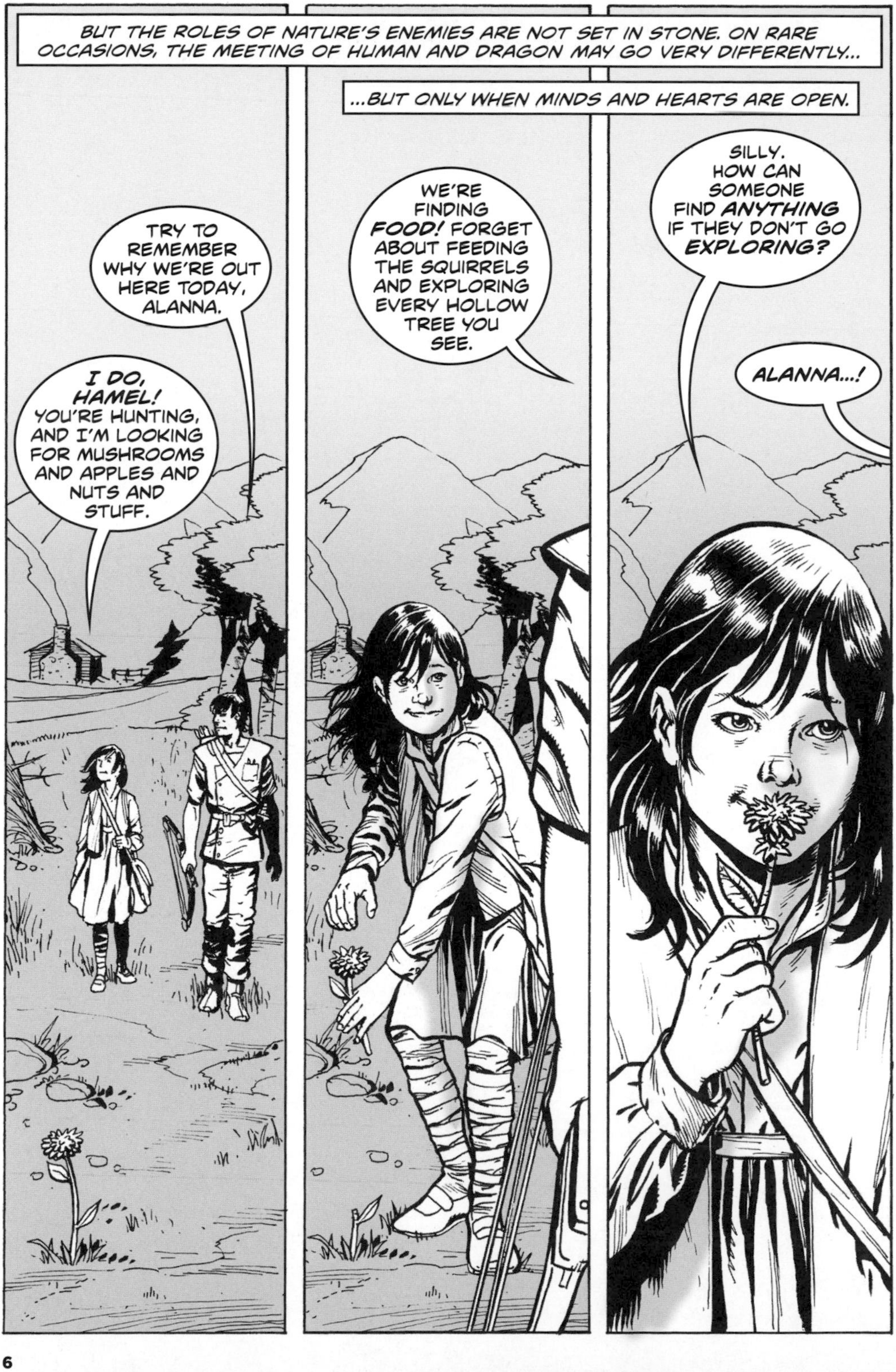
BUT THE ROLES OF NATURE'S ENEMIES ARE NOT SET IN STONE. ON RARE OCCASIONS, THE MEETING OF HUMAN AND DRAGON MAY GO VERY DIFFERENTLY...
TRY TO REMEMBER WHY WE'RE OUT HERE TODAY, ALANNA.
I DO, HAMEL! YOU'RE HUNTING, AND I'M LOOKING FOR MUSHROOMS AND APPLES AND NUTS AND STUFF.
...BUT ONLY WHEN MINDS AND HEARTS ARE OPEN.
WE'RE FINDING FOOD! FORGET ABOUT FEEDING THE SQUIRRELS AND EXPLORING EVERY HOLLOW TREE YOU SEE.
SILLY. HOW CAN SOMEONE FIND ANYTHING IF THEY DON'T GO EXPLORING?
ALANNA...!

CHAPTER ONE

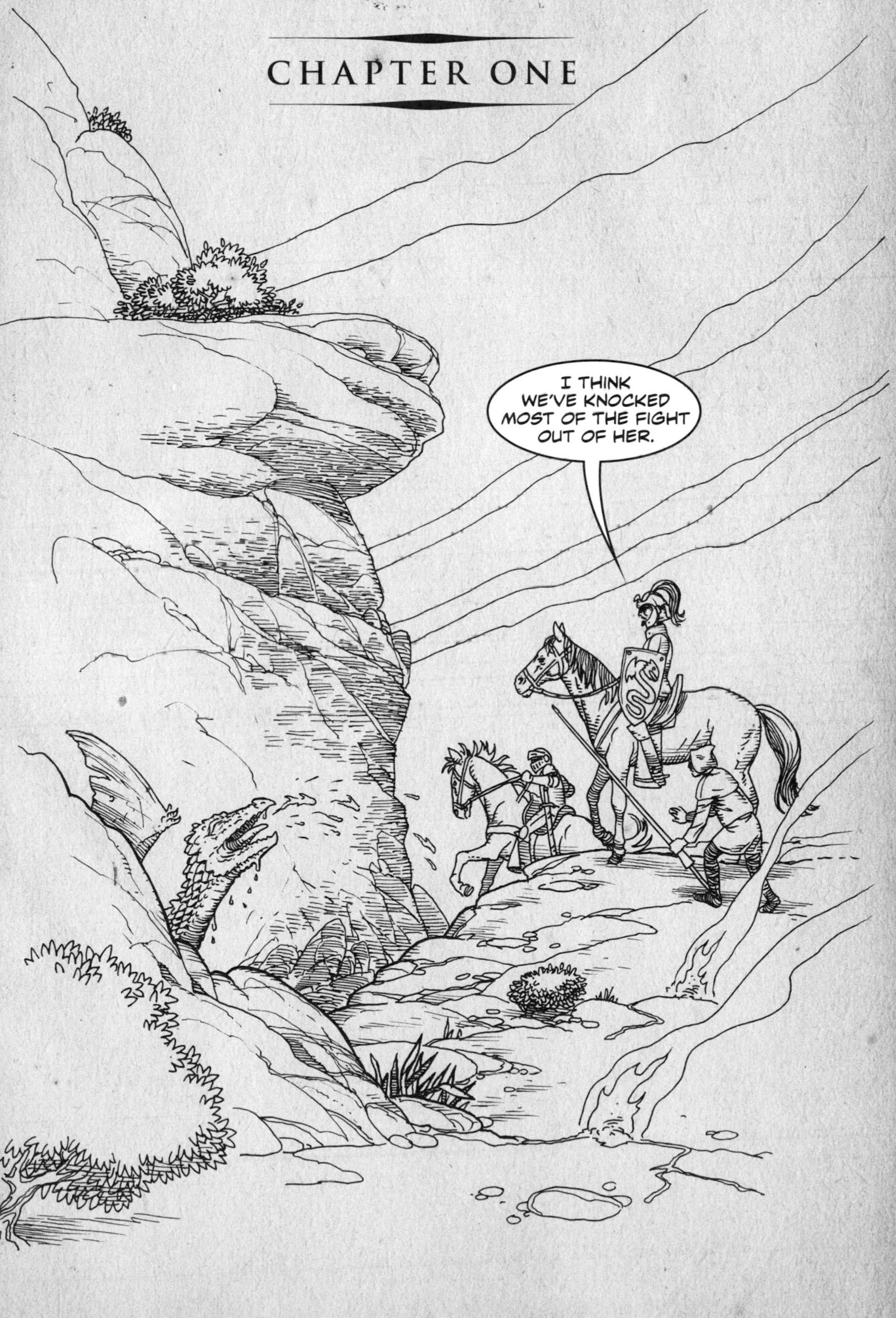
I THINK WE'VE KNOCKED MOST OF THE FIGHT OUT OF HER.

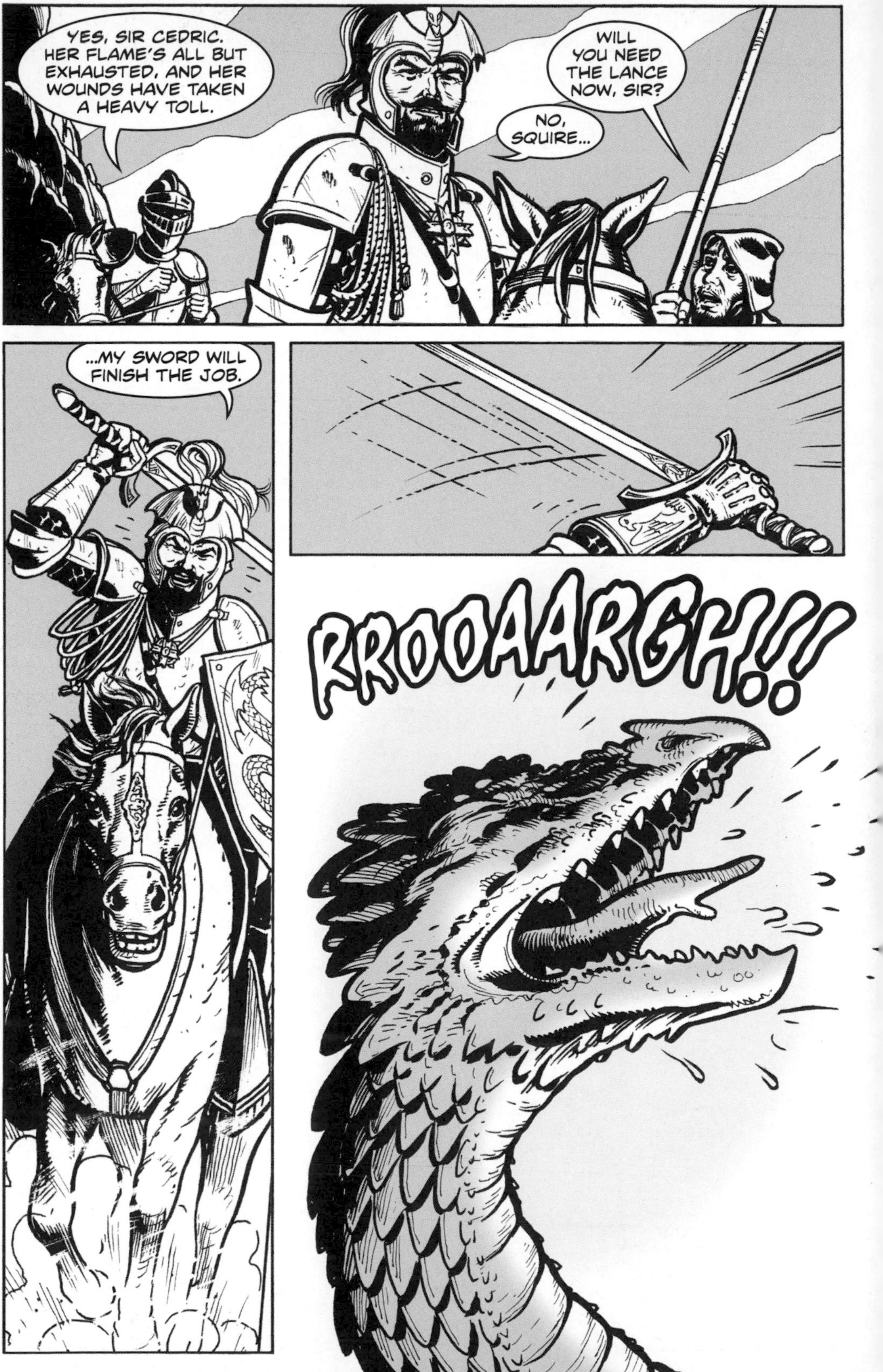
YES, SIR CEDRIC. HER FLAME'S ALL BUT EXHAUSTED, AND HER WOUNDS HAVE TAKEN A HEAVY TOLL.
WILL YOU NEED THE LANCE NOW, SIR?
NO, SQUIRE...
...MY SWORD WILL FINISH THE JOB.
RROOAARGH!!!

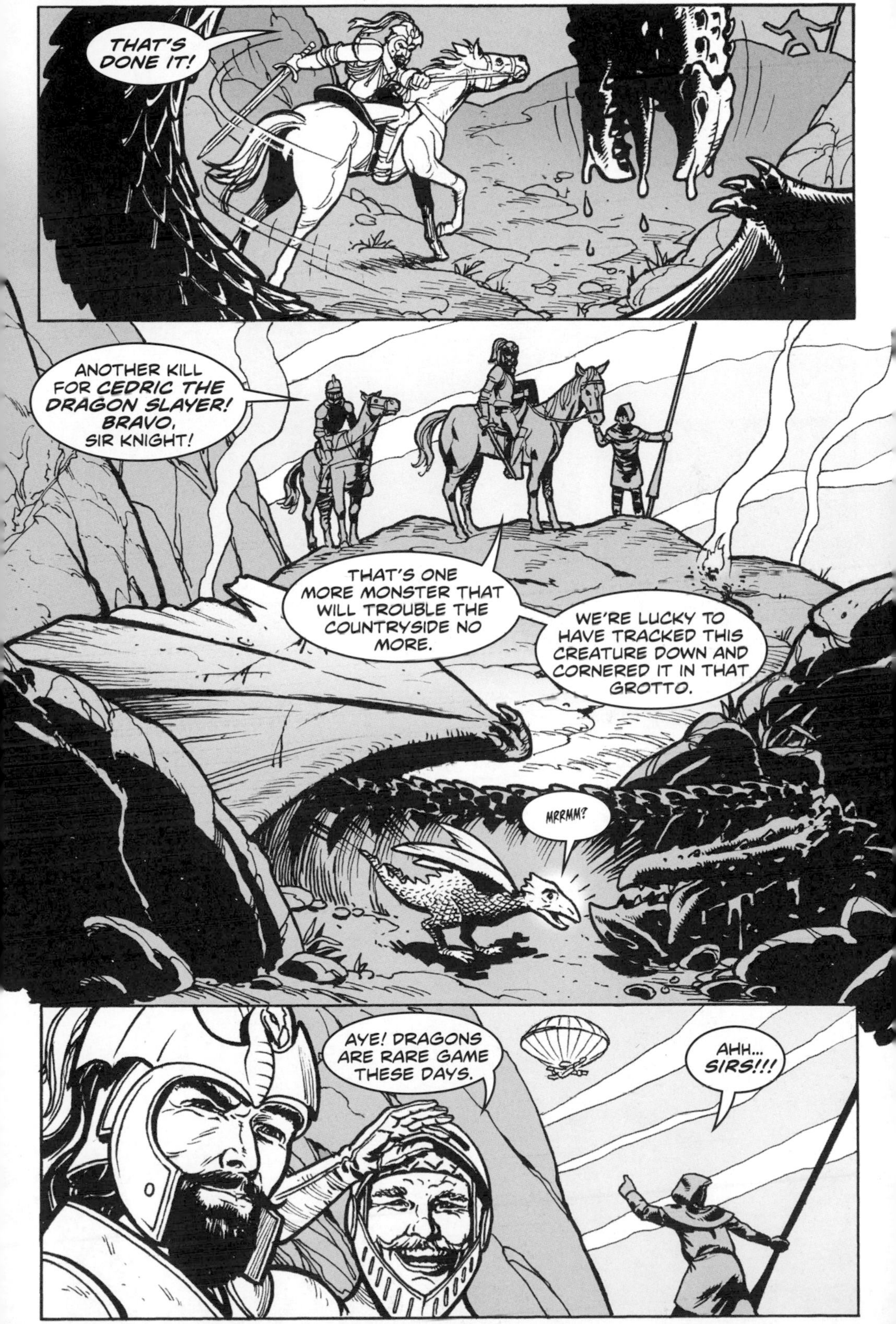
THAT'S DONE IT!
ANOTHER KILL FOR CEDRIC THE DRAGON SLAYER! BRAVO, SIR KNIGHT!
THAT'S ONE MORE MONSTER THAT WILL TROUBLE THE COUNTRYSIDE NO MORE.
WE'RE LUCKY TO HAVE TRACKED THIS CREATURE DOWN AND CORNERED IT IN THAT GROTTO.
MRRMM?
AYE! DRAGONS ARE RARE GAME THESE DAYS.
AHH... SIRS!!!

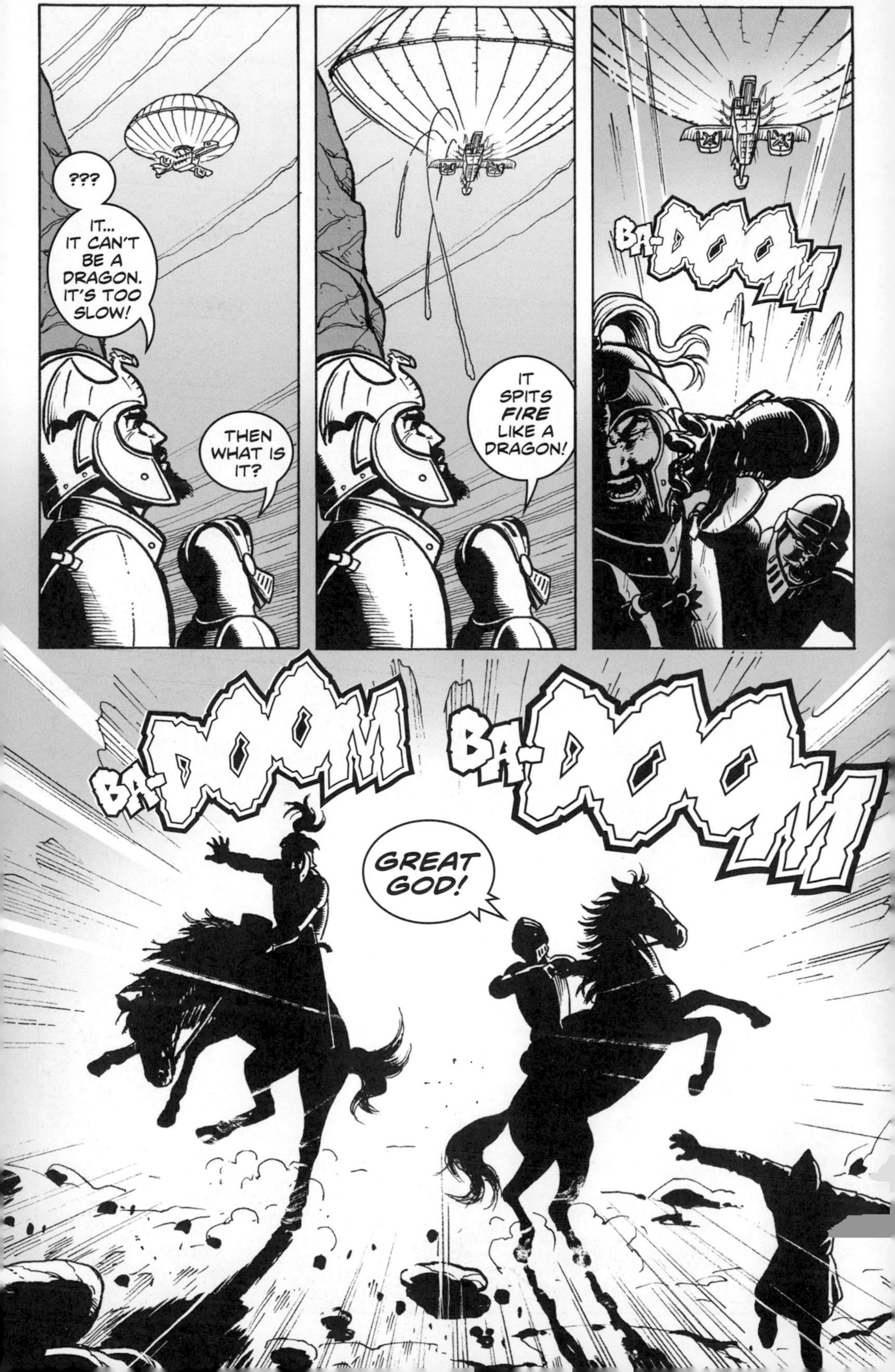

???
IT... IT CAN'T BE A DRAGON. IT'S TOO SLOW!
THEN WHAT IS IT?
IT SPITS FIRE LIKE A DRAGON!
BA-DOOM
BA-DOOM
BA-DOOM
GREAT GOD!

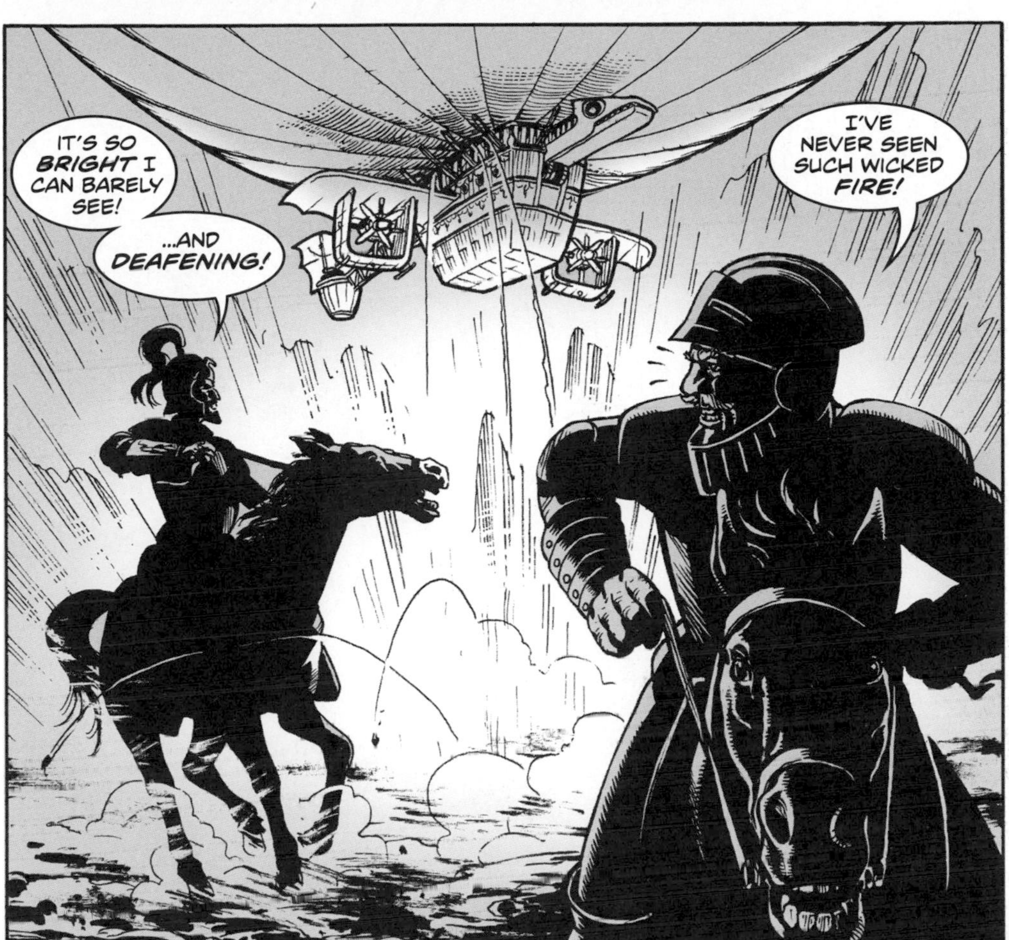
IT'S SO BRIGHT I CAN BARELY SEE!
...AND DEAFENING!
I'VE NEVER SEEN SUCH WICKED FIRE!

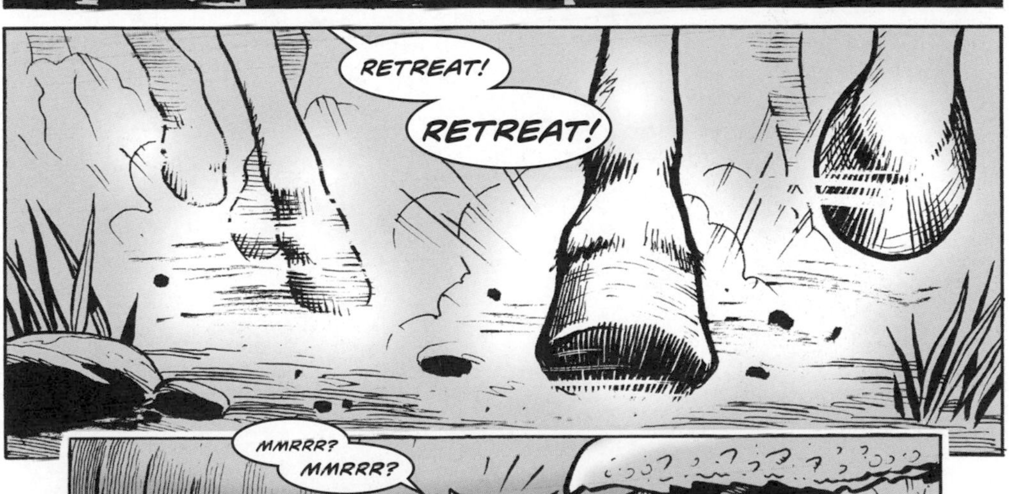
RETREAT!
RETREAT!

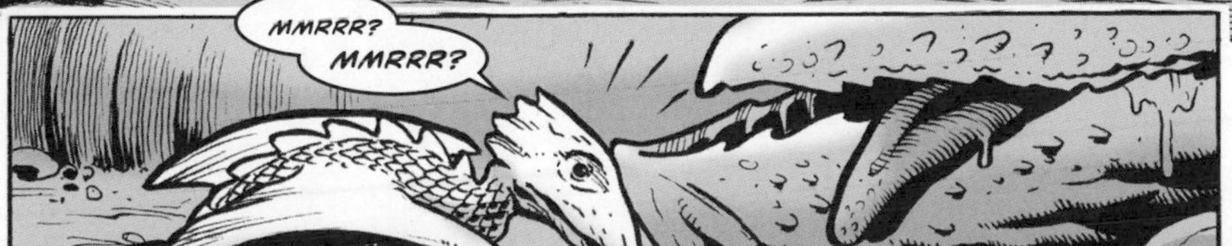
MMRRR? MMRRR?

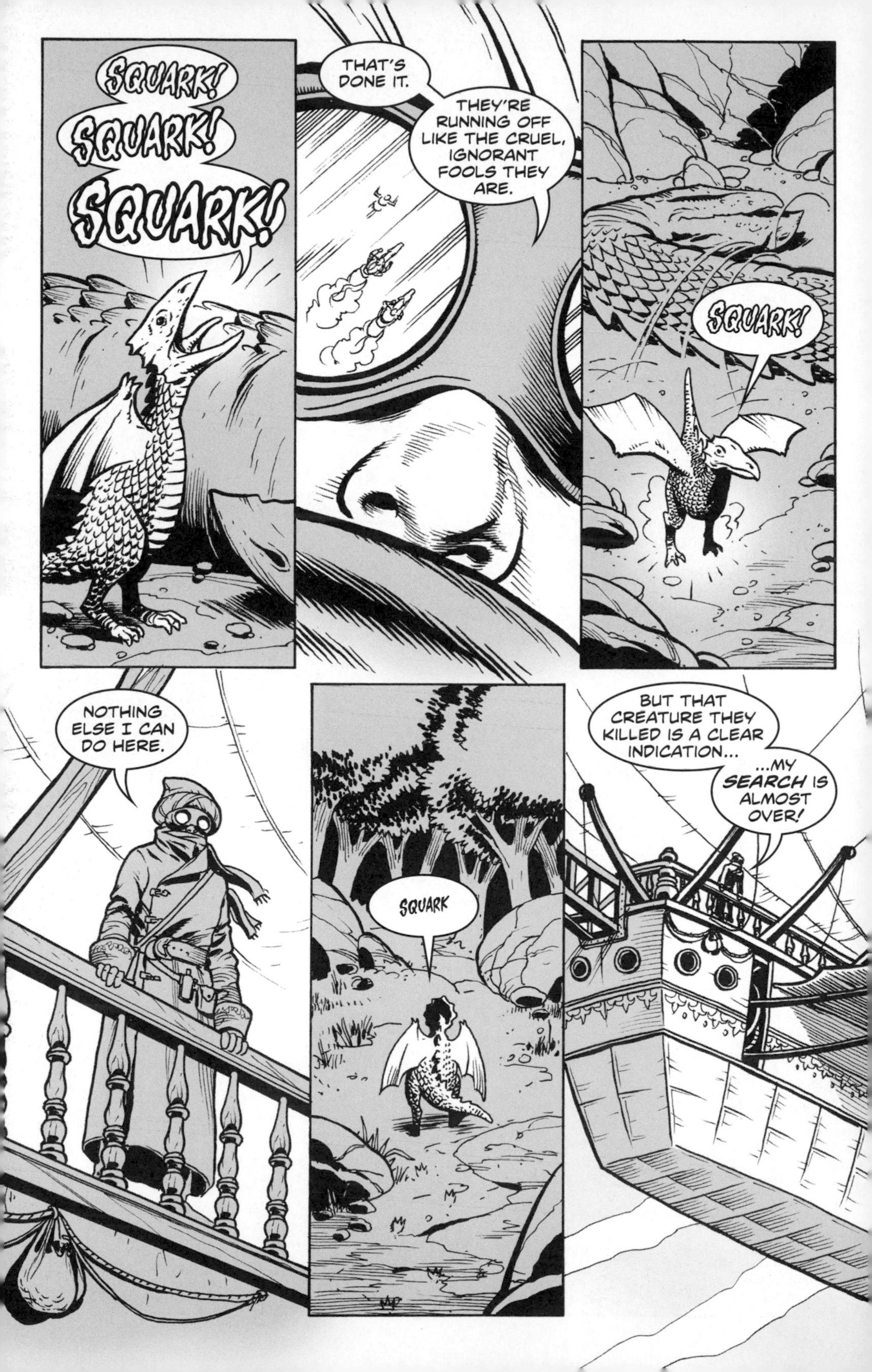
SQUARK!
SQUARK!
SQUARK!
THAT'S DONE IT.
THEY'RE RUNNING OFF LIKE THE CRUEL, IGNORANT FOOLS THEY ARE.
SQUARK!
NOTHING ELSE I CAN DO HERE.
SQUARK
BUT THAT CREATURE THEY KILLED IS A CLEAR INDICATION...
...MY SEARCH IS ALMOST OVER!

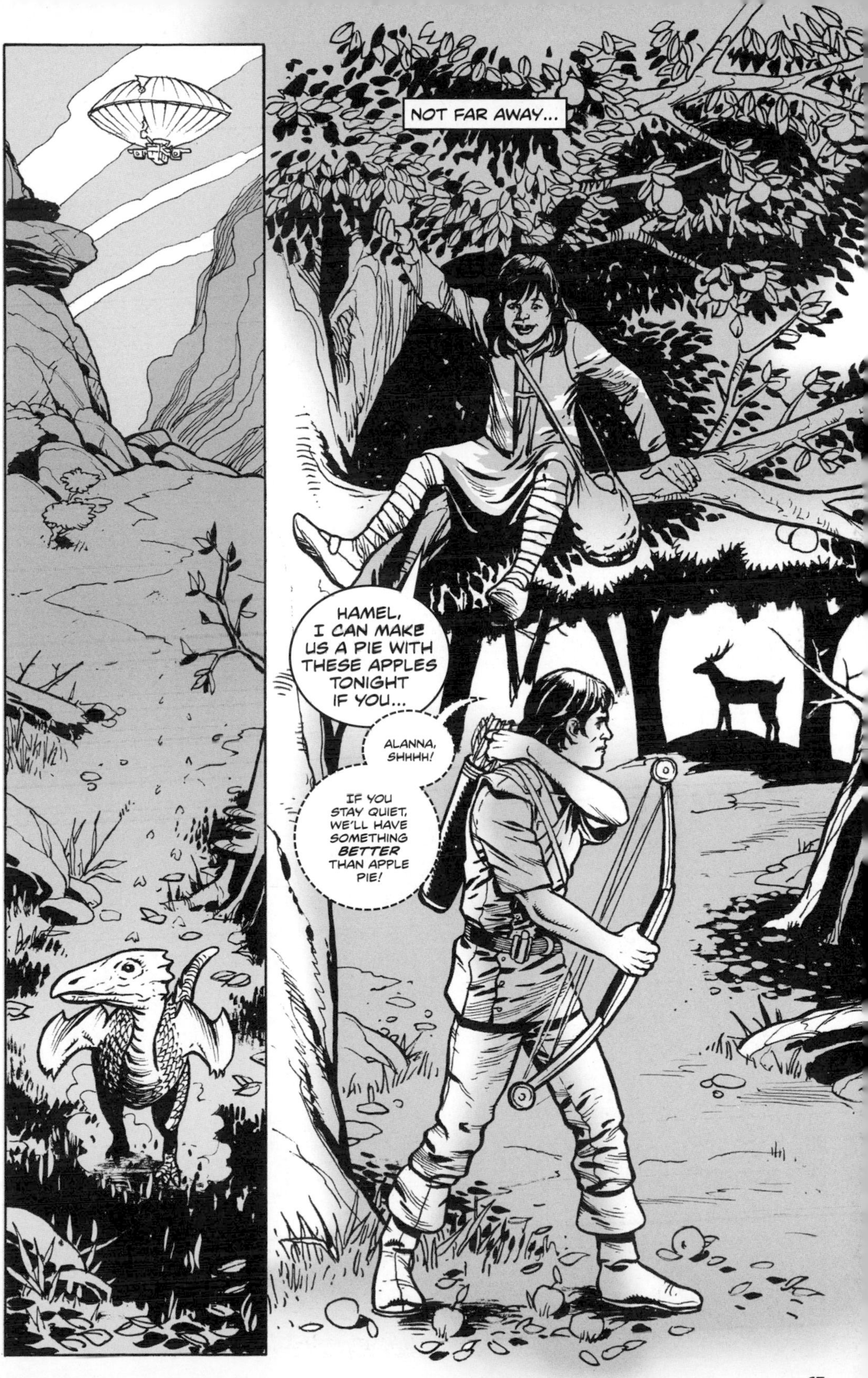
NOT FAR AWAY...
HAMEL, I CAN MAKE US A PIE WITH THESE APPLES TONIGHT IF YOU...
ALANNA, SHHHH!
IF YOU STAY QUIET, WE'LL HAVE SOMETHING *BETTER* THAN APPLE PIE!

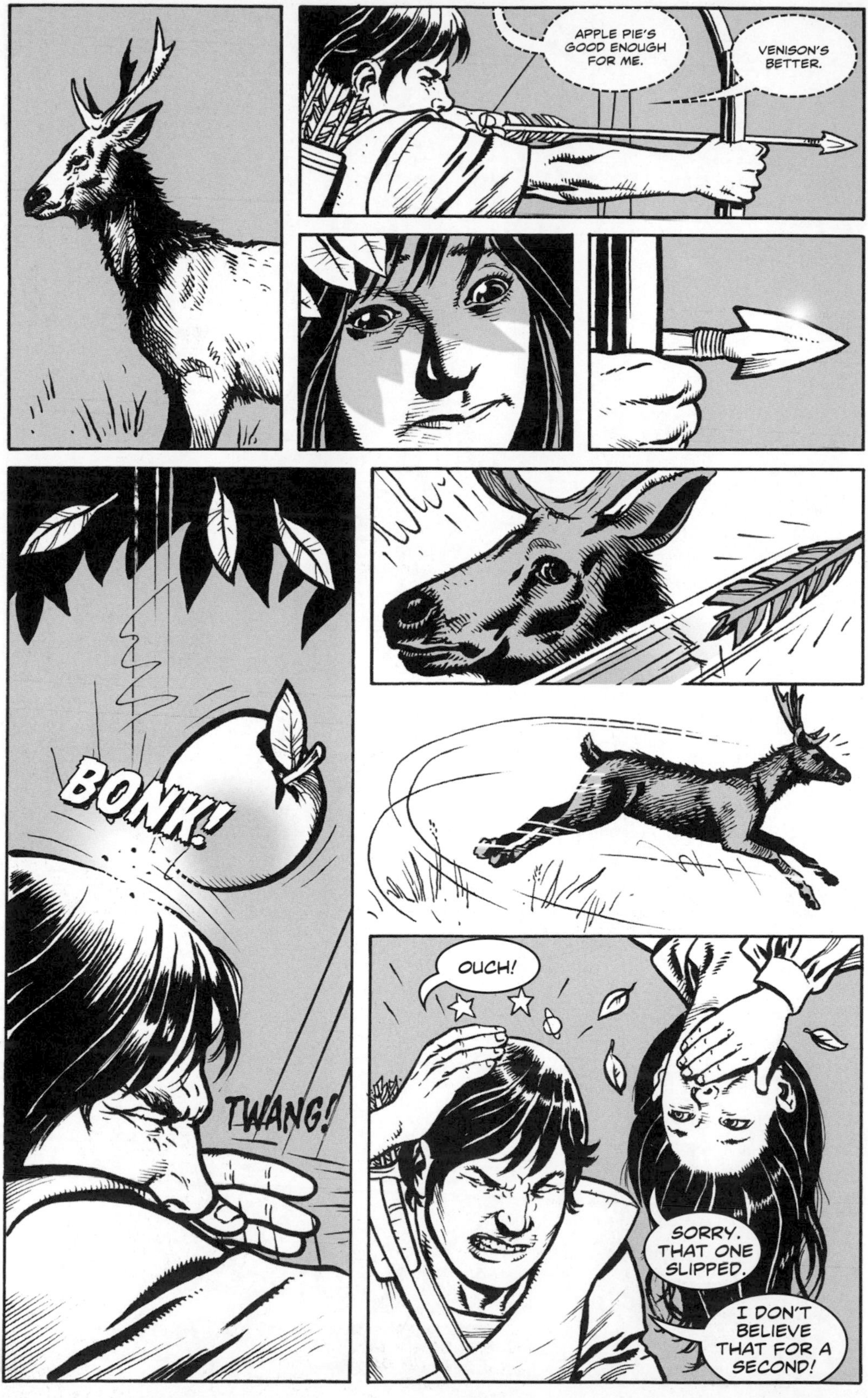
APPLE PIE'S GOOD ENOUGH FOR ME.
VENISON'S BETTER.
BONK!
TWANG!
OUCH!
SORRY. THAT ONE SLIPPED.
I DON'T BELIEVE THAT FOR A SECOND!

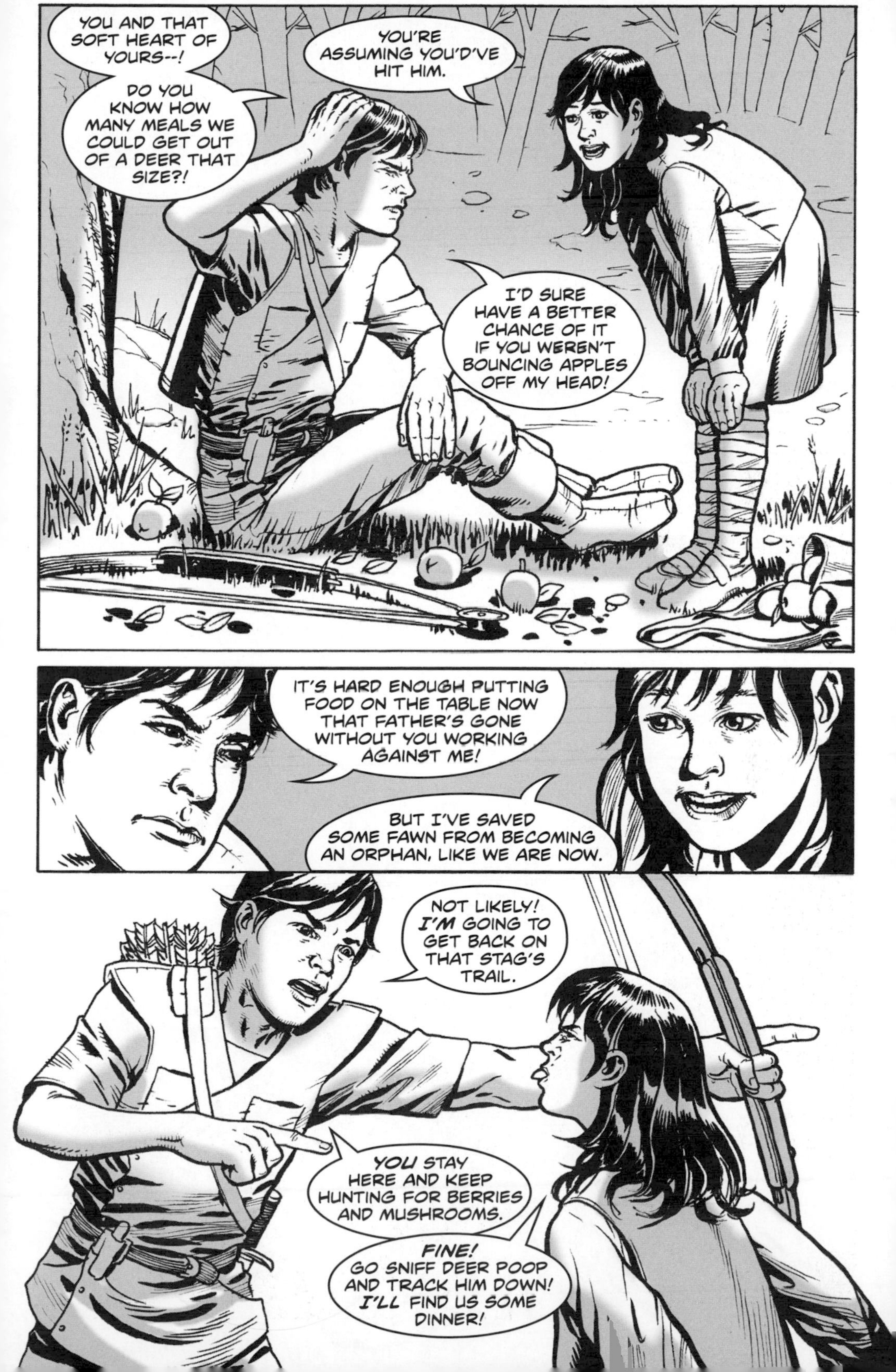
YOU AND THAT SOFT HEART OF YOURS--!
DO YOU KNOW HOW MANY MEALS WE COULD GET OUT OF A DEER THAT SIZE?!
YOU'RE ASSUMING YOU'D'VE HIT HIM.
I'D SURE HAVE A BETTER CHANCE OF IT IF YOU WEREN'T BOUNCING APPLES OFF MY HEAD!
IT'S HARD ENOUGH PUTTING FOOD ON THE TABLE NOW THAT FATHER'S GONE WITHOUT YOU WORKING AGAINST ME!
BUT I'VE SAVED SOME FAWN FROM BECOMING AN ORPHAN, LIKE WE ARE NOW.
NOT LIKELY! I'M GOING TO GET BACK ON THAT STAG'S TRAIL.
YOU STAY HERE AND KEEP HUNTING FOR BERRIES AND MUSHROOMS.
FINE! GO SNIFF DEER POOP AND TRACK HIM DOWN! I'LL FIND US SOME DINNER!

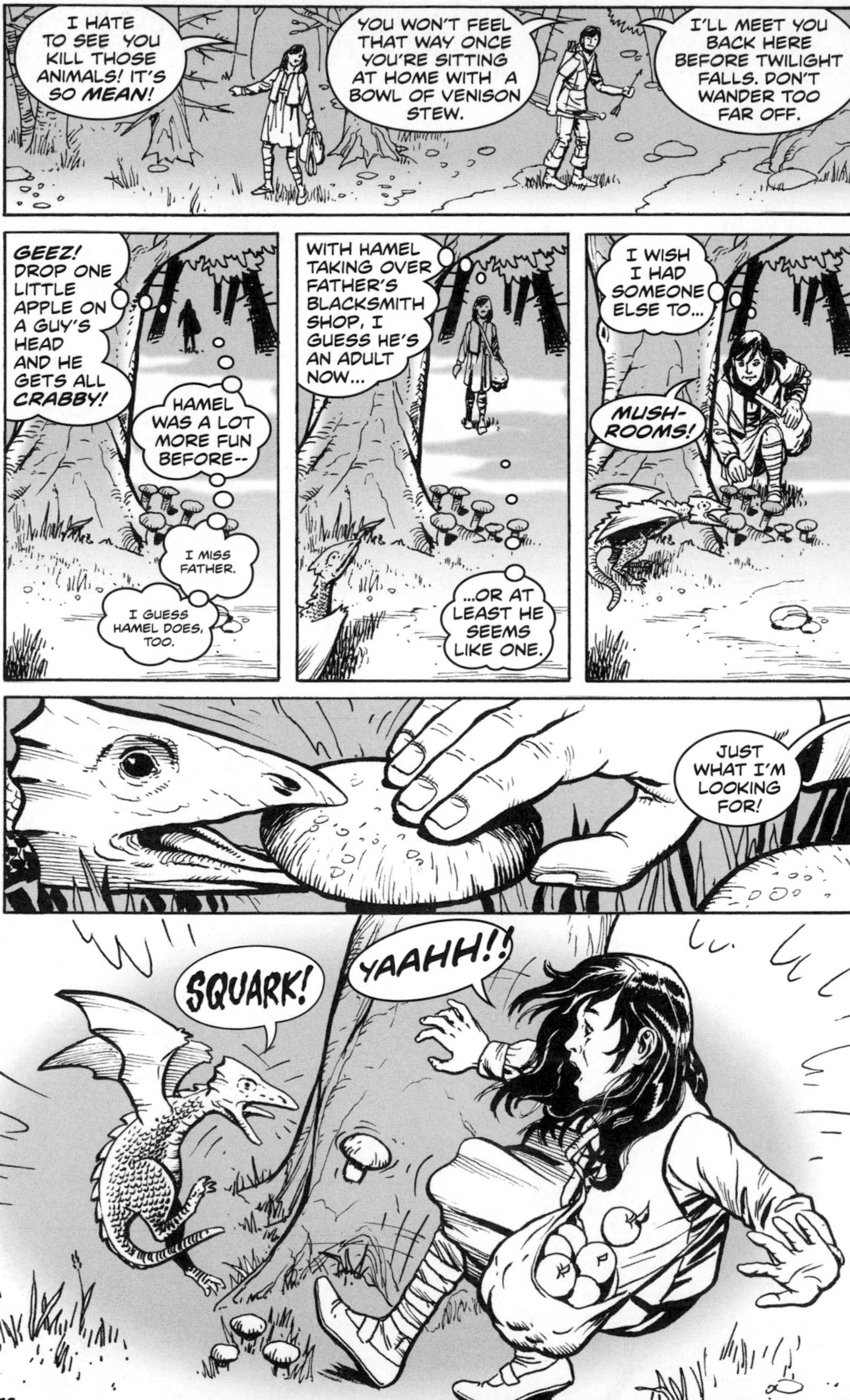

I HATE TO SEE YOU KILL THOSE ANIMALS! IT'S SO *MEAN*!
YOU WON'T FEEL THAT WAY ONCE YOU'RE SITTING AT HOME WITH A BOWL OF VENISON STEW.
I'LL MEET YOU BACK HERE BEFORE TWILIGHT FALLS. DON'T WANDER TOO FAR OFF.
GEEZ! DROP ONE LITTLE APPLE ON A GUY'S HEAD AND HE GETS ALL *CRABBY!*
HAMEL WAS A LOT MORE FUN BEFORE--
I MISS FATHER.
I GUESS HAMEL DOES, TOO.
WITH HAMEL TAKING OVER FATHER'S BLACKSMITH SHOP, I GUESS HE'S AN ADULT NOW...
...OR AT LEAST HE SEEMS LIKE ONE.
I WISH I HAD SOMEONE ELSE TO...
MUSH-ROOMS!
JUST WHAT I'M LOOKING FOR!
SQUARK!
YAAHH!!

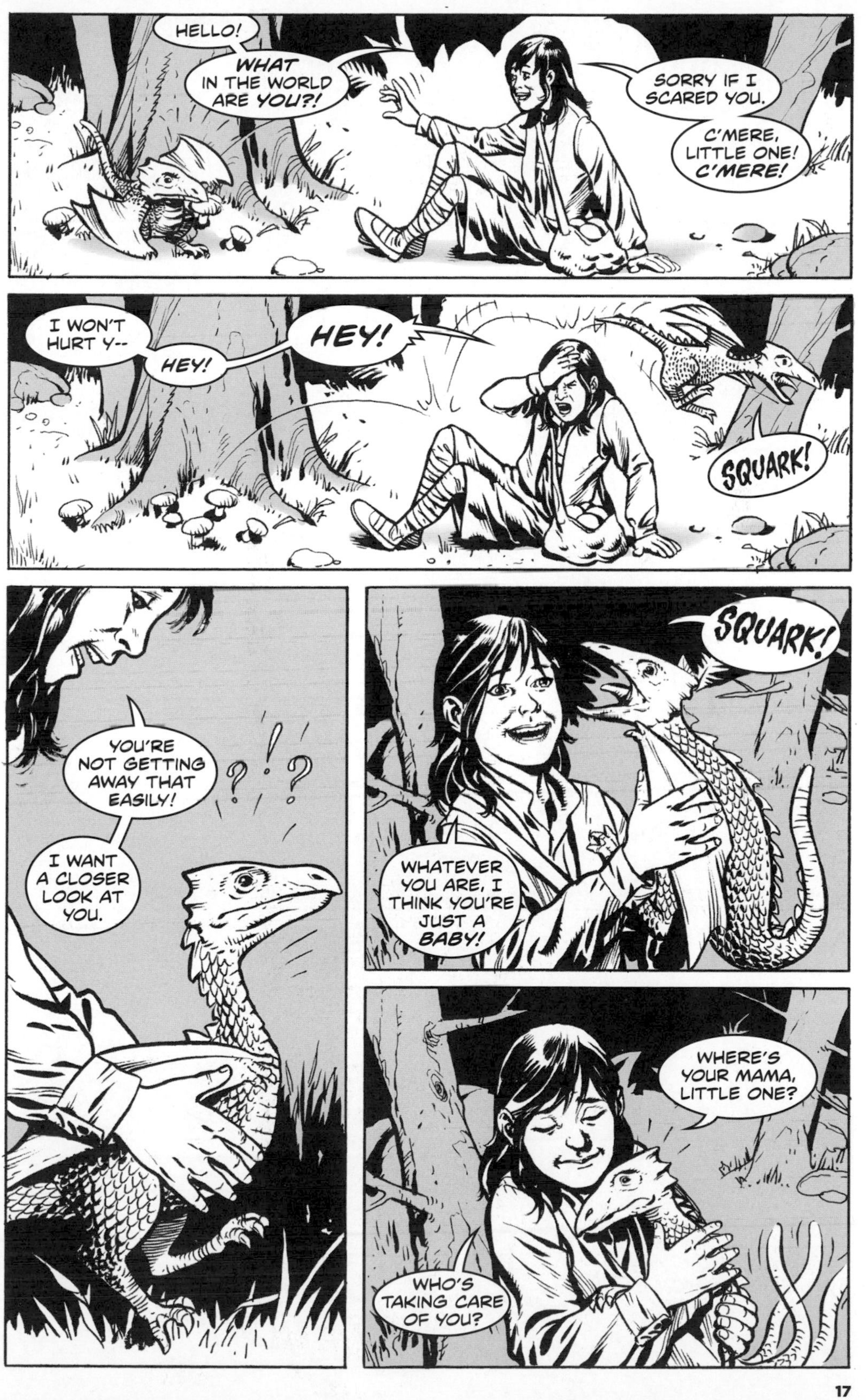
HELLO!
WHAT IN THE WORLD ARE YOU?!
SORRY IF I SCARED YOU.
C'MERE, LITTLE ONE! C'MERE!
I WON'T HURT Y--
HEY!
HEY!
SQUARK!
YOU'RE NOT GETTING AWAY THAT EASILY!
I WANT A CLOSER LOOK AT YOU.
?!?
SQUARK!
WHATEVER YOU ARE, I THINK YOU'RE JUST A BABY!
WHERE'S YOUR MAMA, LITTLE ONE?
WHO'S TAKING CARE OF YOU?

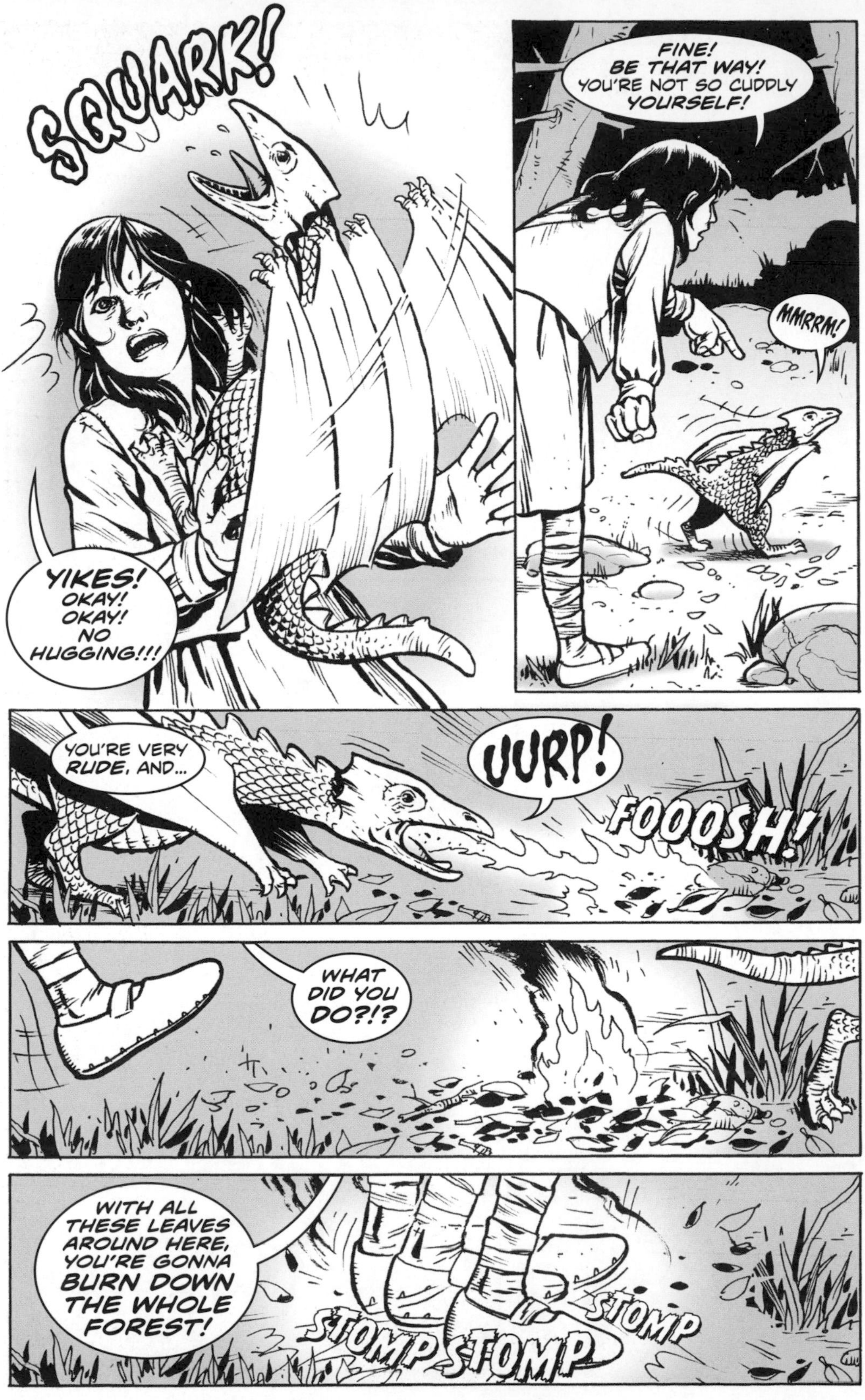
SQUARK!
YIKES! OKAY! OKAY! NO HUGGING!!!
FINE! BE THAT WAY! YOU'RE NOT SO CUDDLY YOURSELF!
MMRRM!
YOU'RE VERY RUDE, AND...
UURP!
FOOOSH!
WHAT DID YOU DO?!?
WITH ALL THESE LEAVES AROUND HERE, YOU'RE GONNA BURN DOWN THE WHOLE FOREST!
STOMP STOMP
STOMP

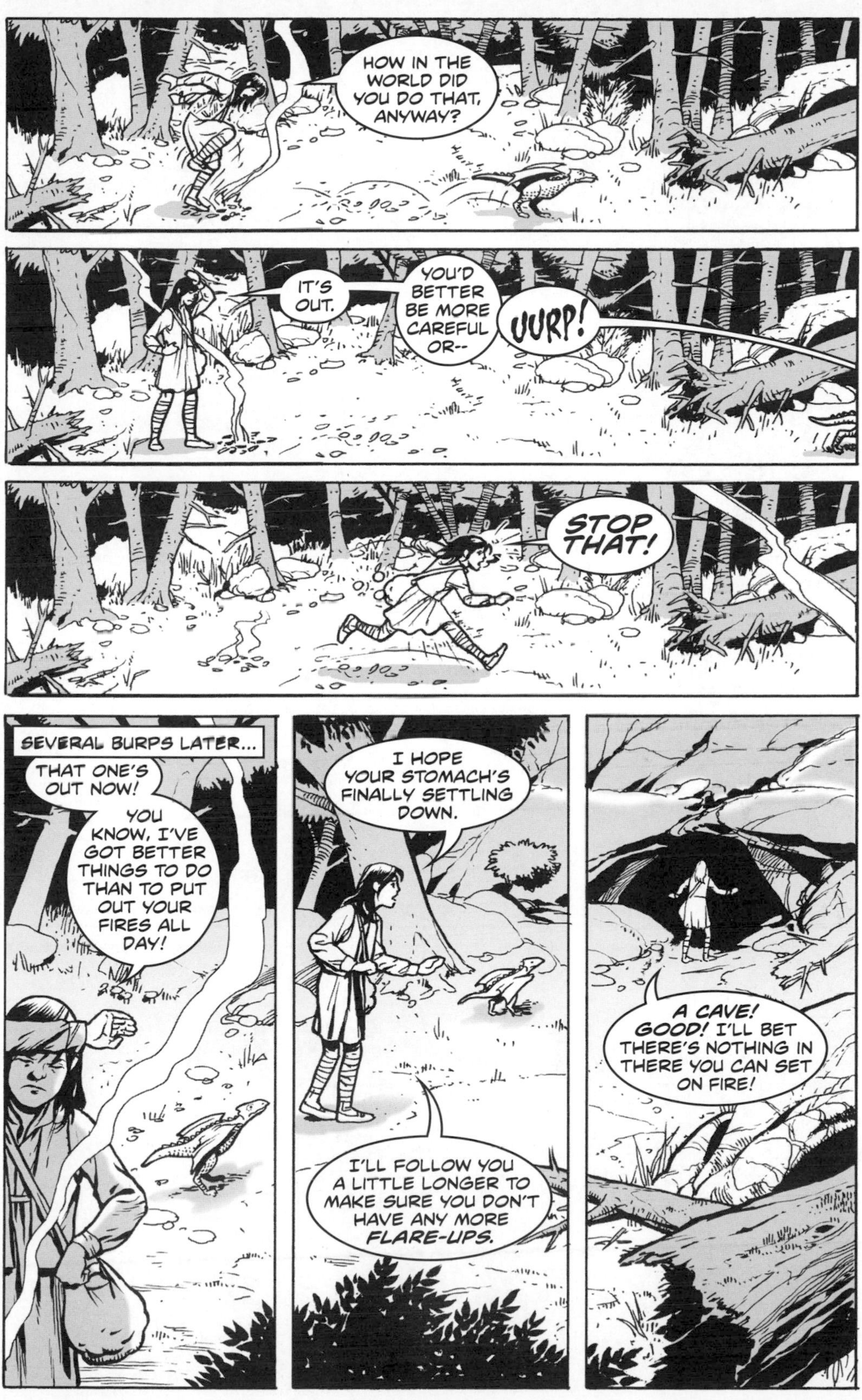
HOW IN THE WORLD DID YOU DO THAT, ANYWAY?
IT'S OUT.
YOU'D BETTER BE MORE CAREFUL OR--
UURP!
STOP THAT!
SEVERAL BURPS LATER...
THAT ONE'S OUT NOW!
YOU KNOW, I'VE GOT BETTER THINGS TO DO THAN TO PUT OUT YOUR FIRES ALL DAY!
I HOPE YOUR STOMACH'S FINALLY SETTLING DOWN.
I'LL FOLLOW YOU A LITTLE LONGER TO MAKE SURE YOU DON'T HAVE ANY MORE FLARE-UPS.
A CAVE! GOOD! I'LL BET THERE'S NOTHING IN THERE YOU CAN SET ON FIRE!

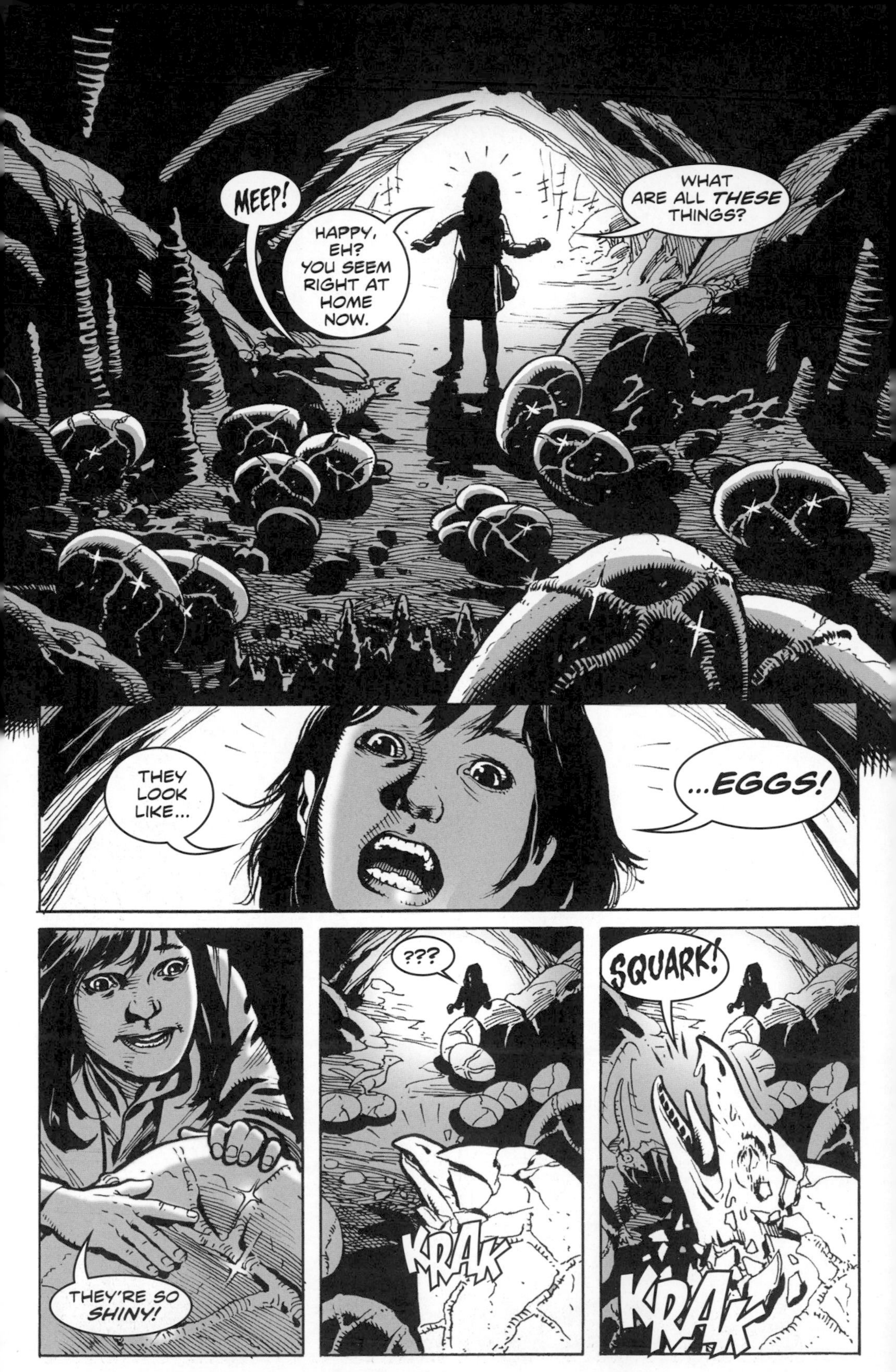
MEEP!
HAPPY, EH? YOU SEEM RIGHT AT HOME NOW.
WHAT ARE ALL THESE THINGS?
THEY LOOK LIKE...
...EGGS!
THEY'RE SO SHINY!
???
KRAK
SQUARK!
KRAK

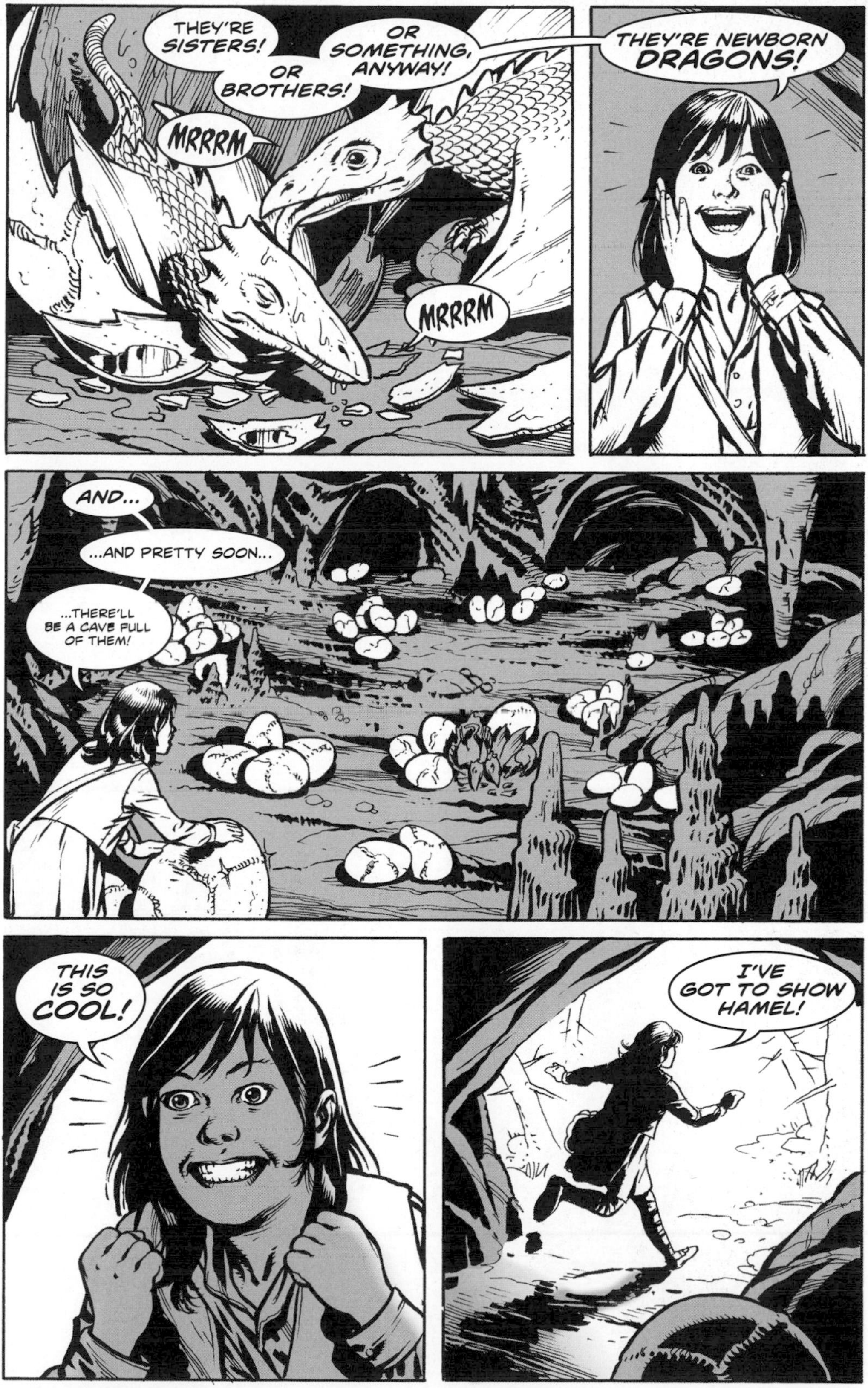
THEY'RE SISTERS!
OR BROTHERS!
OR SOMETHING, ANYWAY!
MRRRM
MRRRM
THEY'RE NEWBORN DRAGONS!
AND...
...AND PRETTY SOON...
...THERE'LL BE A CAVE FULL OF THEM!
THIS IS SO COOL!
I'VE GOT TO SHOW HAMEL!

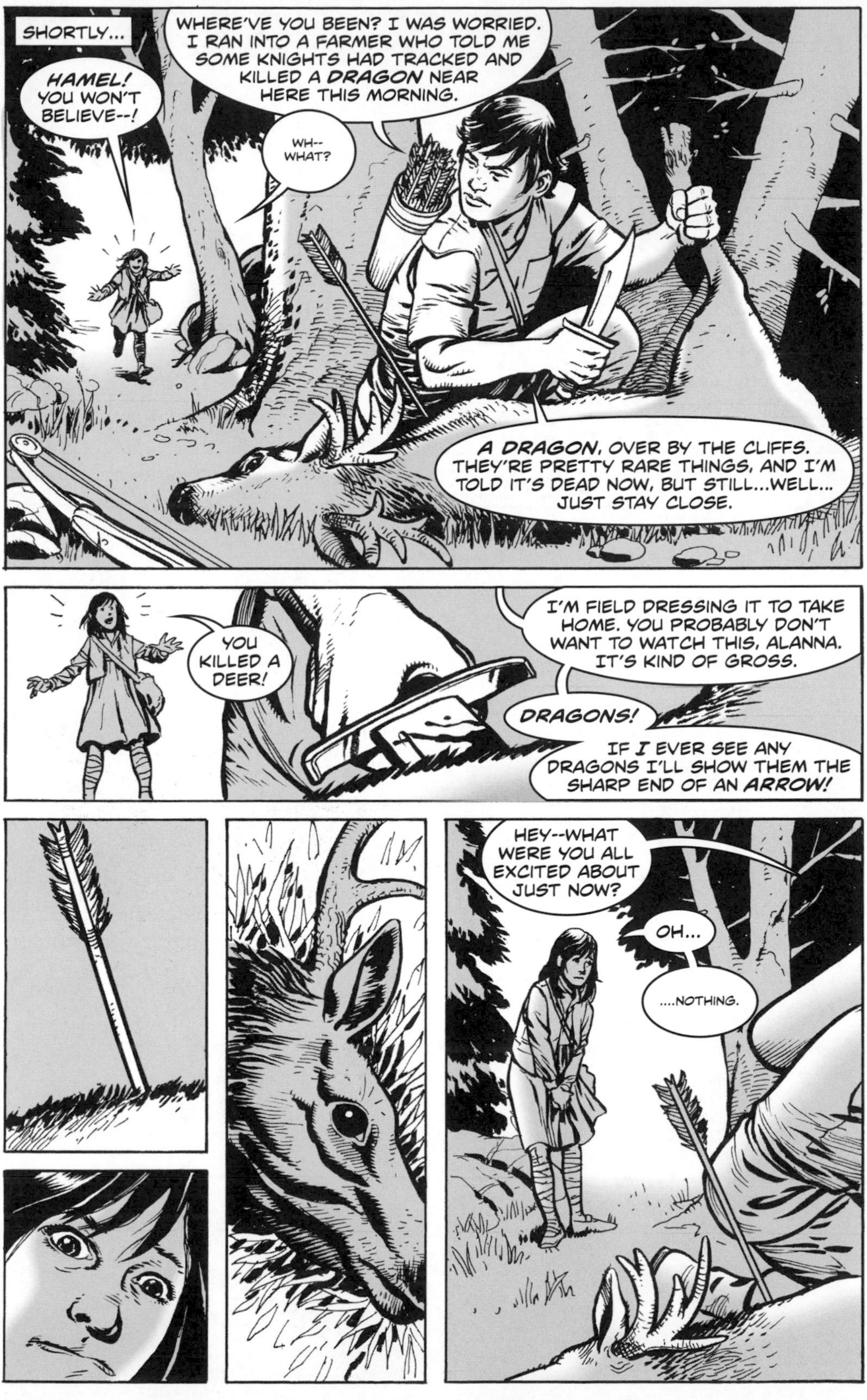
SHORTLY...
HAMEL! YOU WON'T BELIEVE--!
WHERE'VE YOU BEEN? I WAS WORRIED. I RAN INTO A FARMER WHO TOLD ME SOME KNIGHTS HAD TRACKED AND KILLED A DRAGON NEAR HERE THIS MORNING.
WH-- WHAT?
A DRAGON, OVER BY THE CLIFFS. THEY'RE PRETTY RARE THINGS, AND I'M TOLD IT'S DEAD NOW, BUT STILL...WELL... JUST STAY CLOSE.
YOU KILLED A DEER!
I'M FIELD DRESSING IT TO TAKE HOME. YOU PROBABLY DON'T WANT TO WATCH THIS, ALANNA. IT'S KIND OF GROSS.
DRAGONS!
IF I EVER SEE ANY DRAGONS I'LL SHOW THEM THE SHARP END OF AN ARROW!
HEY--WHAT WERE YOU ALL EXCITED ABOUT JUST NOW?
OH...
....NOTHING.

CHAPTER TWO

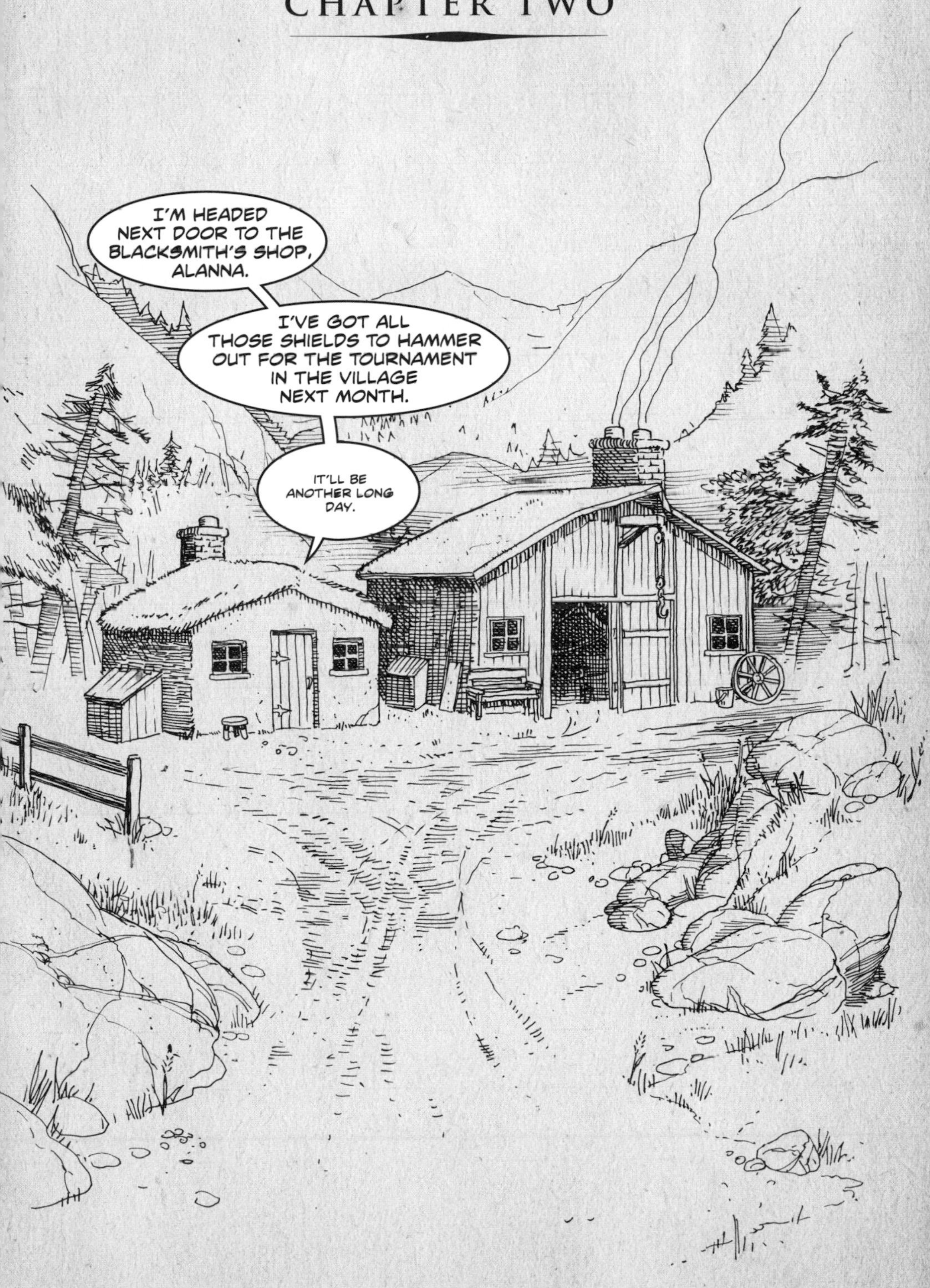
I'M HEADED NEXT DOOR TO THE BLACKSMITH'S SHOP, ALANNA.
I'VE GOT ALL THOSE SHIELDS TO HAMMER OUT FOR THE TOURNAMENT IN THE VILLAGE NEXT MONTH.
IT'LL BE ANOTHER LONG DAY.

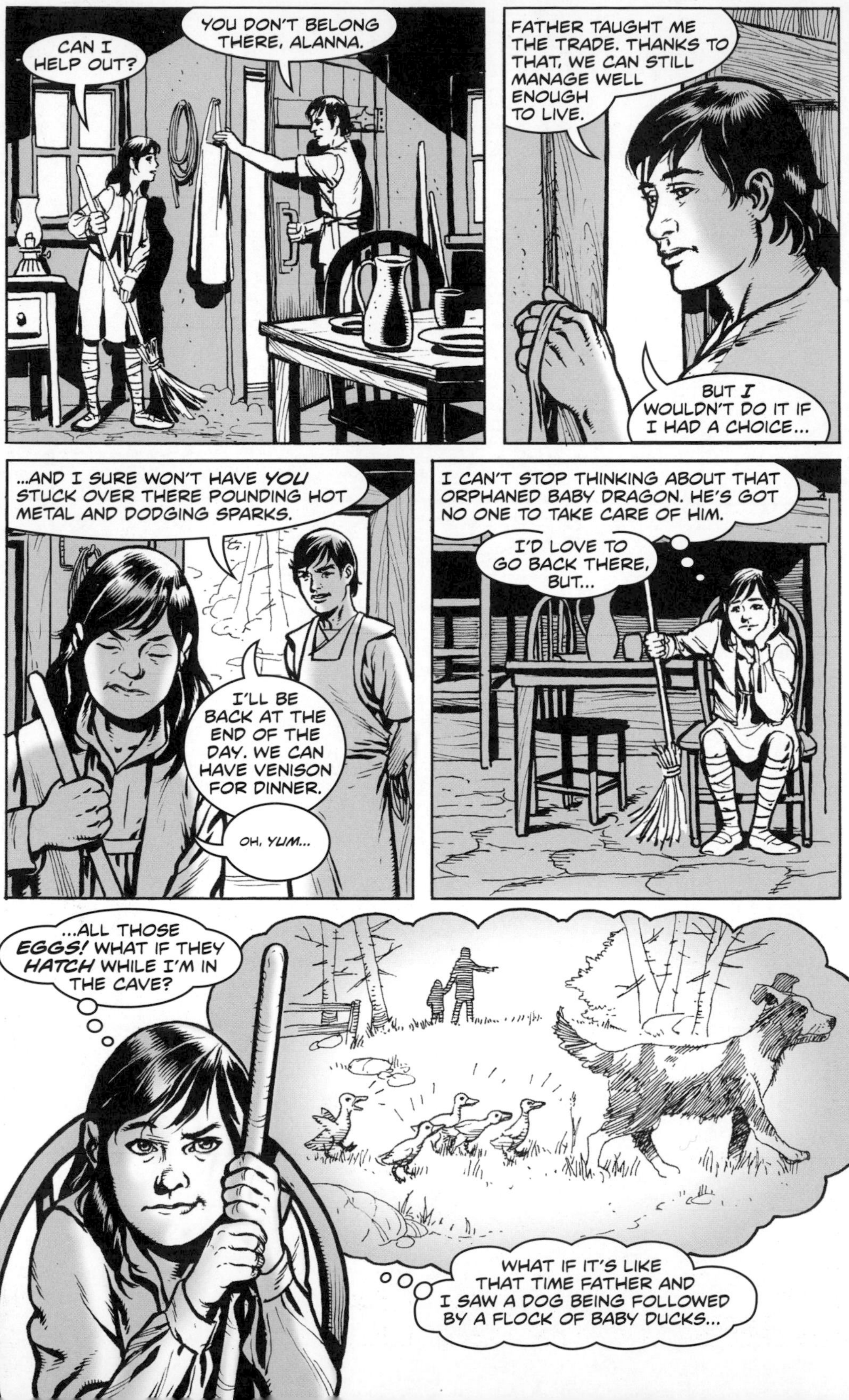
CAN I HELP OUT?
YOU DON'T BELONG THERE, ALANNA.
FATHER TAUGHT ME THE TRADE. THANKS TO THAT, WE CAN STILL MANAGE WELL ENOUGH TO LIVE.
BUT *I* WOULDN'T DO IT IF I HAD A CHOICE...
...AND I SURE WON'T HAVE *YOU* STUCK OVER THERE POUNDING HOT METAL AND DODGING SPARKS.
I'LL BE BACK AT THE END OF THE DAY. WE CAN HAVE VENISON FOR DINNER.
OH, *YUM*...
I CAN'T STOP THINKING ABOUT THAT ORPHANED BABY DRAGON. HE'S GOT NO ONE TO TAKE CARE OF HIM.
I'D LOVE TO GO BACK THERE, BUT...
...ALL THOSE *EGGS!* WHAT IF THEY *HATCH* WHILE I'M IN THE CAVE?
WHAT IF IT'S LIKE THAT TIME FATHER AND I SAW A DOG BEING FOLLOWED BY A FLOCK OF BABY DUCKS...

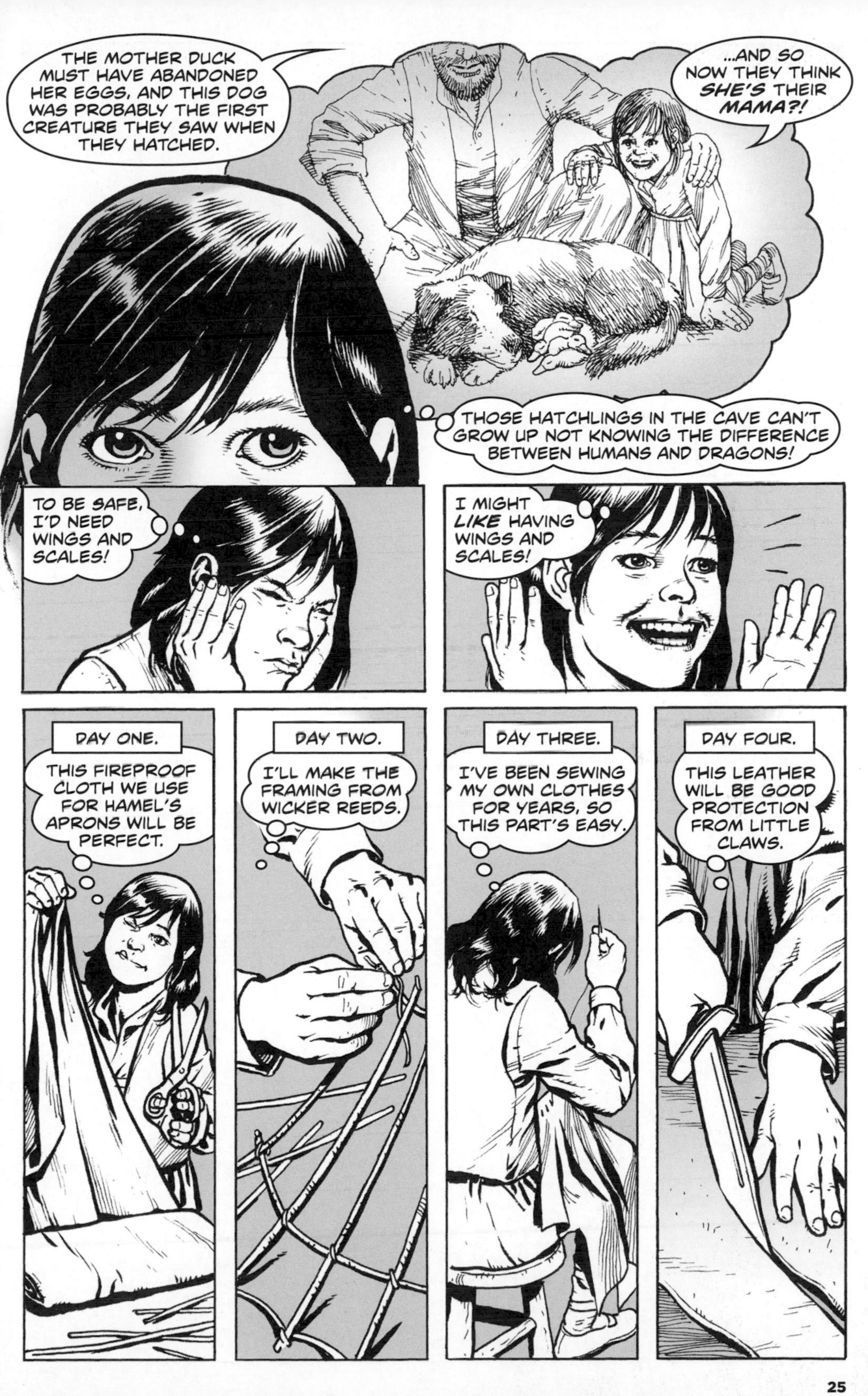
THE MOTHER DUCK MUST HAVE ABANDONED HER EGGS, AND THIS DOG WAS PROBABLY THE FIRST CREATURE THEY SAW WHEN THEY HATCHED.
...AND SO NOW THEY THINK *SHE'S* THEIR *MAMA?!*
THOSE HATCHLINGS IN THE CAVE CAN'T GROW UP NOT KNOWING THE DIFFERENCE BETWEEN HUMANS AND DRAGONS!
TO BE SAFE, I'D NEED WINGS AND SCALES!
I MIGHT *LIKE* HAVING WINGS AND SCALES!
DAY ONE.
THIS FIREPROOF CLOTH WE USE FOR HAMEL'S APRONS WILL BE PERFECT.
DAY TWO.
I'LL MAKE THE FRAMING FROM WICKER REEDS.
DAY THREE.
I'VE BEEN SEWING MY OWN CLOTHES FOR YEARS, SO THIS PART'S EASY.
DAY FOUR.
THIS LEATHER WILL BE GOOD PROTECTION FROM LITTLE CLAWS.

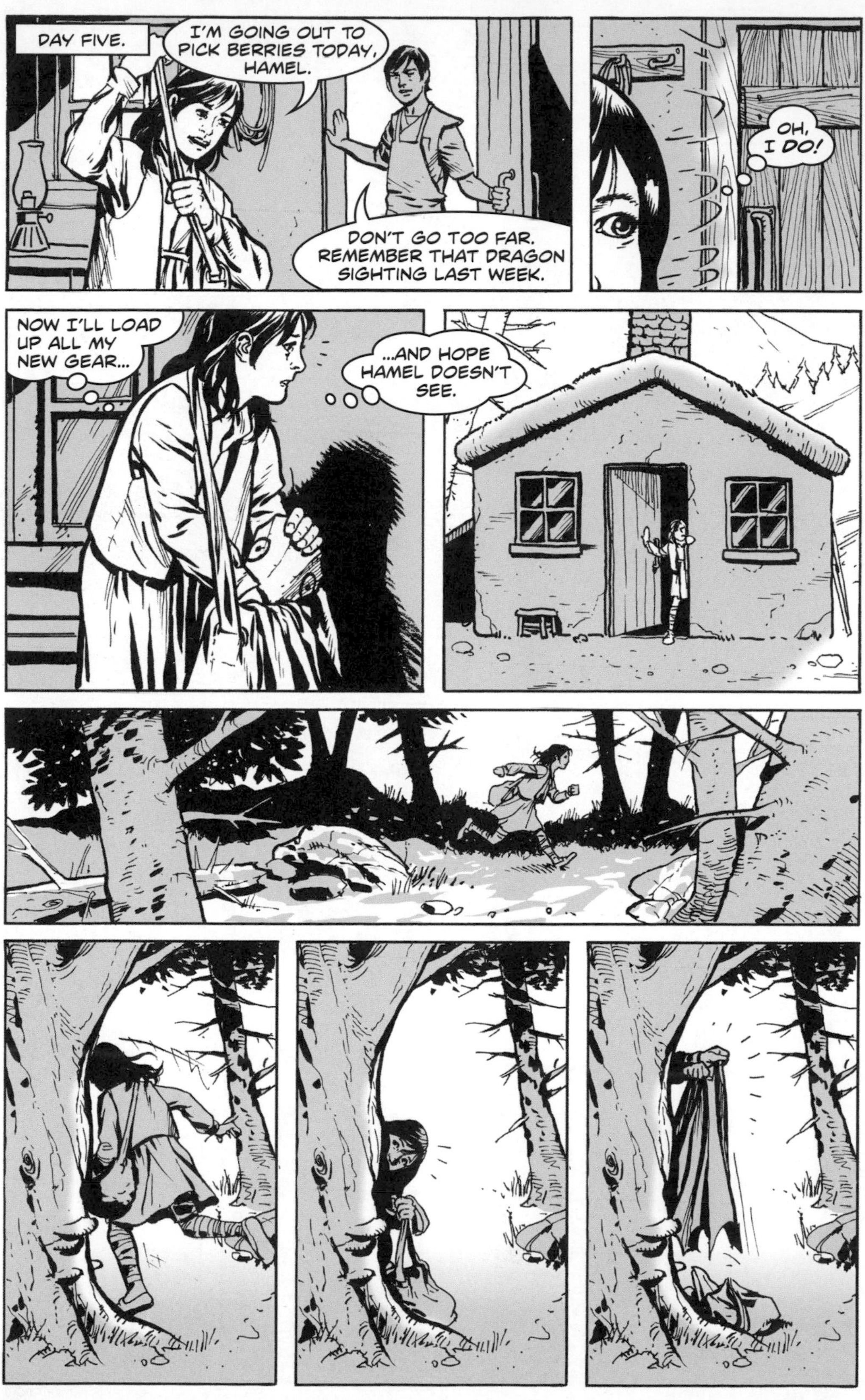
DAY FIVE.
I'M GOING OUT TO PICK BERRIES TODAY, HAMEL.
DON'T GO TOO FAR. REMEMBER THAT DRAGON SIGHTING LAST WEEK.
OH, I DO!
NOW I'LL LOAD UP ALL MY NEW GEAR...
...AND HOPE HAMEL DOESN'T SEE.

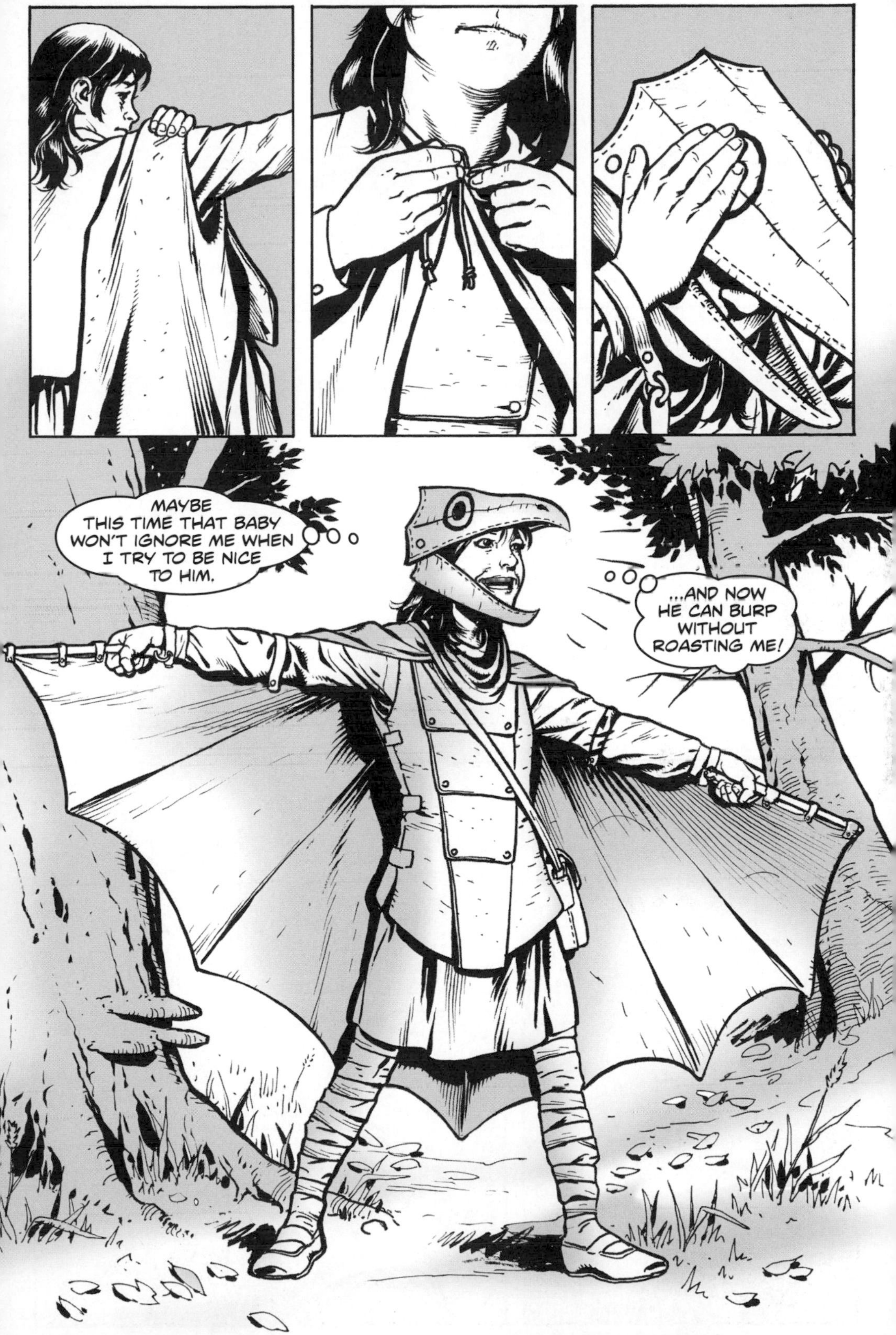

MAYBE THIS TIME THAT BABY WON'T IGNORE ME WHEN I TRY TO BE NICE TO HIM.
...AND NOW HE CAN BURP WITHOUT ROASTING ME!

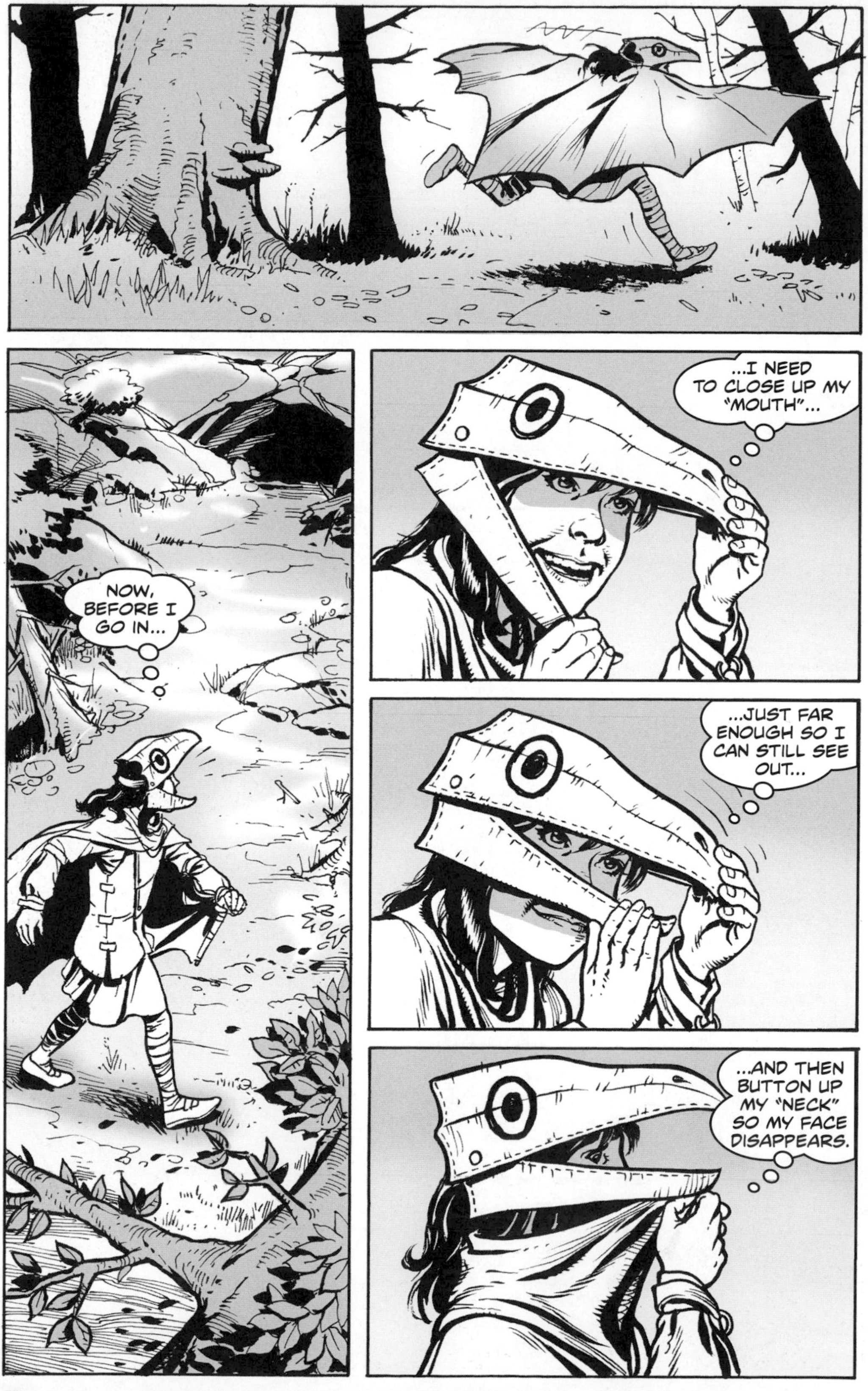
NOW, BEFORE I GO IN...
...I NEED TO CLOSE UP MY "MOUTH"...
...JUST FAR ENOUGH SO I CAN STILL SEE OUT...
...AND THEN BUTTON UP MY "NECK" SO MY FACE DISAPPEARS.

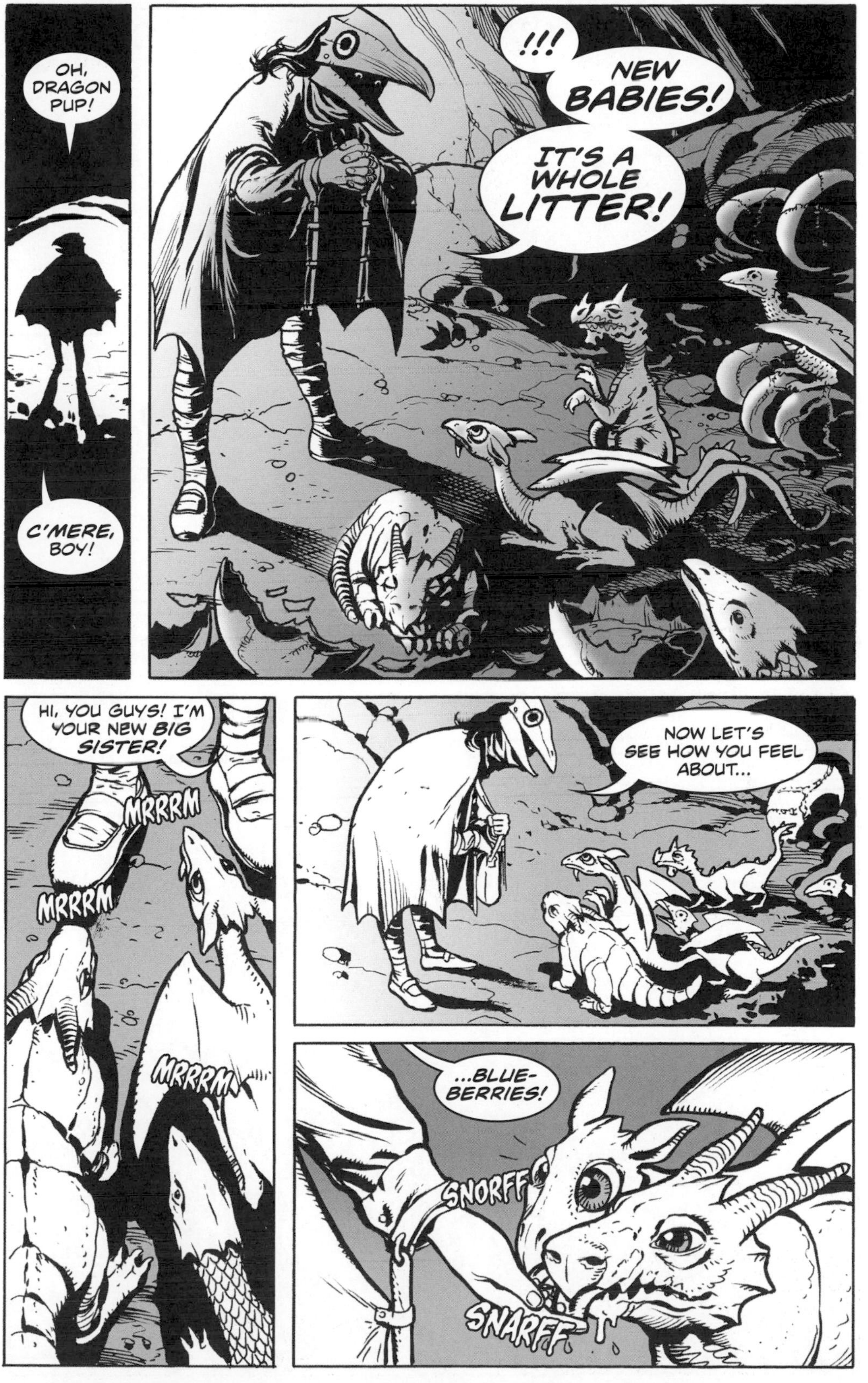
OH, DRAGON PUP!
C'MERE, BOY!
!!!
NEW BABIES!
IT'S A WHOLE LITTER!
HI, YOU GUYS! I'M YOUR NEW BIG SISTER!
MRRRM
MRRRM
MRRRM
NOW LET'S SEE HOW YOU FEEL ABOUT...
...BLUE-BERRIES!
SNORFF
SNARFF

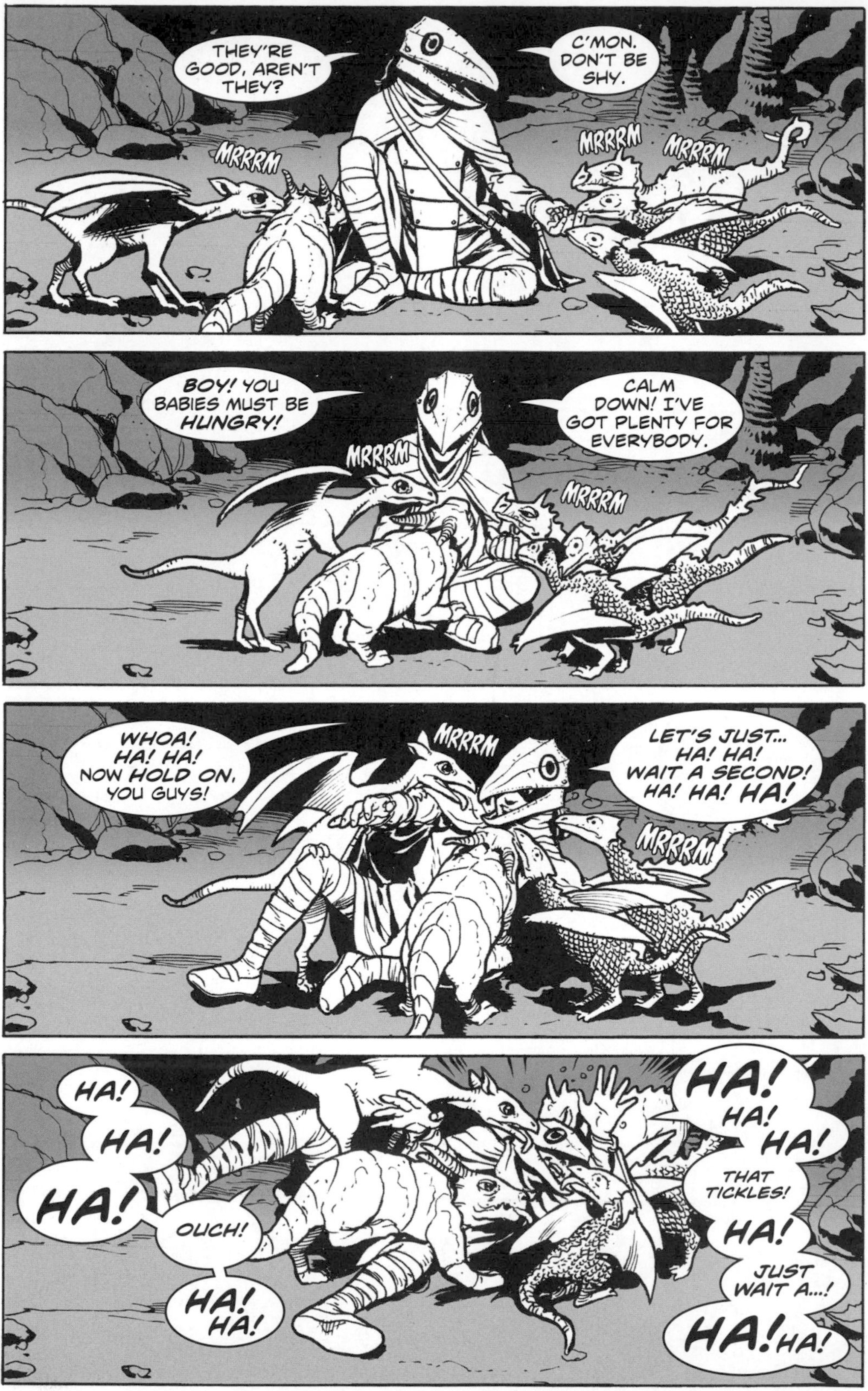
THEY'RE GOOD, AREN'T THEY?
C'MON. DON'T BE SHY.
MRRRM
MRRRM
MRRRM
BOY! YOU BABIES MUST BE HUNGRY!
CALM DOWN! I'VE GOT PLENTY FOR EVERYBODY.
MRRRM
MRRRM
WHOA! HA! HA! NOW HOLD ON, YOU GUYS!
MRRRM
LET'S JUST... HA! HA! WAIT A SECOND! HA! HA! HA!
MRRRM
HA!
HA!
HA!
OUCH!
HA! HA!
HA! HA! HA!
THAT TICKLES!
HA!
JUST WAIT A...!
HA! HA!

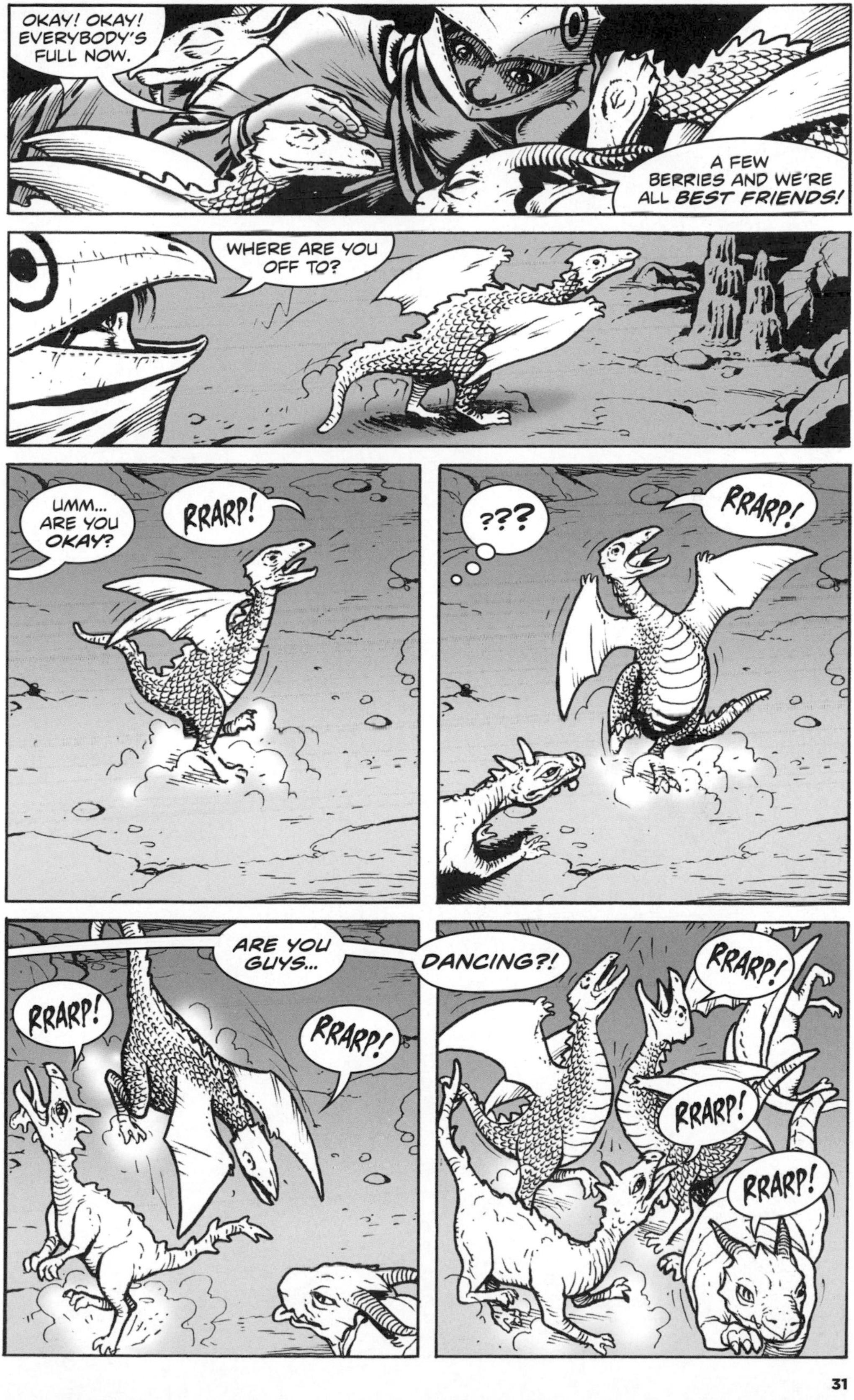
OKAY! OKAY! EVERYBODY'S FULL NOW.
A FEW BERRIES AND WE'RE ALL *BEST FRIENDS!*
WHERE ARE YOU OFF TO?
UMM... ARE YOU *OKAY?*
RRARP!
???
RRARP!
ARE YOU GUYS...
DANCING?!
RRARP!
RRARP!
RRARP!
RRARP!
RRARP!

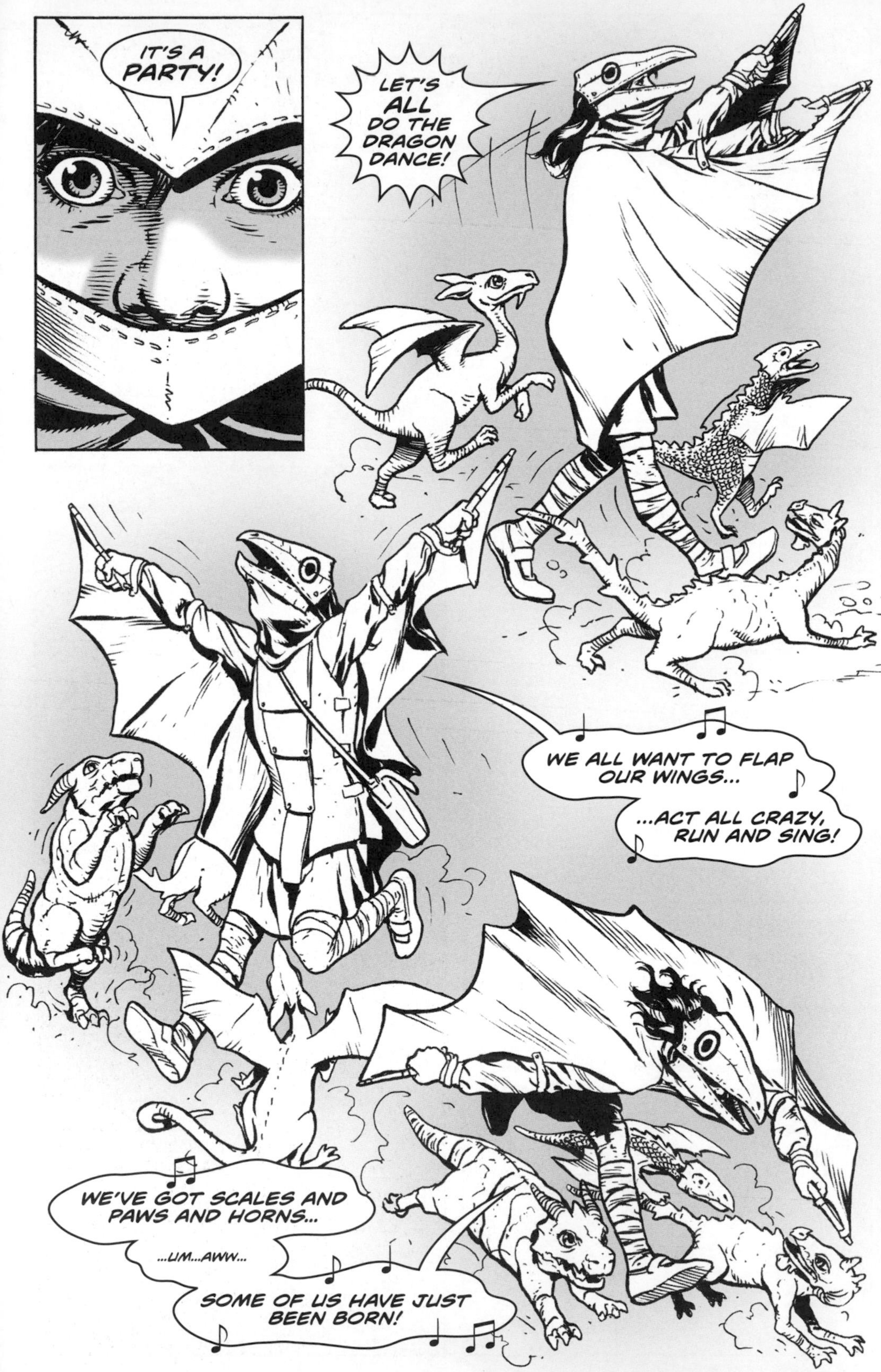
IT'S A PARTY!
LET'S ALL DO THE DRAGON DANCE!
WE ALL WANT TO FLAP OUR WINGS...
...ACT ALL CRAZY, RUN AND SING!
WE'VE GOT SCALES AND PAWS AND HORNS...
...UM...AWW...
SOME OF US HAVE JUST BEEN BORN!

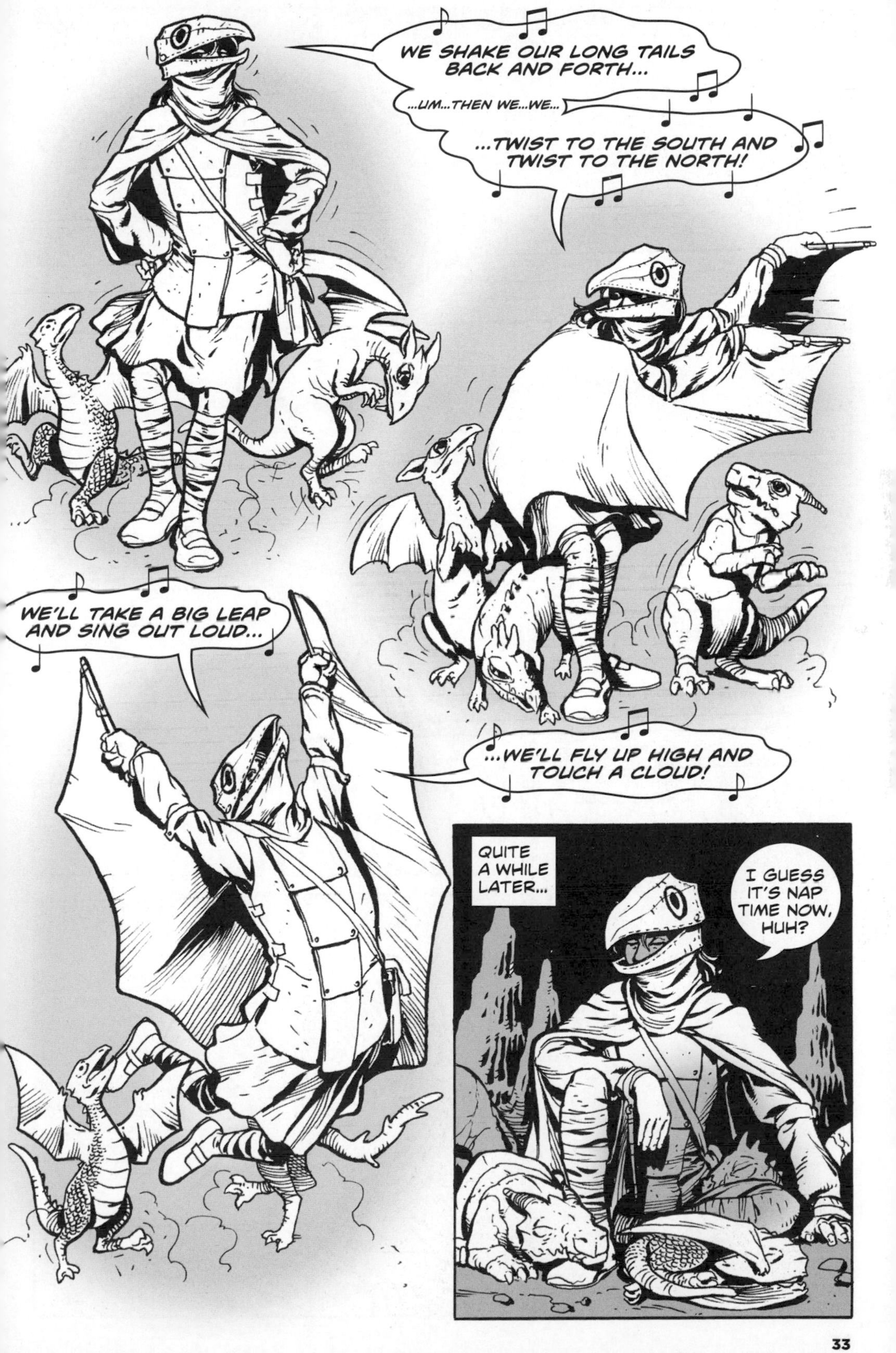
WE SHAKE OUR LONG TAILS BACK AND FORTH...
...UM...THEN WE...WE...
...TWIST TO THE SOUTH AND TWIST TO THE NORTH!
WE'LL TAKE A BIG LEAP AND SING OUT LOUD...
...WE'LL FLY UP HIGH AND TOUCH A CLOUD!
QUITE A WHILE LATER...
I GUESS IT'S NAP TIME NOW, HUH?

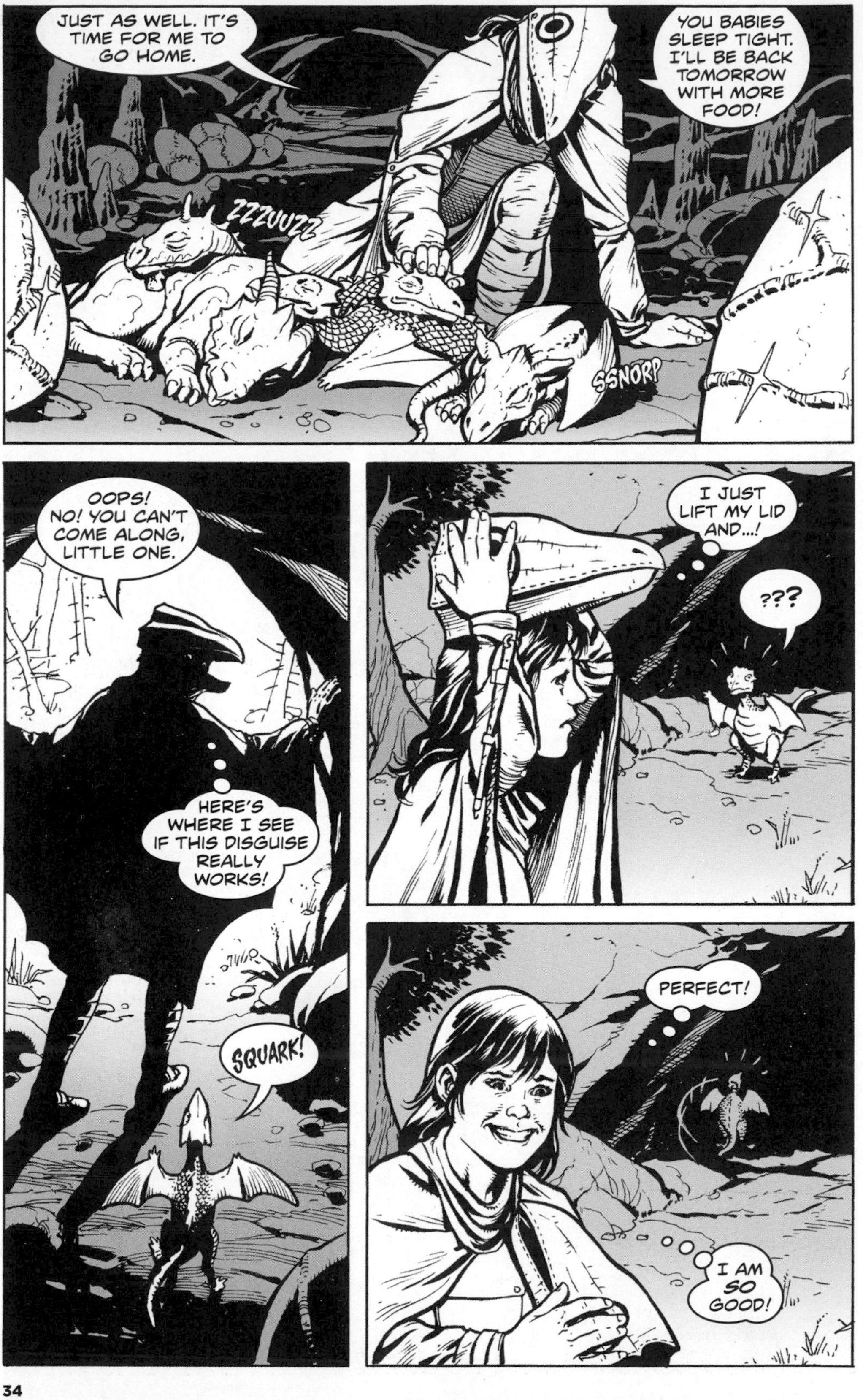

JUST AS WELL. IT'S TIME FOR ME TO GO HOME.
YOU BABIES SLEEP TIGHT. I'LL BE BACK TOMORROW WITH MORE FOOD!
ZZZUUZZ
SSNORP
OOPS! NO! YOU CAN'T COME ALONG, LITTLE ONE.
HERE'S WHERE I SEE IF THIS DISGUISE REALLY WORKS!
SQUARK!
I JUST LIFT MY LID AND...!
???
PERFECT!
I AM SO GOOD!

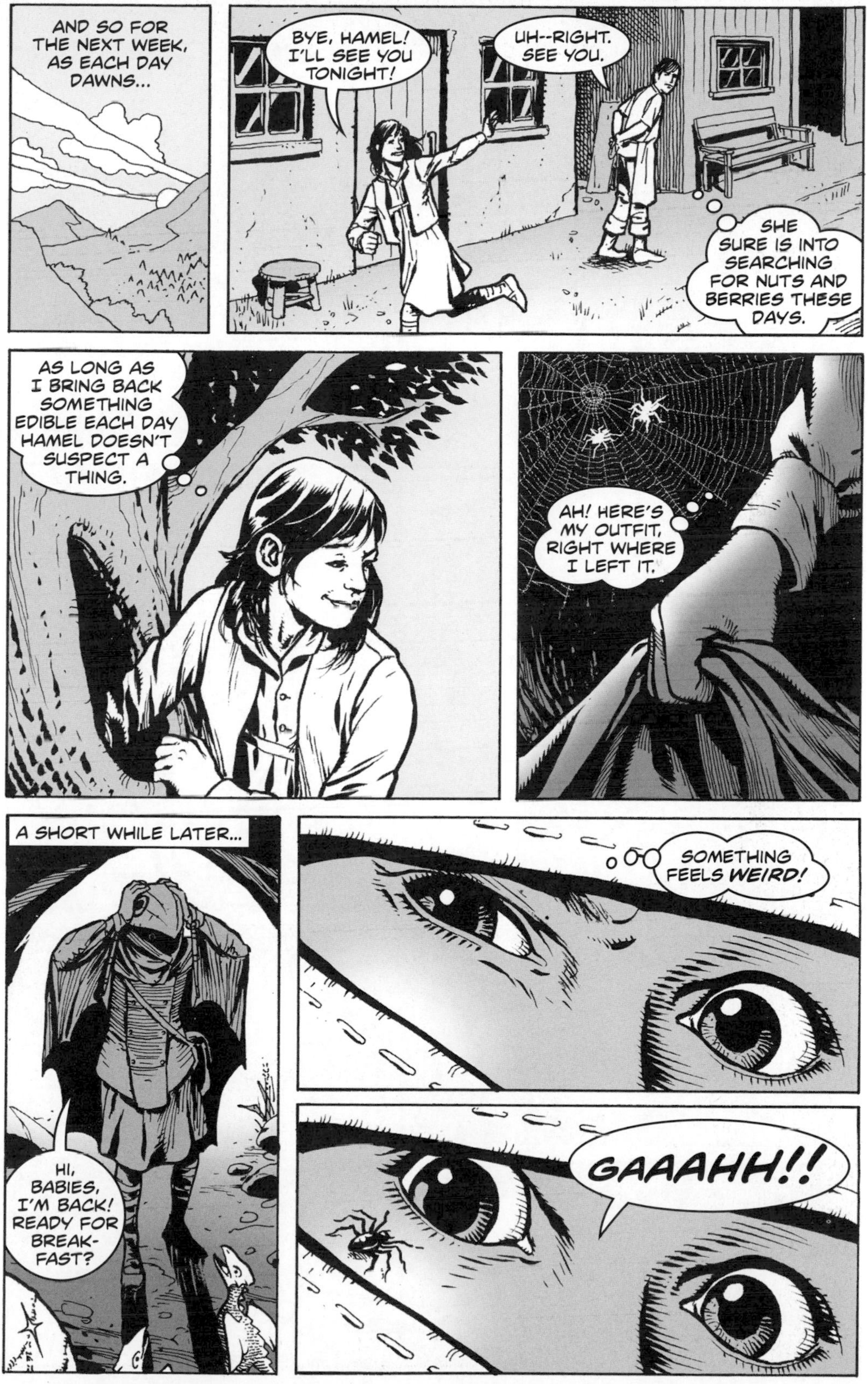
AND SO FOR THE NEXT WEEK, AS EACH DAY DAWNS...
BYE, HAMEL! I'LL SEE YOU TONIGHT!
UH--RIGHT. SEE YOU.
SHE SURE IS INTO SEARCHING FOR NUTS AND BERRIES THESE DAYS.
AS LONG AS I BRING BACK SOMETHING EDIBLE EACH DAY HAMEL DOESN'T SUSPECT A THING.
AH! HERE'S MY OUTFIT, RIGHT WHERE I LEFT IT.
A SHORT WHILE LATER...
HI, BABIES, I'M BACK! READY FOR BREAK-FAST?
SOMETHING FEELS ***WEIRD!***
GAAAHH!!

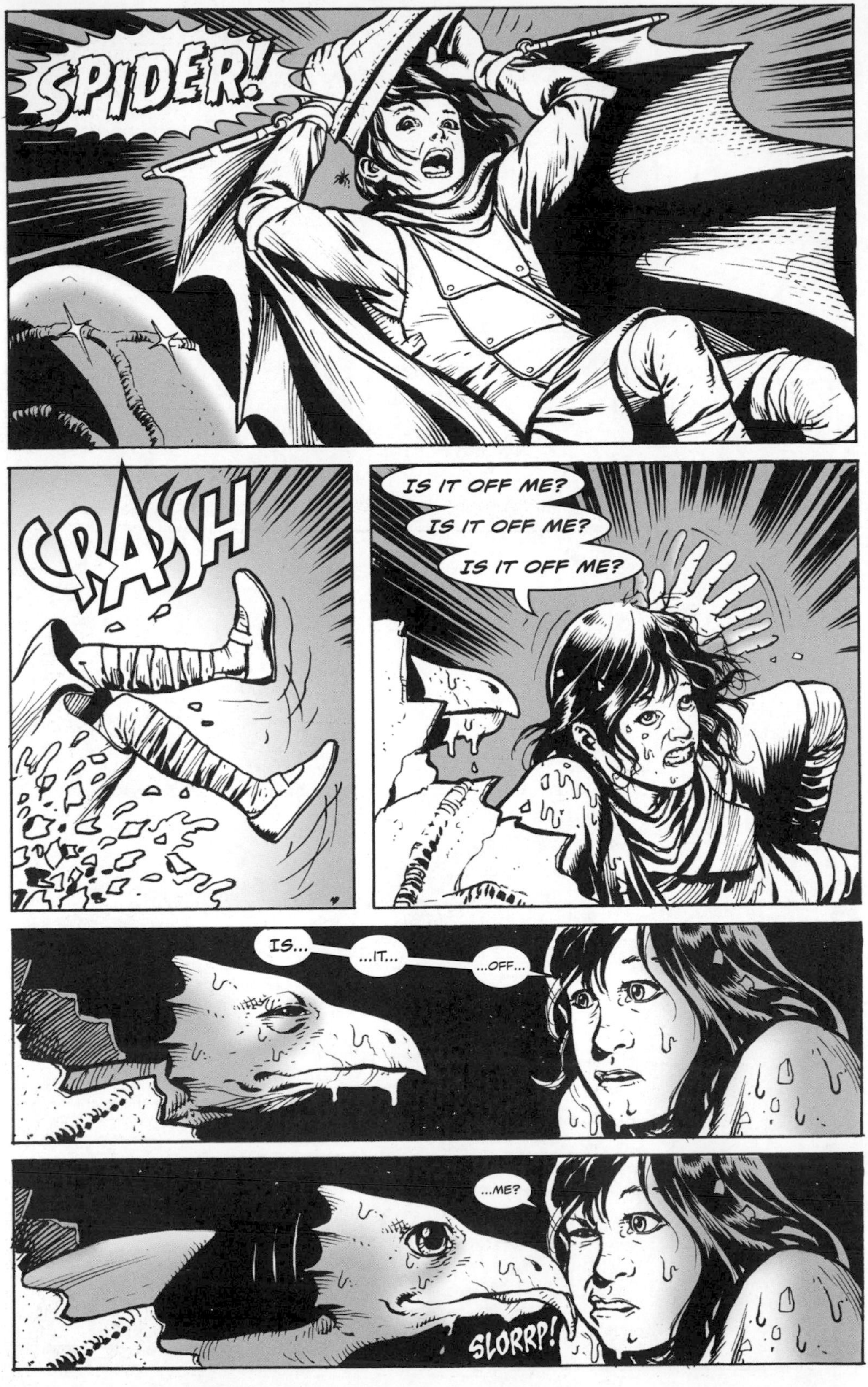
SPIDER!
CRASH
IS IT OFF ME?
IS IT OFF ME?
IS IT OFF ME?
IS...
...IT...
...OFF...
...ME?
SLORRP!

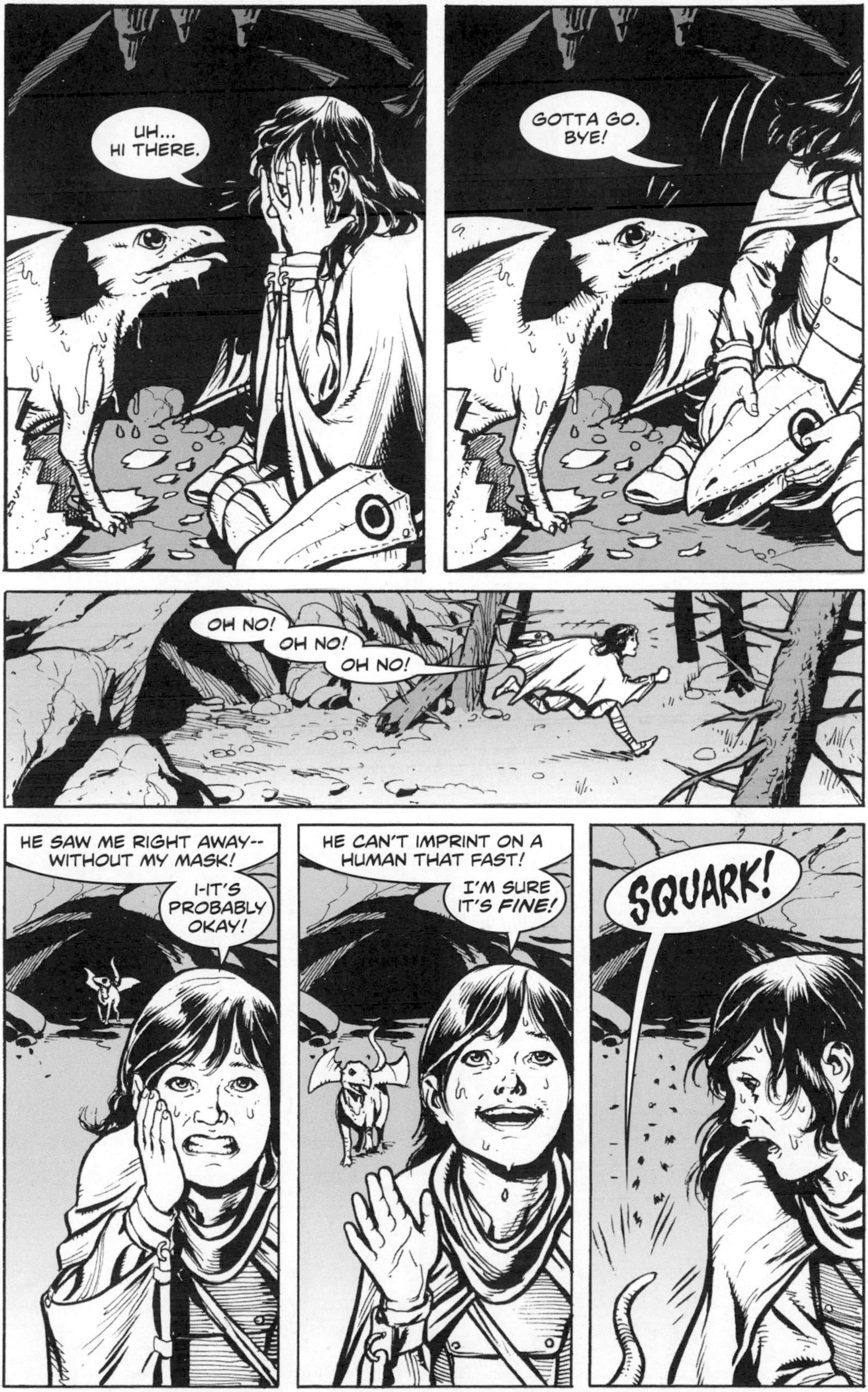
UH... HI THERE.
GOTTA GO. BYE!
OH NO!
OH NO!
OH NO!
HE SAW ME RIGHT AWAY-- WITHOUT MY MASK!
I-IT'S PROBABLY OKAY!
HE CAN'T IMPRINT ON A HUMAN THAT FAST!
I'M SURE IT'S FINE!
SQUARK!

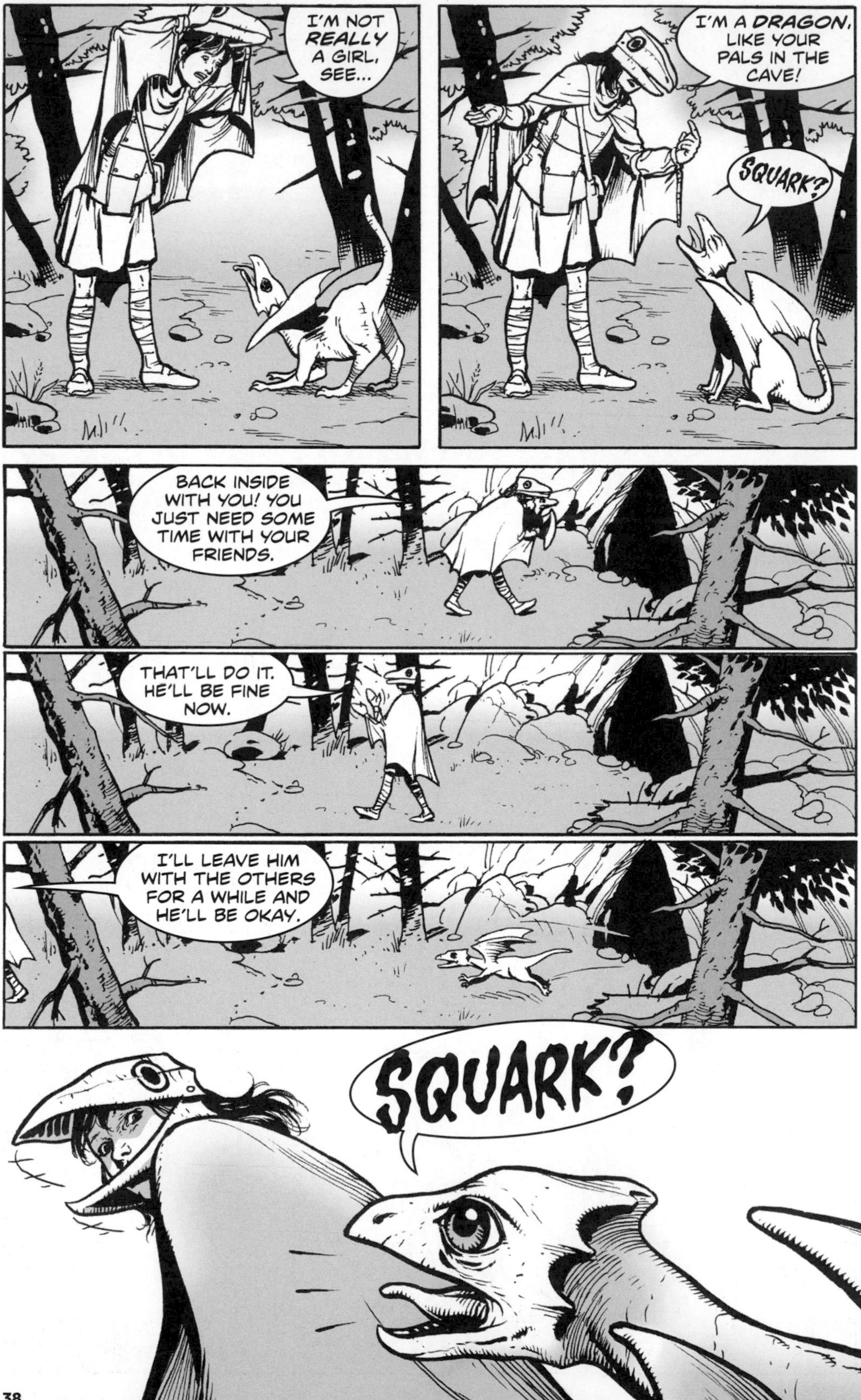
I'M NOT REALLY A GIRL, SEE...
I'M A DRAGON, LIKE YOUR PALS IN THE CAVE!
SQUARK?
BACK INSIDE WITH YOU! YOU JUST NEED SOME TIME WITH YOUR FRIENDS.
THAT'LL DO IT. HE'LL BE FINE NOW.
I'LL LEAVE HIM WITH THE OTHERS FOR A WHILE AND HE'LL BE OKAY.
SQUARK?

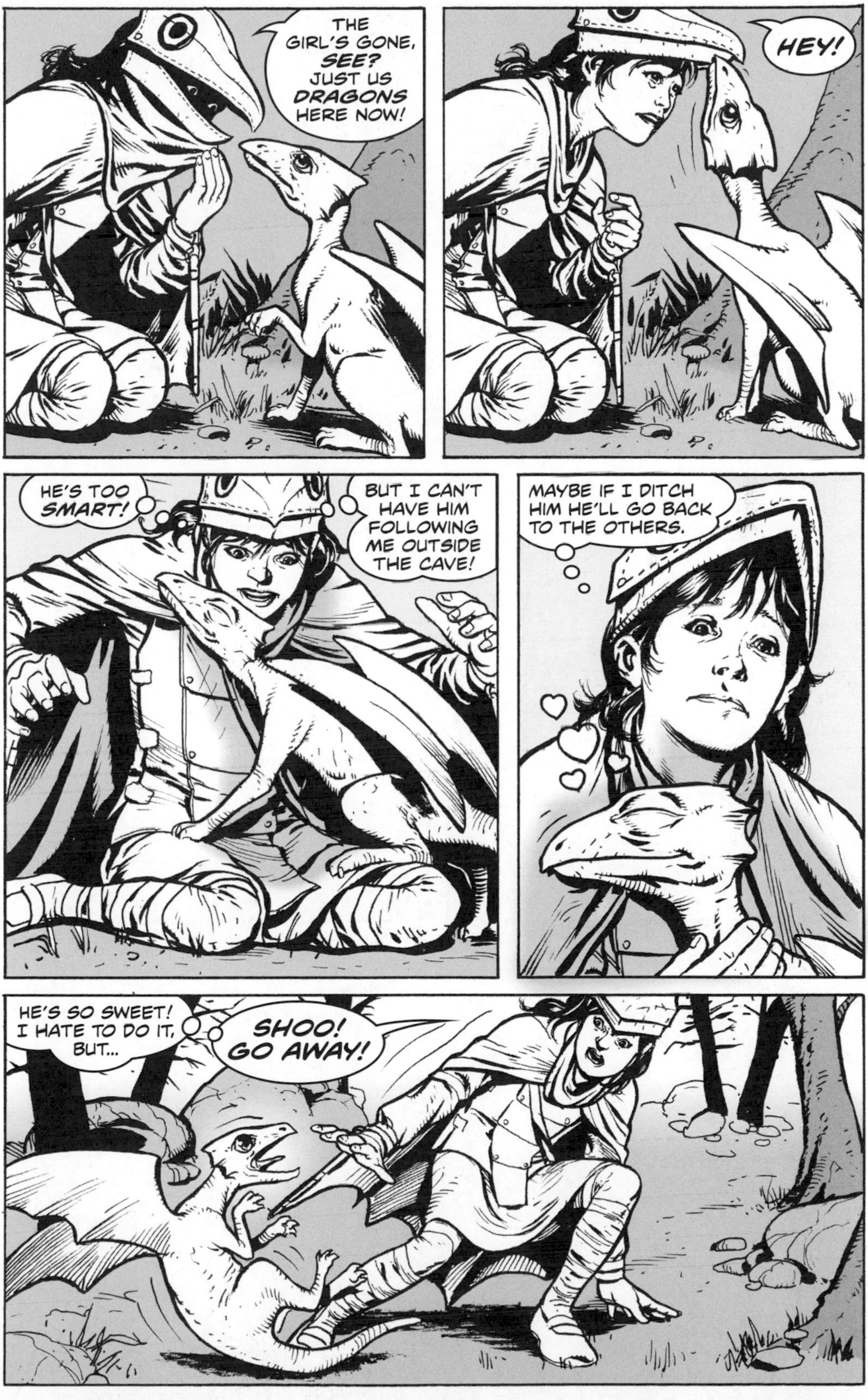
THE GIRL'S GONE, SEE? JUST US DRAGONS HERE NOW!
HEY!
HE'S TOO SMART!
BUT I CAN'T HAVE HIM FOLLOWING ME OUTSIDE THE CAVE!
MAYBE IF I DITCH HIM HE'LL GO BACK TO THE OTHERS.
HE'S SO SWEET! I HATE TO DO IT, BUT...
SHOO! GO AWAY!

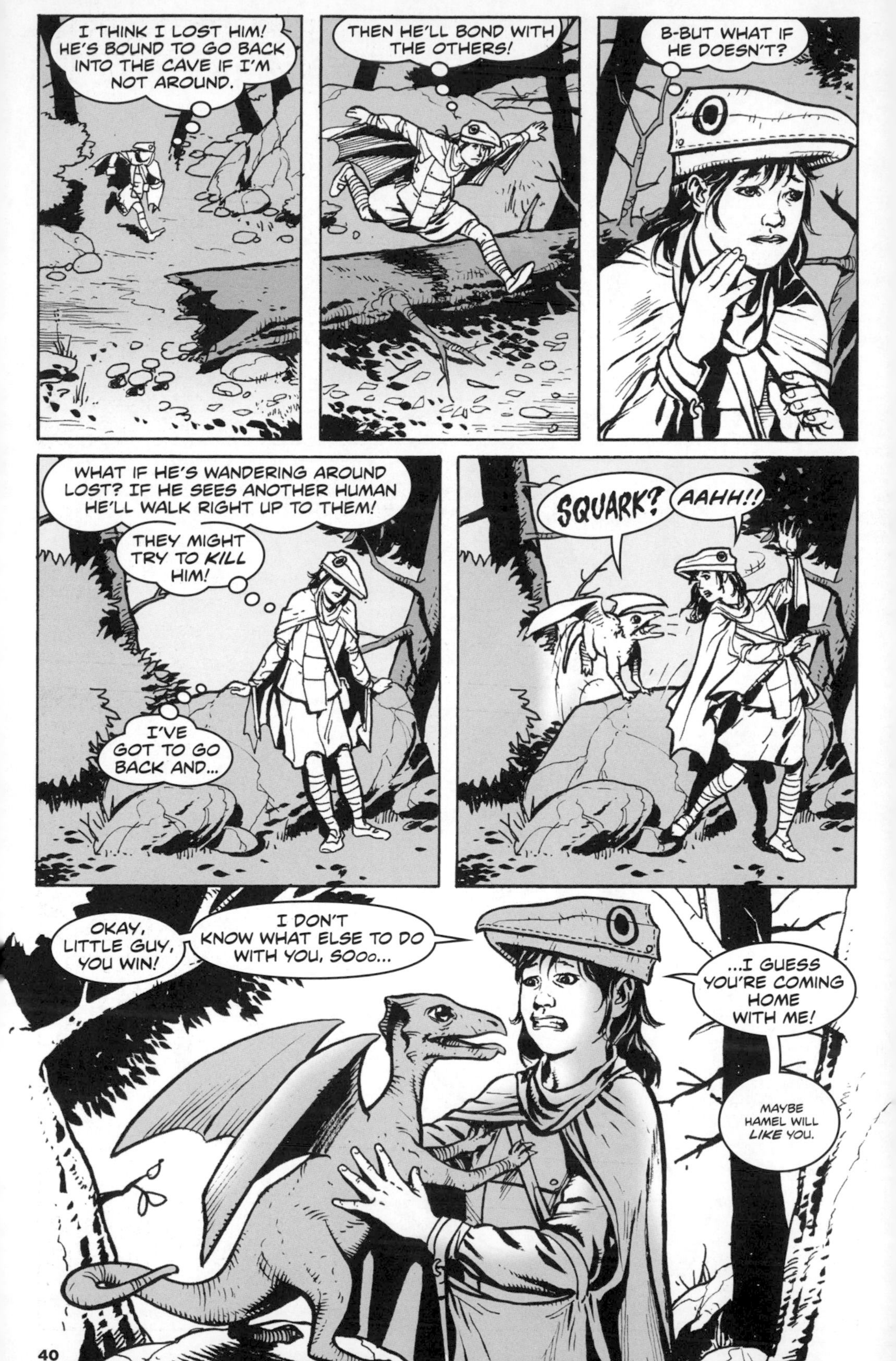
I THINK I LOST HIM! HE'S BOUND TO GO BACK INTO THE CAVE IF I'M NOT AROUND.
THEN HE'LL BOND WITH THE OTHERS!
B-BUT WHAT IF HE DOESN'T?
WHAT IF HE'S WANDERING AROUND LOST? IF HE SEES ANOTHER HUMAN HE'LL WALK RIGHT UP TO THEM!
THEY MIGHT TRY TO KILL HIM!
I'VE GOT TO GO BACK AND...
SQUARK?
AAHH!!
OKAY, LITTLE GUY, YOU WIN!
I DON'T KNOW WHAT ELSE TO DO WITH YOU, SOOo...
...I GUESS YOU'RE COMING HOME WITH ME!
MAYBE HAMEL WILL LIKE YOU.

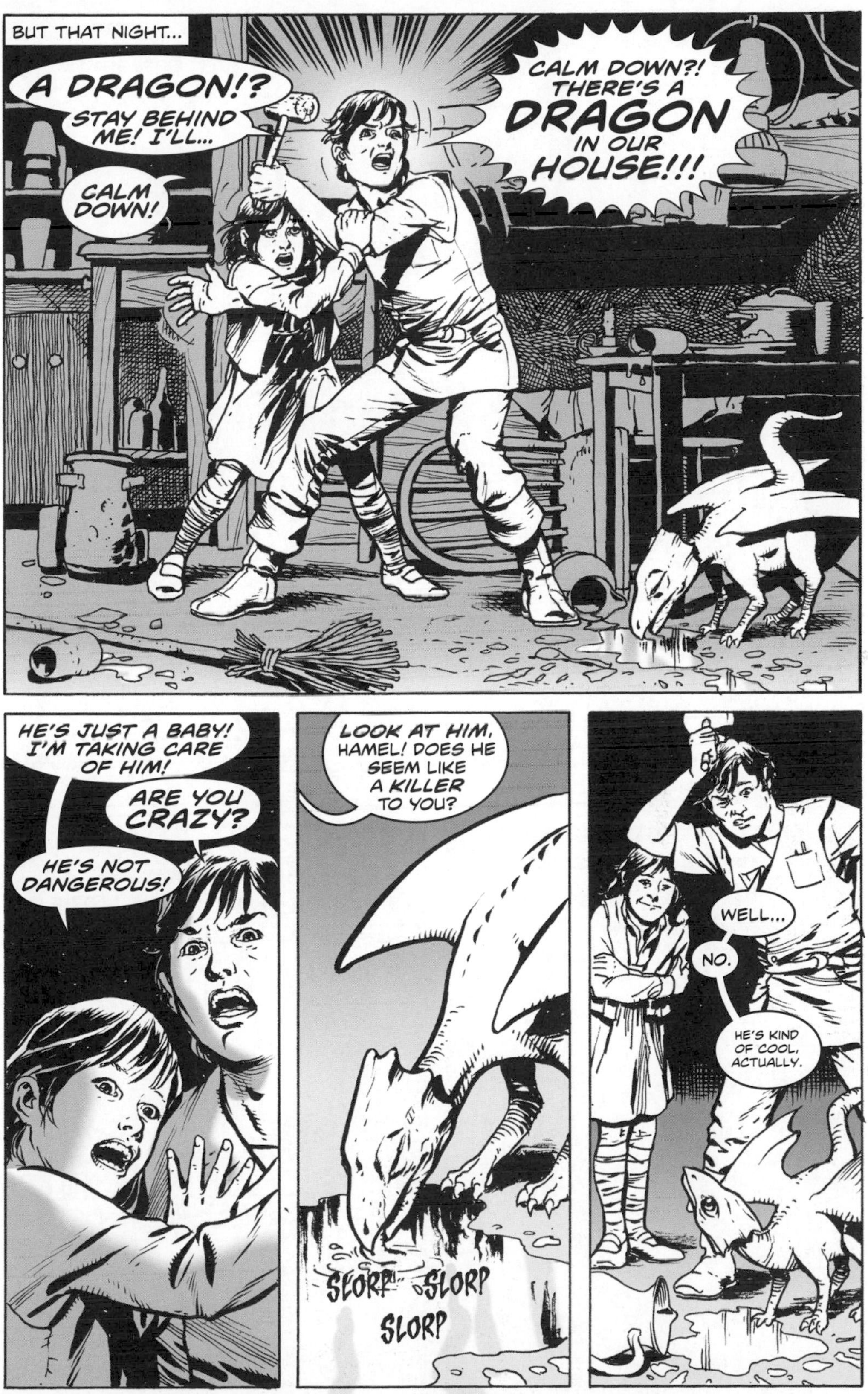
BUT THAT NIGHT...
A DRAGON!? STAY BEHIND ME! I'LL...
CALM DOWN!
CALM DOWN?! THERE'S A DRAGON IN OUR HOUSE!!!
HE'S JUST A BABY! I'M TAKING CARE OF HIM!
ARE YOU CRAZY?
HE'S NOT DANGEROUS!
LOOK AT HIM, HAMEL! DOES HE SEEM LIKE A KILLER TO YOU?
SLORP SLORP
SLORP
WELL...
NO.
HE'S KIND OF COOL, ACTUALLY.

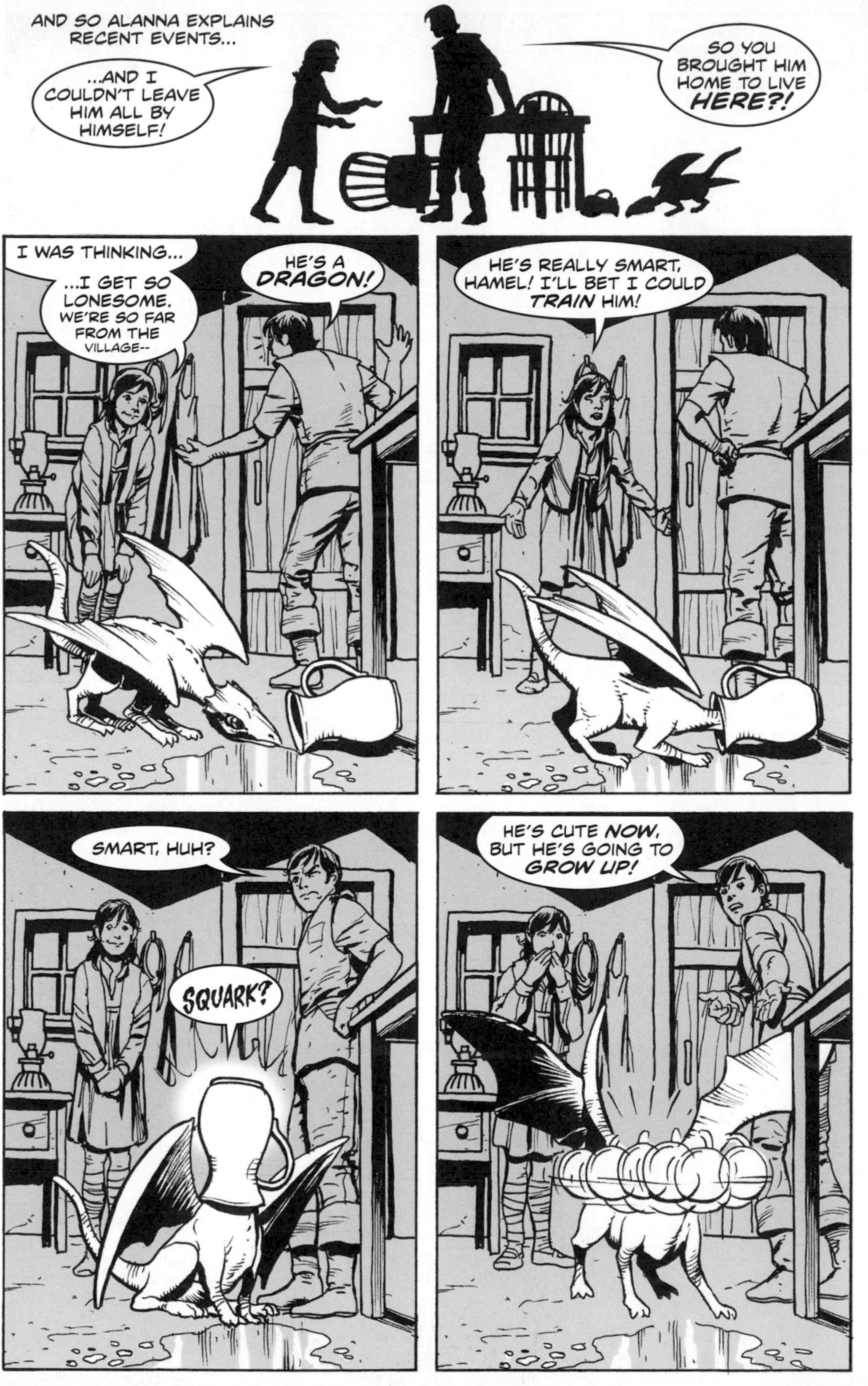
AND SO ALANNA EXPLAINS RECENT EVENTS...
...AND I COULDN'T LEAVE HIM ALL BY HIMSELF!
SO YOU BROUGHT HIM HOME TO LIVE HERE?!
I WAS THINKING...
...I GET SO LONESOME. WE'RE SO FAR FROM THE VILLAGE--
HE'S A DRAGON!
HE'S REALLY SMART, HAMEL! I'LL BET I COULD TRAIN HIM!
SMART, HUH?
SQUARK?
HE'S CUTE NOW, BUT HE'S GOING TO GROW UP!

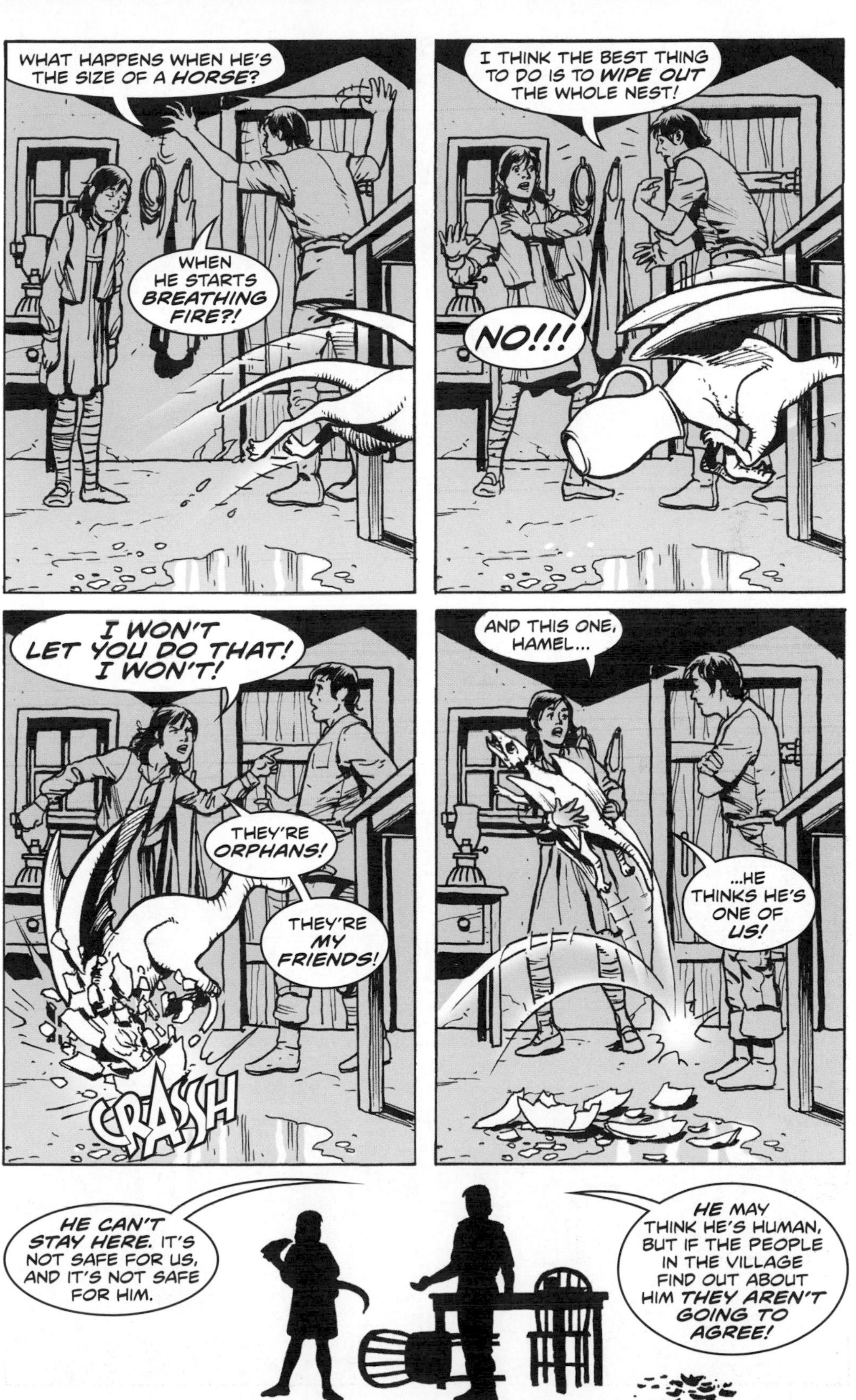
WHAT HAPPENS WHEN HE'S THE SIZE OF A HORSE?
WHEN HE STARTS BREATHING FIRE?!
I THINK THE BEST THING TO DO IS TO WIPE OUT THE WHOLE NEST!
NO!!!
I WON'T LET YOU DO THAT! I WON'T!
THEY'RE ORPHANS!
THEY'RE MY FRIENDS!
CRASH
AND THIS ONE, HAMEL...
...HE THINKS HE'S ONE OF US!
HE CAN'T STAY HERE. IT'S NOT SAFE FOR US, AND IT'S NOT SAFE FOR HIM.
HE MAY THINK HE'S HUMAN, BUT IF THE PEOPLE IN THE VILLAGE FIND OUT ABOUT HIM THEY AREN'T GOING TO AGREE!

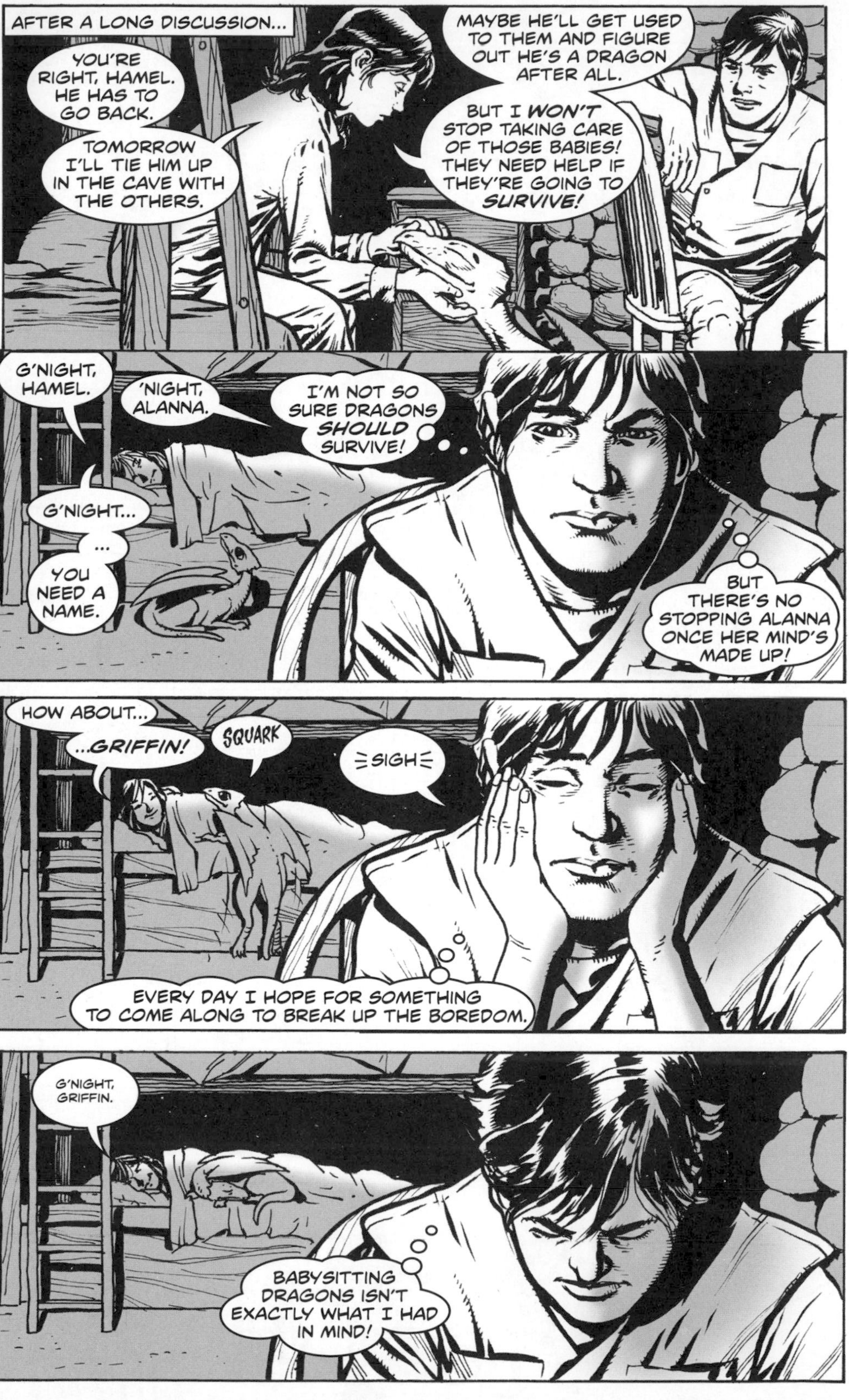
AFTER A LONG DISCUSSION...
YOU'RE RIGHT, HAMEL. HE HAS TO GO BACK.
TOMORROW I'LL TIE HIM UP IN THE CAVE WITH THE OTHERS.
MAYBE HE'LL GET USED TO THEM AND FIGURE OUT HE'S A DRAGON AFTER ALL.
BUT I WON'T STOP TAKING CARE OF THOSE BABIES! THEY NEED HELP IF THEY'RE GOING TO SURVIVE!
G'NIGHT, HAMEL.
'NIGHT, ALANNA.
I'M NOT SO SURE DRAGONS SHOULD SURVIVE!
G'NIGHT...
...
YOU NEED A NAME.
BUT THERE'S NO STOPPING ALANNA ONCE HER MIND'S MADE UP!
HOW ABOUT...
...GRIFFIN!
SQUARK
SIGH
EVERY DAY I HOPE FOR SOMETHING TO COME ALONG TO BREAK UP THE BOREDOM.
G'NIGHT, GRIFFIN.
BABYSITTING DRAGONS ISN'T EXACTLY WHAT I HAD IN MIND!

CHAPTER THREE

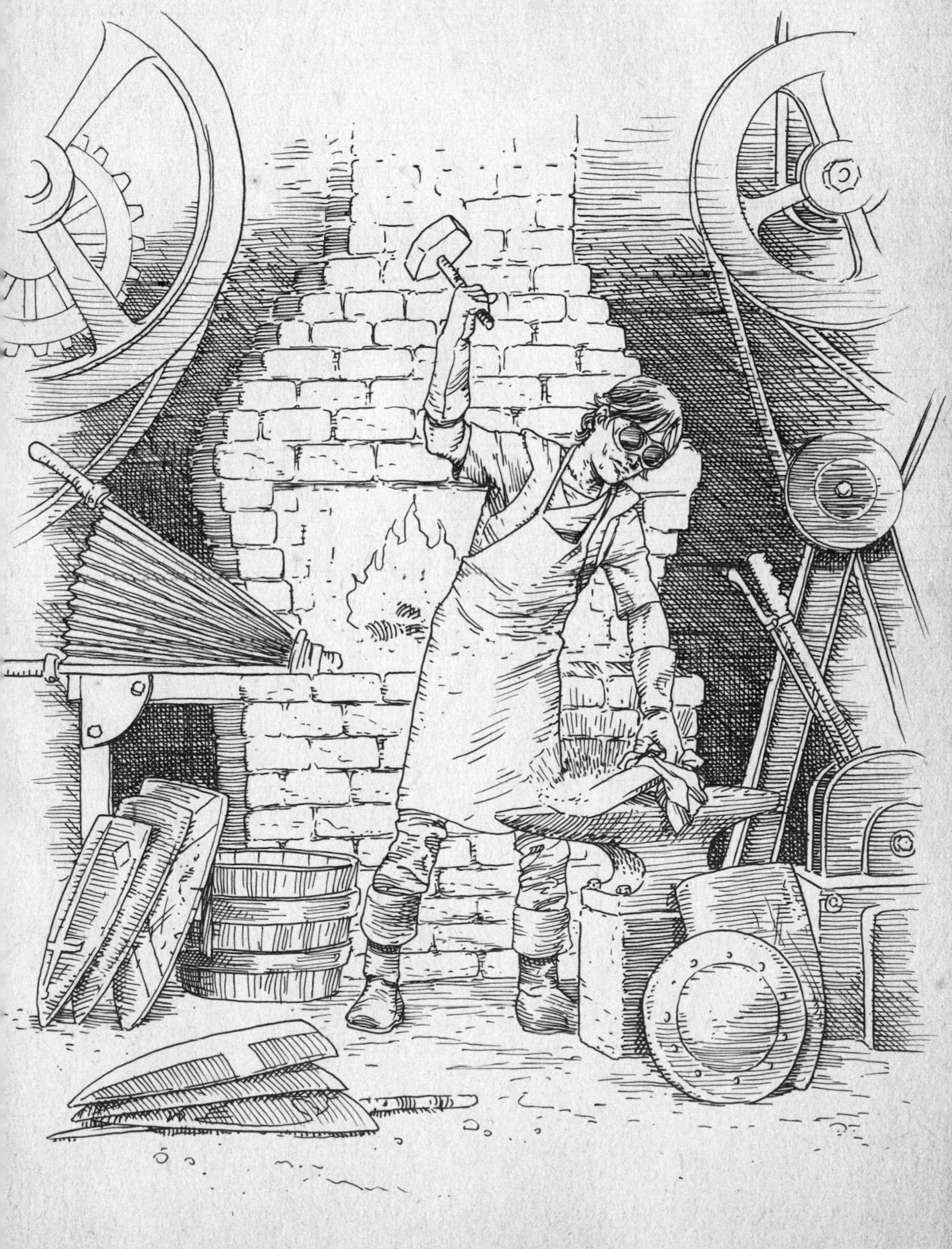

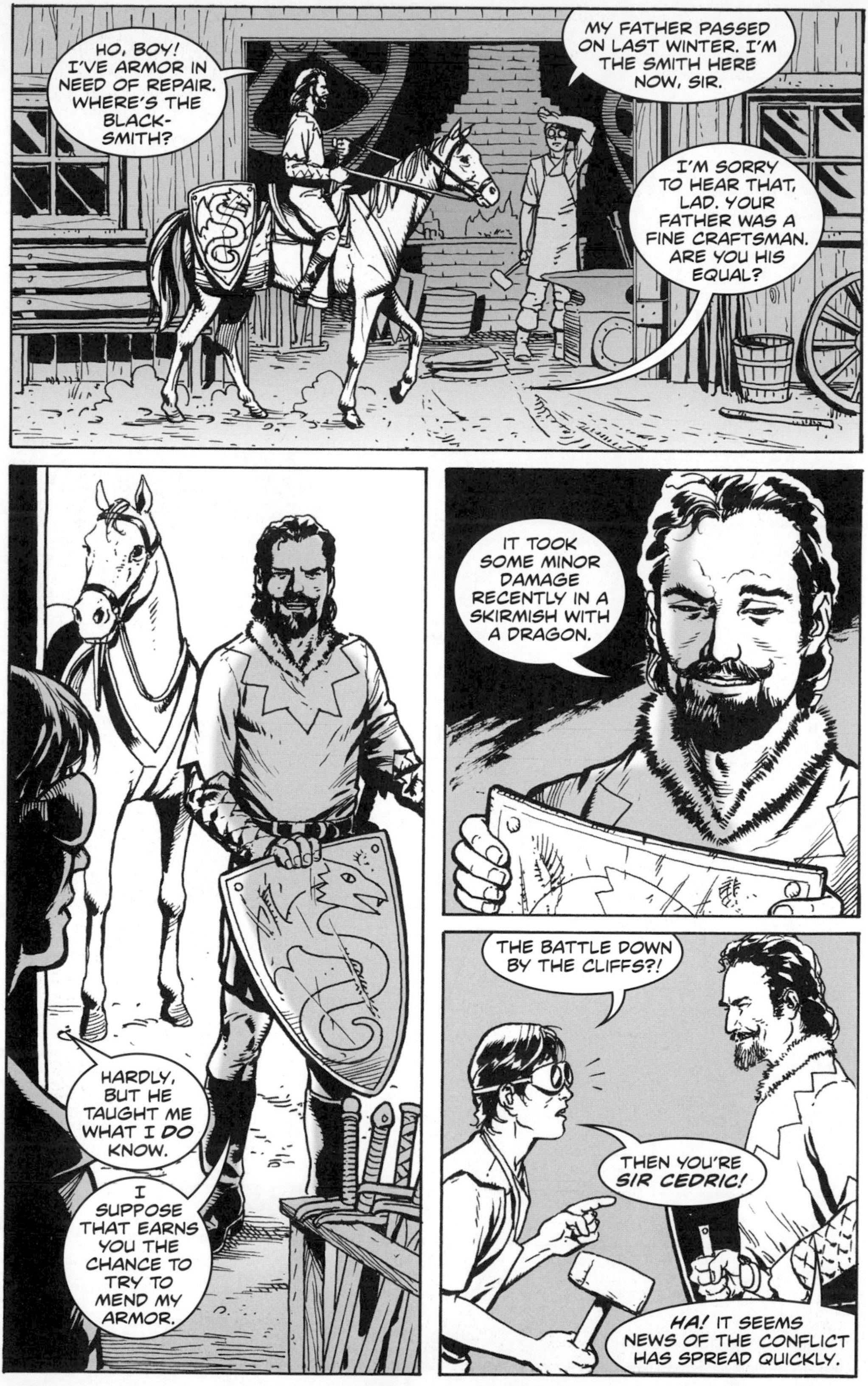
HO, BOY! I'VE ARMOR IN NEED OF REPAIR. WHERE'S THE BLACK-SMITH?
MY FATHER PASSED ON LAST WINTER. I'M THE SMITH HERE NOW, SIR.
I'M SORRY TO HEAR THAT, LAD. YOUR FATHER WAS A FINE CRAFTSMAN. ARE YOU HIS EQUAL?
HARDLY, BUT HE TAUGHT ME WHAT I *DO* KNOW.
I SUPPOSE THAT EARNS YOU THE CHANCE TO TRY TO MEND MY ARMOR.
IT TOOK SOME MINOR DAMAGE RECENTLY IN A SKIRMISH WITH A DRAGON.
THE BATTLE DOWN BY THE CLIFFS?!
THEN YOU'RE *SIR CEDRIC!*
HA! IT SEEMS NEWS OF THE CONFLICT HAS SPREAD QUICKLY.

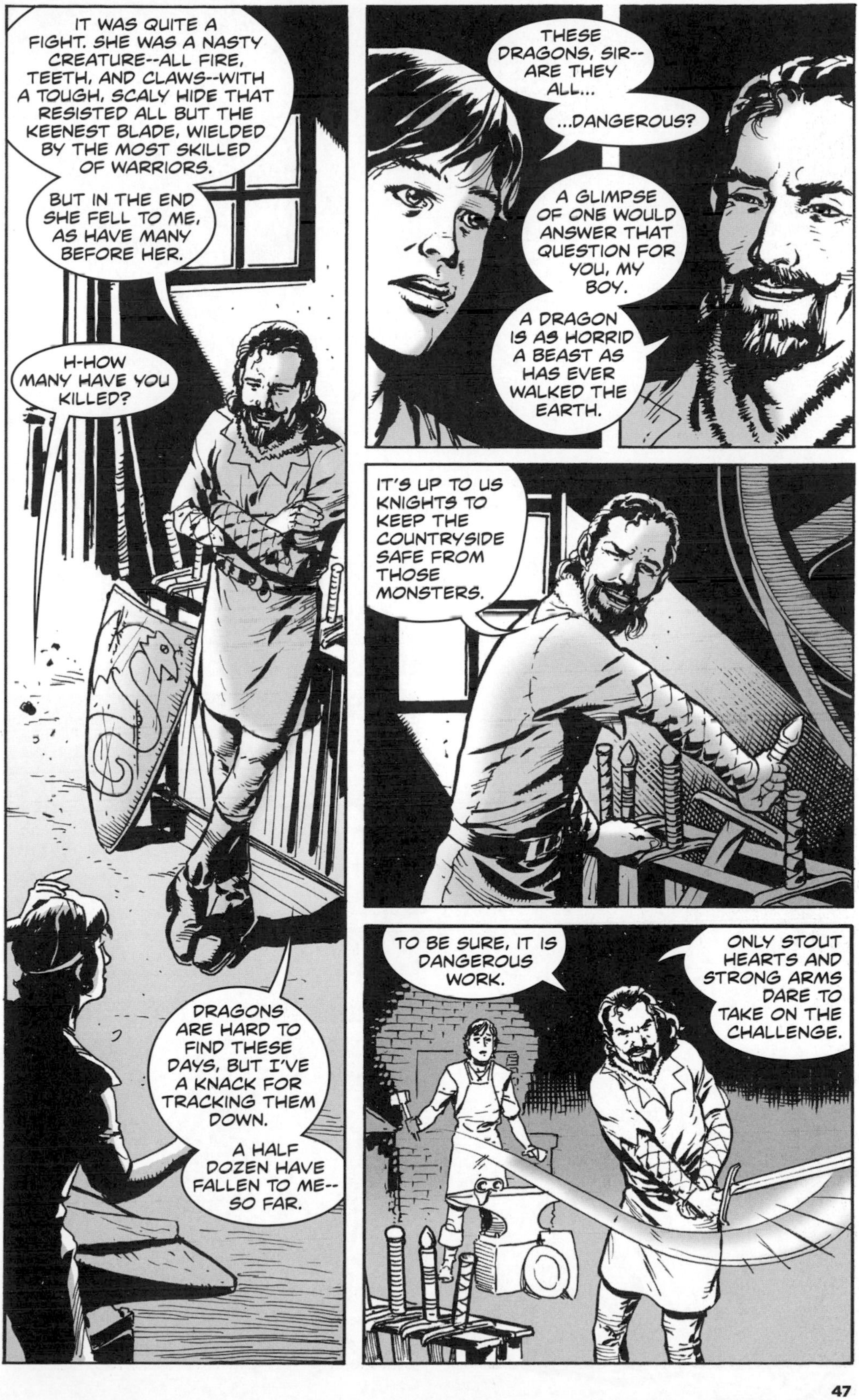
IT WAS QUITE A FIGHT. SHE WAS A NASTY CREATURE--ALL FIRE, TEETH, AND CLAWS--WITH A TOUGH, SCALY HIDE THAT RESISTED ALL BUT THE KEENEST BLADE, WIELDED BY THE MOST SKILLED OF WARRIORS.
BUT IN THE END SHE FELL TO ME, AS HAVE MANY BEFORE HER.
H-HOW MANY HAVE YOU KILLED?
DRAGONS ARE HARD TO FIND THESE DAYS, BUT I'VE A KNACK FOR TRACKING THEM DOWN.
A HALF DOZEN HAVE FALLEN TO ME--SO FAR.
THESE DRAGONS, SIR--ARE THEY ALL...
...DANGEROUS?
A GLIMPSE OF ONE WOULD ANSWER THAT QUESTION FOR YOU, MY BOY.
A DRAGON IS AS HORRID A BEAST AS HAS EVER WALKED THE EARTH.
IT'S UP TO US KNIGHTS TO KEEP THE COUNTRYSIDE SAFE FROM THOSE MONSTERS.
TO BE SURE, IT IS DANGEROUS WORK.
ONLY STOUT HEARTS AND STRONG ARMS DARE TO TAKE ON THE CHALLENGE.

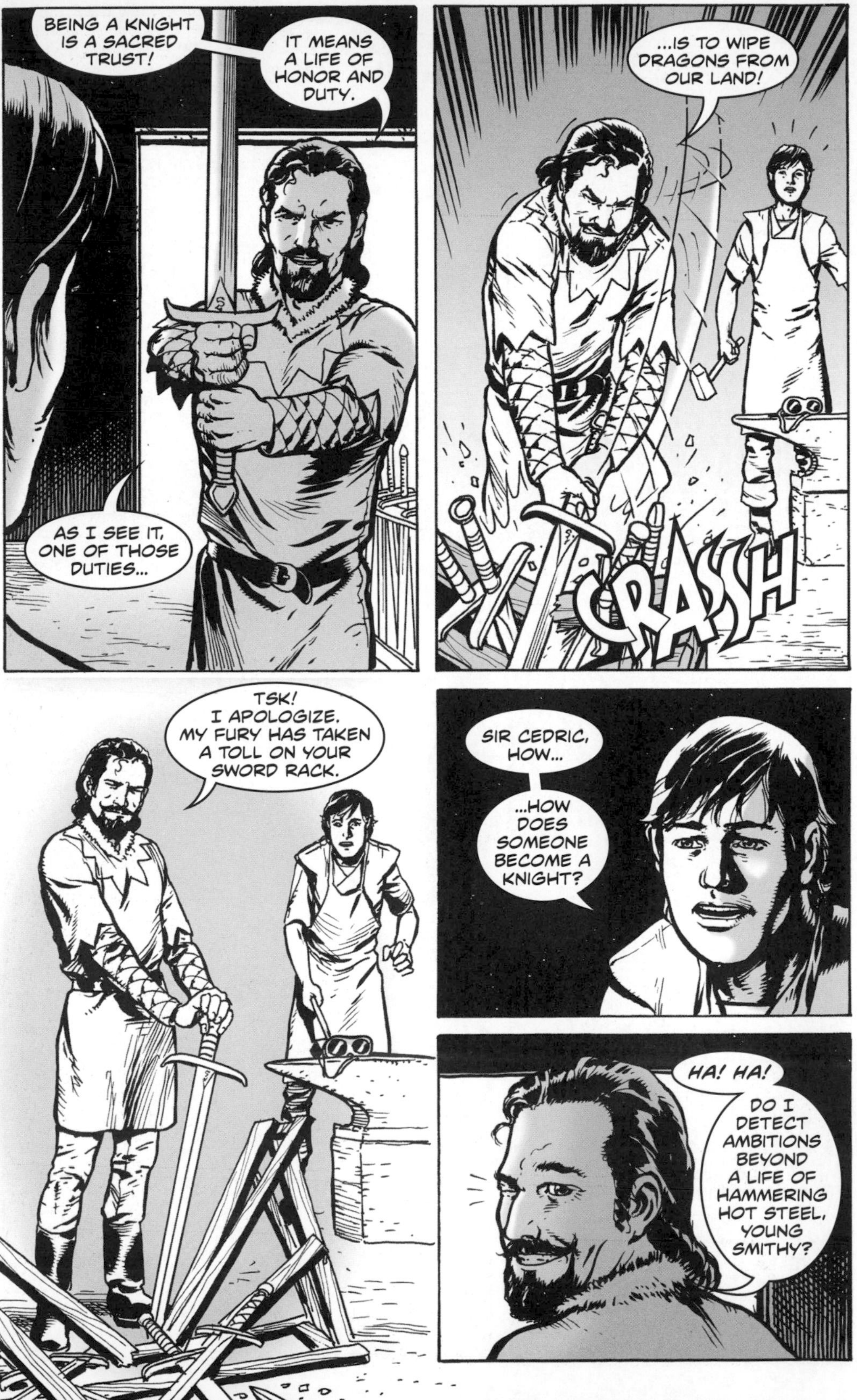
BEING A KNIGHT IS A SACRED TRUST!
IT MEANS A LIFE OF HONOR AND DUTY.
AS I SEE IT, ONE OF THOSE DUTIES...
...IS TO WIPE DRAGONS FROM OUR LAND!
CRASH
TSK! I APOLOGIZE. MY FURY HAS TAKEN A TOLL ON YOUR SWORD RACK.
SIR CEDRIC, HOW...
...HOW DOES SOMEONE BECOME A KNIGHT?
HA! HA!
DO I DETECT AMBITIONS BEYOND A LIFE OF HAMMERING HOT STEEL, YOUNG SMITHY?

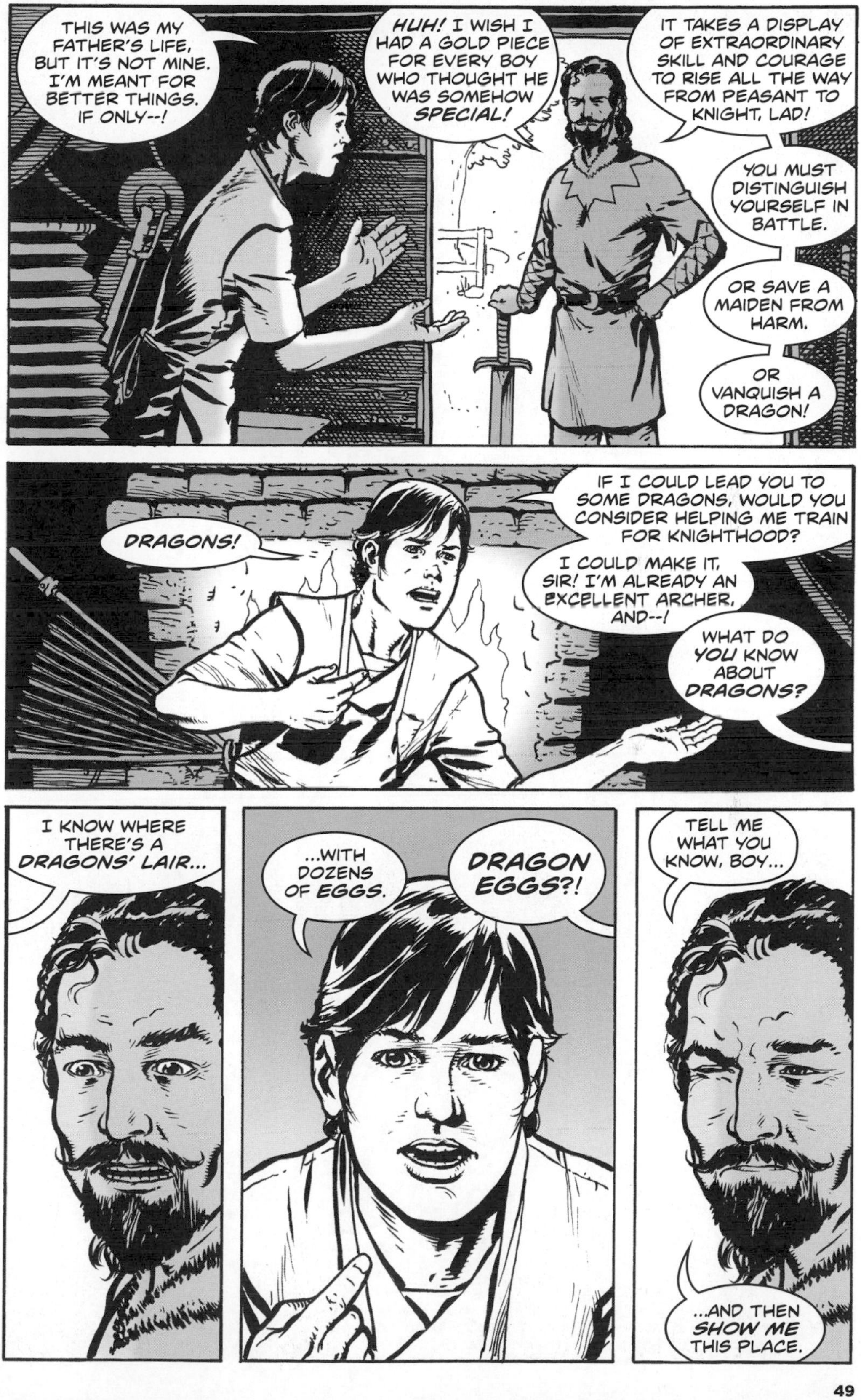
THIS WAS MY FATHER'S LIFE, BUT IT'S NOT MINE. I'M MEANT FOR BETTER THINGS. IF ONLY--!
HUH! I WISH I HAD A GOLD PIECE FOR EVERY BOY WHO THOUGHT HE WAS SOMEHOW SPECIAL!
IT TAKES A DISPLAY OF EXTRAORDINARY SKILL AND COURAGE TO RISE ALL THE WAY FROM PEASANT TO KNIGHT, LAD!
YOU MUST DISTINGUISH YOURSELF IN BATTLE.
OR SAVE A MAIDEN FROM HARM.
OR VANQUISH A DRAGON!
DRAGONS!
IF I COULD LEAD YOU TO SOME DRAGONS, WOULD YOU CONSIDER HELPING ME TRAIN FOR KNIGHTHOOD?
I COULD MAKE IT, SIR! I'M ALREADY AN EXCELLENT ARCHER, AND--!
WHAT DO YOU KNOW ABOUT DRAGONS?
I KNOW WHERE THERE'S A DRAGONS' LAIR...
...WITH DOZENS OF EGGS.
DRAGON EGGS?!
TELL ME WHAT YOU KNOW, BOY...
...AND THEN SHOW ME THIS PLACE.

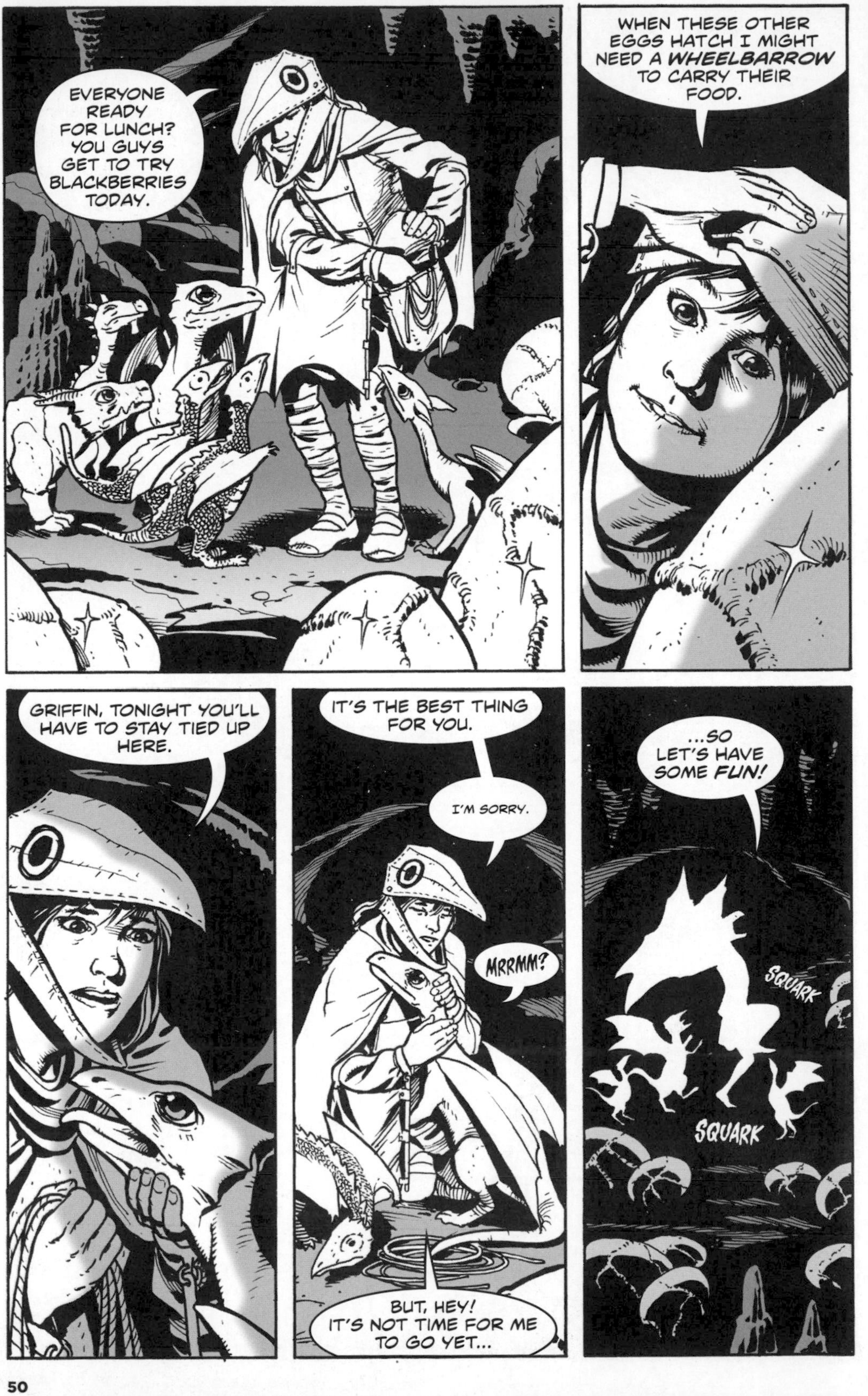
EVERYONE READY FOR LUNCH? YOU GUYS GET TO TRY BLACKBERRIES TODAY.
WHEN THESE OTHER EGGS HATCH I MIGHT NEED A *WHEELBARROW* TO CARRY THEIR FOOD.
GRIFFIN, TONIGHT YOU'LL HAVE TO STAY TIED UP HERE.
IT'S THE BEST THING FOR YOU.
I'M SORRY.
MRRMM?
BUT, HEY! IT'S NOT TIME FOR ME TO GO YET...
...SO LET'S HAVE SOME *FUN!*
SQUARK
SQUARK

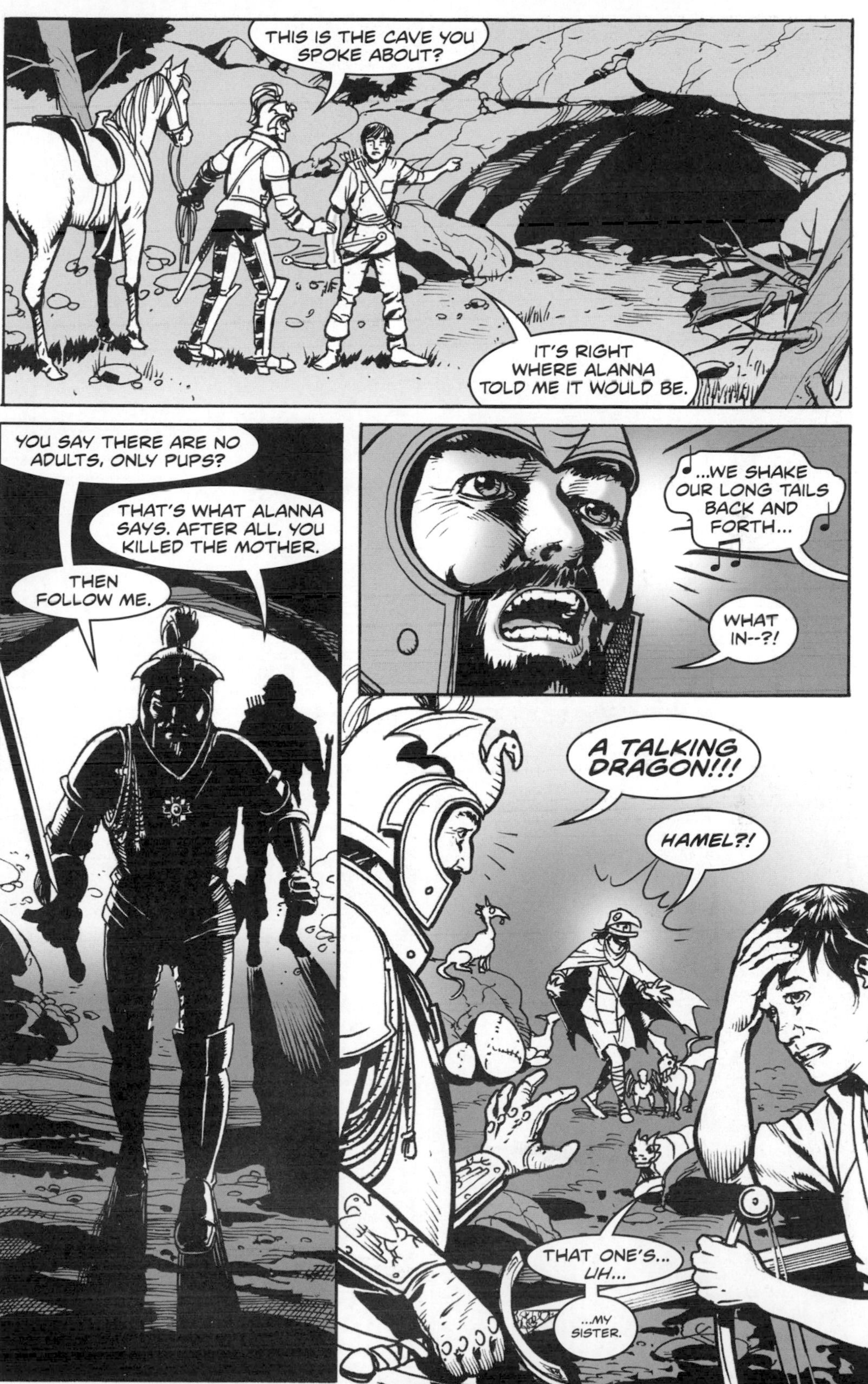
THIS IS THE CAVE YOU SPOKE ABOUT?
IT'S RIGHT WHERE ALANNA TOLD ME IT WOULD BE.
YOU SAY THERE ARE NO ADULTS, ONLY PUPS?
THAT'S WHAT ALANNA SAYS. AFTER ALL, YOU KILLED THE MOTHER.
THEN FOLLOW ME.
...WE SHAKE OUR LONG TAILS BACK AND FORTH...
WHAT IN--?!
A TALKING DRAGON!!!
HAMEL?!
THAT ONE'S... UH...
...MY SISTER.

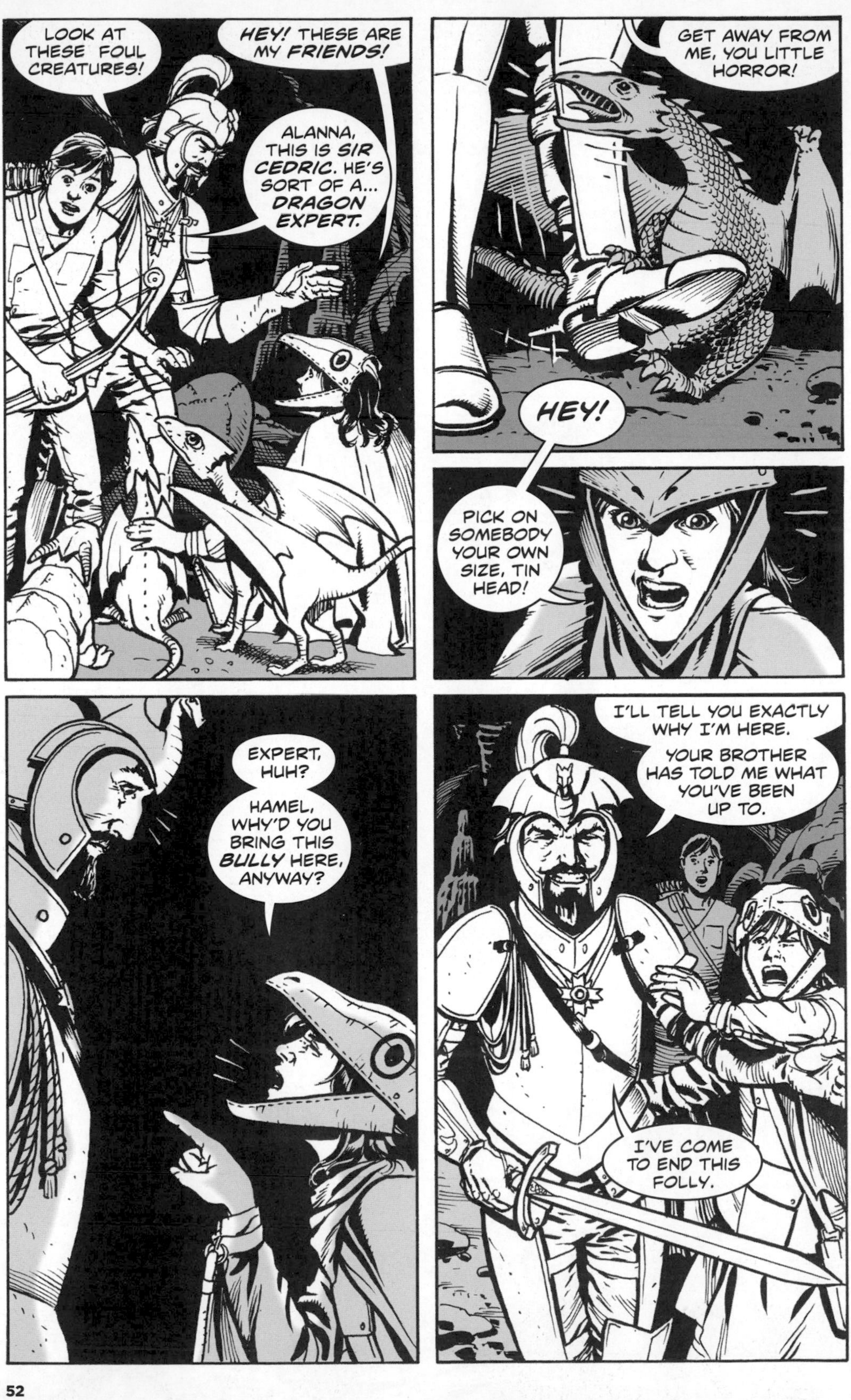
LOOK AT THESE FOUL CREATURES!
HEY! THESE ARE MY FRIENDS!
ALANNA, THIS IS SIR CEDRIC. HE'S SORT OF A... DRAGON EXPERT.
GET AWAY FROM ME, YOU LITTLE HORROR!
HEY!
PICK ON SOMEBODY YOUR OWN SIZE, TIN HEAD!
EXPERT, HUH?
HAMEL, WHY'D YOU BRING THIS BULLY HERE, ANYWAY?
I'LL TELL YOU EXACTLY WHY I'M HERE.
YOUR BROTHER HAS TOLD ME WHAT YOU'VE BEEN UP TO.
I'VE COME TO END THIS FOLLY.

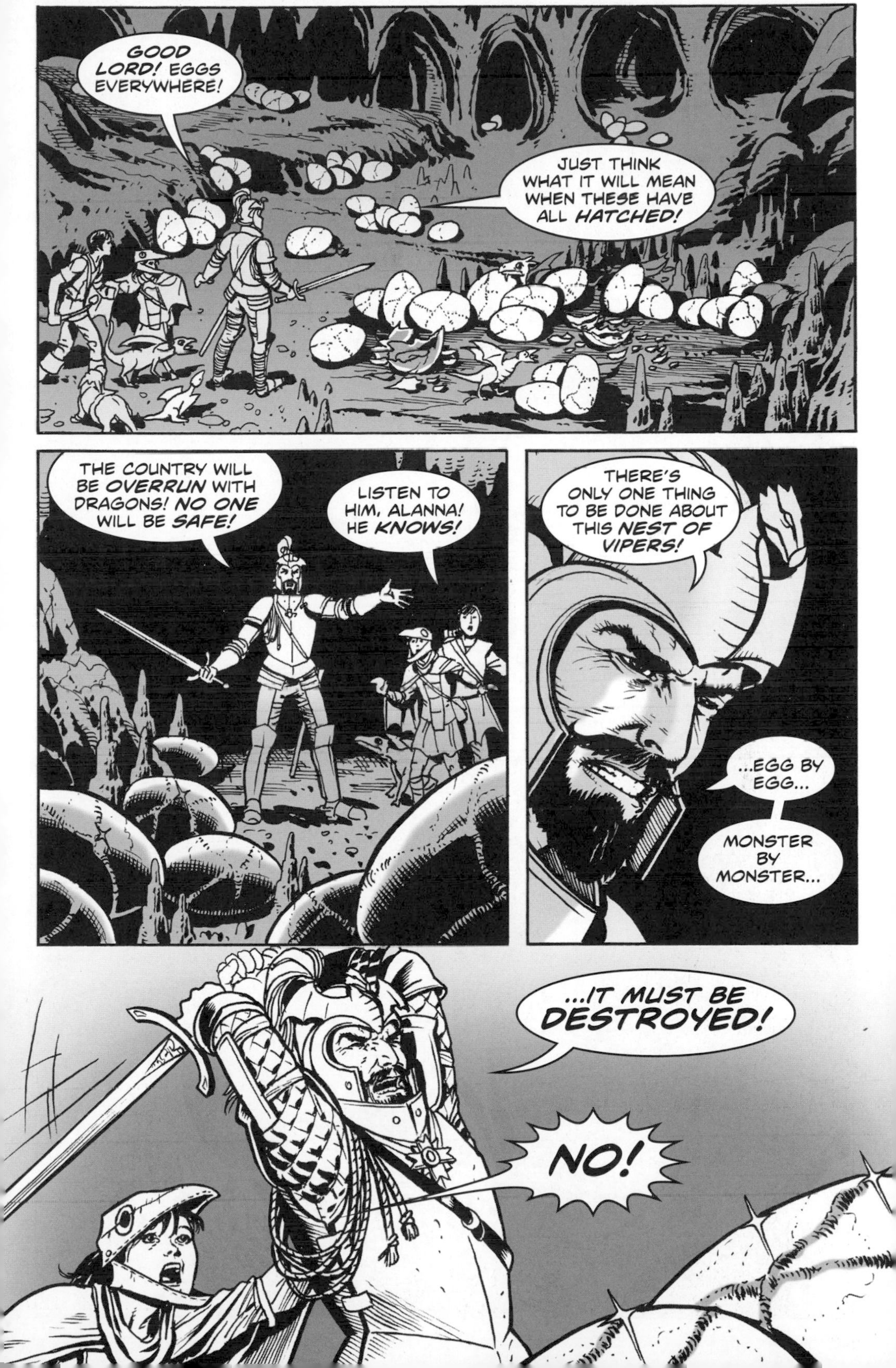
GOOD LORD! EGGS EVERYWHERE!
JUST THINK WHAT IT WILL MEAN WHEN THESE HAVE ALL HATCHED!
THE COUNTRY WILL BE OVERRUN WITH DRAGONS! NO ONE WILL BE SAFE!
LISTEN TO HIM, ALANNA! HE KNOWS!
THERE'S ONLY ONE THING TO BE DONE ABOUT THIS NEST OF VIPERS!
...EGG BY EGG...
MONSTER BY MONSTER...
...IT MUST BE DESTROYED!
NO!

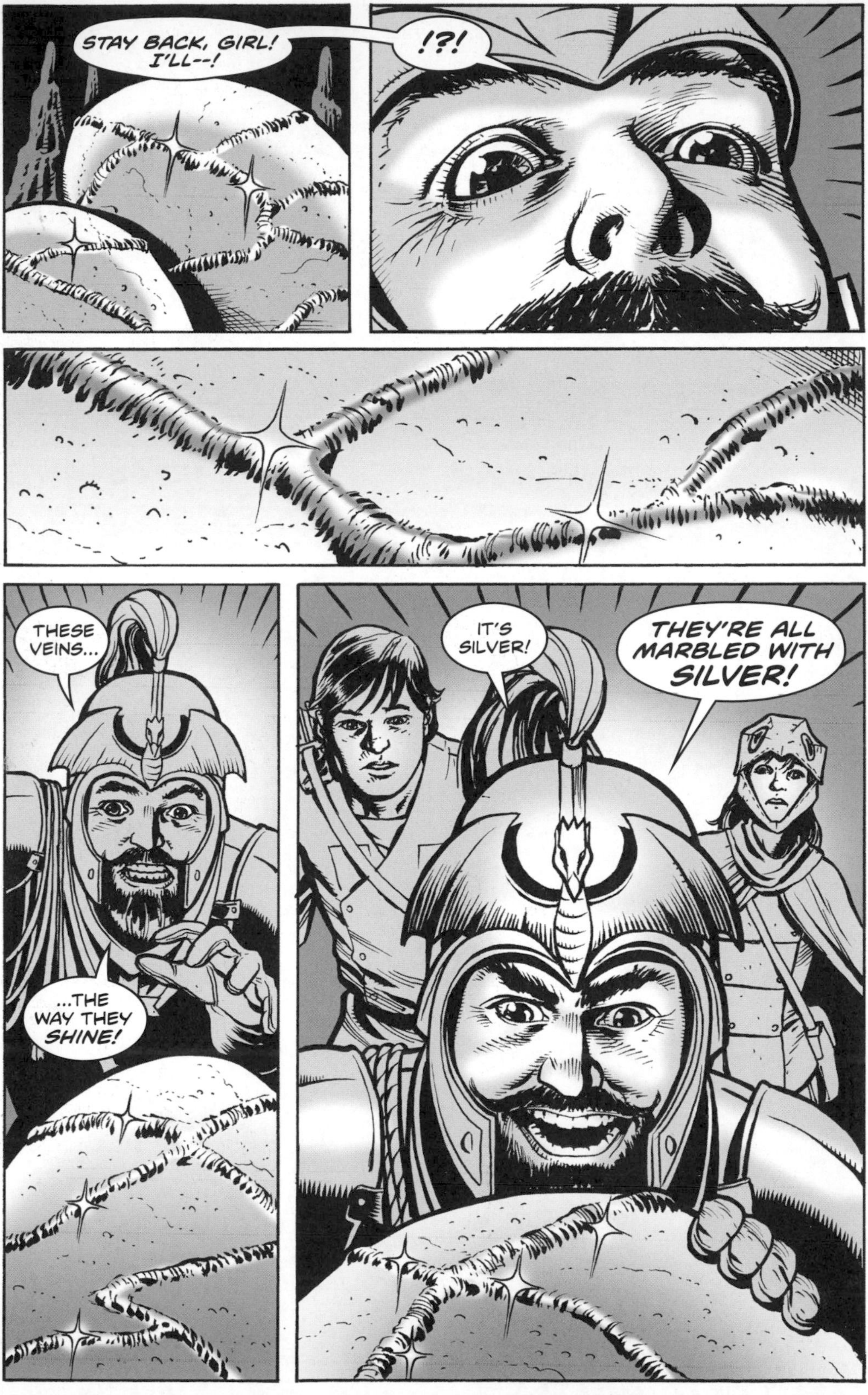
STAY BACK, GIRL! I'LL--!
!?!
THESE VEINS...
...THE WAY THEY SHINE!
IT'S SILVER!
THEY'RE ALL MARBLED WITH SILVER!

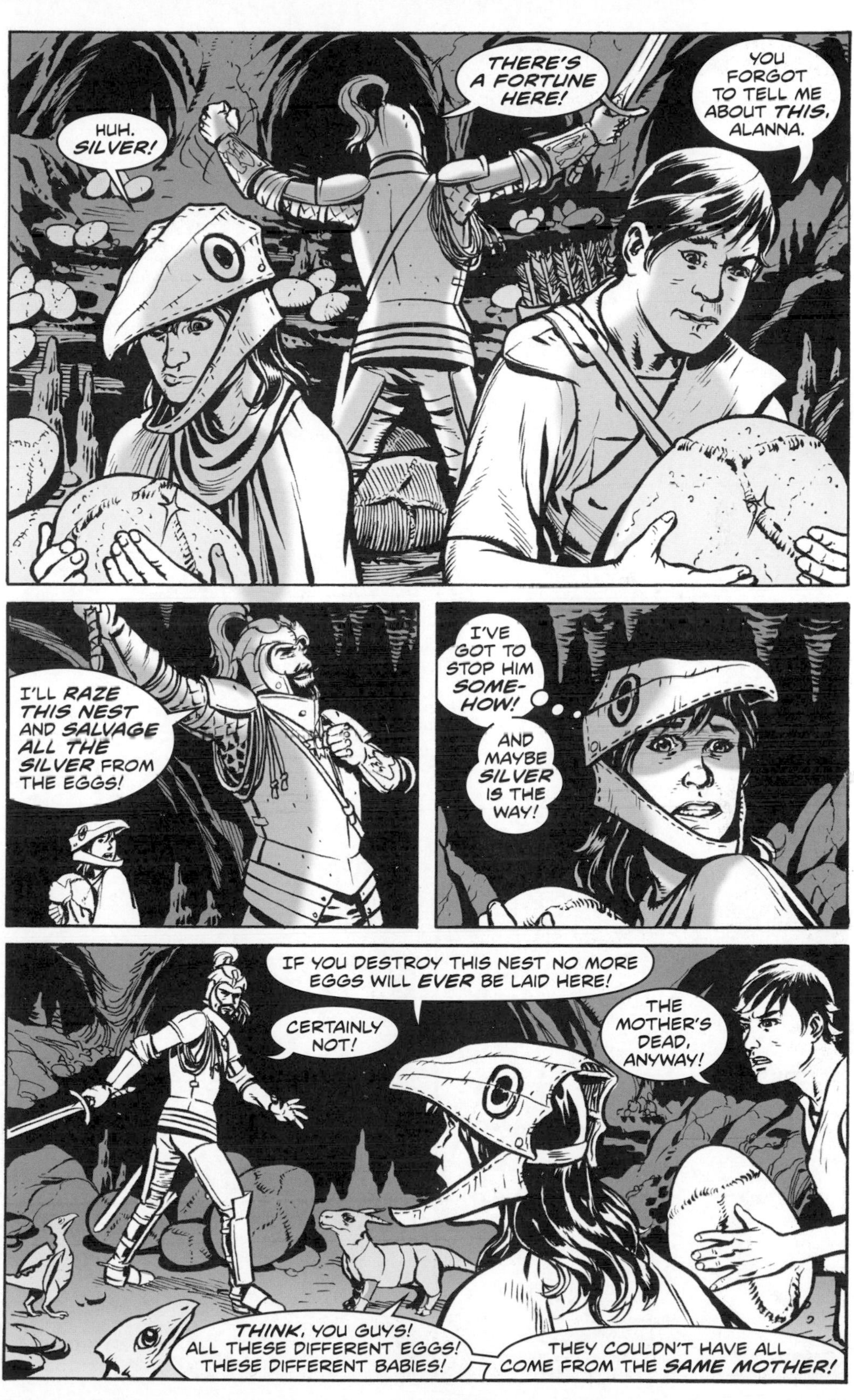
HUH. SILVER!
THERE'S A FORTUNE HERE!
YOU FORGOT TO TELL ME ABOUT THIS, ALANNA.
I'LL RAZE THIS NEST AND SALVAGE ALL THE SILVER FROM THE EGGS!
I'VE GOT TO STOP HIM SOMEHOW!
AND MAYBE SILVER IS THE WAY!
IF YOU DESTROY THIS NEST NO MORE EGGS WILL EVER BE LAID HERE!
CERTAINLY NOT!
THE MOTHER'S DEAD, ANYWAY!
THINK, YOU GUYS! ALL THESE DIFFERENT EGGS! THESE DIFFERENT BABIES!
THEY COULDN'T HAVE ALL COME FROM THE SAME MOTHER!

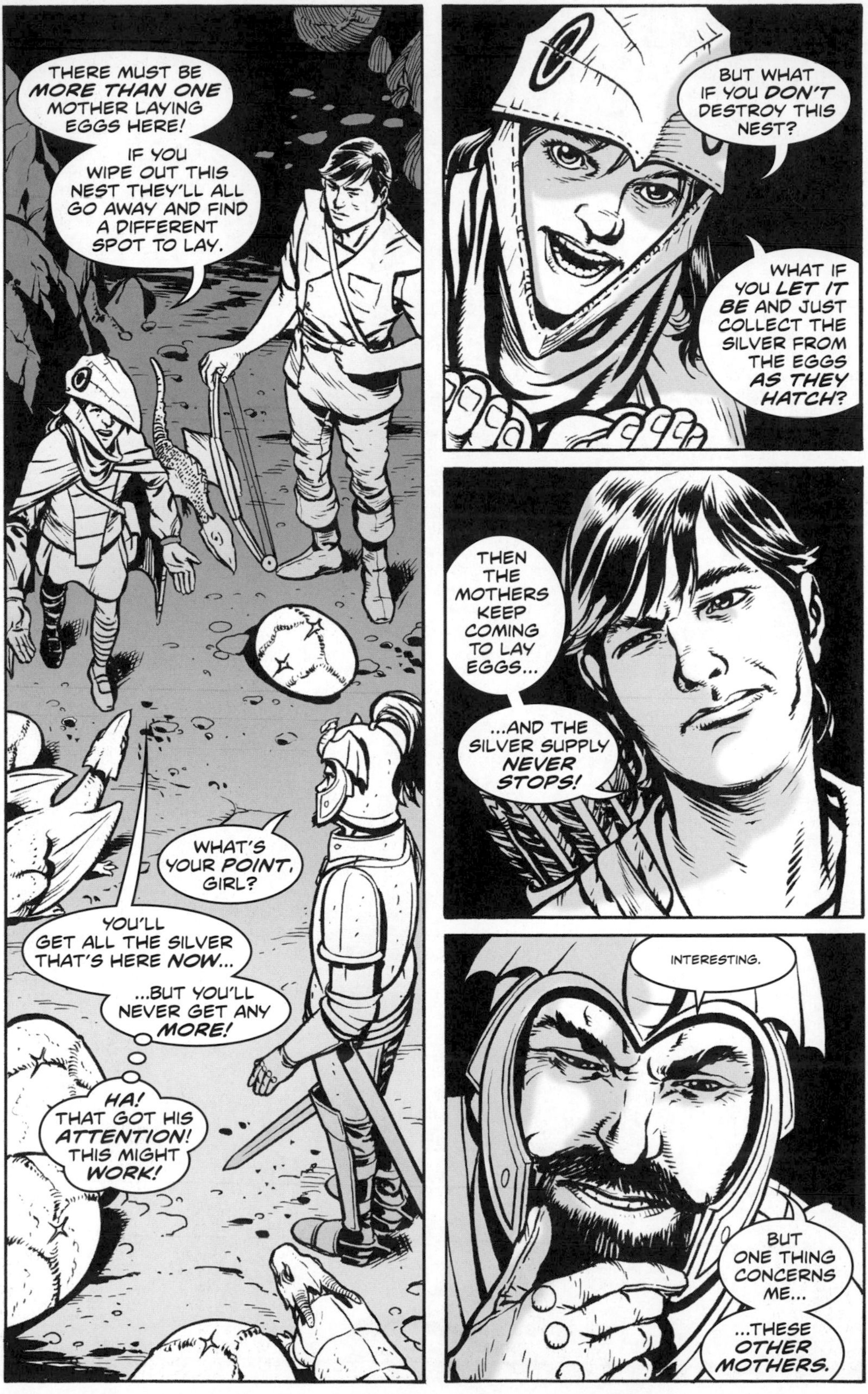
THERE MUST BE MORE THAN ONE MOTHER LAYING EGGS HERE!
IF YOU WIPE OUT THIS NEST THEY'LL ALL GO AWAY AND FIND A DIFFERENT SPOT TO LAY.
WHAT'S YOUR POINT, GIRL?
YOU'LL GET ALL THE SILVER THAT'S HERE NOW...
...BUT YOU'LL NEVER GET ANY MORE!
HA! THAT GOT HIS ATTENTION! THIS MIGHT WORK!
BUT WHAT IF YOU DON'T DESTROY THIS NEST?
WHAT IF YOU LET IT BE AND JUST COLLECT THE SILVER FROM THE EGGS AS THEY HATCH?
THEN THE MOTHERS KEEP COMING TO LAY EGGS...
...AND THE SILVER SUPPLY NEVER STOPS!
INTERESTING.
BUT ONE THING CONCERNS ME...
...THESE OTHER MOTHERS.

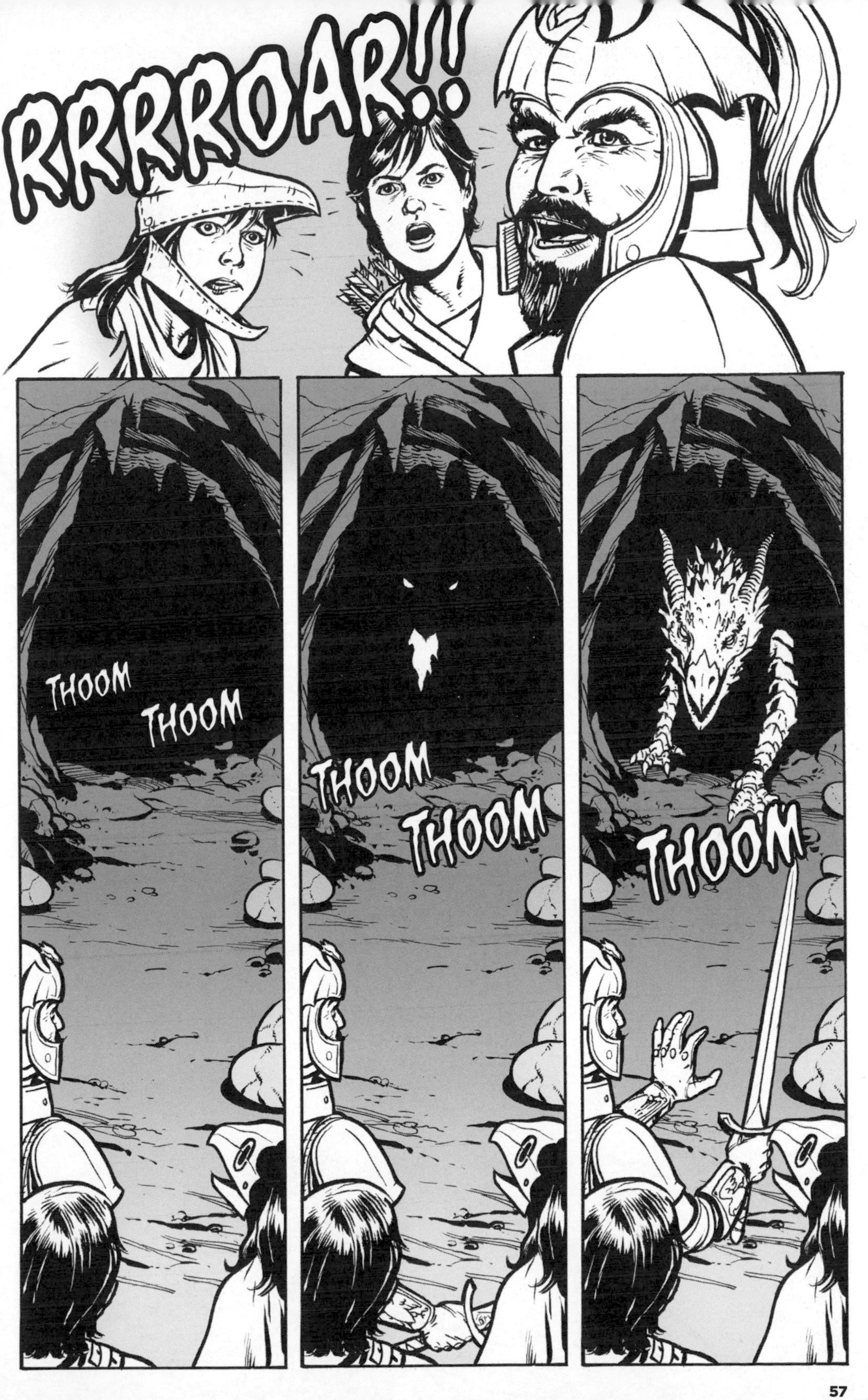

RRRROAR!!
THOOM
THOOM
THOOM
THOOM
THOOM

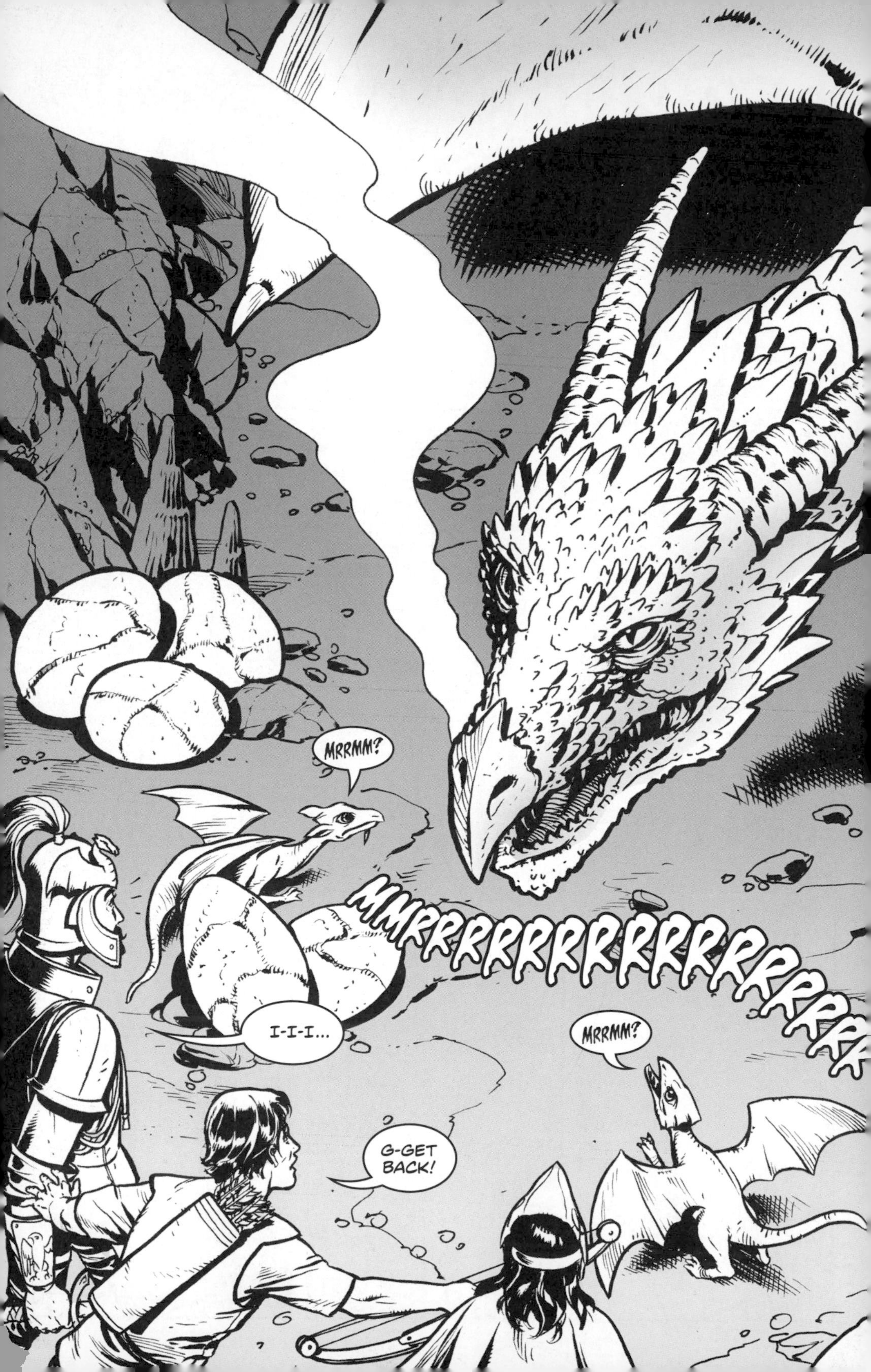
MRRMM?
MMRRRRRRRRRRRRRRRRRRK
I-I-I...
MRRMM?
G-GET BACK!

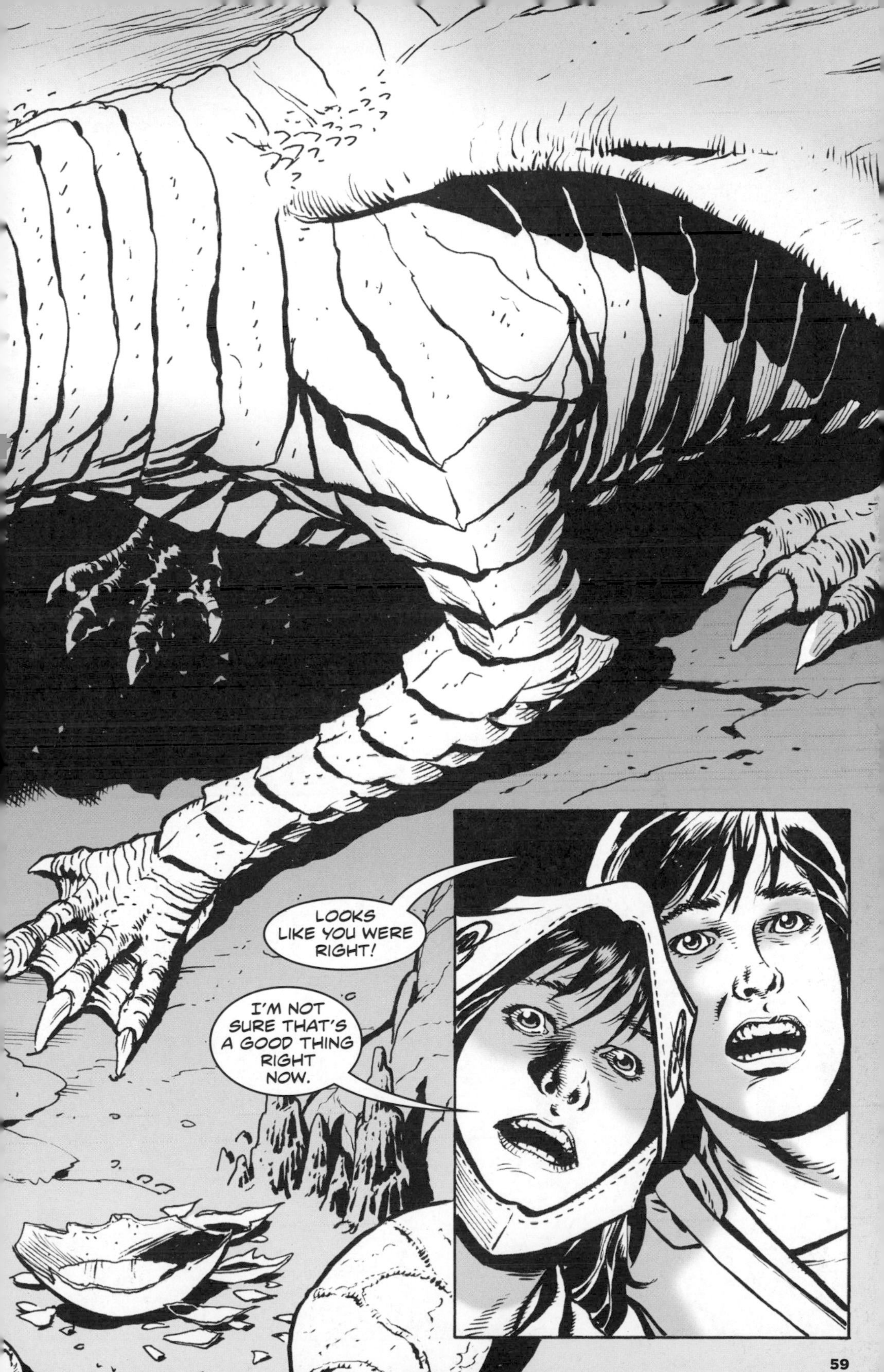
LOOKS LIKE YOU WERE RIGHT!
I'M NOT SURE THAT'S A GOOD THING RIGHT NOW.

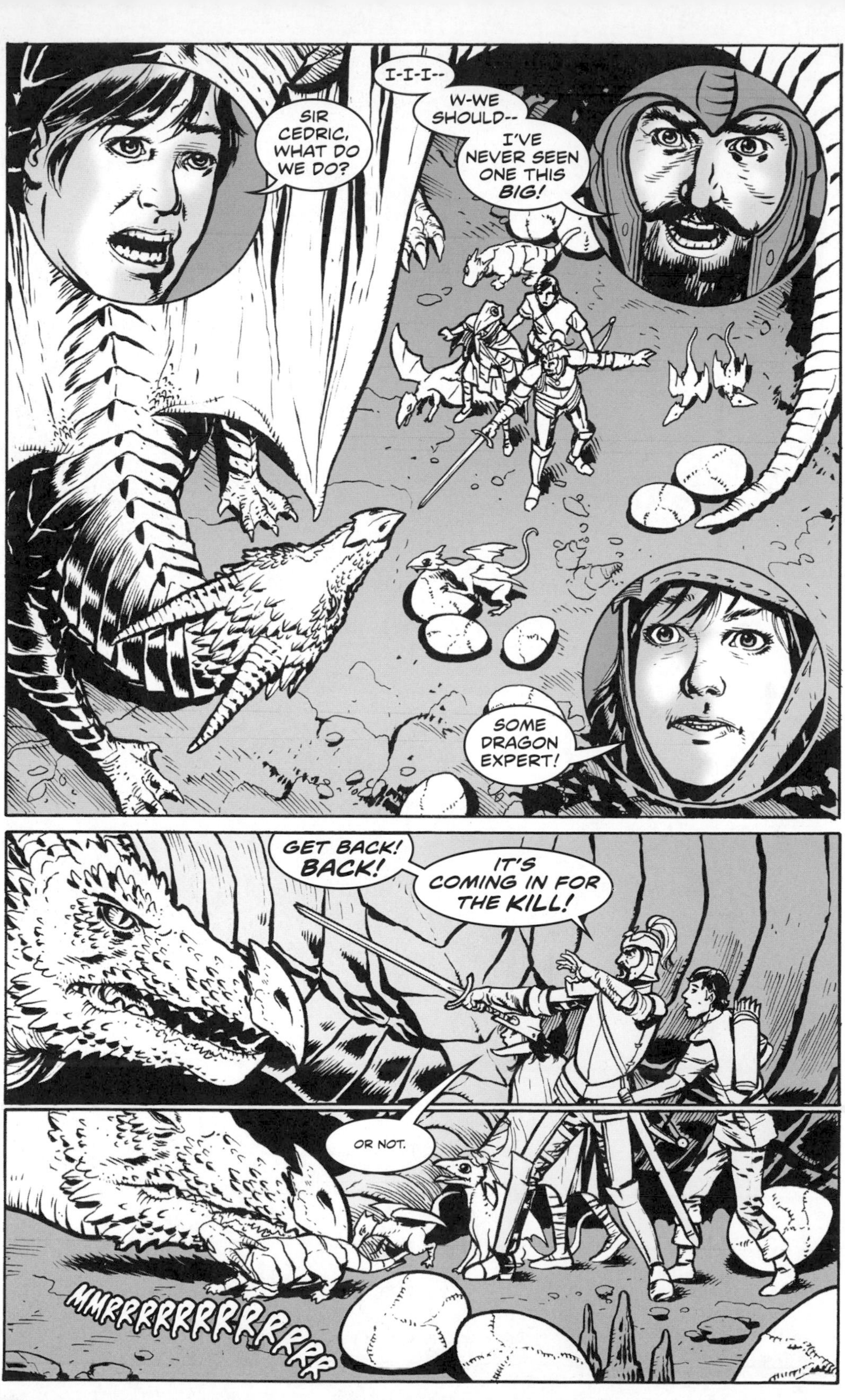
SIR CEDRIC, WHAT DO WE DO?
I-I-I--
W-WE SHOULD--
I'VE NEVER SEEN ONE THIS BIG!
SOME DRAGON EXPERT!
GET BACK! BACK!
IT'S COMING IN FOR THE KILL!
OR NOT.
MMRRRRRRRRRRRRR

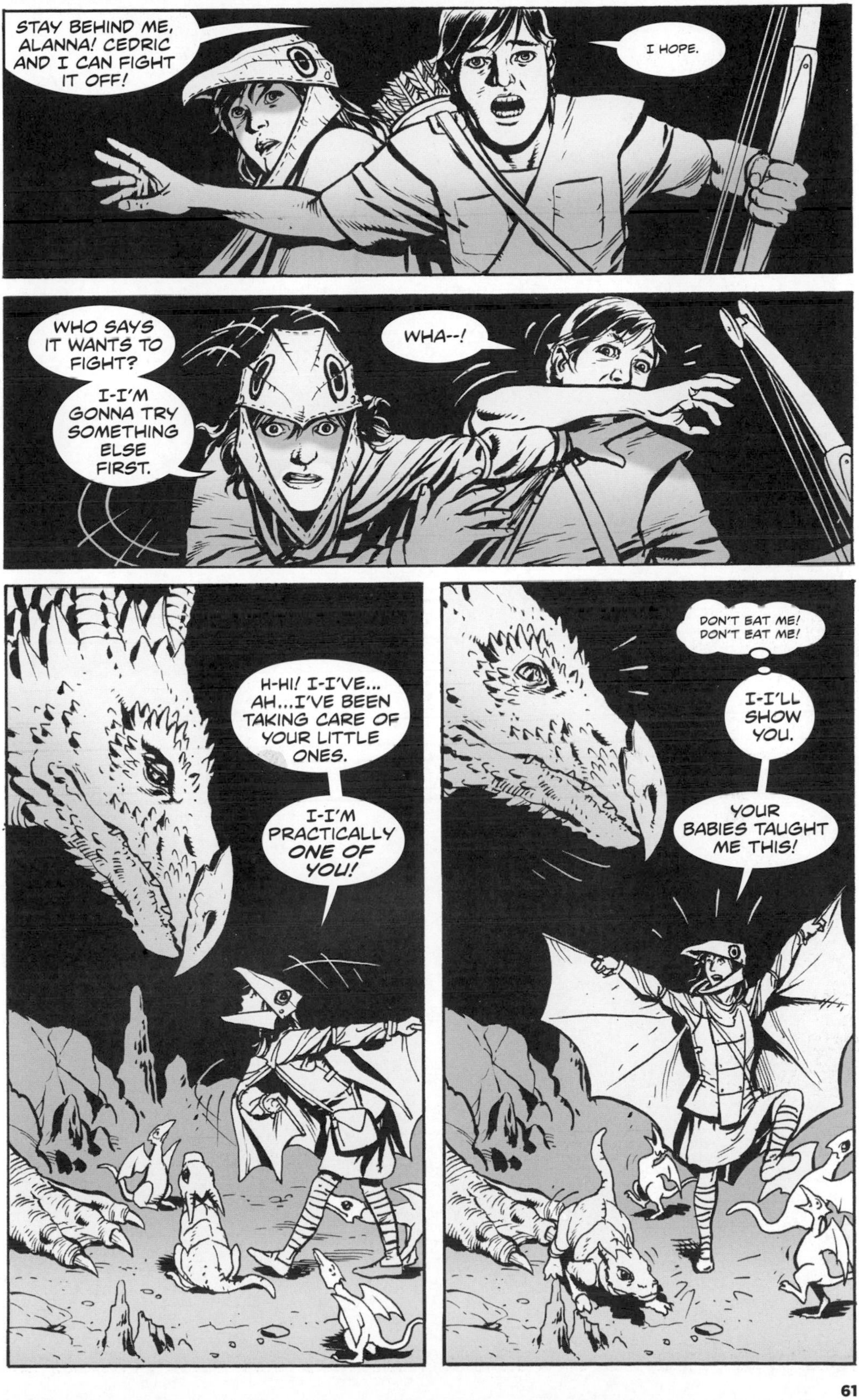
STAY BEHIND ME, ALANNA! CEDRIC AND I CAN FIGHT IT OFF!
I HOPE.
WHO SAYS IT WANTS TO FIGHT?
I-I'M GONNA TRY SOMETHING ELSE FIRST.
WHA--!
H-HI! I-I'VE... AH...I'VE BEEN TAKING CARE OF YOUR LITTLE ONES.
I-I'M PRACTICALLY ONE OF YOU!
DON'T EAT ME! DON'T EAT ME!
I-I'LL SHOW YOU.
YOUR BABIES TAUGHT ME THIS!

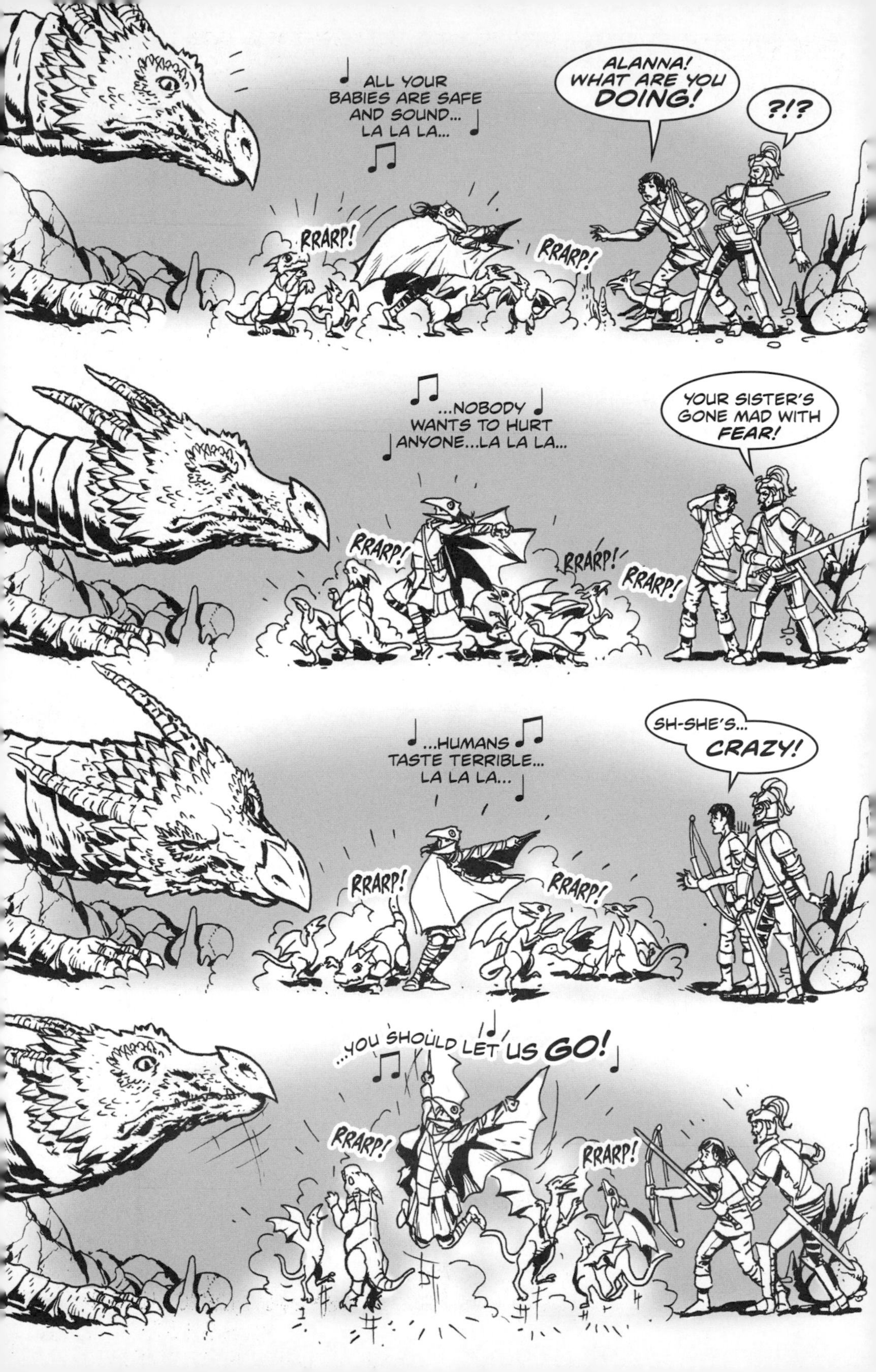

ALL YOUR BABIES ARE SAFE AND SOUND... LA LA LA...
ALANNA! WHAT ARE YOU DOING!
?!?
RRARP!
RRARP!
...NOBODY WANTS TO HURT ANYONE...LA LA LA...
YOUR SISTER'S GONE MAD WITH FEAR!
RRARP!
RRARP!
RRARP!
...HUMANS TASTE TERRIBLE... LA LA LA...
SH-SHE'S... CRAZY!
RRARP!
RRARP!
...YOU SHOULD LET US GO!
RRARP!
RRARP!

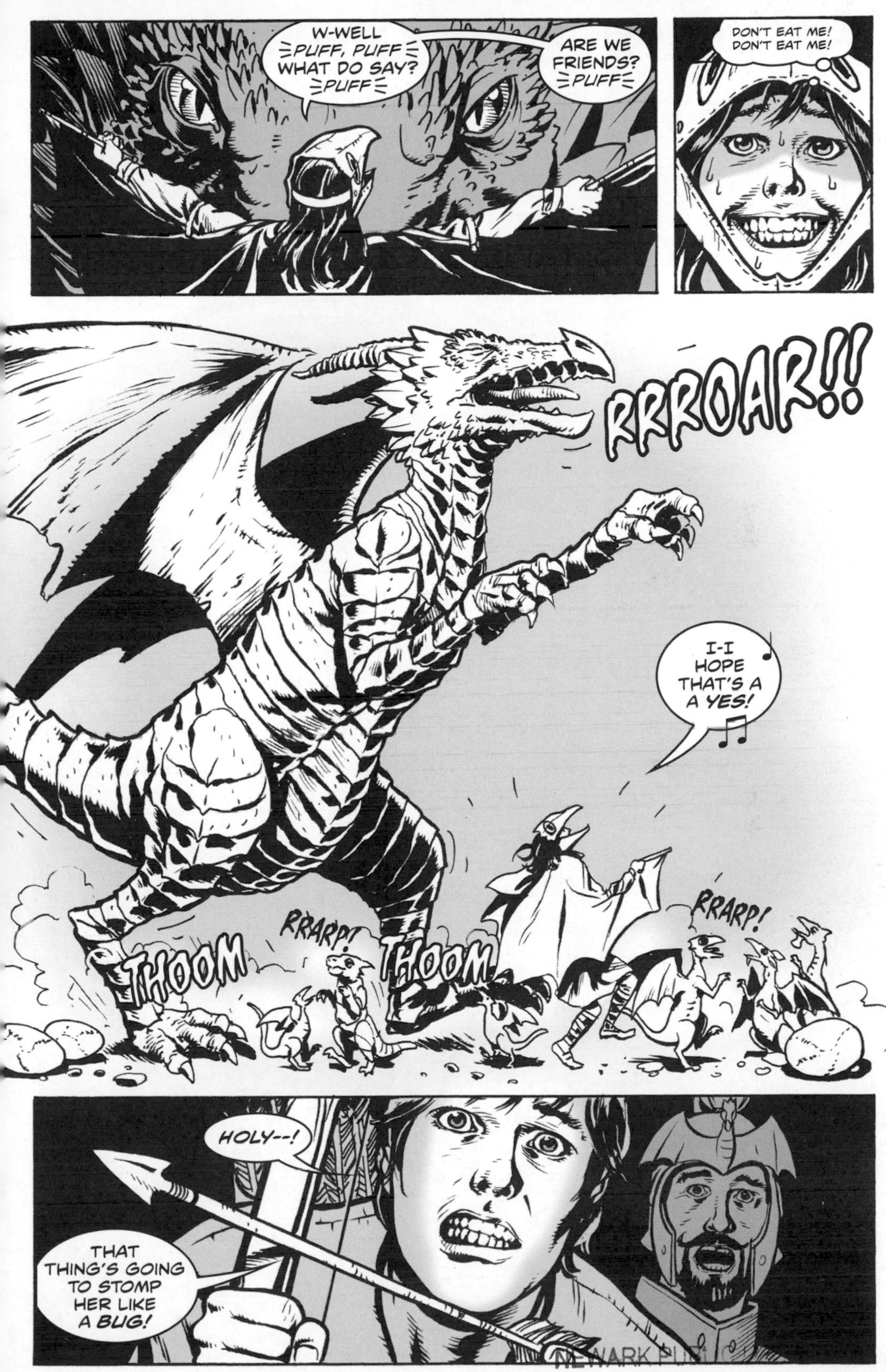
W-WELL
PUFF, PUFF
WHAT DO SAY?
PUFF
ARE WE
FRIENDS?
PUFF
DON'T EAT ME!
DON'T EAT ME!
RRROAR!!
I-I
HOPE
THAT'S A
A YES!
RRARP!
THOOM
THOOM
RRARP!
HOLY--!
THAT
THING'S GOING
TO STOMP
HER LIKE
A BUG!

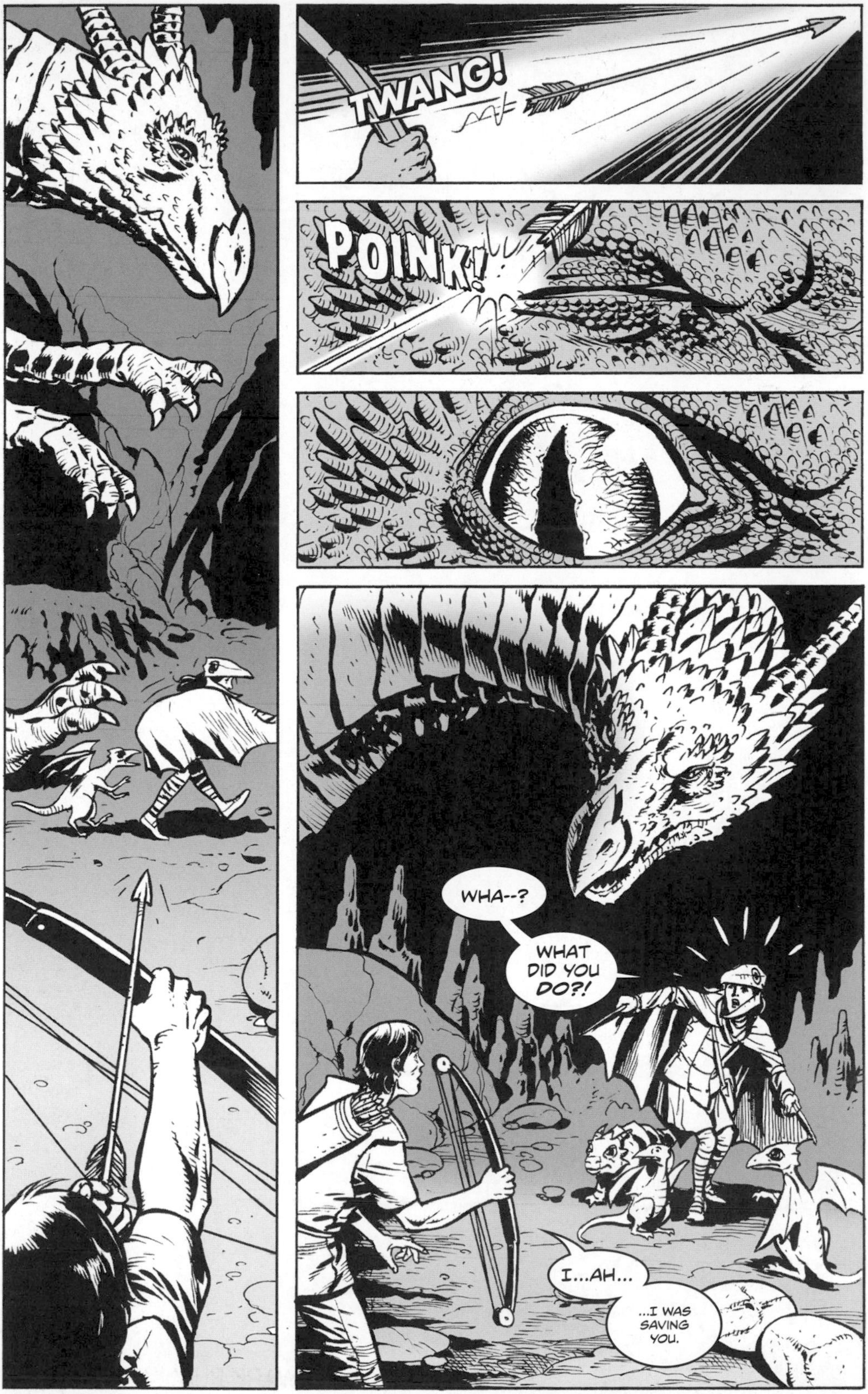
TWANG!
POINK!
WHA--?
WHAT DID YOU DO?!
I...AH...
...I WAS SAVING YOU.

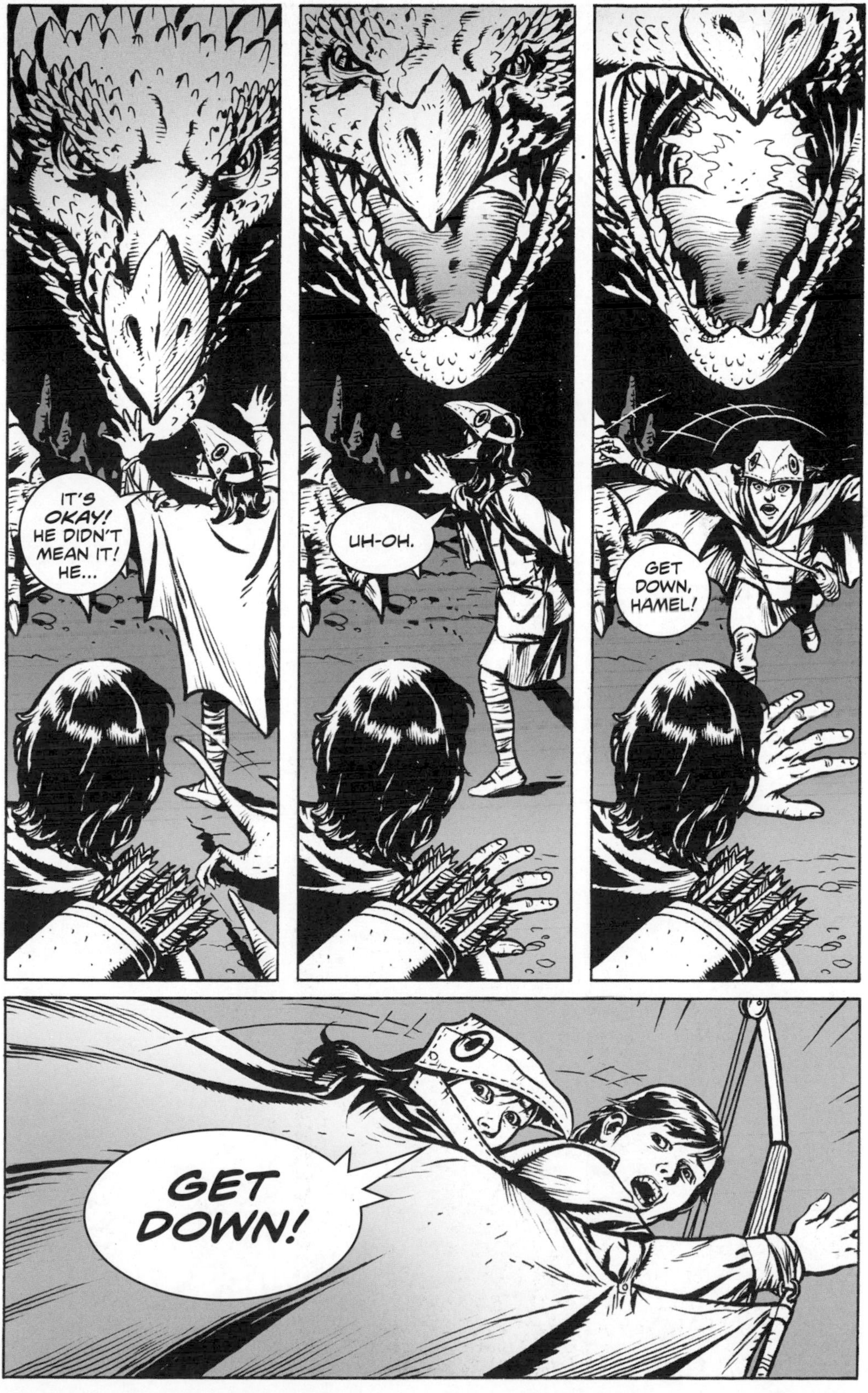
IT'S OKAY! HE DIDN'T MEAN IT! HE...
UH-OH.
GET DOWN, HAMEL!
GET DOWN!

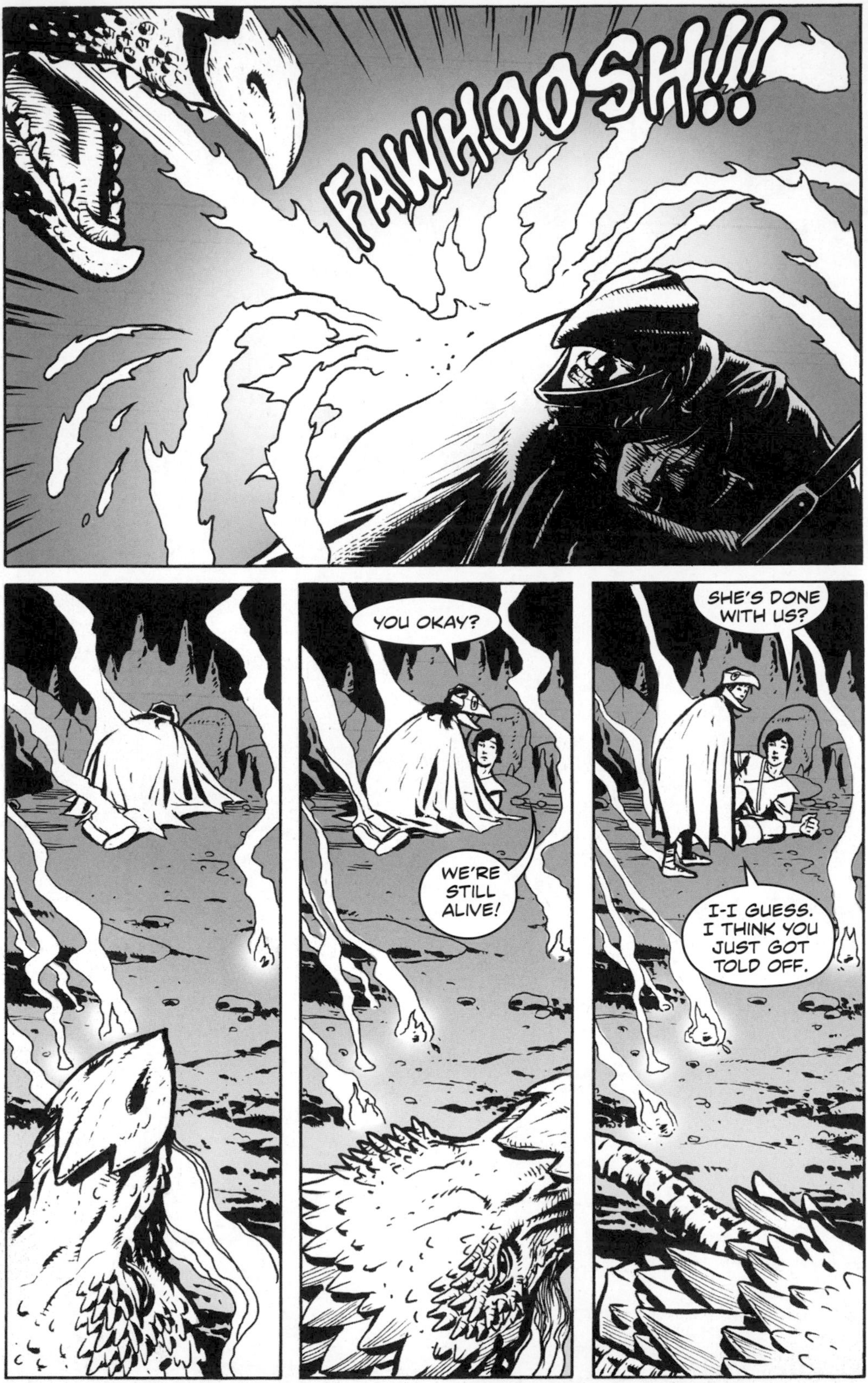
FAWHOOSH!!!
YOU OKAY?
WE'RE STILL ALIVE!
SHE'S DONE WITH US?
I-I GUESS. I THINK YOU JUST GOT TOLD OFF.

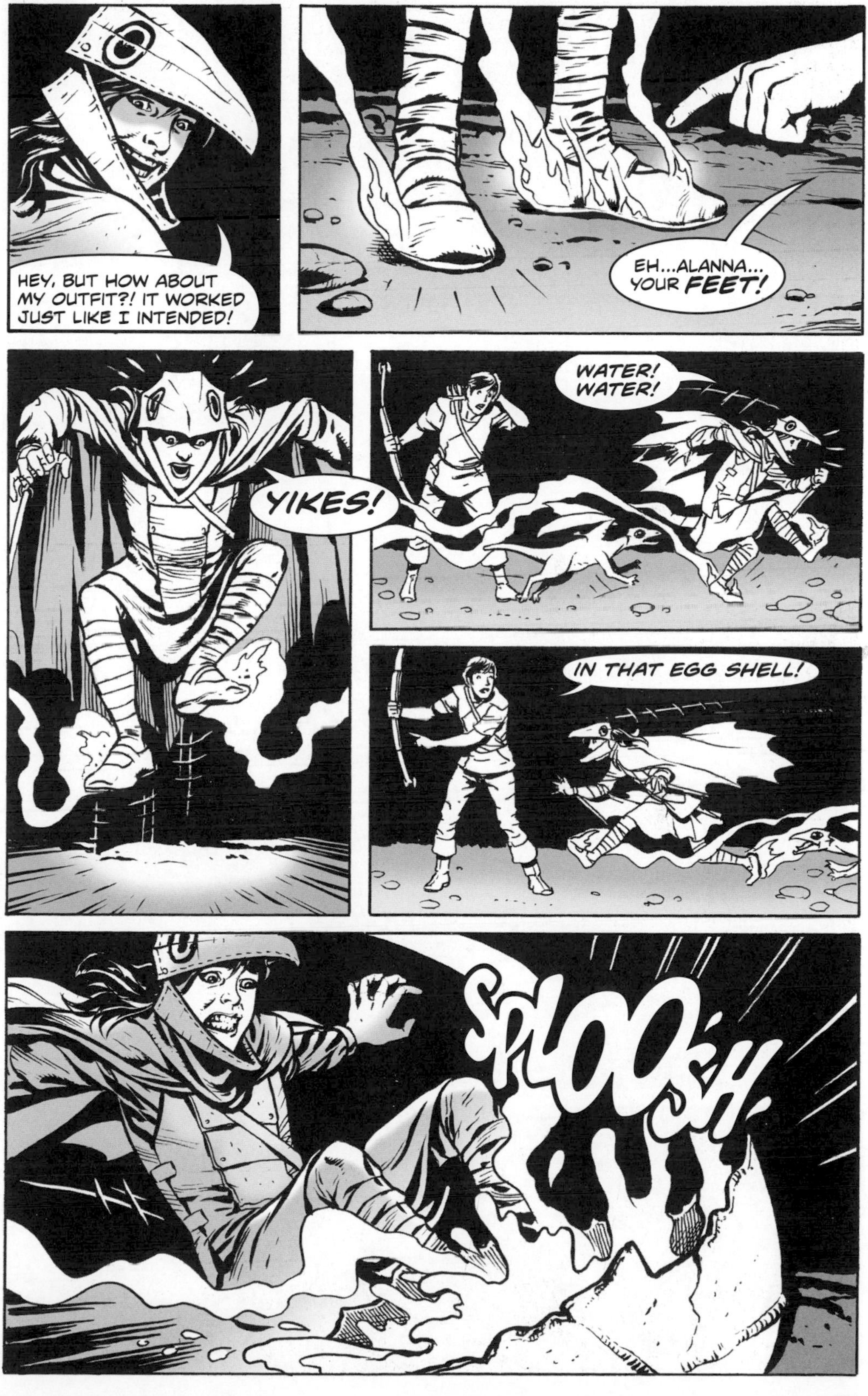
HEY, BUT HOW ABOUT MY OUTFIT?! IT WORKED JUST LIKE I INTENDED!
EH...ALANNA... YOUR FEET!
YIKES!
WATER! WATER!
IN THAT EGG SHELL!
SPLOOSH

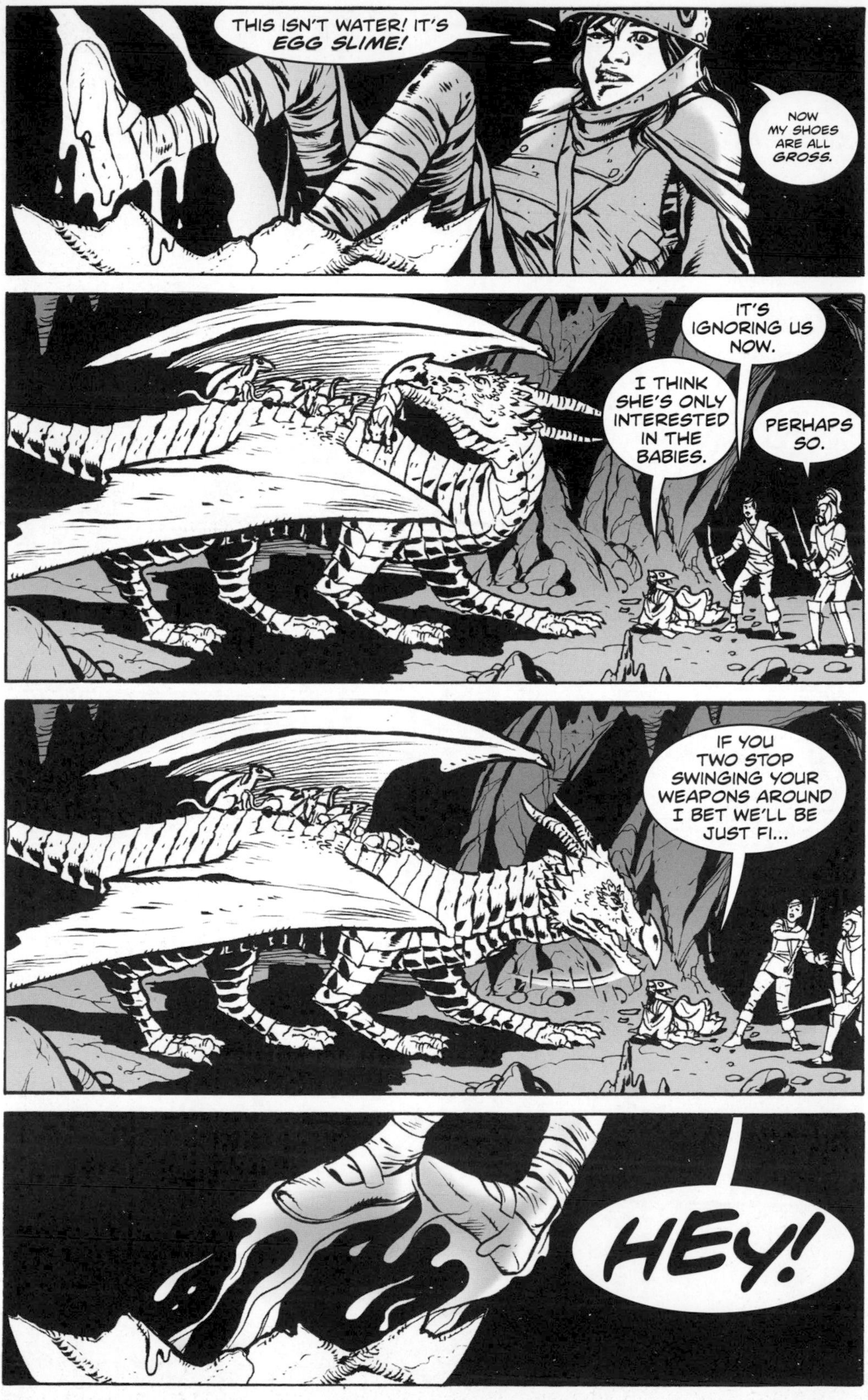
THIS ISN'T WATER! IT'S EGG SLIME!
NOW MY SHOES ARE ALL GROSS.
IT'S IGNORING US NOW.
I THINK SHE'S ONLY INTERESTED IN THE BABIES.
PERHAPS SO.
IF YOU TWO STOP SWINGING YOUR WEAPONS AROUND I BET WE'LL BE JUST FI...
HEY!

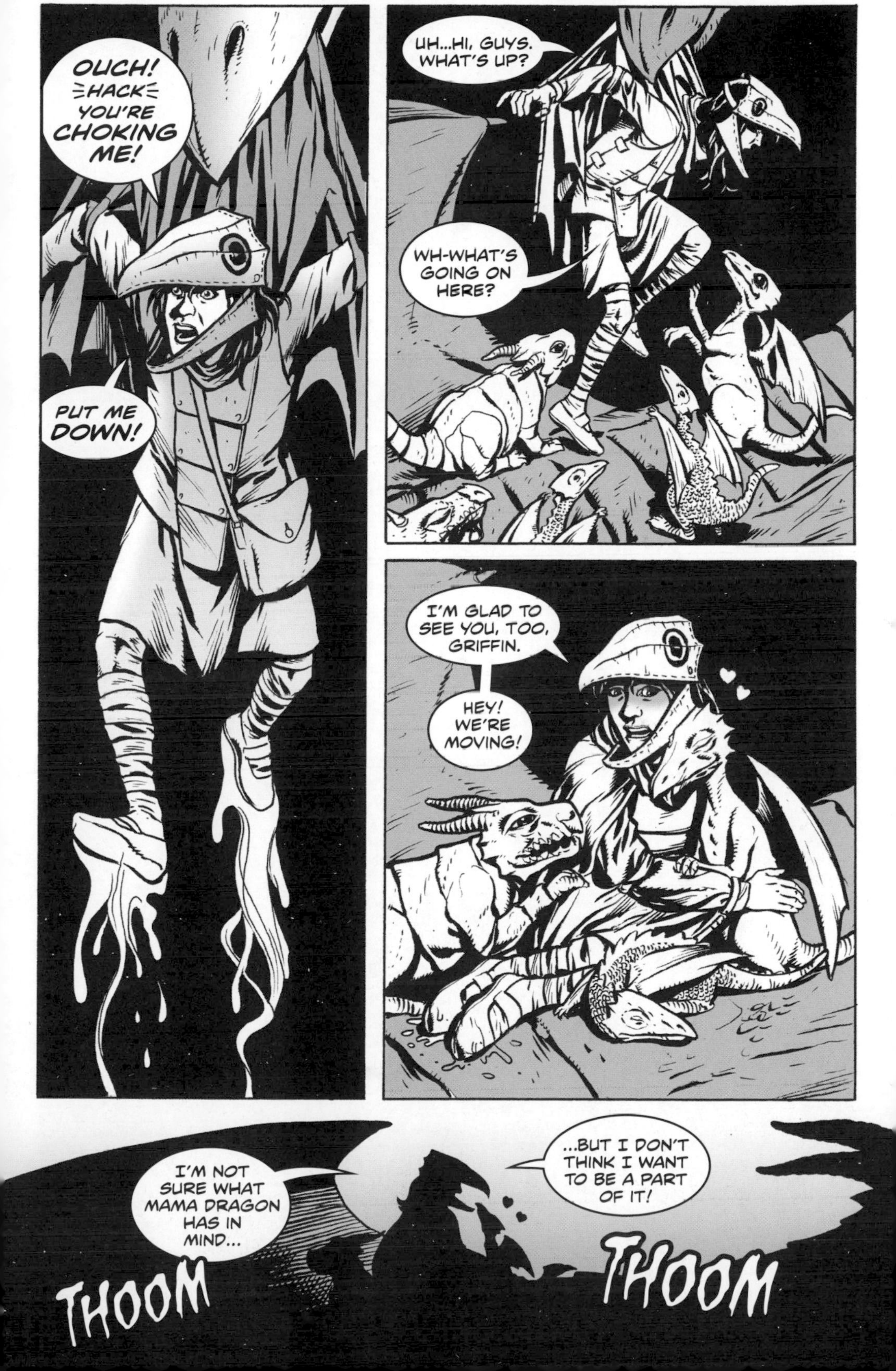
OUCH! HACK YOU'RE CHOKING ME!
PUT ME DOWN!
UH...HI, GUYS. WHAT'S UP?
WH-WHAT'S GOING ON HERE?
I'M GLAD TO SEE YOU, TOO, GRIFFIN.
HEY! WE'RE MOVING!
I'M NOT SURE WHAT MAMA DRAGON HAS IN MIND...
...BUT I DON'T THINK I WANT TO BE A PART OF IT!
THOOM
THOOM

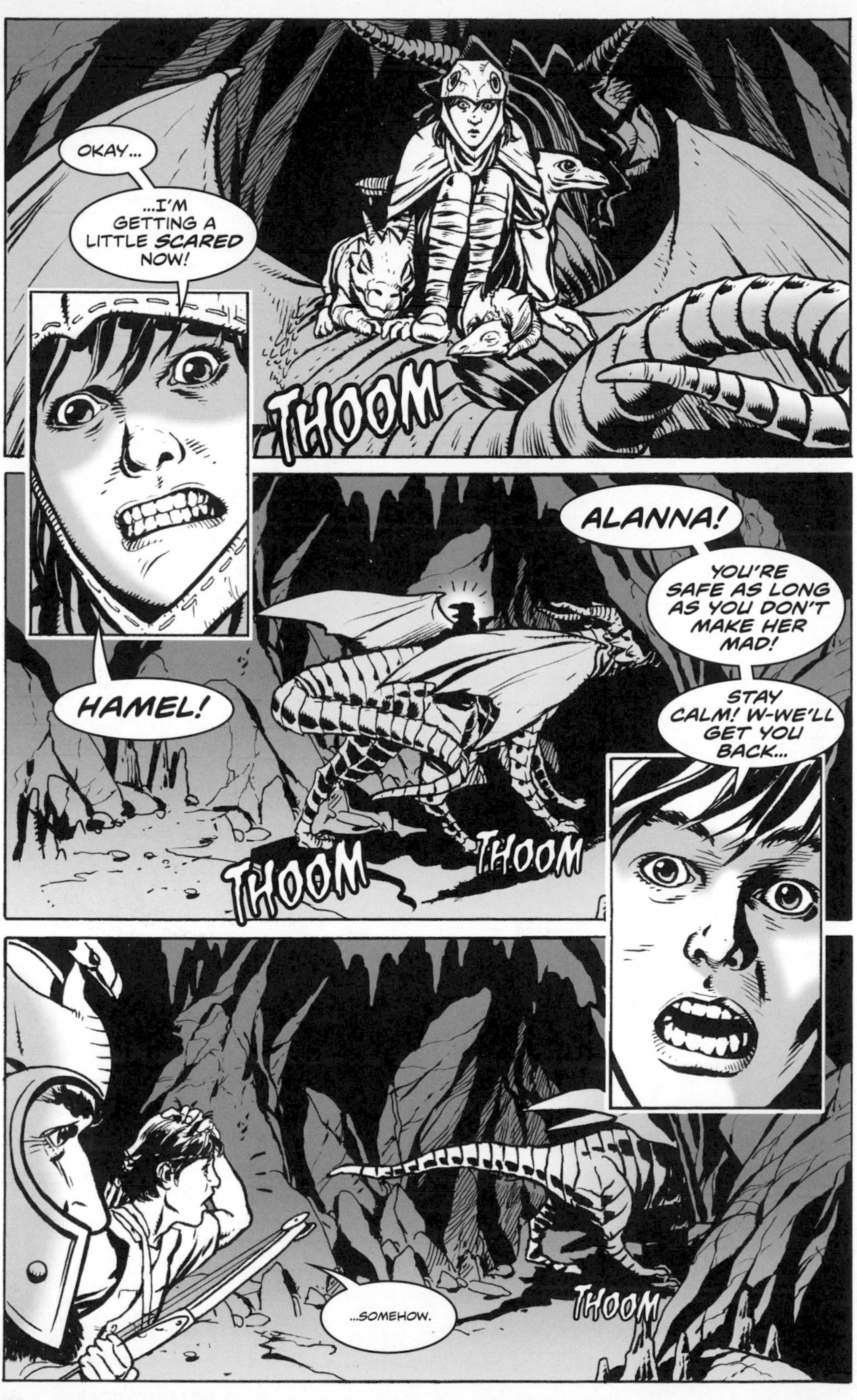

OKAY...
...I'M GETTING A LITTLE SCARED NOW!
THOOM
HAMEL!
ALANNA!
YOU'RE SAFE AS LONG AS YOU DON'T MAKE HER MAD!
STAY CALM! W-WE'LL GET YOU BACK...
THOOM
THOOM
...SOMEHOW.
THOOM

CHAPTER FOUR

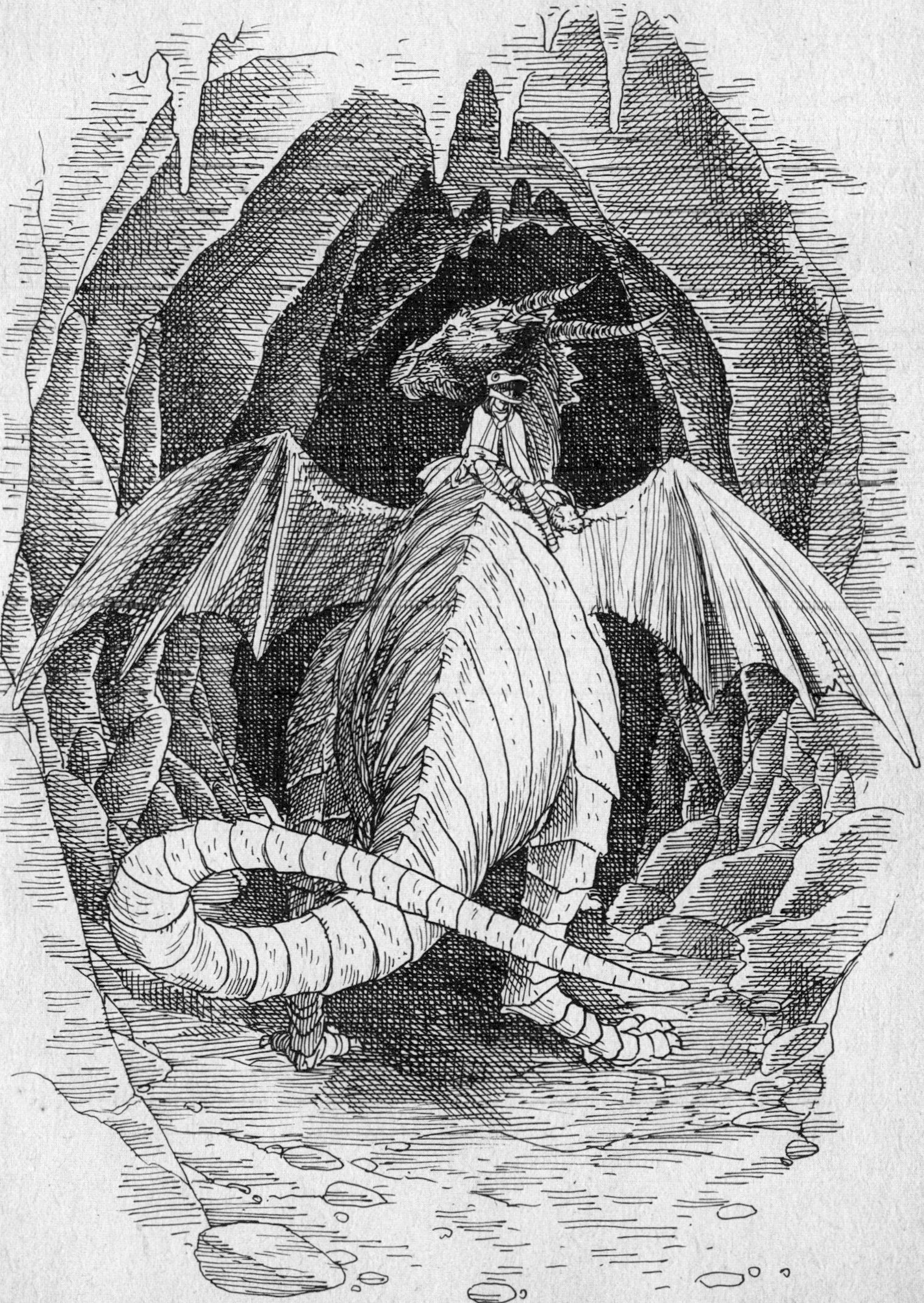

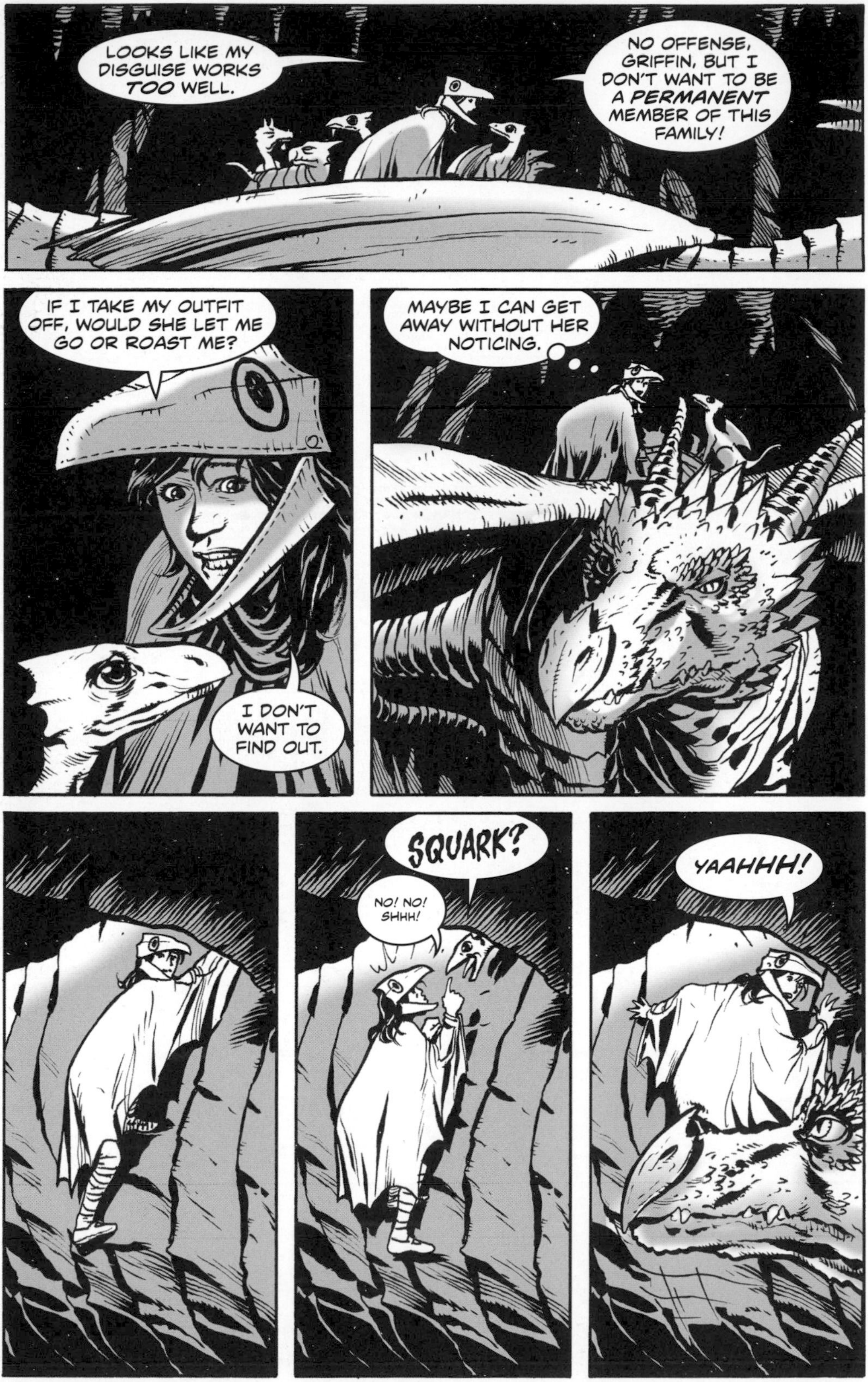
LOOKS LIKE MY DISGUISE WORKS TOO WELL.
NO OFFENSE, GRIFFIN, BUT I DON'T WANT TO BE A PERMANENT MEMBER OF THIS FAMILY!
IF I TAKE MY OUTFIT OFF, WOULD SHE LET ME GO OR ROAST ME?
I DON'T WANT TO FIND OUT.
MAYBE I CAN GET AWAY WITHOUT HER NOTICING.
SQUARK?
NO! NO! SHHH!
YAAHHH!

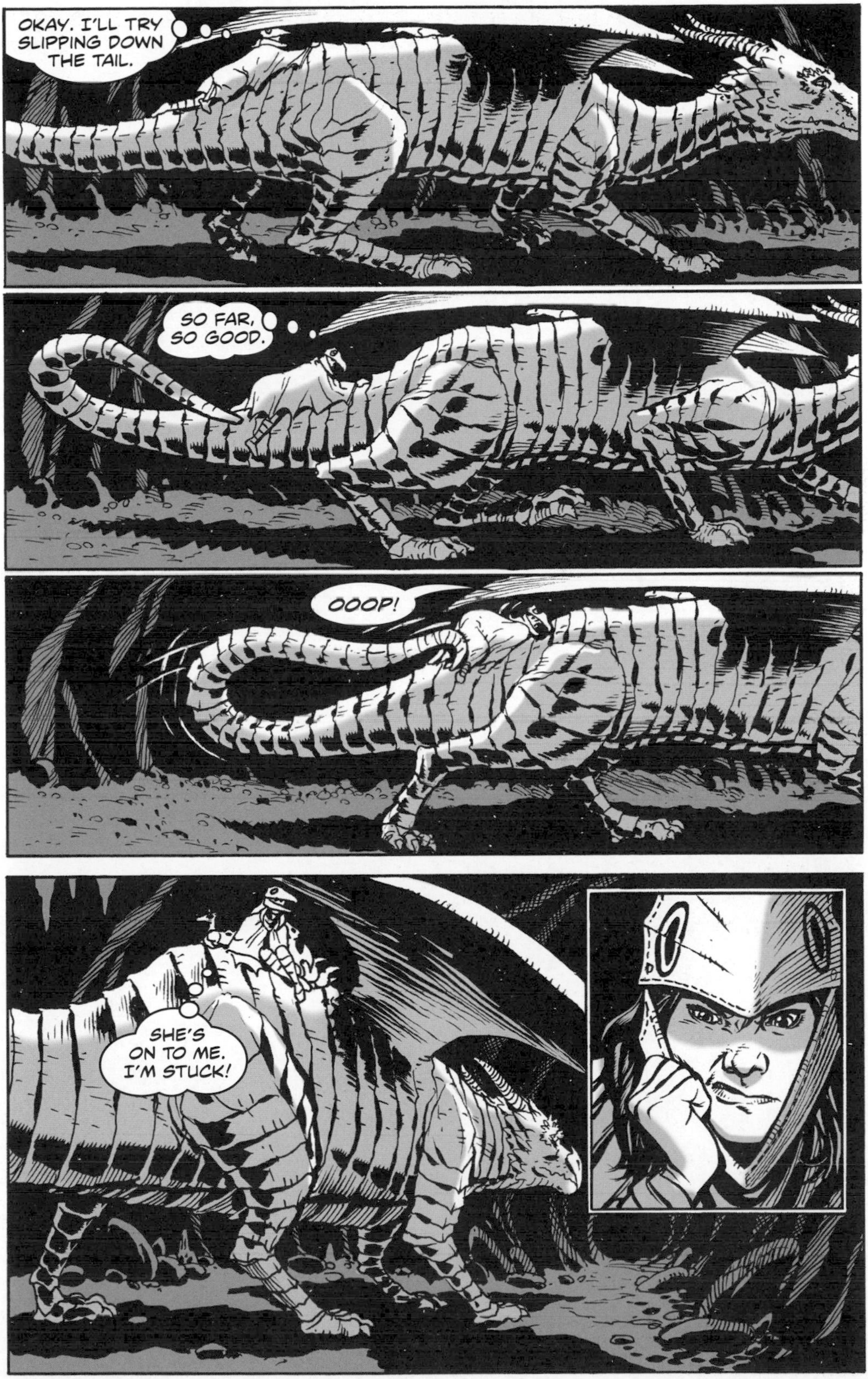
OKAY. I'LL TRY SLIPPING DOWN THE TAIL.
SO FAR, SO GOOD.
OOOP!
SHE'S ON TO ME. I'M STUCK!

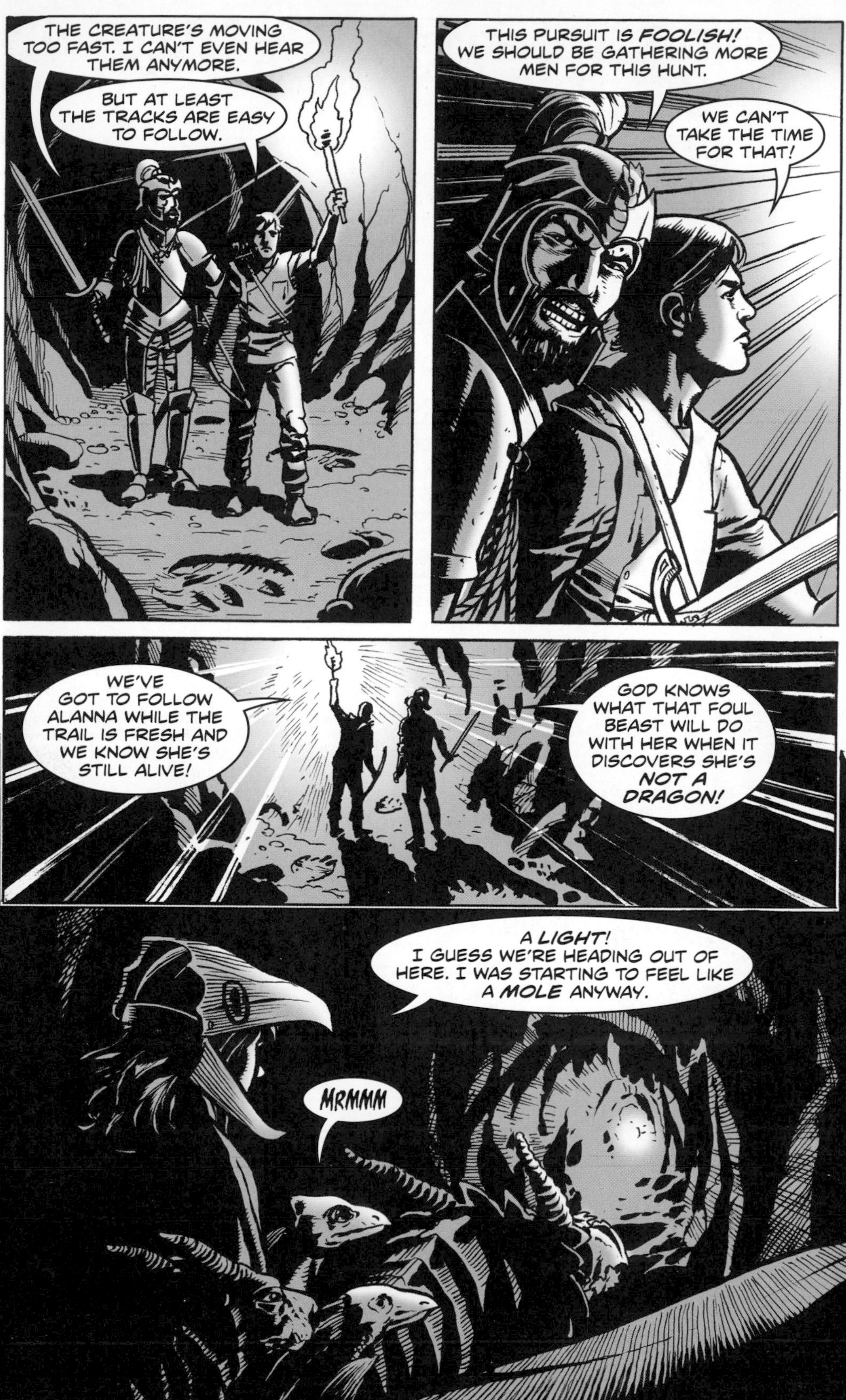
THE CREATURE'S MOVING TOO FAST. I CAN'T EVEN HEAR THEM ANYMORE.
BUT AT LEAST THE TRACKS ARE EASY TO FOLLOW.
THIS PURSUIT IS *FOOLISH!* WE SHOULD BE GATHERING MORE MEN FOR THIS HUNT.
WE CAN'T TAKE THE TIME FOR THAT!
WE'VE GOT TO FOLLOW ALANNA WHILE THE TRAIL IS FRESH AND WE KNOW SHE'S STILL ALIVE!
GOD KNOWS WHAT THAT FOUL BEAST WILL DO WITH HER WHEN IT DISCOVERS SHE'S *NOT A DRAGON!*
A *LIGHT!* I GUESS WE'RE HEADING OUT OF HERE. I WAS STARTING TO FEEL LIKE A *MOLE* ANYWAY.
MRMMM

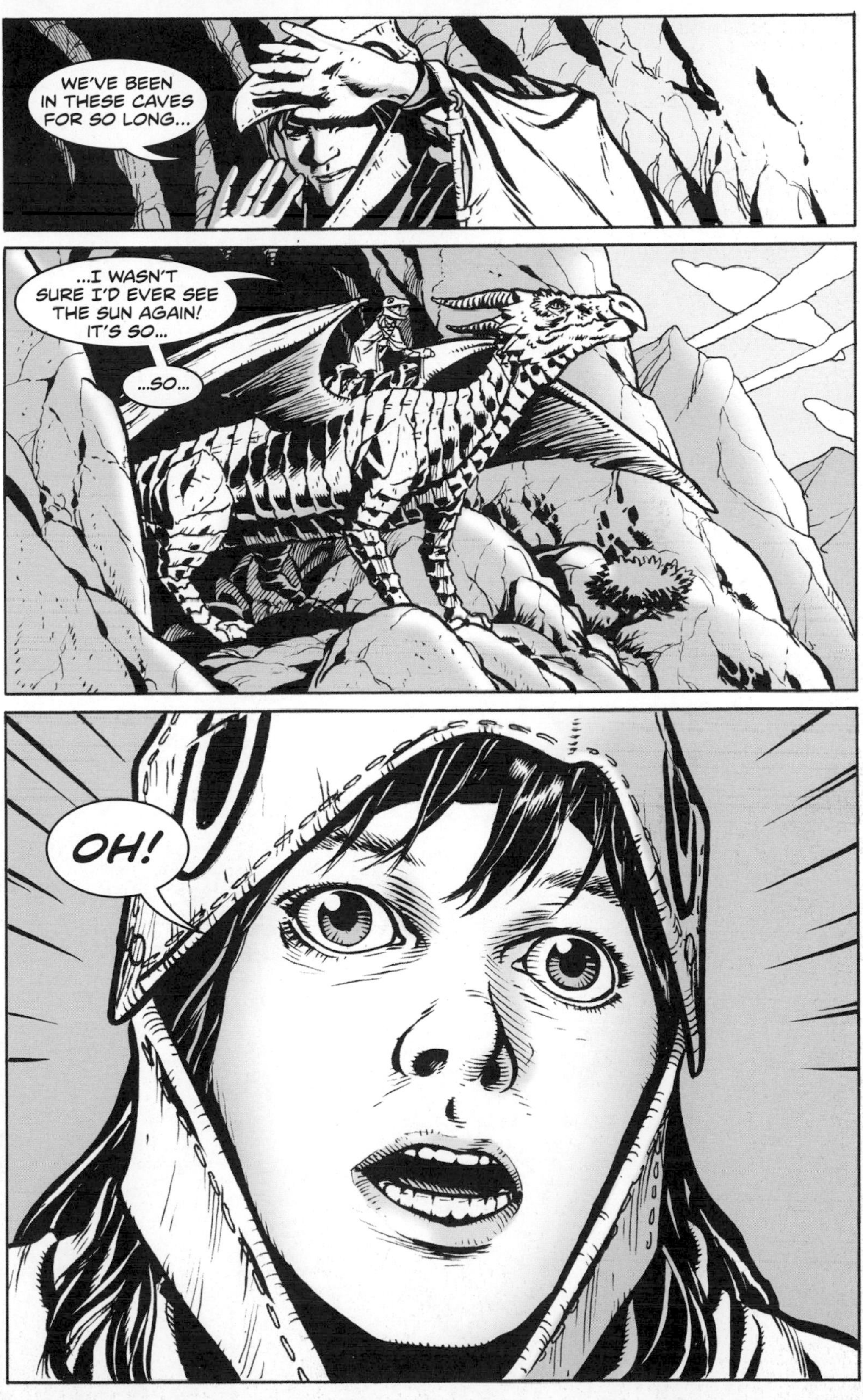
WE'VE BEEN IN THESE CAVES FOR SO LONG...
...I WASN'T SURE I'D EVER SEE THE SUN AGAIN! IT'S SO...
...SO...
OH!

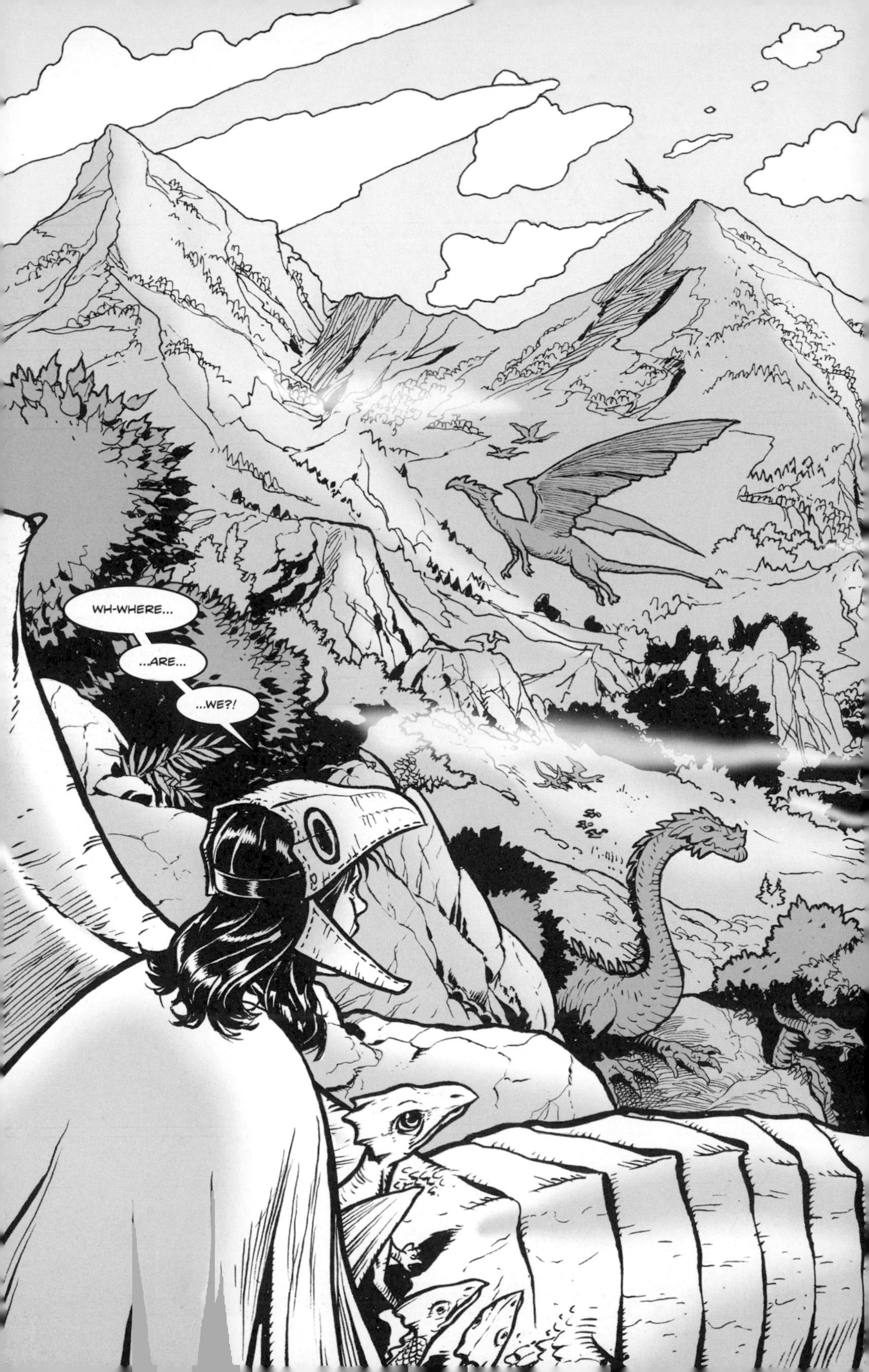
WH-WHERE...
...ARE...
...WE?!

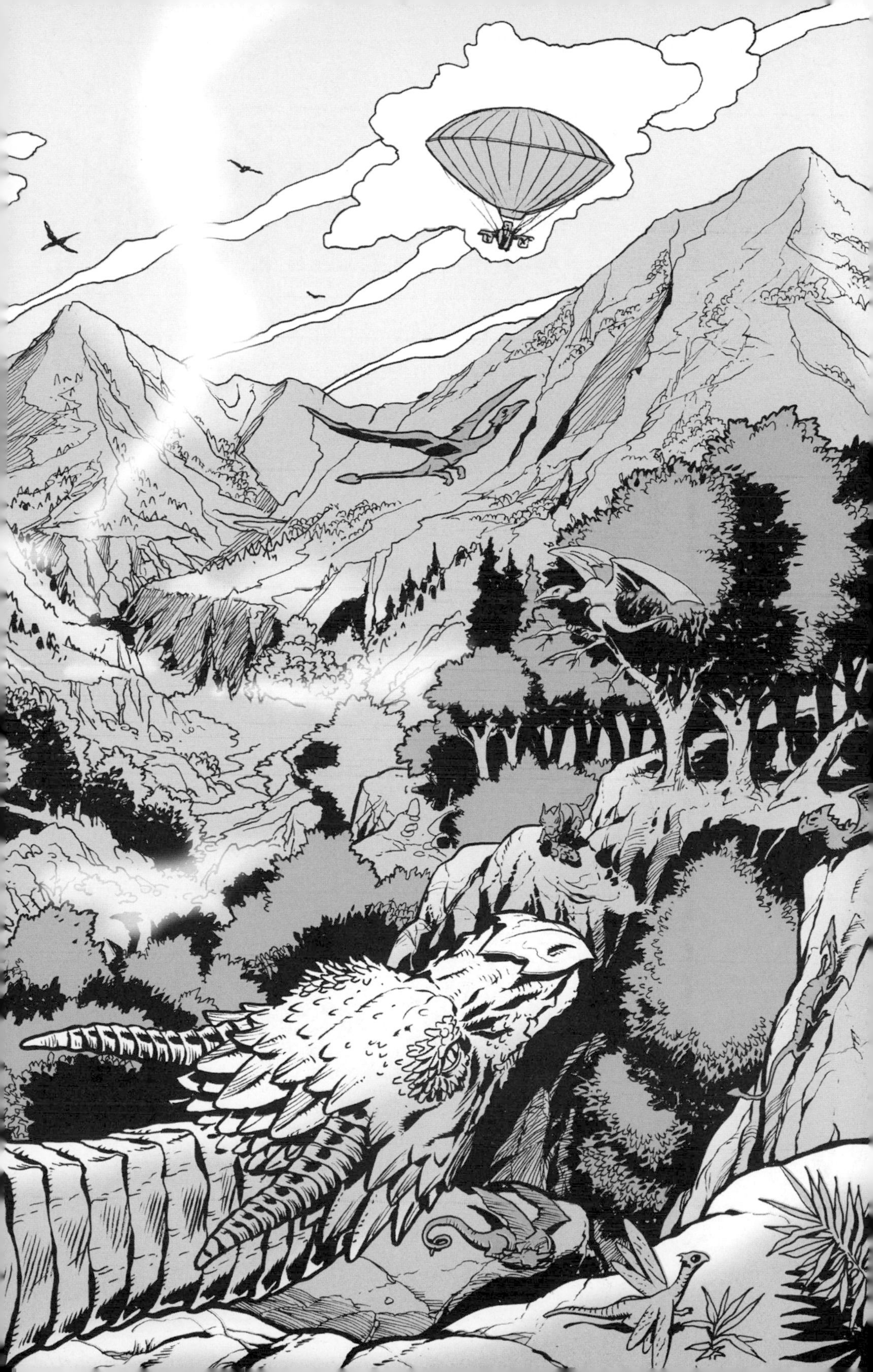

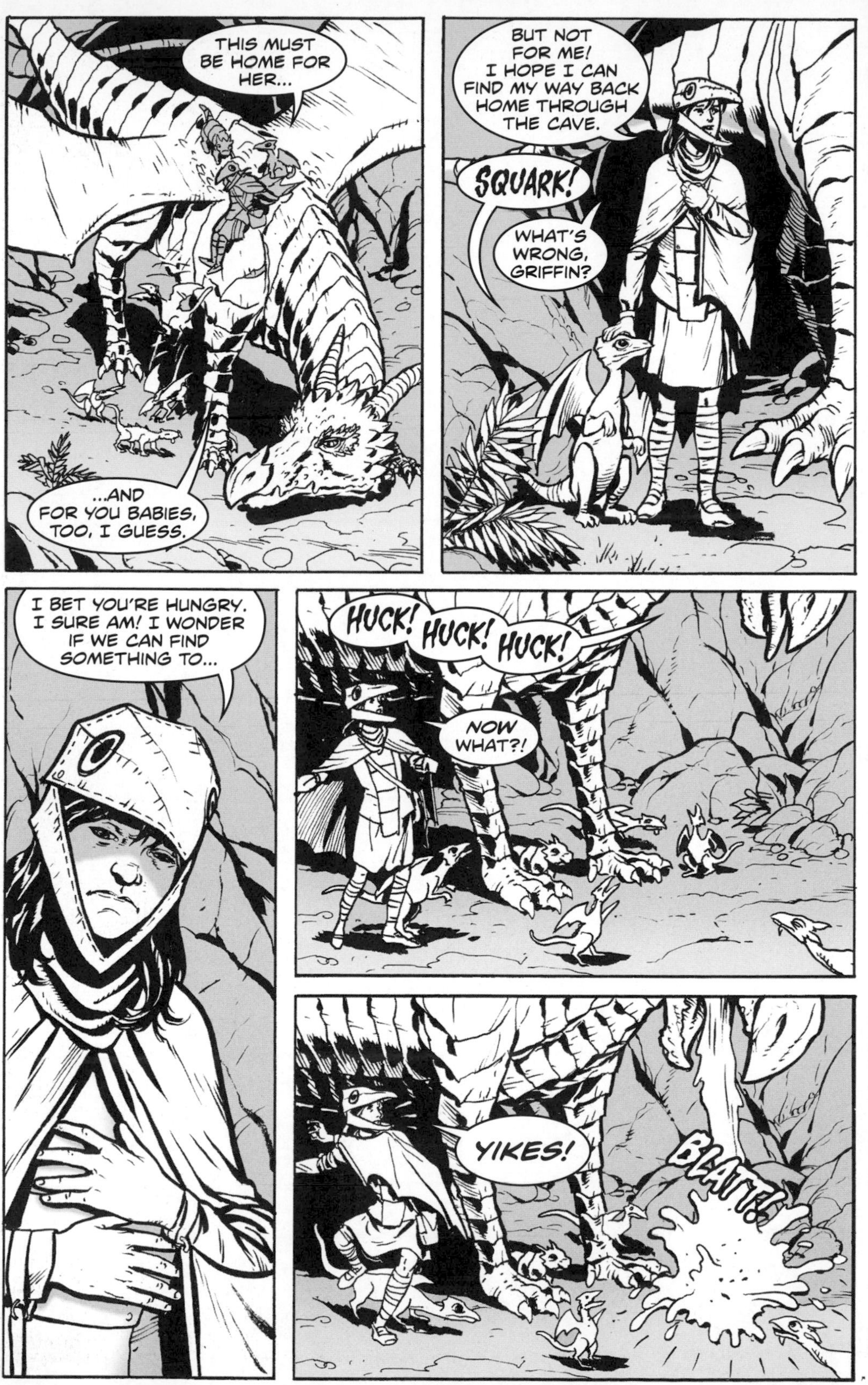
THIS MUST BE HOME FOR HER...
...AND FOR YOU BABIES, TOO, I GUESS.
BUT NOT FOR ME! I HOPE I CAN FIND MY WAY BACK HOME THROUGH THE CAVE.
SQUARK!
WHAT'S WRONG, GRIFFIN?
I BET YOU'RE HUNGRY. I SURE AM! I WONDER IF WE CAN FIND SOMETHING TO...
HUCK!
HUCK!
HUCK!
NOW WHAT?!
YIKES!
BLATT!

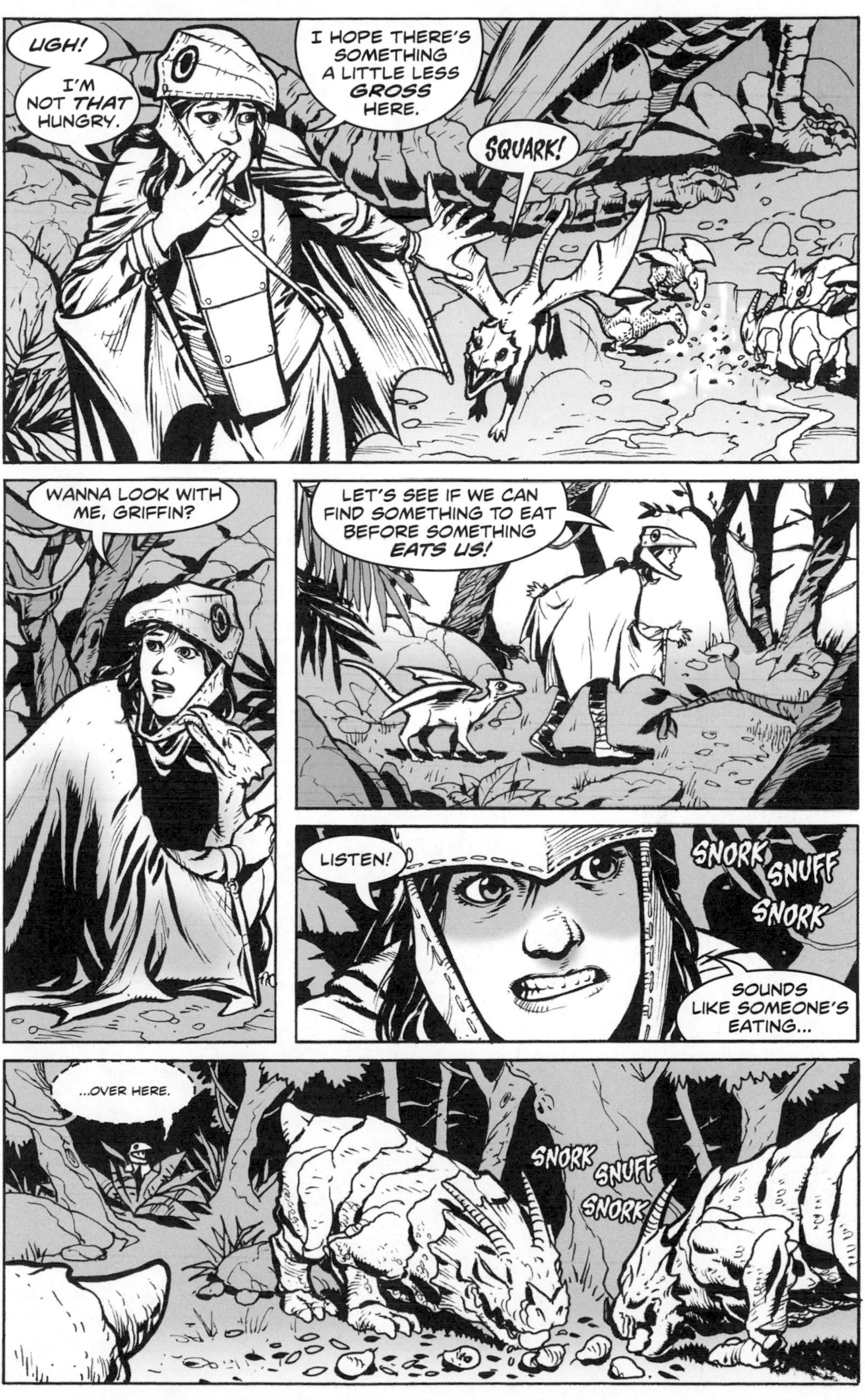
UGH!
I'M NOT THAT HUNGRY.
I HOPE THERE'S SOMETHING A LITTLE LESS GROSS HERE.
SQUARK!
WANNA LOOK WITH ME, GRIFFIN?
LET'S SEE IF WE CAN FIND SOMETHING TO EAT BEFORE SOMETHING EATS US!
LISTEN!
SNORK SNUFF SNORK
SOUNDS LIKE SOMEONE'S EATING...
...OVER HERE.
SNORK SNUFF SNORK

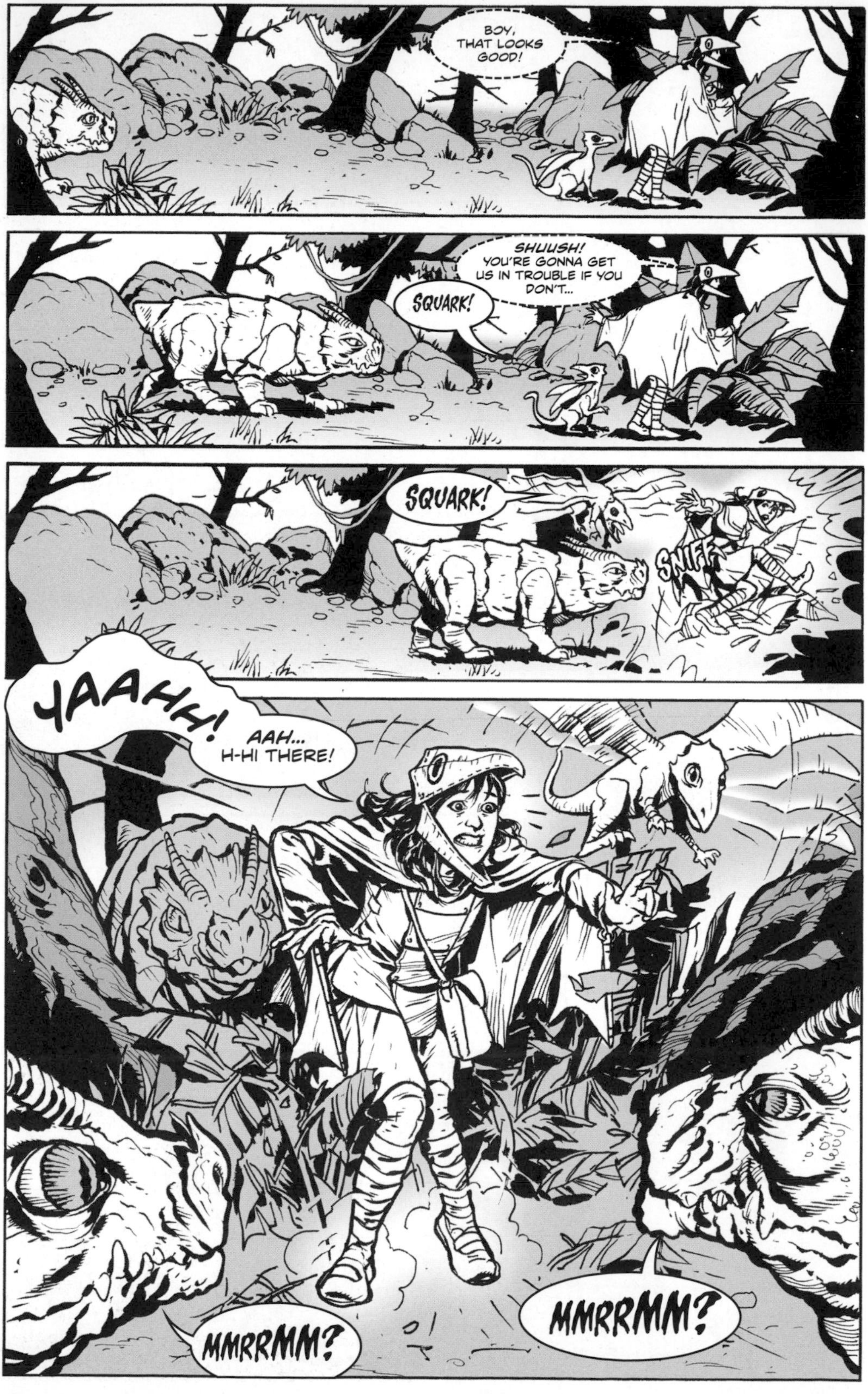
BOY, THAT LOOKS GOOD!
SHUUSH! YOU'RE GONNA GET US IN TROUBLE IF YOU DON'T...
SQUARK!
SQUARK!
SNIFF
YAAHH!
AAH... H-HI THERE!
MMRRMM?
MMRRMM?

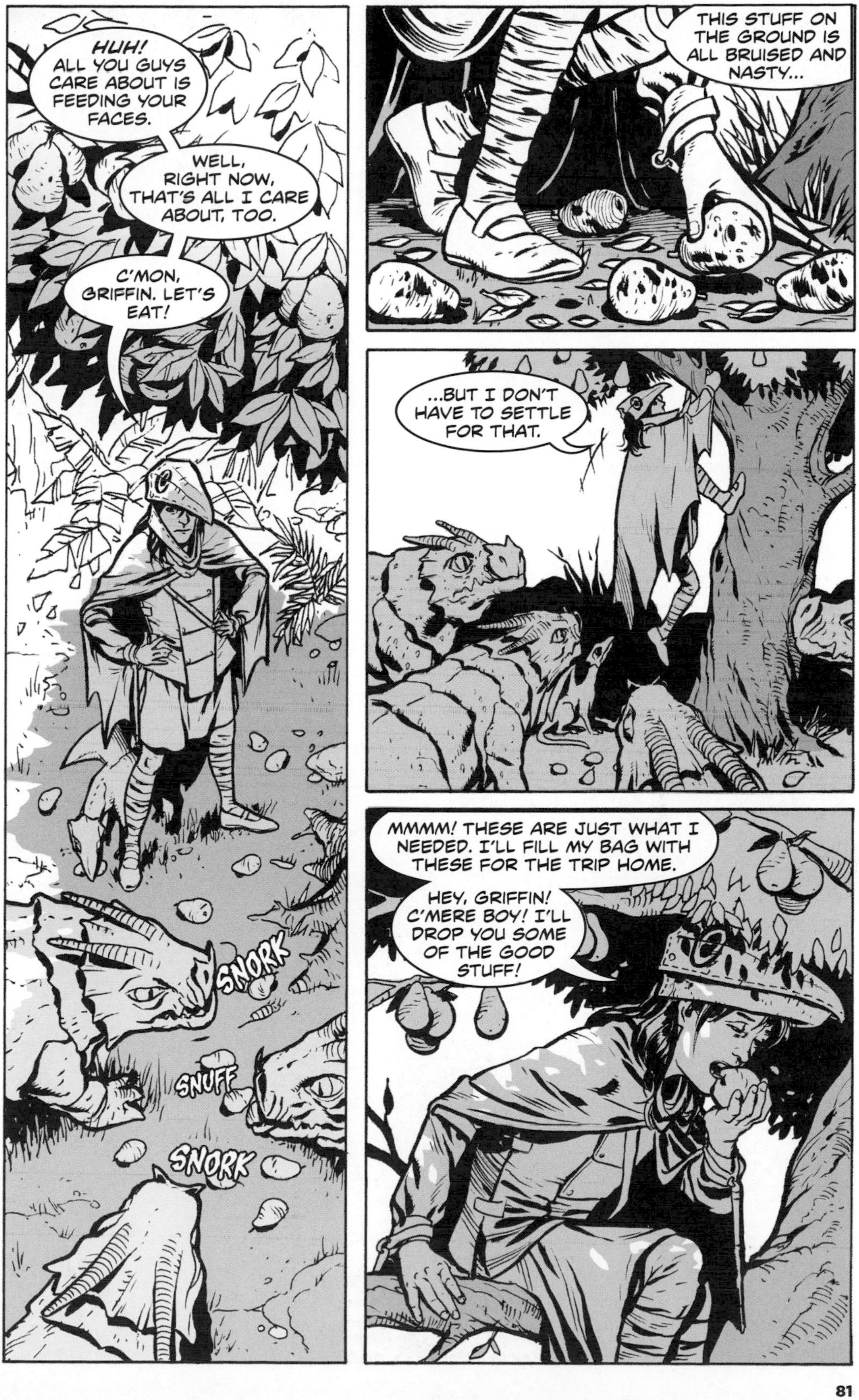
HUH! ALL YOU GUYS CARE ABOUT IS FEEDING YOUR FACES.
WELL, RIGHT NOW, THAT'S ALL I CARE ABOUT, TOO.
C'MON, GRIFFIN. LET'S EAT!
SNORK
SNUFF
SNORK
THIS STUFF ON THE GROUND IS ALL BRUISED AND NASTY...
...BUT I DON'T HAVE TO SETTLE FOR THAT.
MMMM! THESE ARE JUST WHAT I NEEDED. I'LL FILL MY BAG WITH THESE FOR THE TRIP HOME.
HEY, GRIFFIN! C'MERE BOY! I'LL DROP YOU SOME OF THE GOOD STUFF!

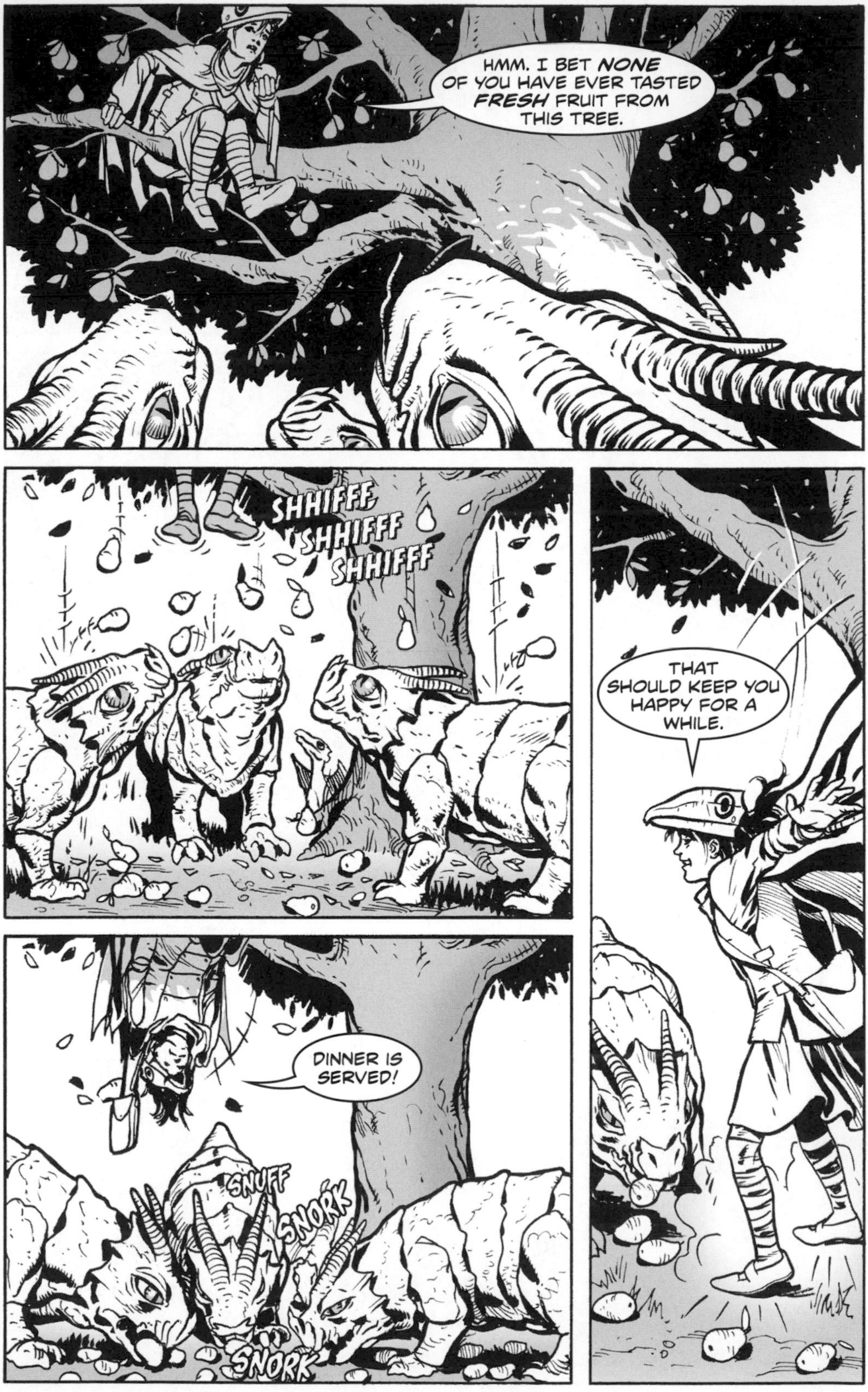
HMM. I BET NONE OF YOU HAVE EVER TASTED FRESH FRUIT FROM THIS TREE.
SHHIFFF
SHHIFFF
SHHIFFF
THAT SHOULD KEEP YOU HAPPY FOR A WHILE.
DINNER IS SERVED!
SNUFF
SNORK
SNORK

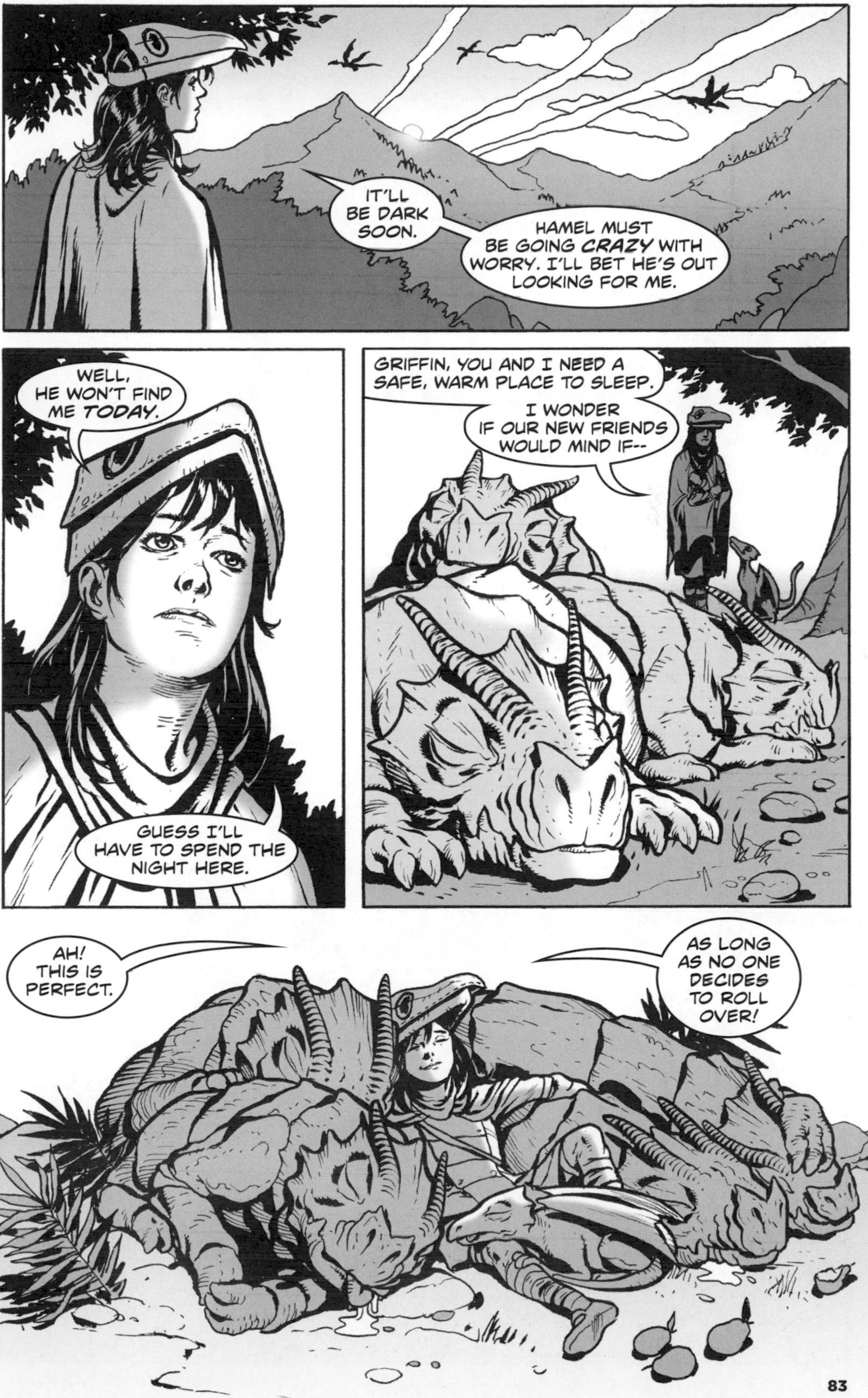
IT'LL BE DARK SOON.
HAMEL MUST BE GOING CRAZY WITH WORRY. I'LL BET HE'S OUT LOOKING FOR ME.
WELL, HE WON'T FIND ME TODAY.
GUESS I'LL HAVE TO SPEND THE NIGHT HERE.
GRIFFIN, YOU AND I NEED A SAFE, WARM PLACE TO SLEEP.
I WONDER IF OUR NEW FRIENDS WOULD MIND IF--
AH! THIS IS PERFECT.
AS LONG AS NO ONE DECIDES TO ROLL OVER!

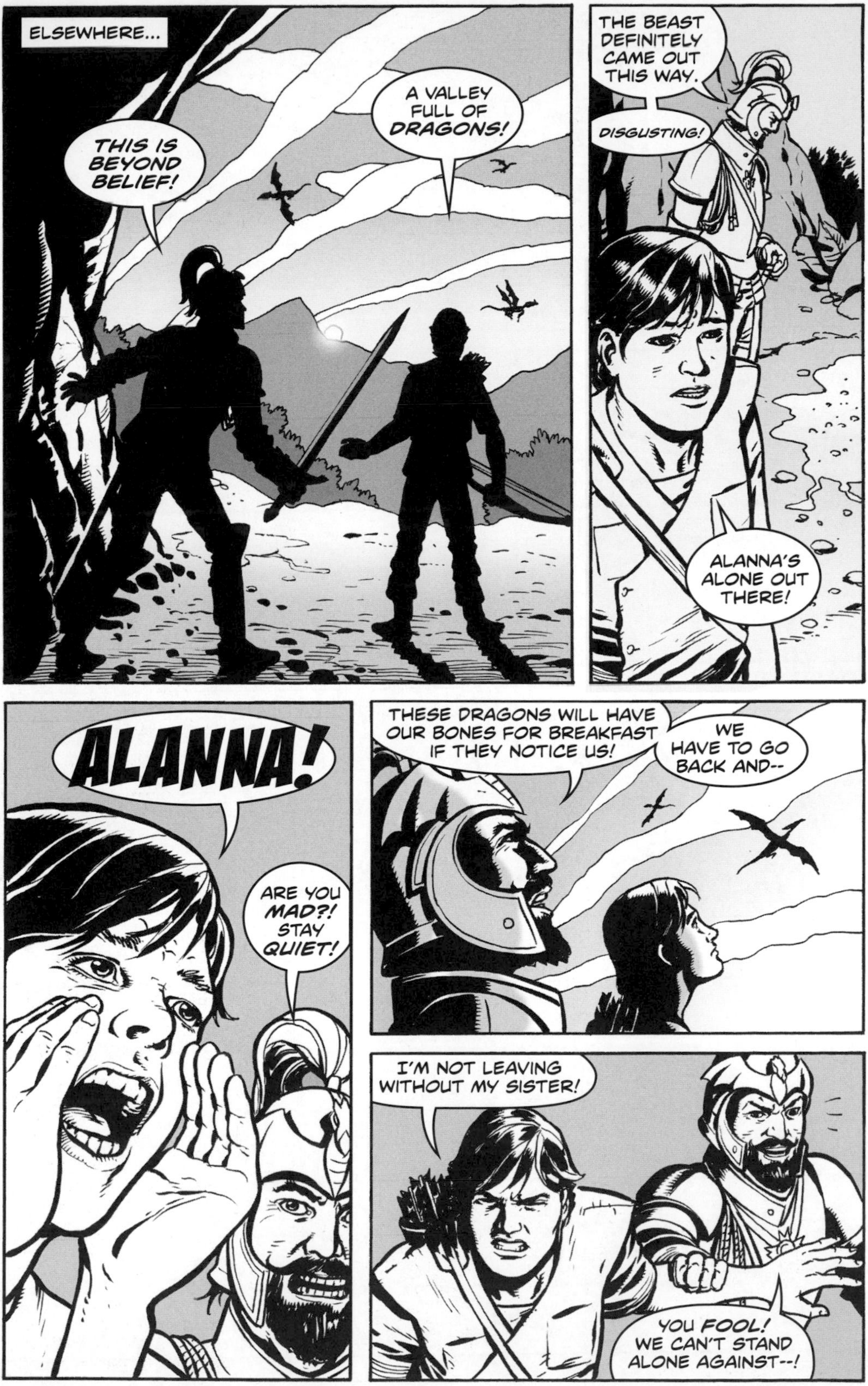

ELSEWHERE...
THIS IS BEYOND BELIEF!
A VALLEY FULL OF DRAGONS!
THE BEAST DEFINITELY CAME OUT THIS WAY.
DISGUSTING!
ALANNA'S ALONE OUT THERE!
ALANNA!
ARE YOU MAD?! STAY QUIET!
THESE DRAGONS WILL HAVE OUR BONES FOR BREAKFAST IF THEY NOTICE US!
WE HAVE TO GO BACK AND--
I'M NOT LEAVING WITHOUT MY SISTER!
YOU FOOL! WE CAN'T STAND ALONE AGAINST--!

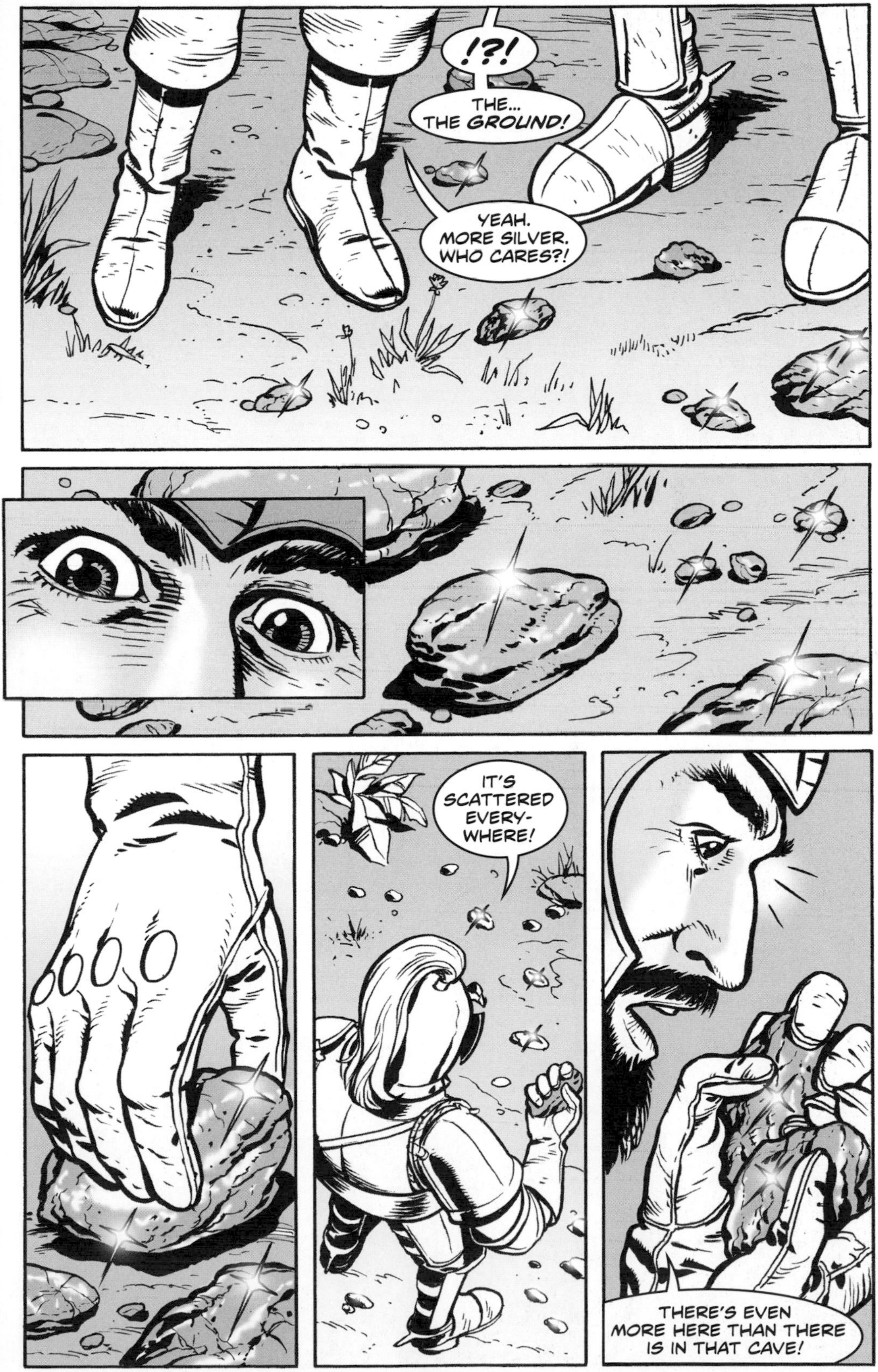
!?!
THE... THE GROUND!
YEAH. MORE SILVER. WHO CARES?!
IT'S SCATTERED EVERY-WHERE!
THERE'S EVEN MORE HERE THAN THERE IS IN THAT CAVE!

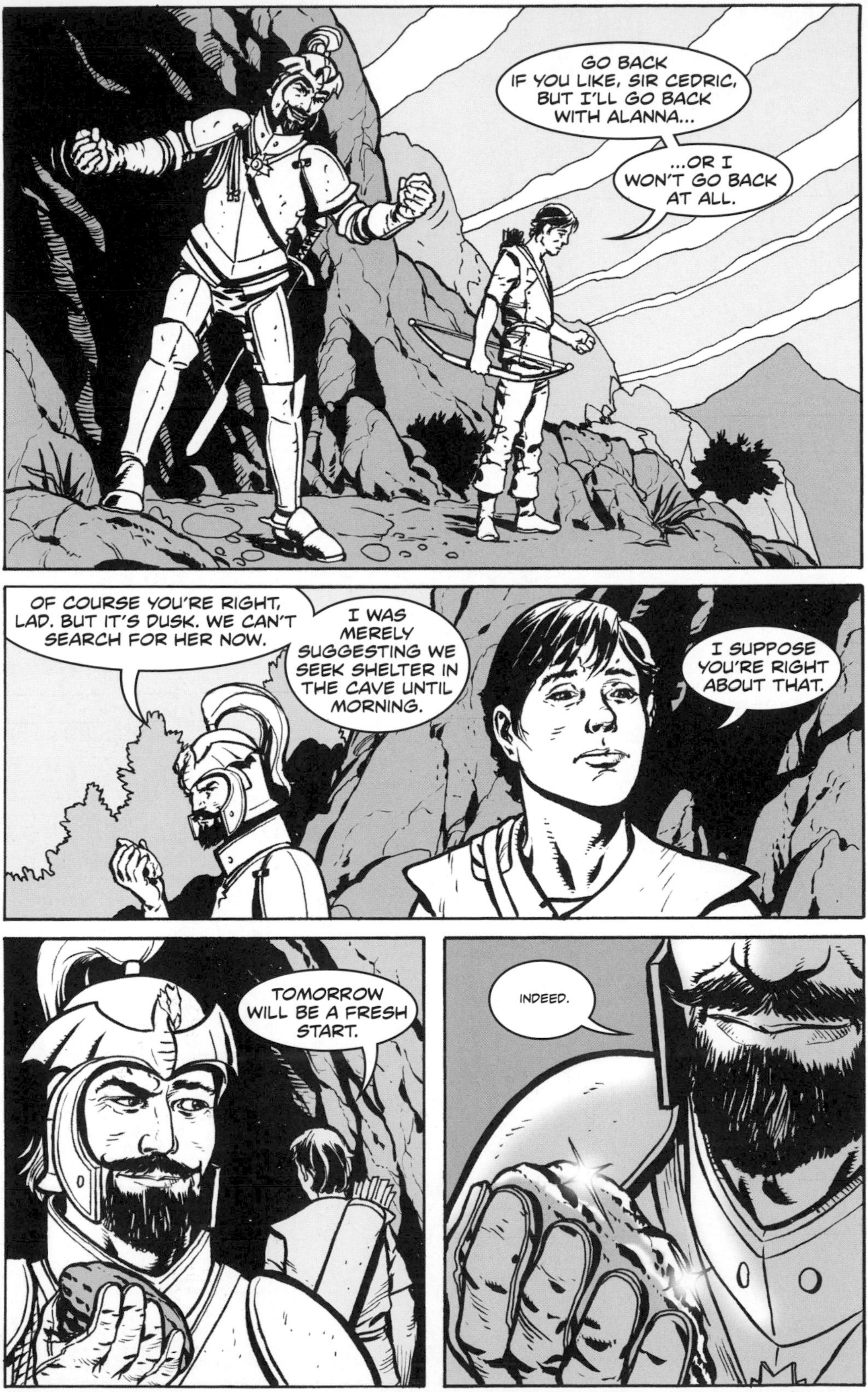
GO BACK IF YOU LIKE, SIR CEDRIC, BUT I'LL GO BACK WITH ALANNA...
...OR I WON'T GO BACK AT ALL.
OF COURSE YOU'RE RIGHT, LAD. BUT IT'S DUSK. WE CAN'T SEARCH FOR HER NOW.
I WAS MERELY SUGGESTING WE SEEK SHELTER IN THE CAVE UNTIL MORNING.
I SUPPOSE YOU'RE RIGHT ABOUT THAT.
TOMORROW WILL BE A FRESH START.
INDEED.

CHAPTER FIVE

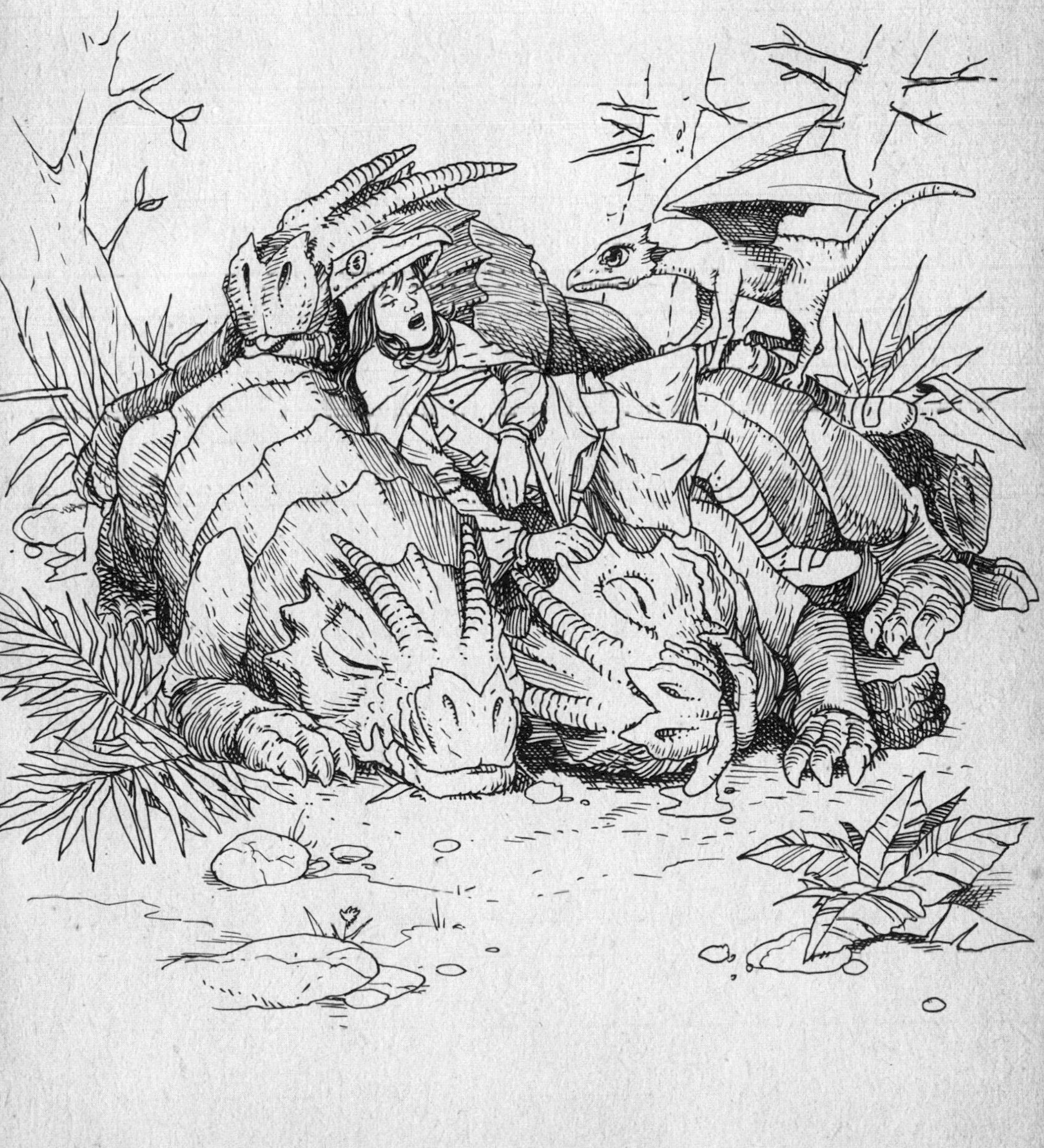

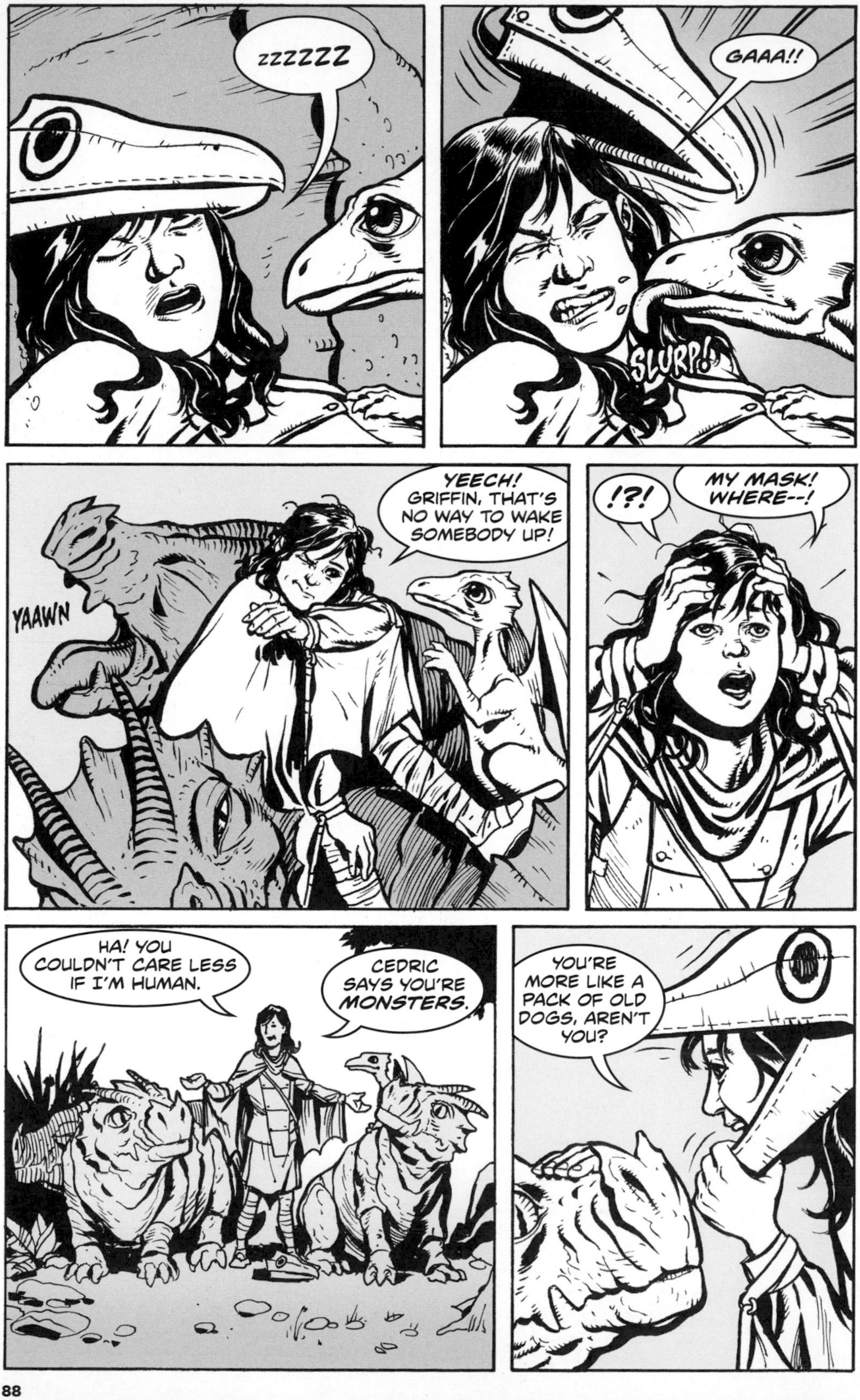
ZZZZZZ
GAAA!!
SLURP!
YEECH! GRIFFIN, THAT'S NO WAY TO WAKE SOMEBODY UP!
YAAWN
!?!
MY MASK! WHERE--!
HA! YOU COULDN'T CARE LESS IF I'M HUMAN.
CEDRIC SAYS YOU'RE MONSTERS.
YOU'RE MORE LIKE A PACK OF OLD DOGS, AREN'T YOU?

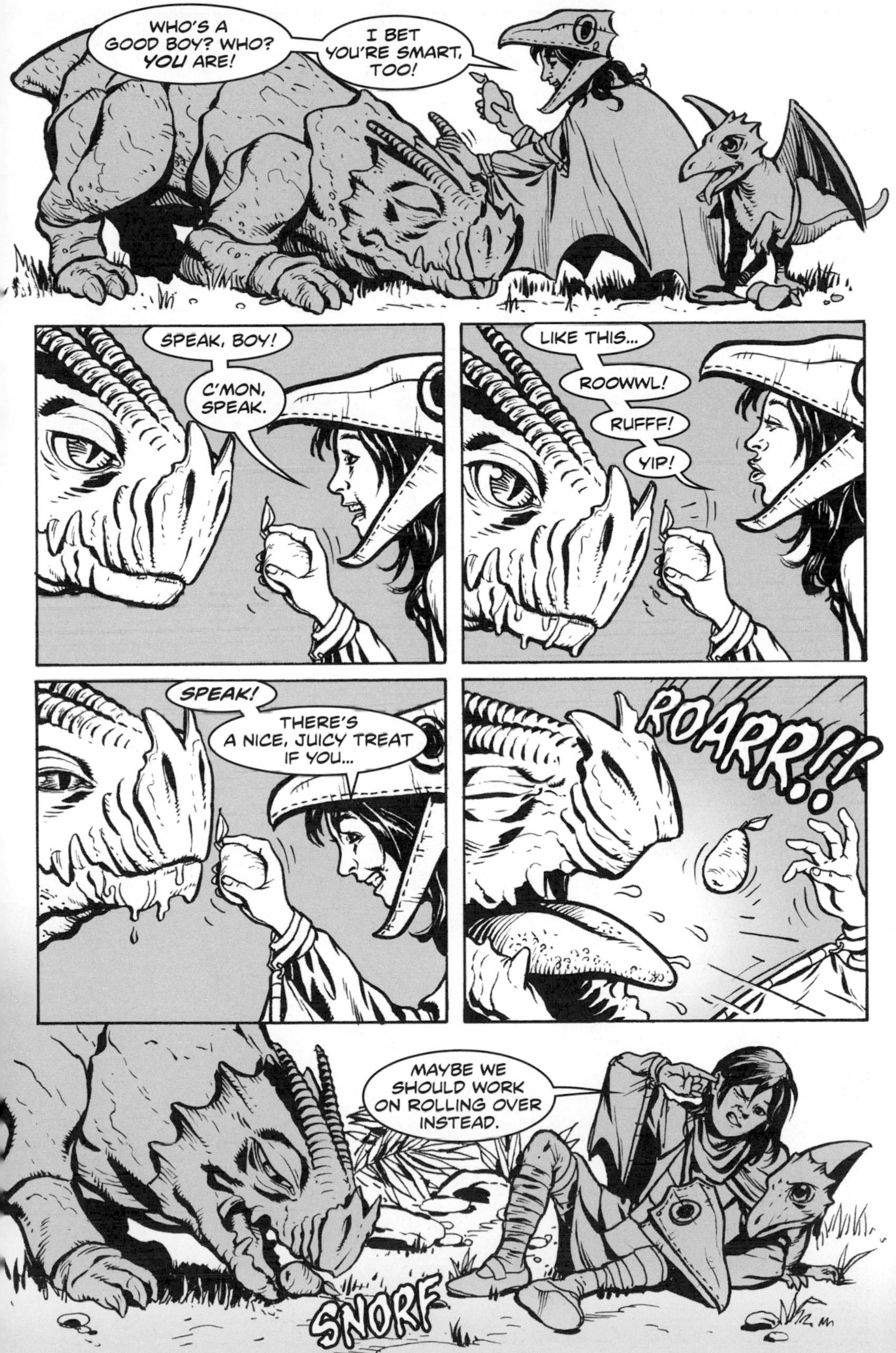
WHO'S A GOOD BOY? WHO? *YOU* ARE!
I BET YOU'RE SMART, TOO!
SPEAK, BOY!
C'MON, SPEAK.
LIKE THIS...
ROOWWL!
RUFFF!
YIP!
SPEAK!
THERE'S A NICE, JUICY TREAT IF YOU...
ROARR!!
MAYBE WE SHOULD WORK ON ROLLING OVER INSTEAD.
SNORF

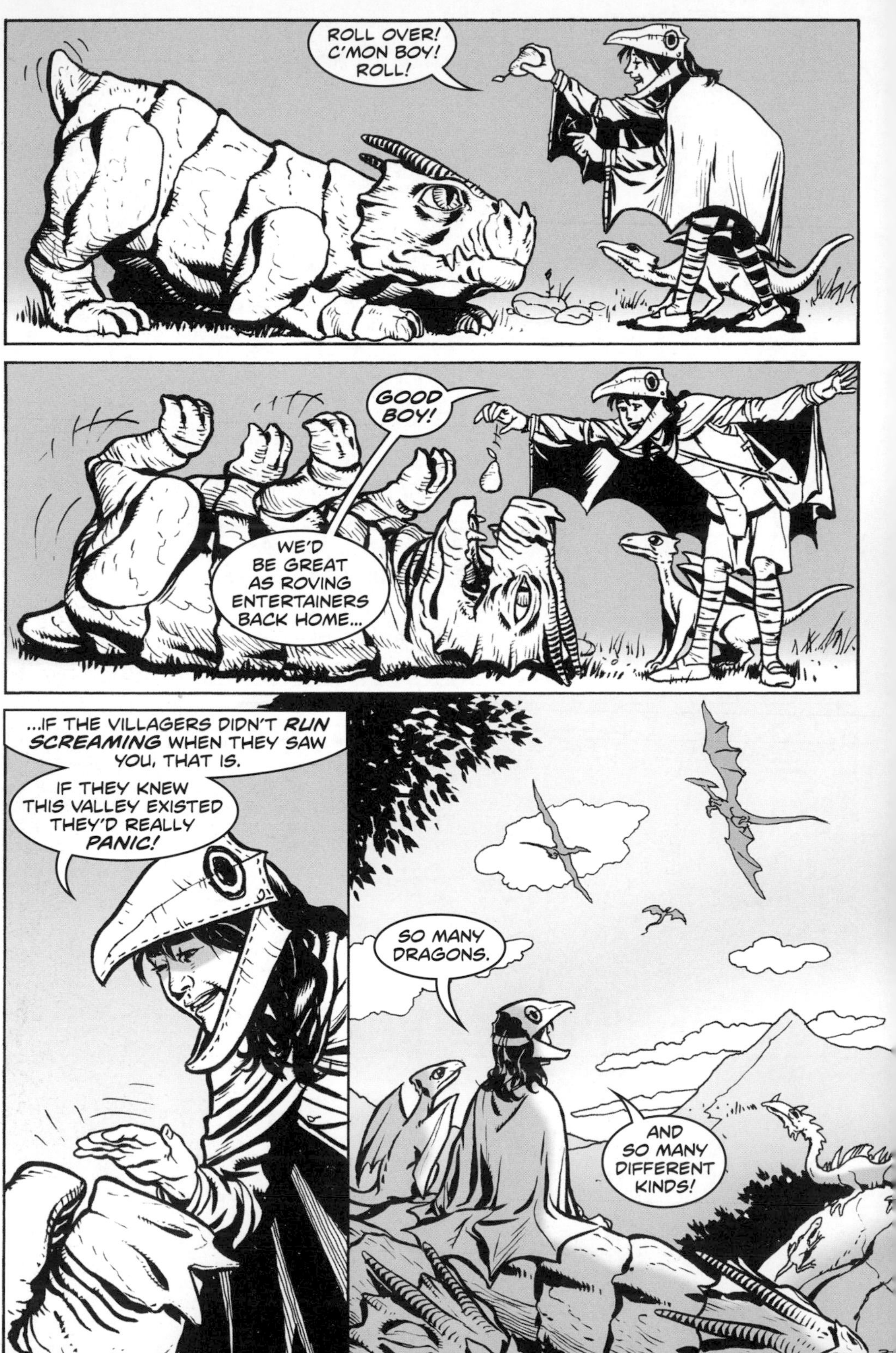
ROLL OVER! C'MON BOY! ROLL!
GOOD BOY!
WE'D BE GREAT AS ROVING ENTERTAINERS BACK HOME...
...IF THE VILLAGERS DIDN'T RUN SCREAMING WHEN THEY SAW YOU, THAT IS.
IF THEY KNEW THIS VALLEY EXISTED THEY'D REALLY PANIC!
SO MANY DRAGONS.
AND SO MANY DIFFERENT KINDS!

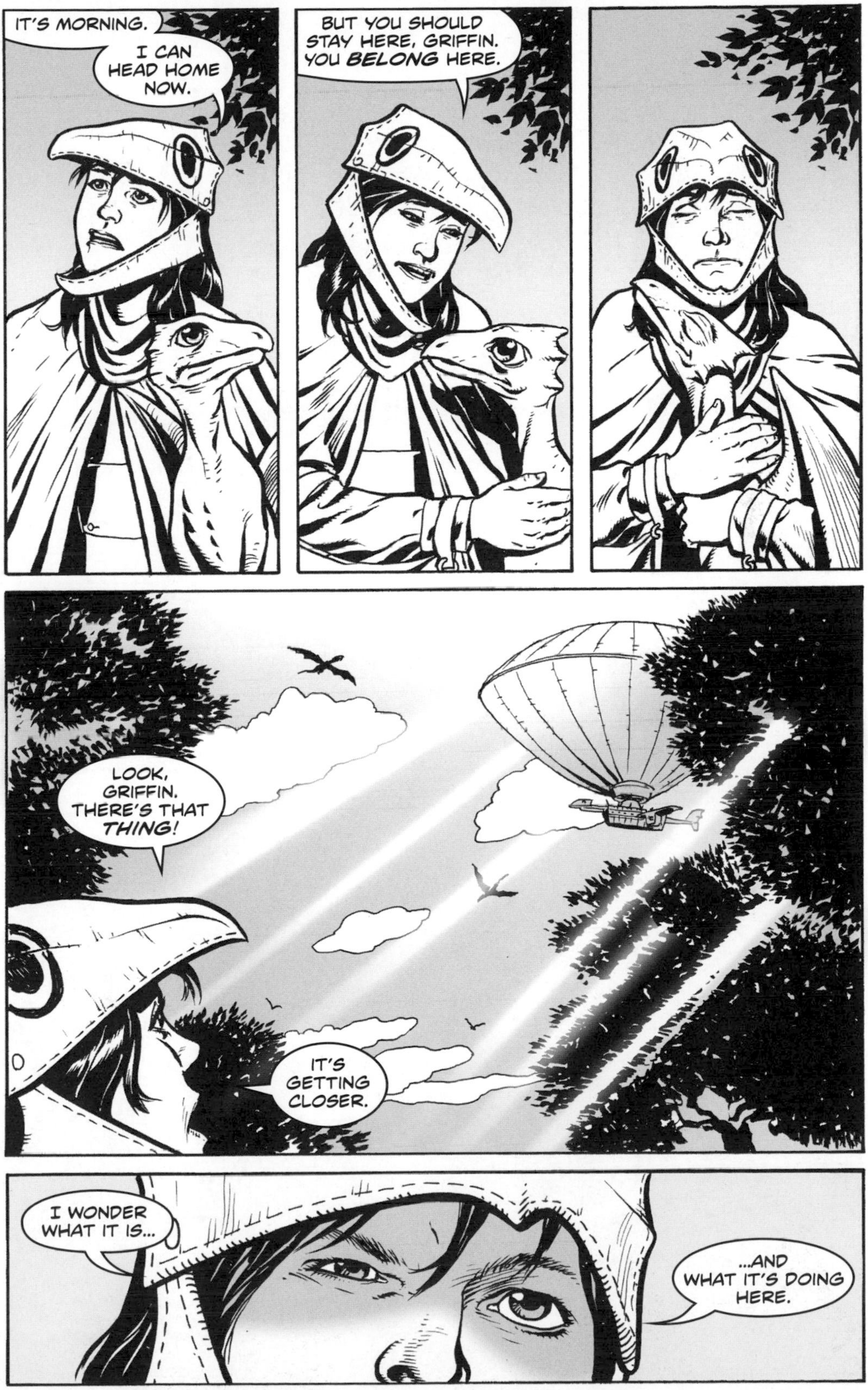
IT'S MORNING.
I CAN HEAD HOME NOW.
BUT YOU SHOULD STAY HERE, GRIFFIN. YOU *BELONG* HERE.
LOOK, GRIFFIN. THERE'S THAT *THING*!
IT'S GETTING CLOSER.
I WONDER WHAT IT IS...
...AND WHAT IT'S DOING HERE.

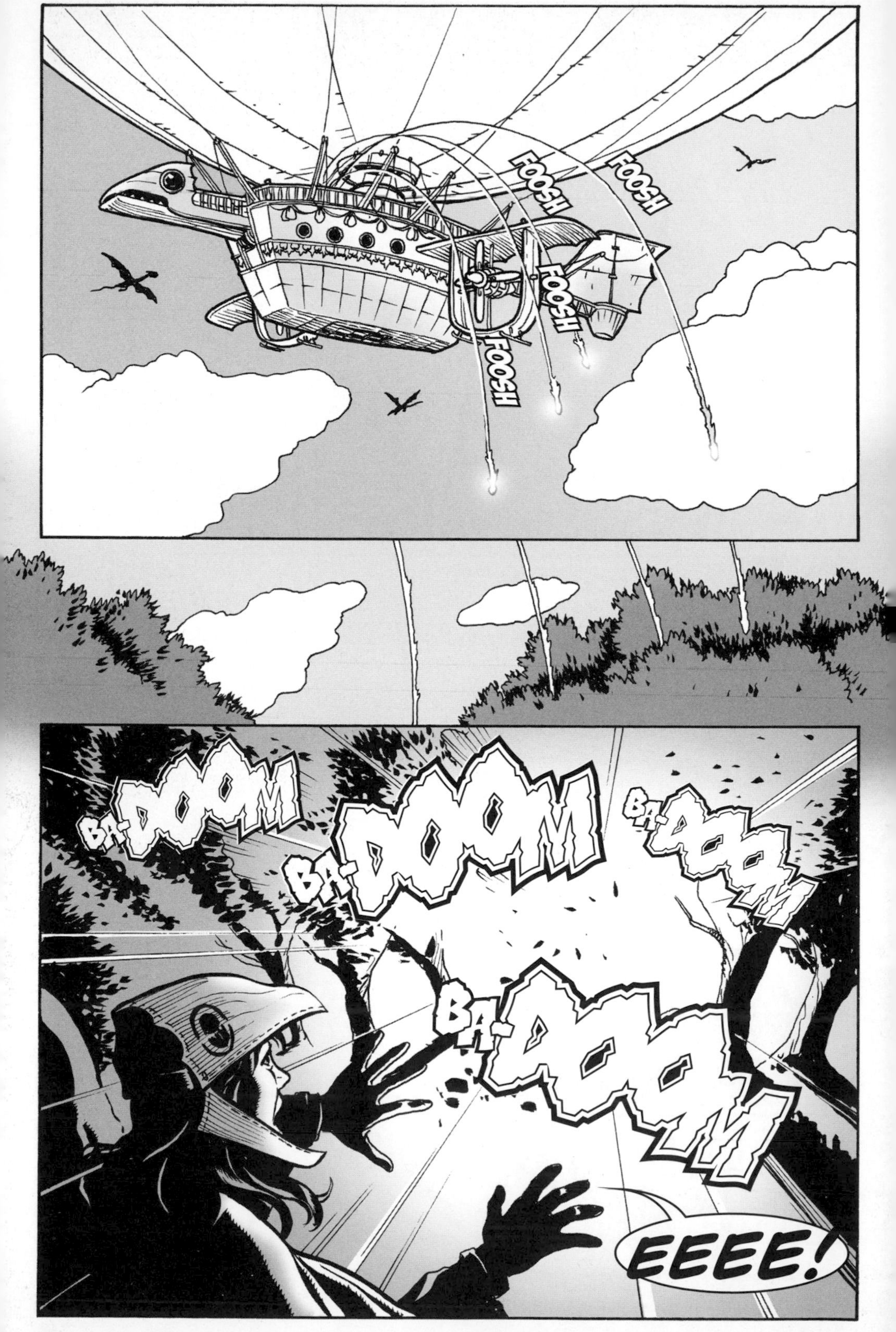
FOOSH
FOOSH
FOOSH
FOOSH
BA-DOOM
BA-DOOM
BA-DOOM
BA-DOOM
EEEE!

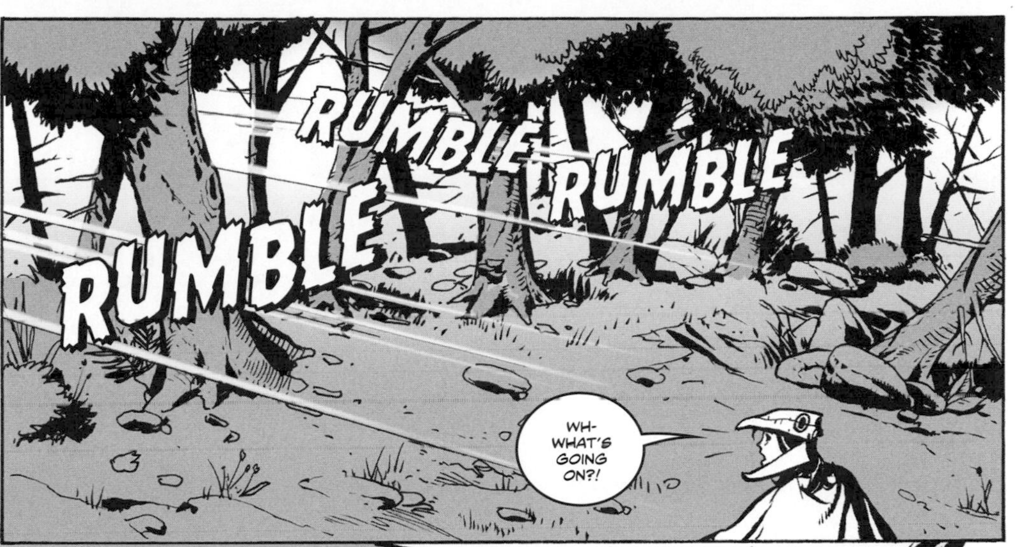
RUMBLE
RUMBLE
RUMBLE
WH- WHAT'S GOING ON?!
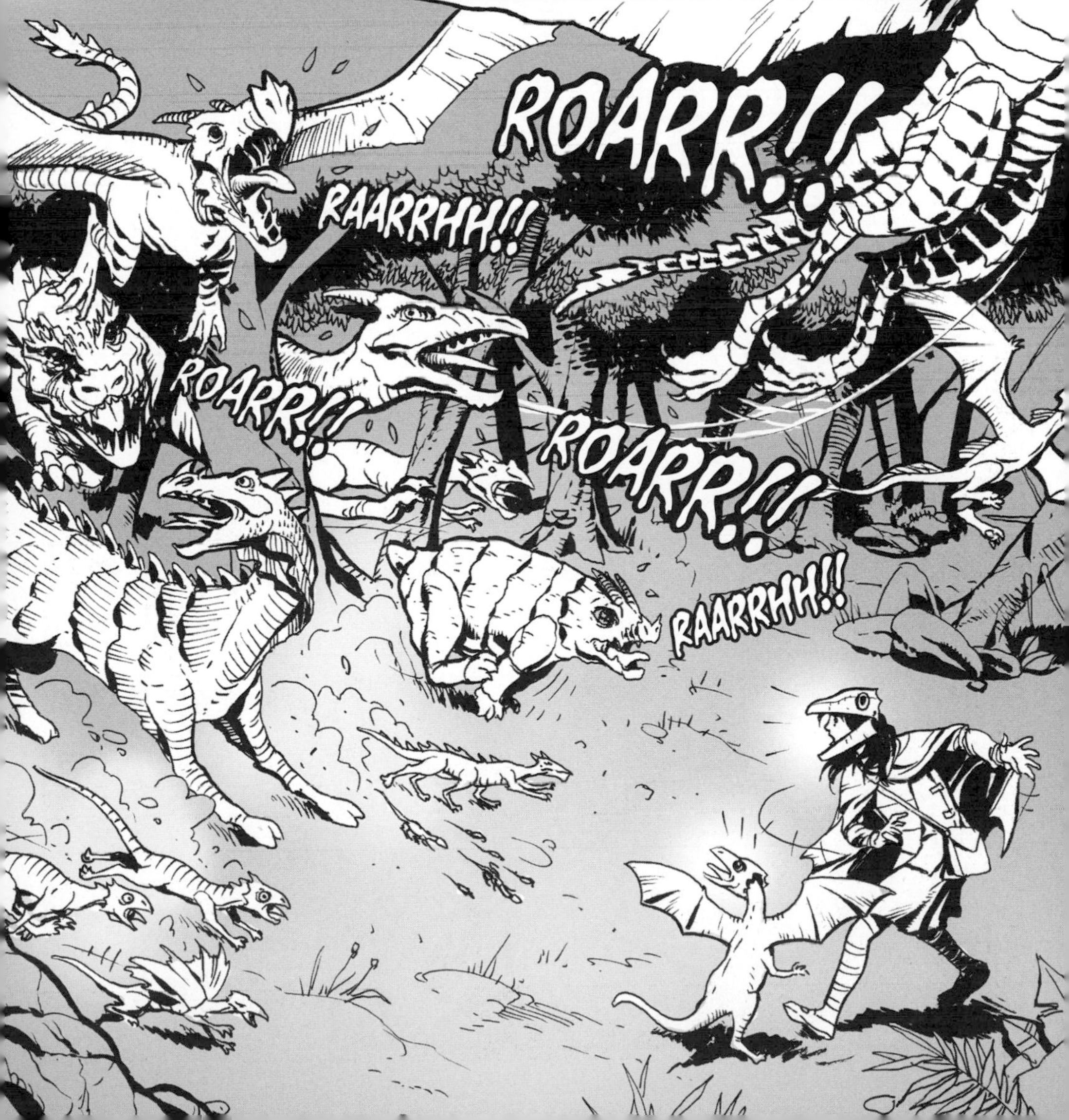
ROARR!!
RAARRHH!!
ROARR!!
ROARR!!
RAARRHH!!

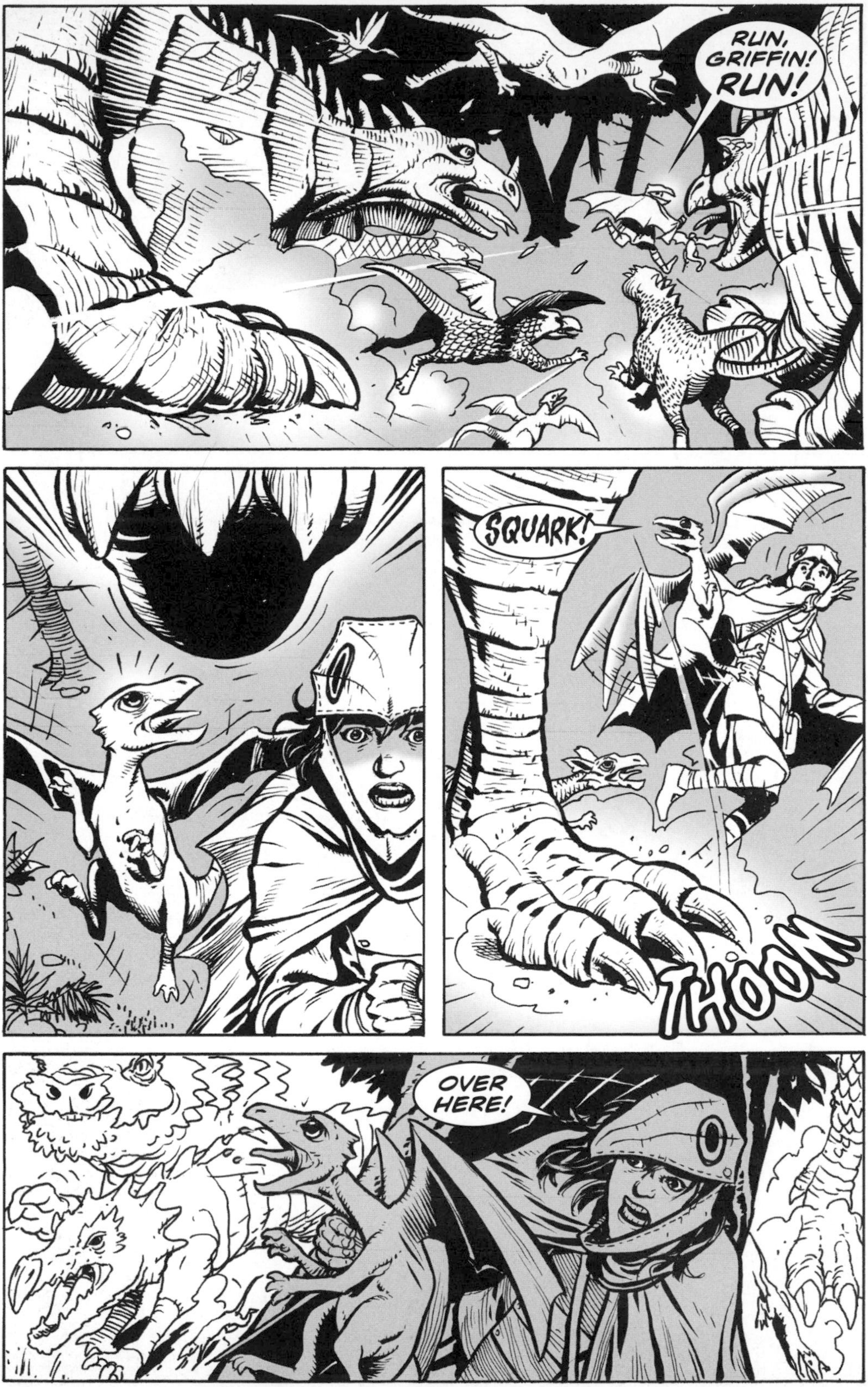
RUN, GRIFFIN! RUN!
SQUARK!
THOOM
OVER HERE!

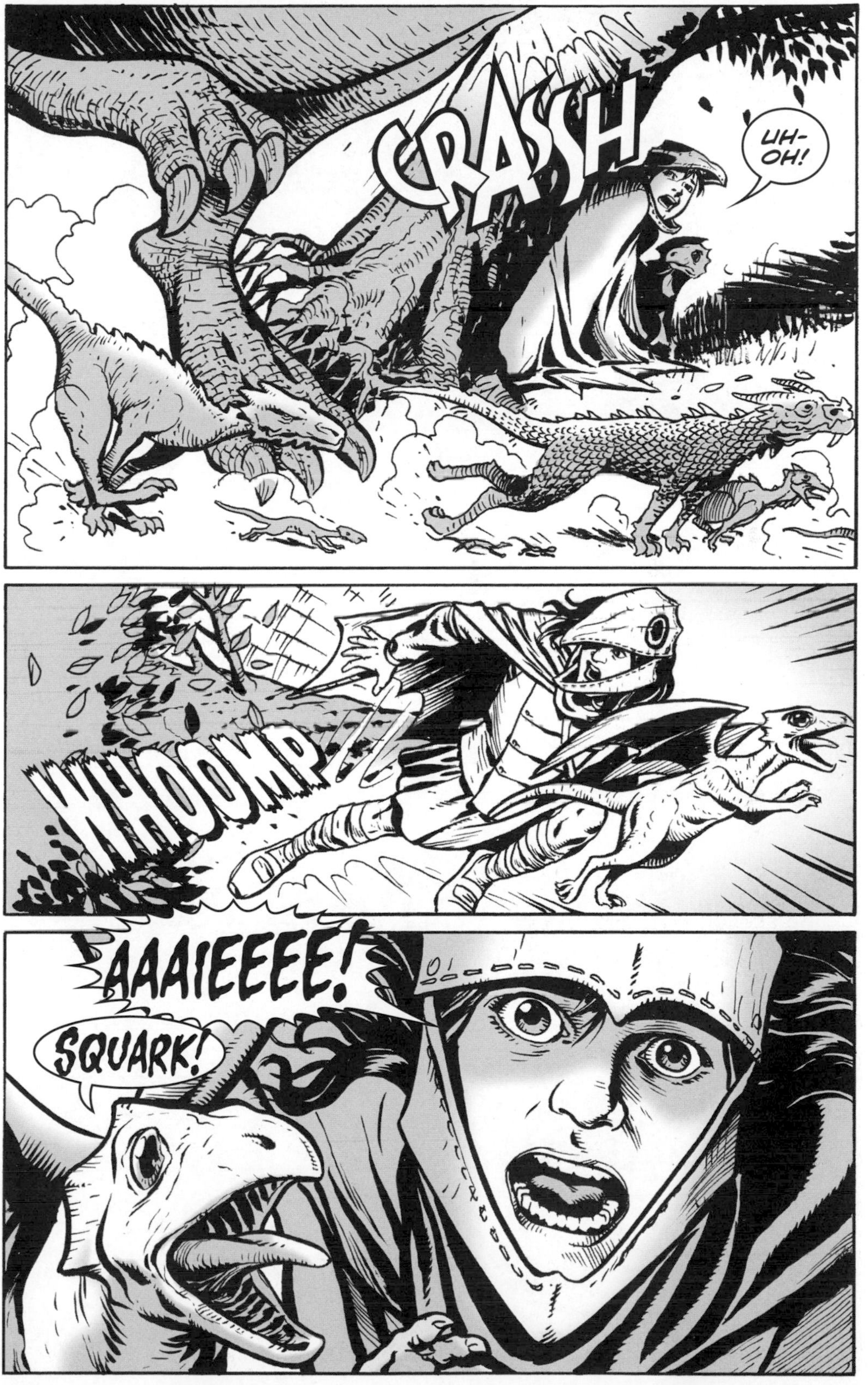
CRASH
UH-OH!
WHOOMP
AAAIEEEE!
SQUARK!

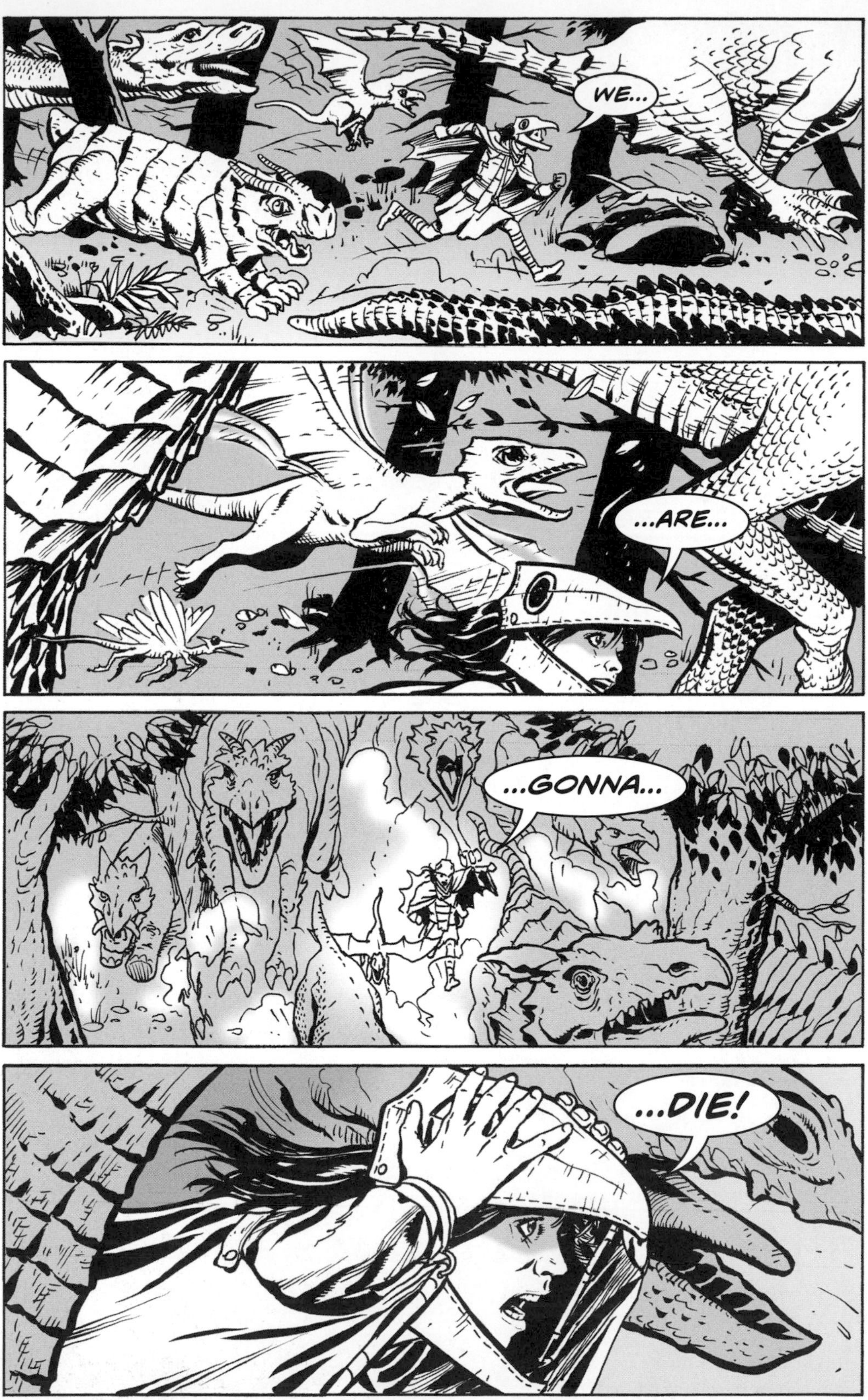
WE...
...ARE...
...GONNA...
...DIE!

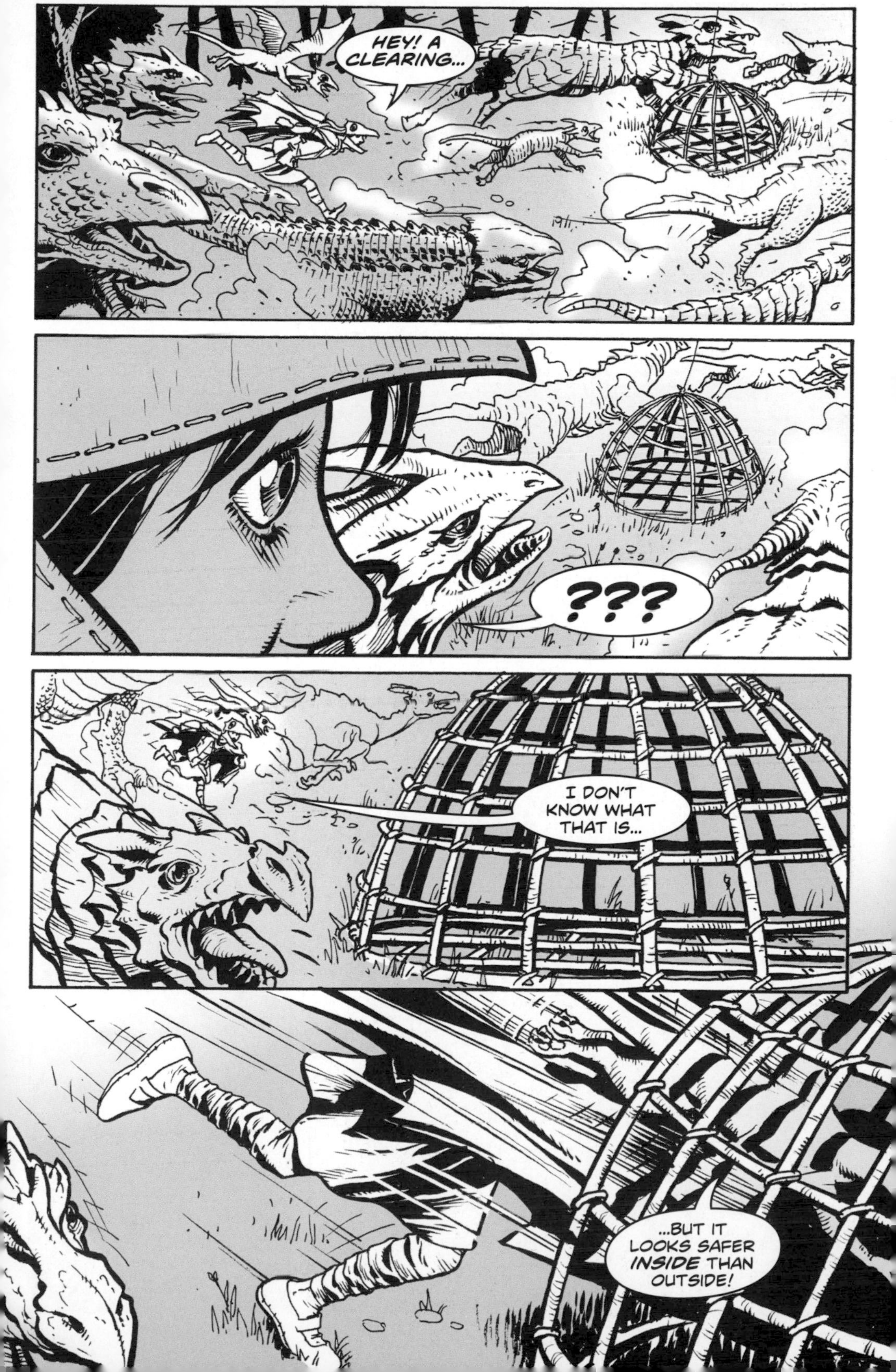
HEY! A CLEARING...
???
I DON'T KNOW WHAT THAT IS...
...BUT IT LOOKS SAFER INSIDE THAN OUTSIDE!

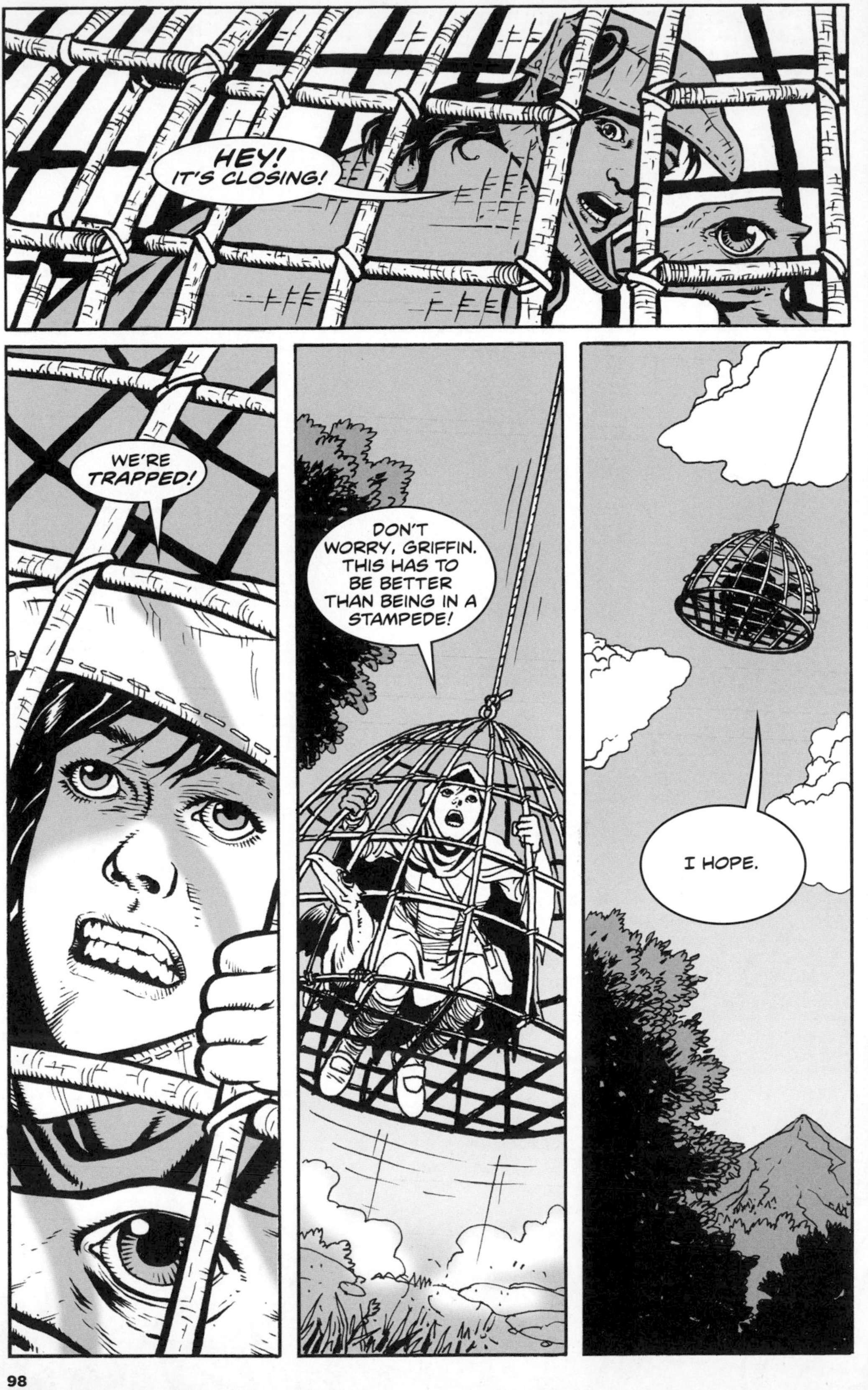
HEY! IT'S CLOSING!
WE'RE TRAPPED!
DON'T WORRY, GRIFFIN. THIS HAS TO BE BETTER THAN BEING IN A STAMPEDE!
I HOPE.

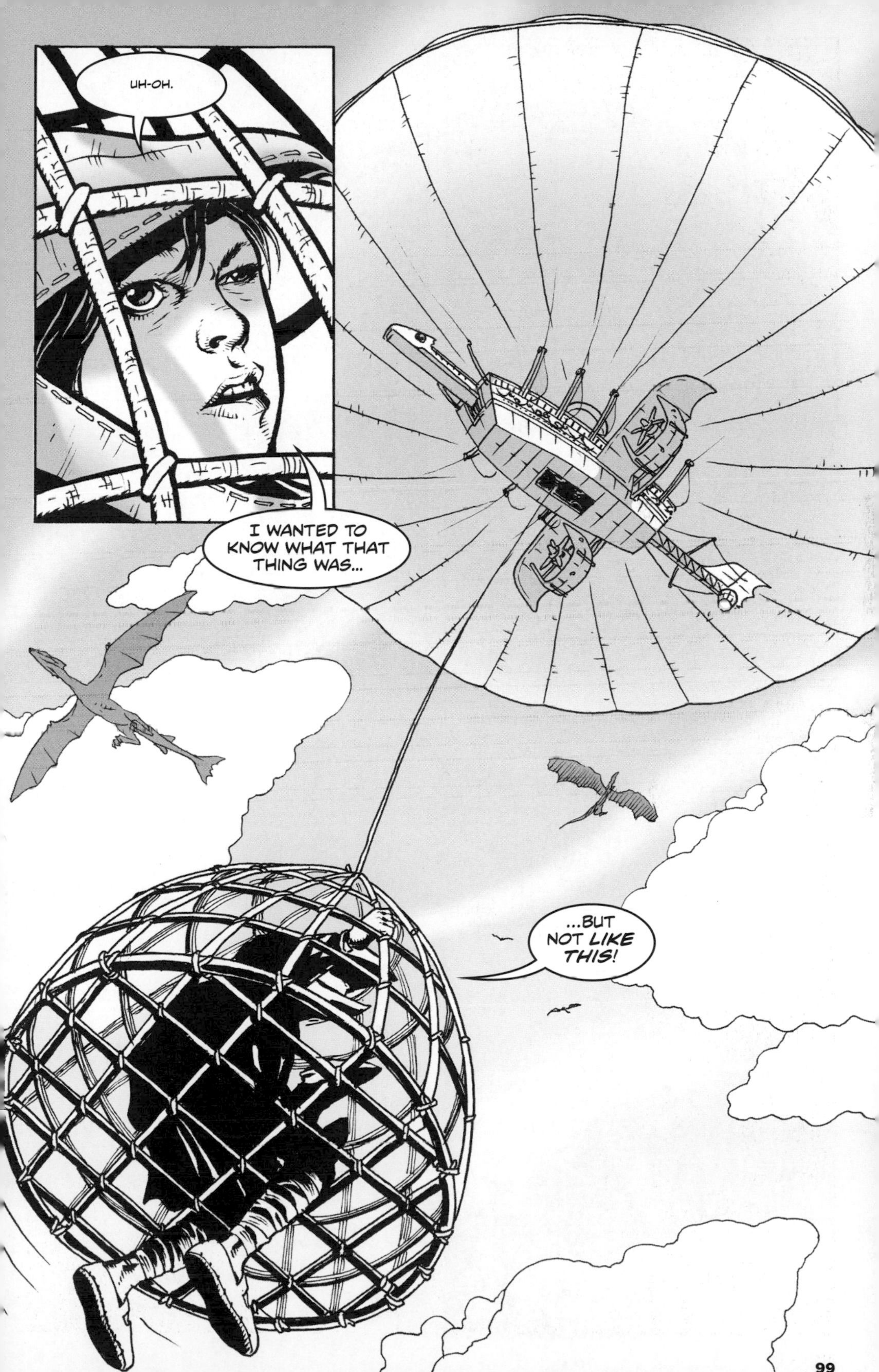
UH-OH.
I WANTED TO KNOW WHAT THAT THING WAS...
...BUT NOT LIKE THIS!

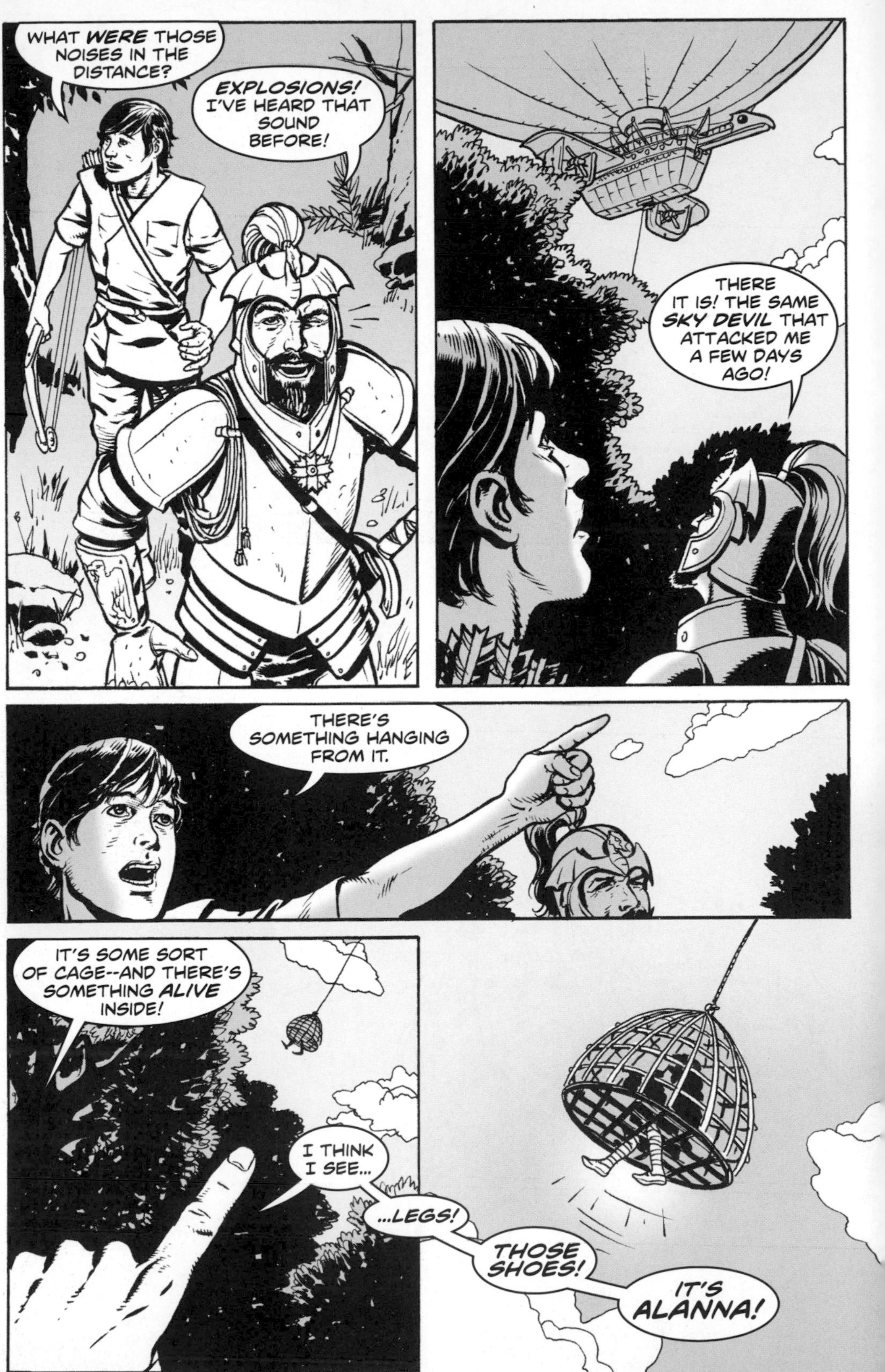
WHAT WERE THOSE NOISES IN THE DISTANCE?
EXPLOSIONS! I'VE HEARD THAT SOUND BEFORE!
THERE IT IS! THE SAME SKY DEVIL THAT ATTACKED ME A FEW DAYS AGO!
THERE'S SOMETHING HANGING FROM IT.
IT'S SOME SORT OF CAGE--AND THERE'S SOMETHING ALIVE INSIDE!
I THINK I SEE...
...LEGS!
THOSE SHOES!
IT'S ALANNA!

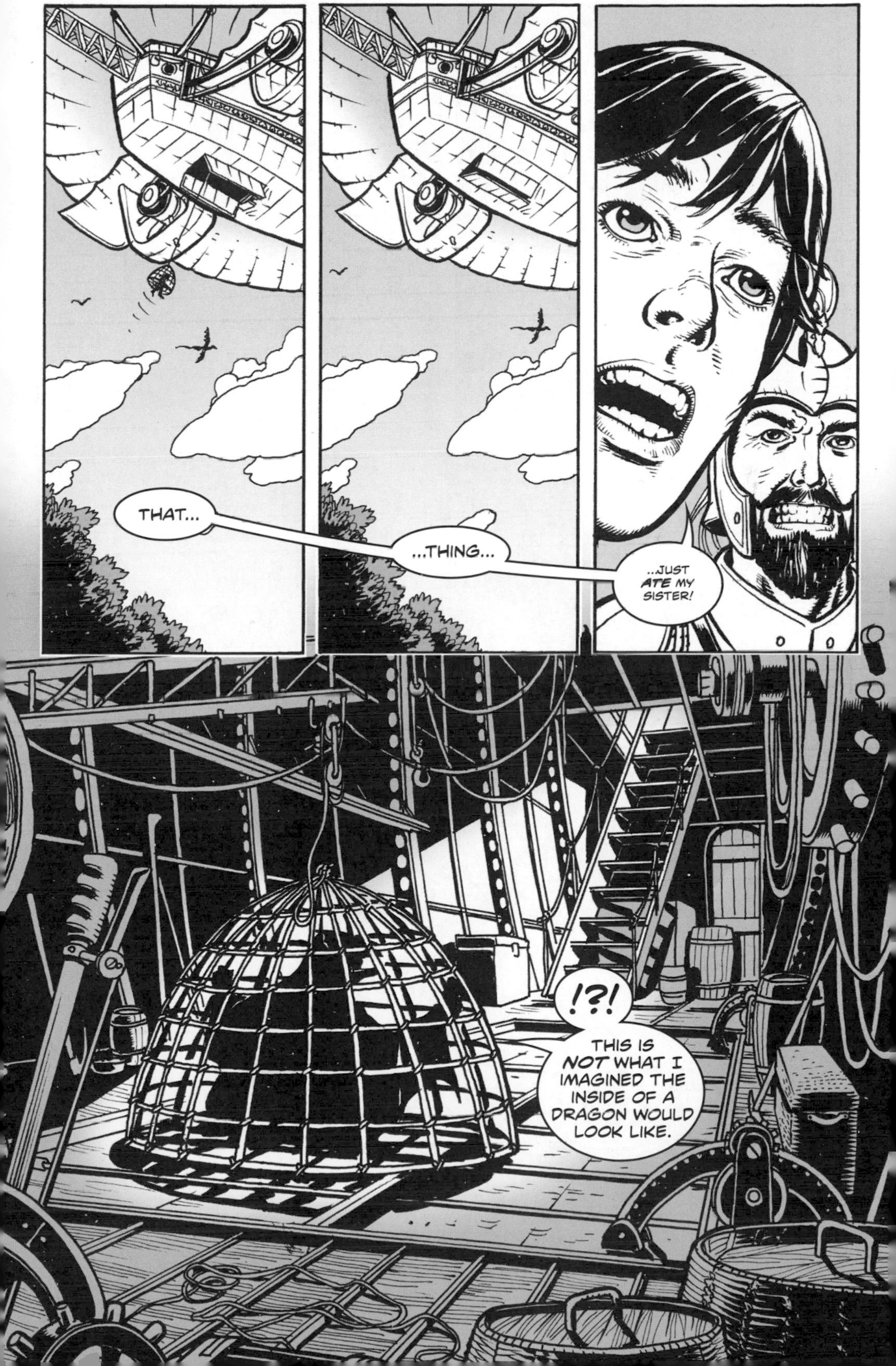
THAT...
...THING...
...JUST ATE MY SISTER!
!?!
THIS IS NOT WHAT I IMAGINED THE INSIDE OF A DRAGON WOULD LOOK LIKE.

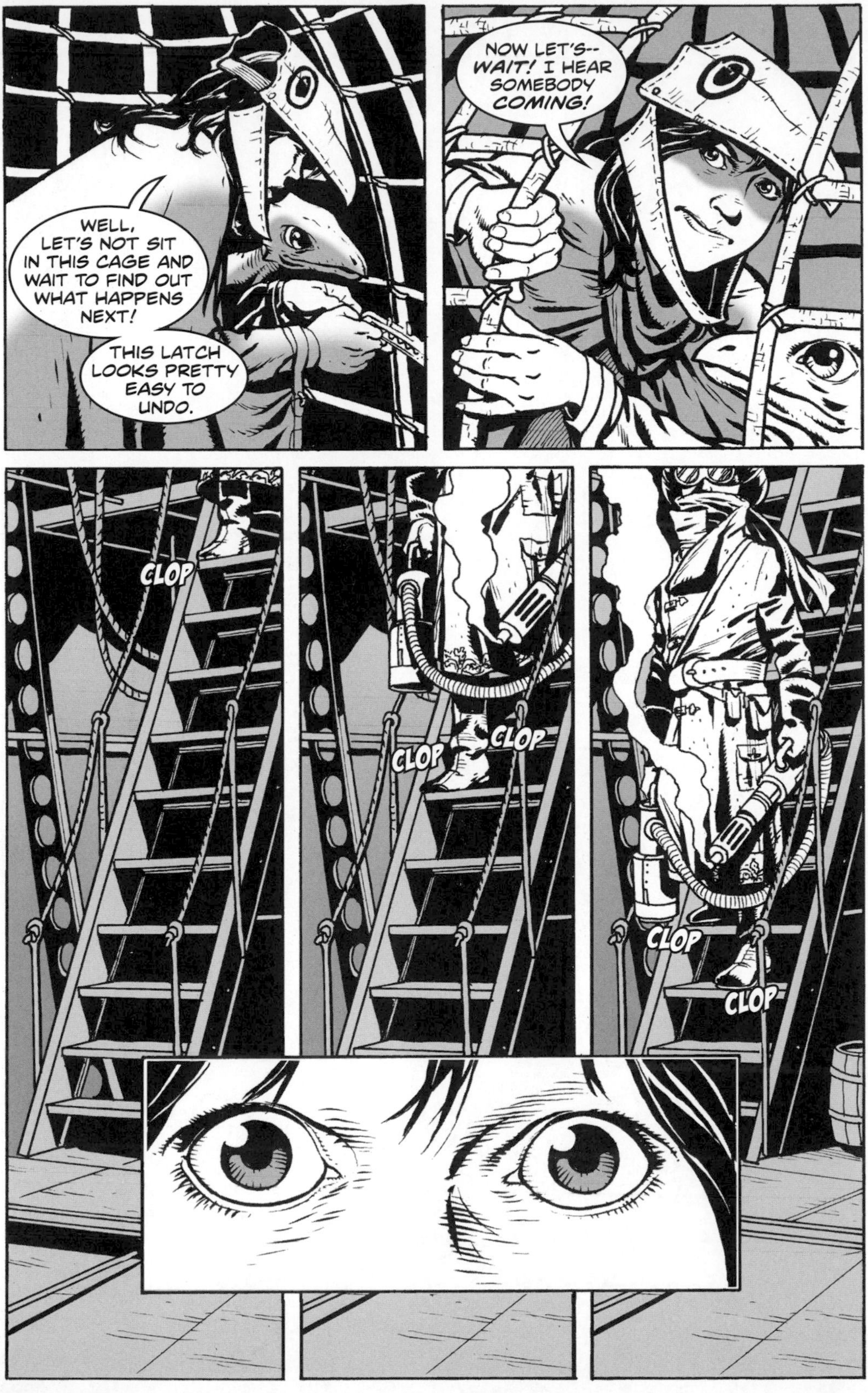
WELL, LET'S NOT SIT IN THIS CAGE AND WAIT TO FIND OUT WHAT HAPPENS NEXT!
THIS LATCH LOOKS PRETTY EASY TO UNDO.
NOW LET'S-- WAIT! I HEAR SOMEBODY COMING!
CLOP
CLOP
CLOP
CLOP
CLOP

CHAPTER SIX

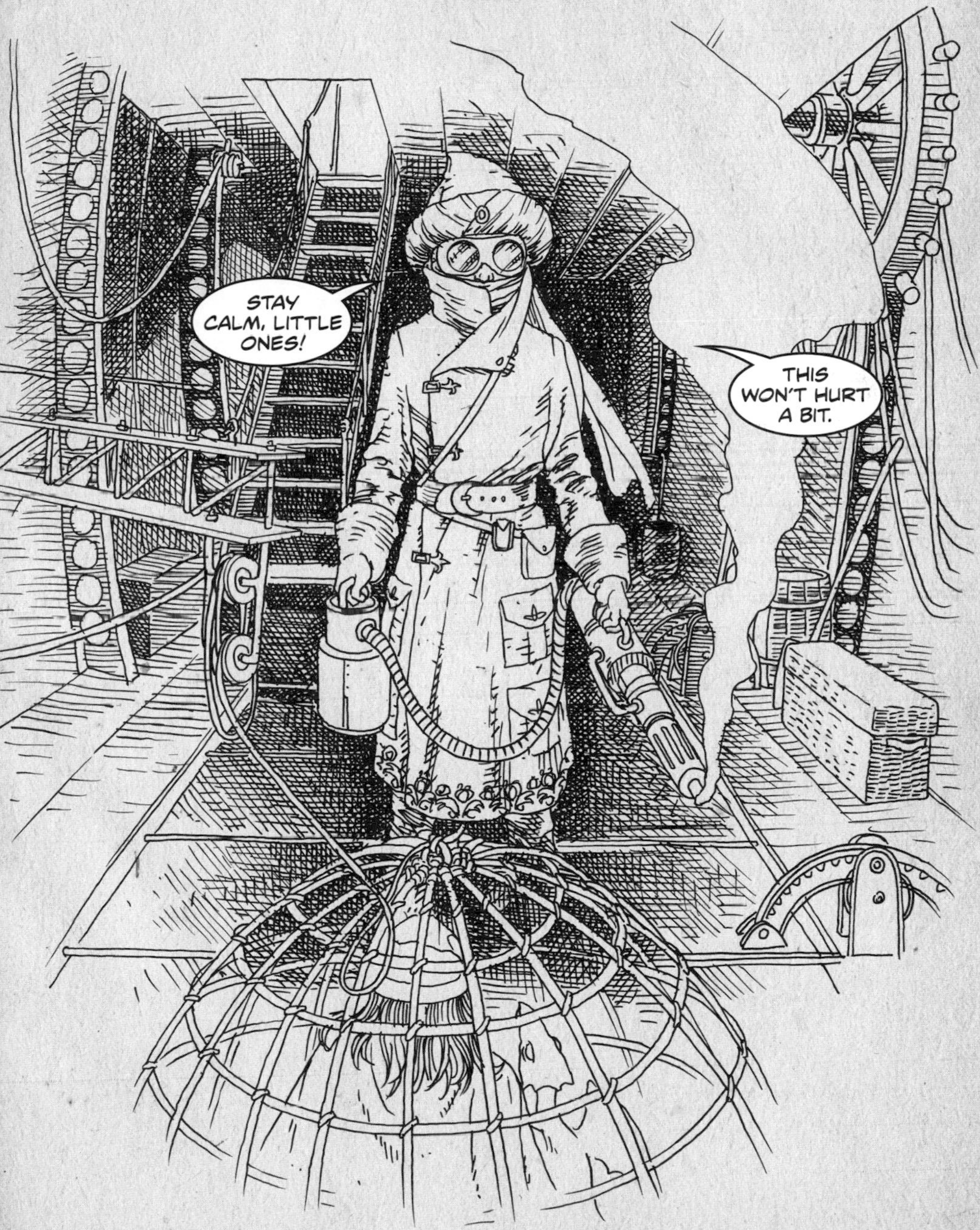
STAY CALM, LITTLE ONES!
THIS WON'T HURT A BIT.

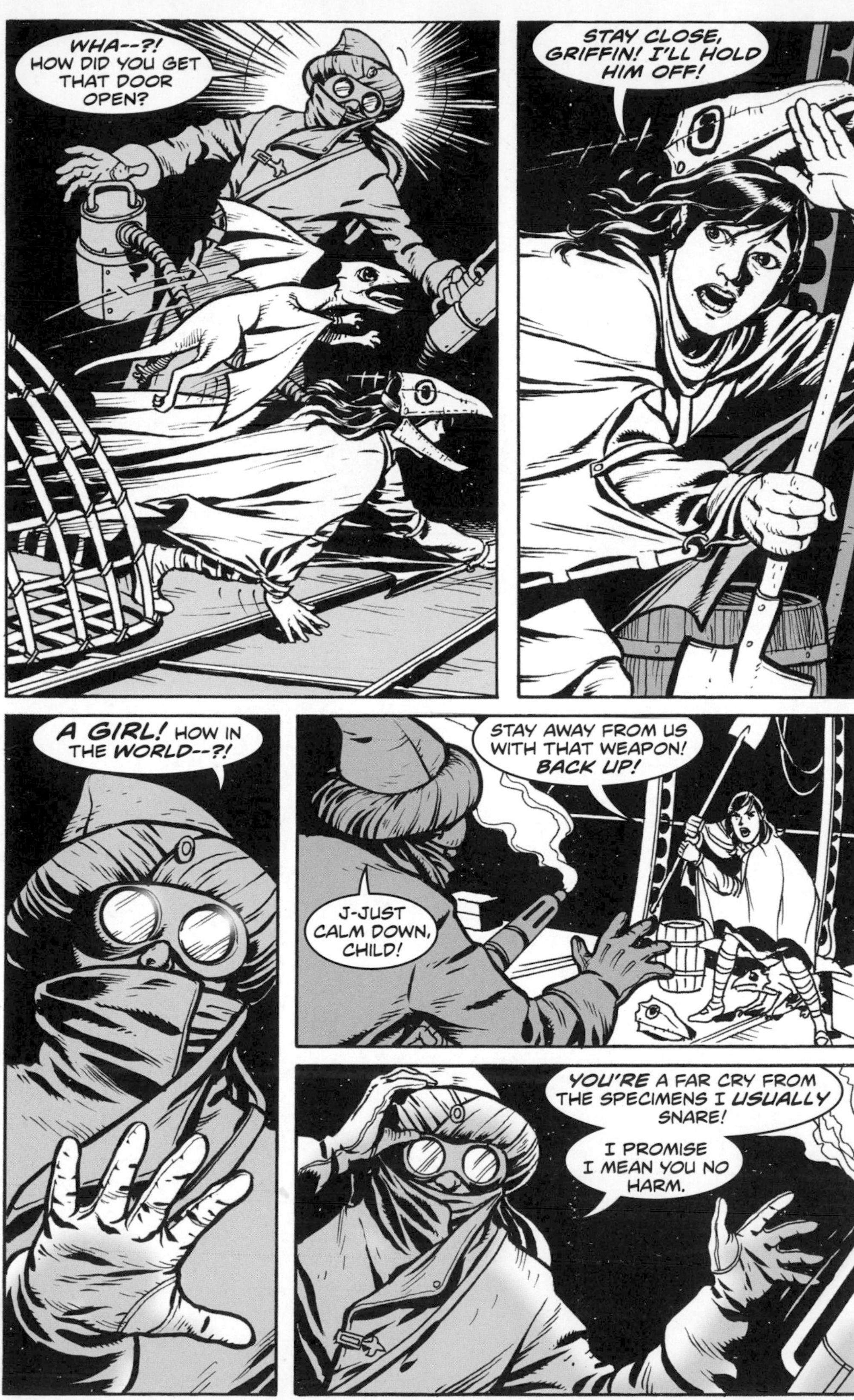
WHA--?! HOW DID YOU GET THAT DOOR OPEN?
STAY CLOSE, GRIFFIN! I'LL HOLD HIM OFF!
A GIRL! HOW IN THE WORLD--?!
STAY AWAY FROM US WITH THAT WEAPON! BACK UP!
J-JUST CALM DOWN, CHILD!
YOU'RE A FAR CRY FROM THE SPECIMENS I USUALLY SNARE!
I PROMISE I MEAN YOU NO HARM.

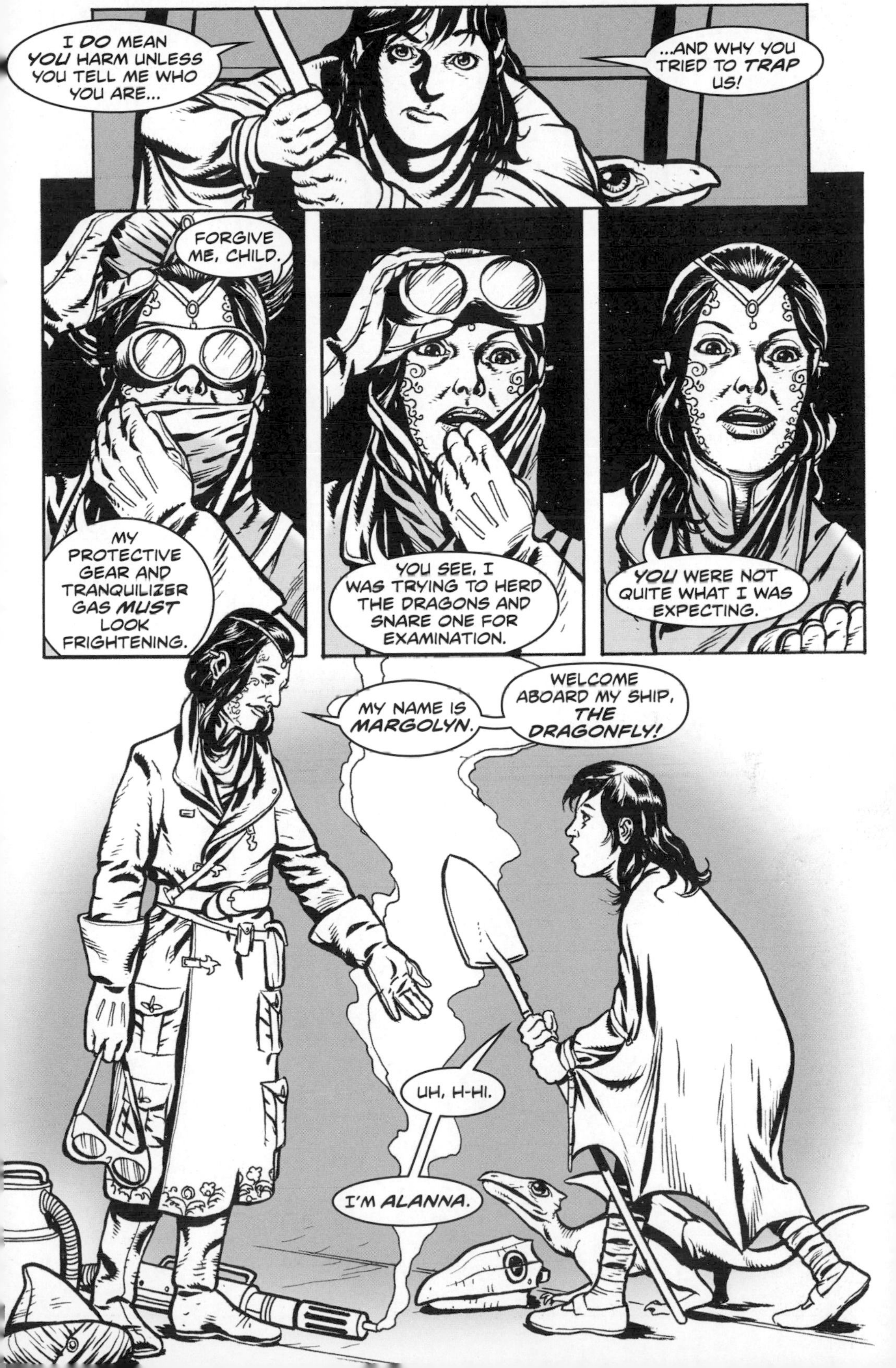
I DO MEAN YOU HARM UNLESS YOU TELL ME WHO YOU ARE...
...AND WHY YOU TRIED TO TRAP US!
FORGIVE ME, CHILD.
MY PROTECTIVE GEAR AND TRANQUILIZER GAS MUST LOOK FRIGHTENING.
YOU SEE, I WAS TRYING TO HERD THE DRAGONS AND SNARE ONE FOR EXAMINATION.
YOU WERE NOT QUITE WHAT I WAS EXPECTING.
MY NAME IS MARGOLYN.
WELCOME ABOARD MY SHIP, THE DRAGONFLY!
UH, H-HI.
I'M ALANNA.

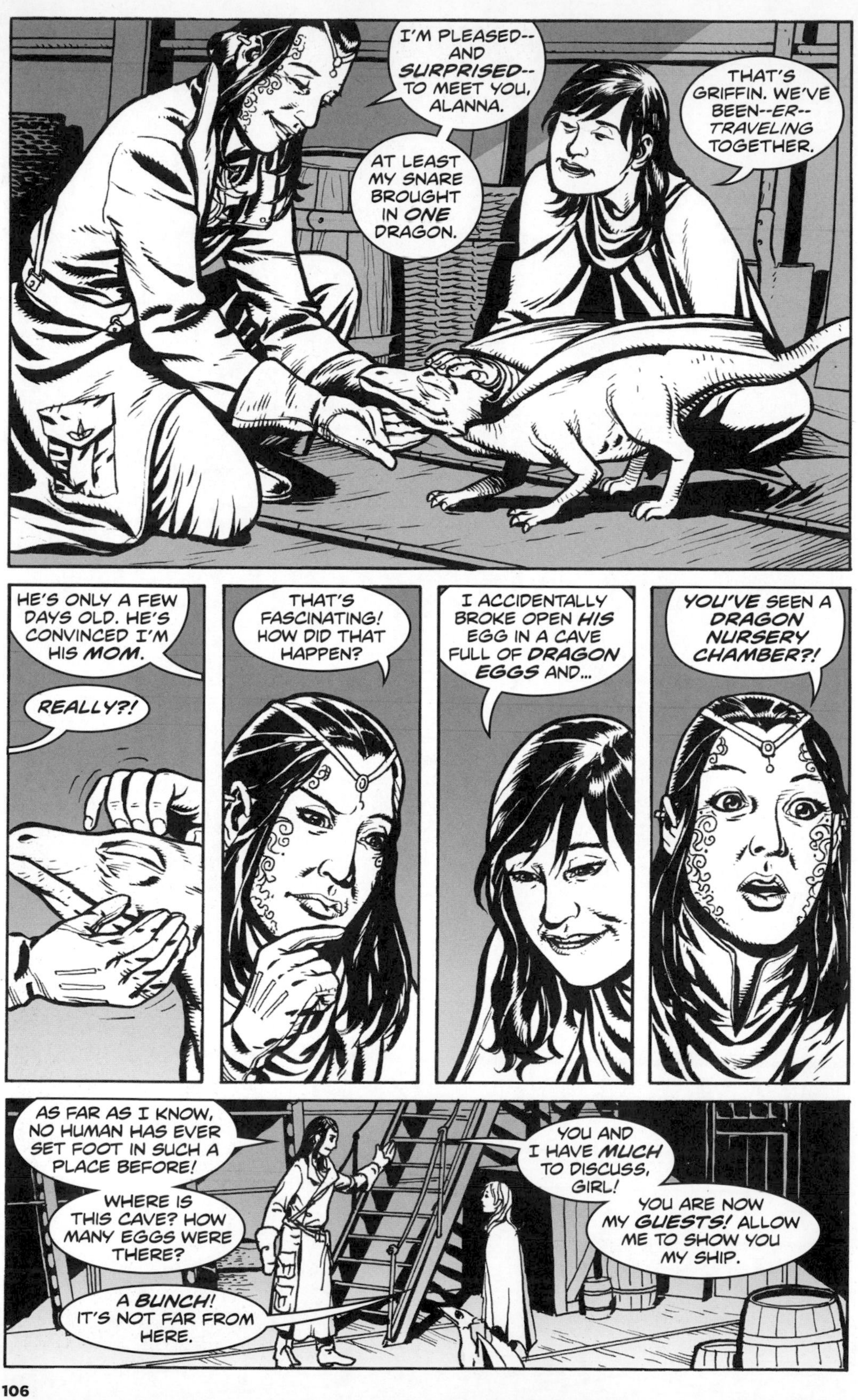

I'M PLEASED-- AND SURPRISED-- TO MEET YOU, ALANNA.
AT LEAST MY SNARE BROUGHT IN ONE DRAGON.
THAT'S GRIFFIN. WE'VE BEEN--ER-- TRAVELING TOGETHER.
HE'S ONLY A FEW DAYS OLD. HE'S CONVINCED I'M HIS MOM.
REALLY?!
THAT'S FASCINATING! HOW DID THAT HAPPEN?
I ACCIDENTALLY BROKE OPEN HIS EGG IN A CAVE FULL OF DRAGON EGGS AND...
YOU'VE SEEN A DRAGON NURSERY CHAMBER?!
AS FAR AS I KNOW, NO HUMAN HAS EVER SET FOOT IN SUCH A PLACE BEFORE!
WHERE IS THIS CAVE? HOW MANY EGGS WERE THERE?
A BUNCH! IT'S NOT FAR FROM HERE.
YOU AND I HAVE MUCH TO DISCUSS, GIRL!
YOU ARE NOW MY GUESTS! ALLOW ME TO SHOW YOU MY SHIP.

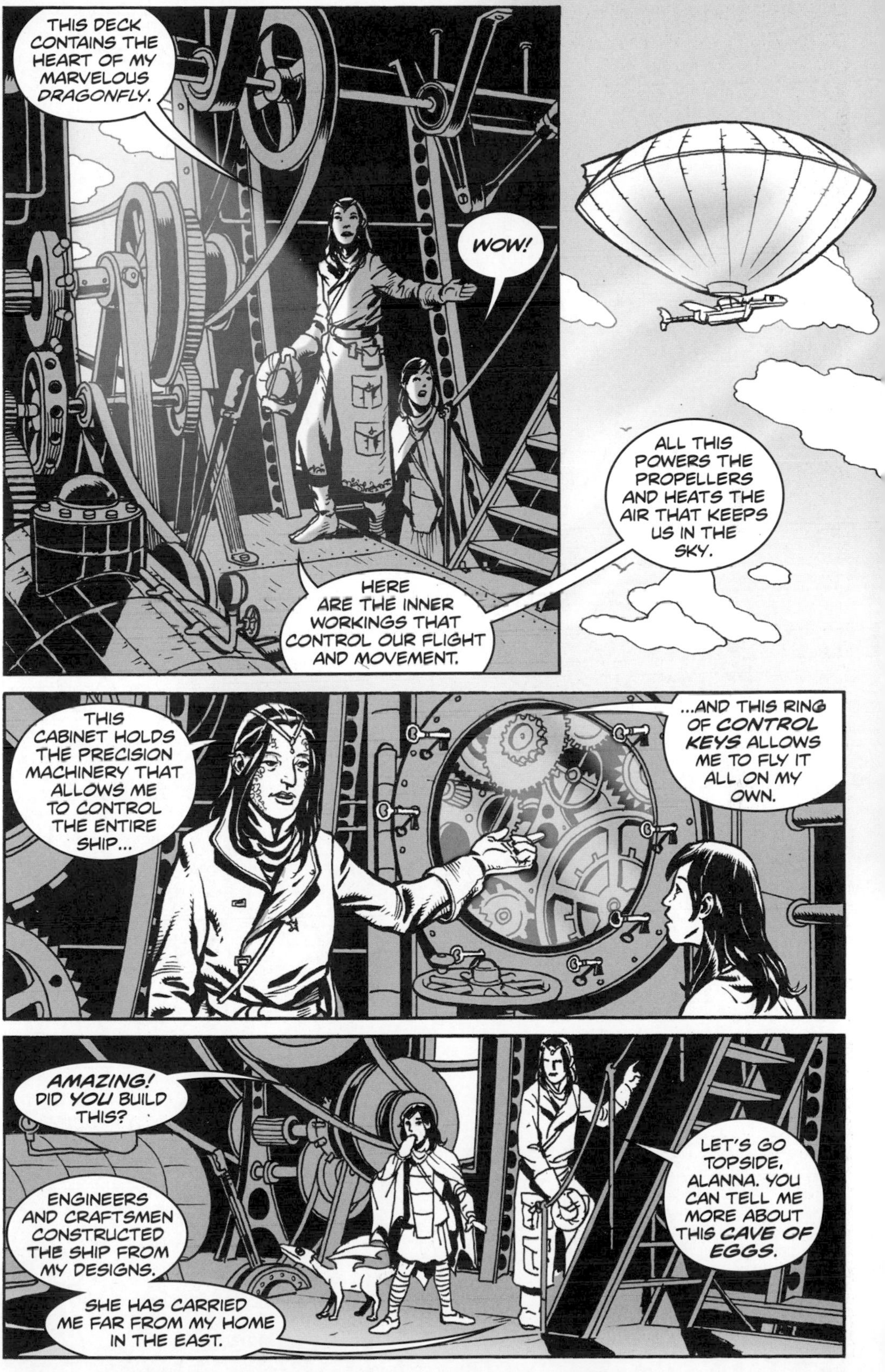
THIS DECK CONTAINS THE HEART OF MY MARVELOUS *DRAGONFLY*.
WOW!
HERE ARE THE INNER WORKINGS THAT CONTROL OUR FLIGHT AND MOVEMENT.
ALL THIS POWERS THE PROPELLERS AND HEATS THE AIR THAT KEEPS US IN THE SKY.
THIS CABINET HOLDS THE PRECISION MACHINERY THAT ALLOWS ME TO CONTROL THE ENTIRE SHIP...
...AND THIS RING OF *CONTROL KEYS* ALLOWS ME TO FLY IT ALL ON MY OWN.
AMAZING! DID *YOU* BUILD THIS?
ENGINEERS AND CRAFTSMEN CONSTRUCTED THE SHIP FROM MY DESIGNS.
SHE HAS CARRIED ME FAR FROM MY HOME IN THE EAST.
LET'S GO TOPSIDE, ALANNA. YOU CAN TELL ME MORE ABOUT THIS *CAVE OF EGGS*.

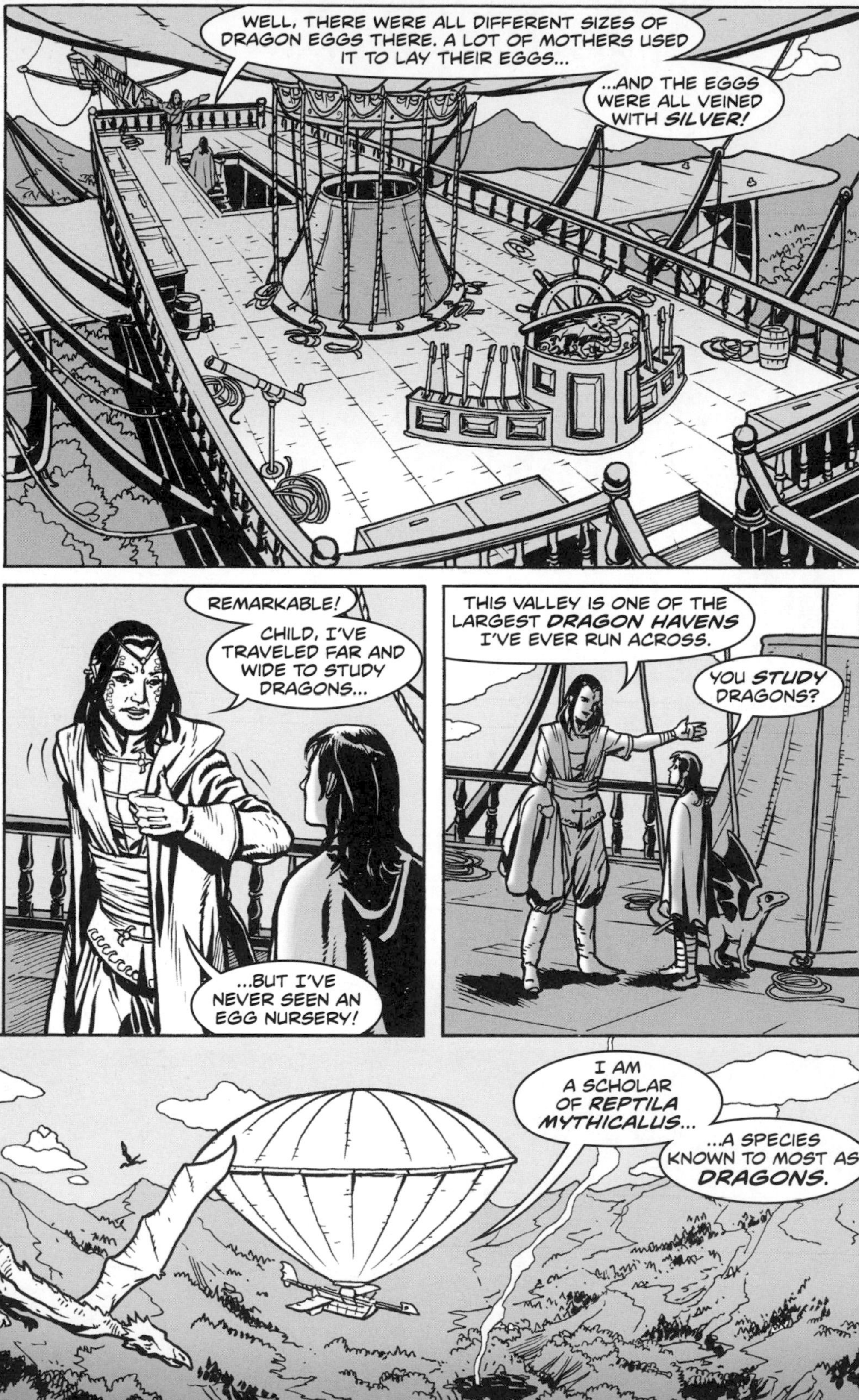
WELL, THERE WERE ALL DIFFERENT SIZES OF DRAGON EGGS THERE. A LOT OF MOTHERS USED IT TO LAY THEIR EGGS...
...AND THE EGGS WERE ALL VEINED WITH SILVER!
REMARKABLE!
CHILD, I'VE TRAVELED FAR AND WIDE TO STUDY DRAGONS...
...BUT I'VE NEVER SEEN AN EGG NURSERY!
THIS VALLEY IS ONE OF THE LARGEST DRAGON HAVENS I'VE EVER RUN ACROSS.
YOU STUDY DRAGONS?
I AM A SCHOLAR OF REPTILA MYTHICALUS...
...A SPECIES KNOWN TO MOST AS DRAGONS.

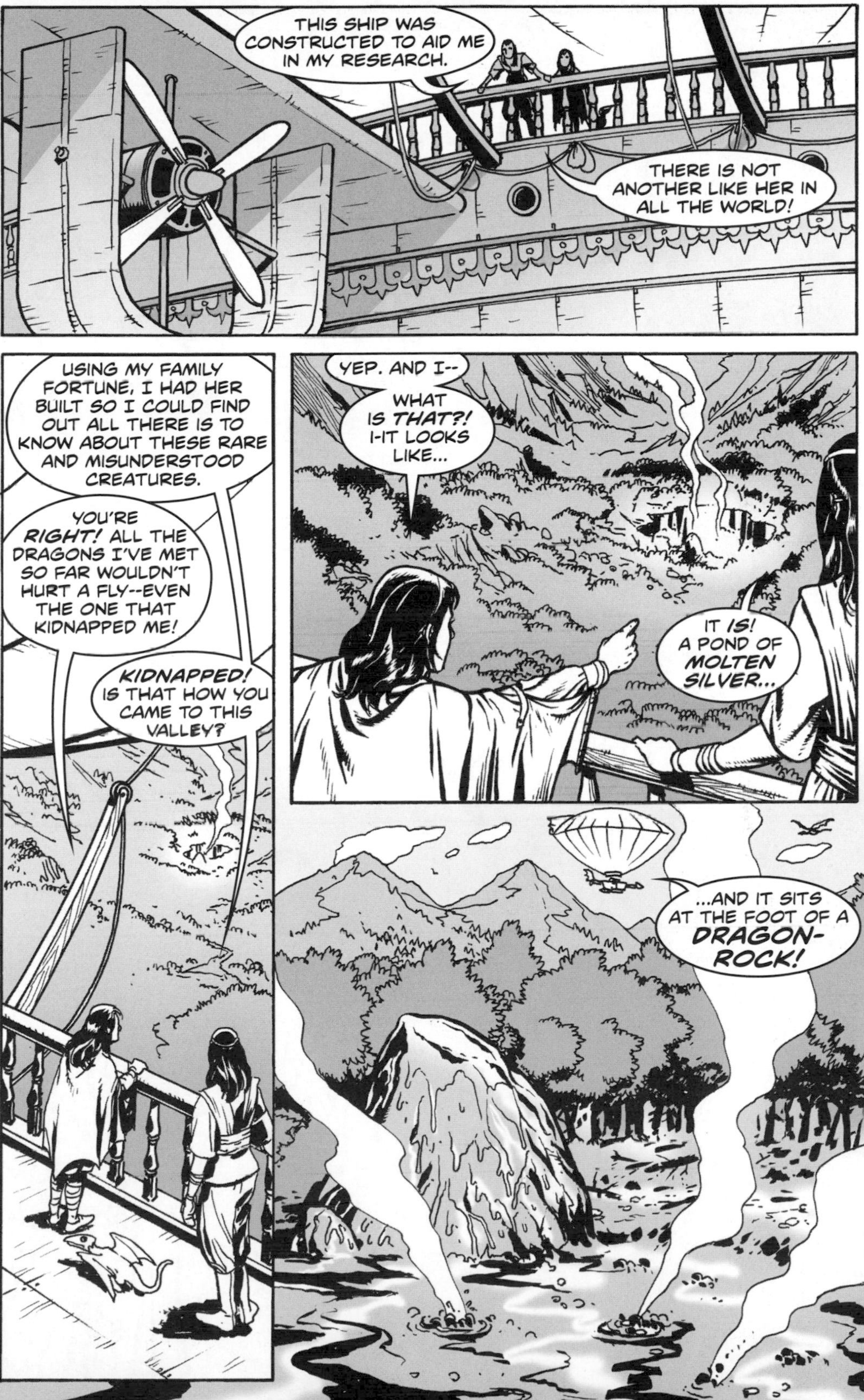
THIS SHIP WAS CONSTRUCTED TO AID ME IN MY RESEARCH.
THERE IS NOT ANOTHER LIKE HER IN ALL THE WORLD!
USING MY FAMILY FORTUNE, I HAD HER BUILT SO I COULD FIND OUT ALL THERE IS TO KNOW ABOUT THESE RARE AND MISUNDERSTOOD CREATURES.
YOU'RE RIGHT! ALL THE DRAGONS I'VE MET SO FAR WOULDN'T HURT A FLY--EVEN THE ONE THAT KIDNAPPED ME!
KIDNAPPED! IS THAT HOW YOU CAME TO THIS VALLEY?
YEP. AND I--
WHAT IS THAT?! I-IT LOOKS LIKE...
IT IS! A POND OF MOLTEN SILVER...
...AND IT SITS AT THE FOOT OF A DRAGON-ROCK!

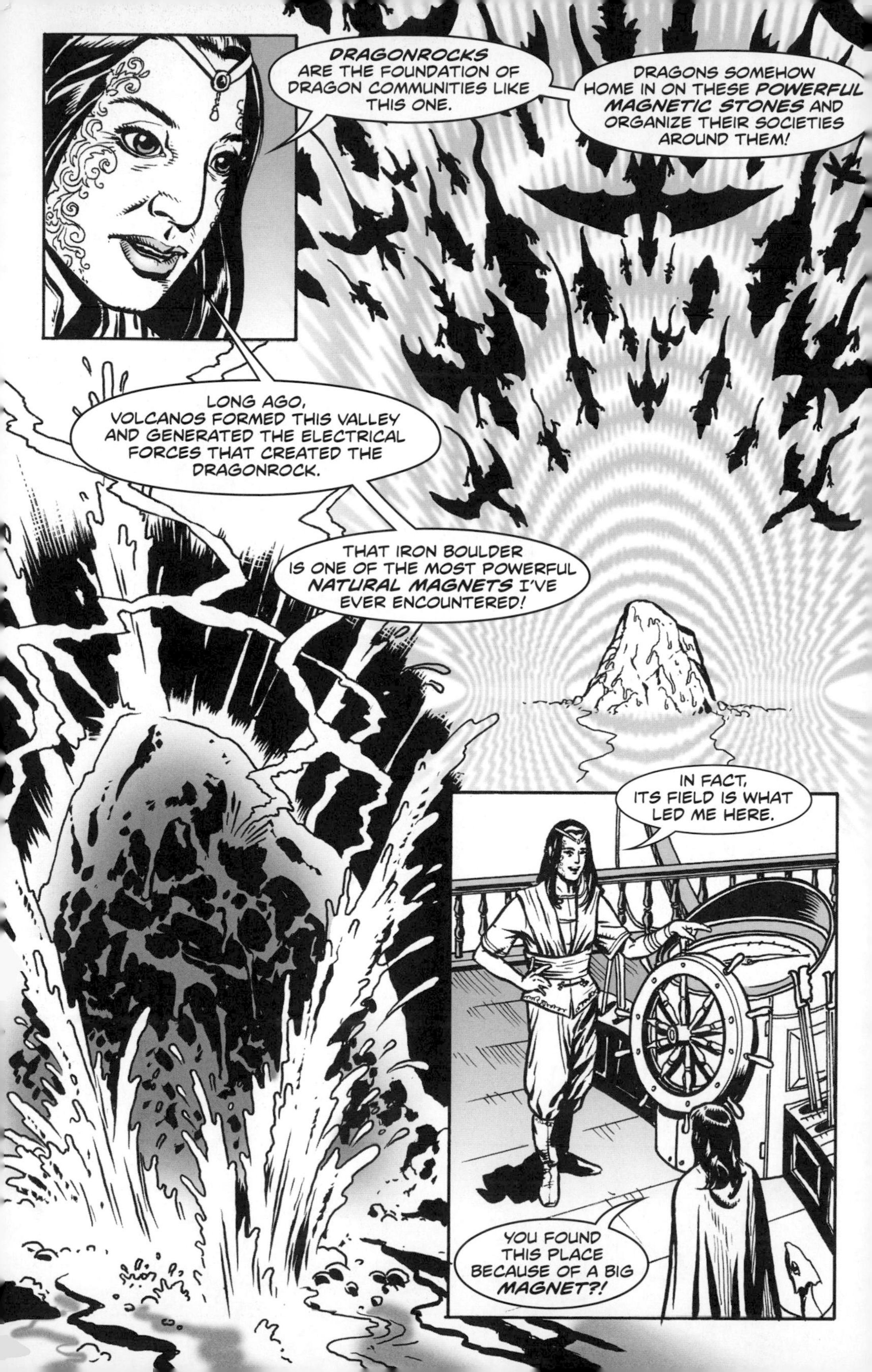
DRAGONROCKS ARE THE FOUNDATION OF DRAGON COMMUNITIES LIKE THIS ONE.
DRAGONS SOMEHOW HOME IN ON THESE POWERFUL MAGNETIC STONES AND ORGANIZE THEIR SOCIETIES AROUND THEM!
LONG AGO, VOLCANOS FORMED THIS VALLEY AND GENERATED THE ELECTRICAL FORCES THAT CREATED THE DRAGONROCK.
THAT IRON BOULDER IS ONE OF THE MOST POWERFUL NATURAL MAGNETS I'VE EVER ENCOUNTERED!
IN FACT, ITS FIELD IS WHAT LED ME HERE.
YOU FOUND THIS PLACE BECAUSE OF A BIG MAGNET?!

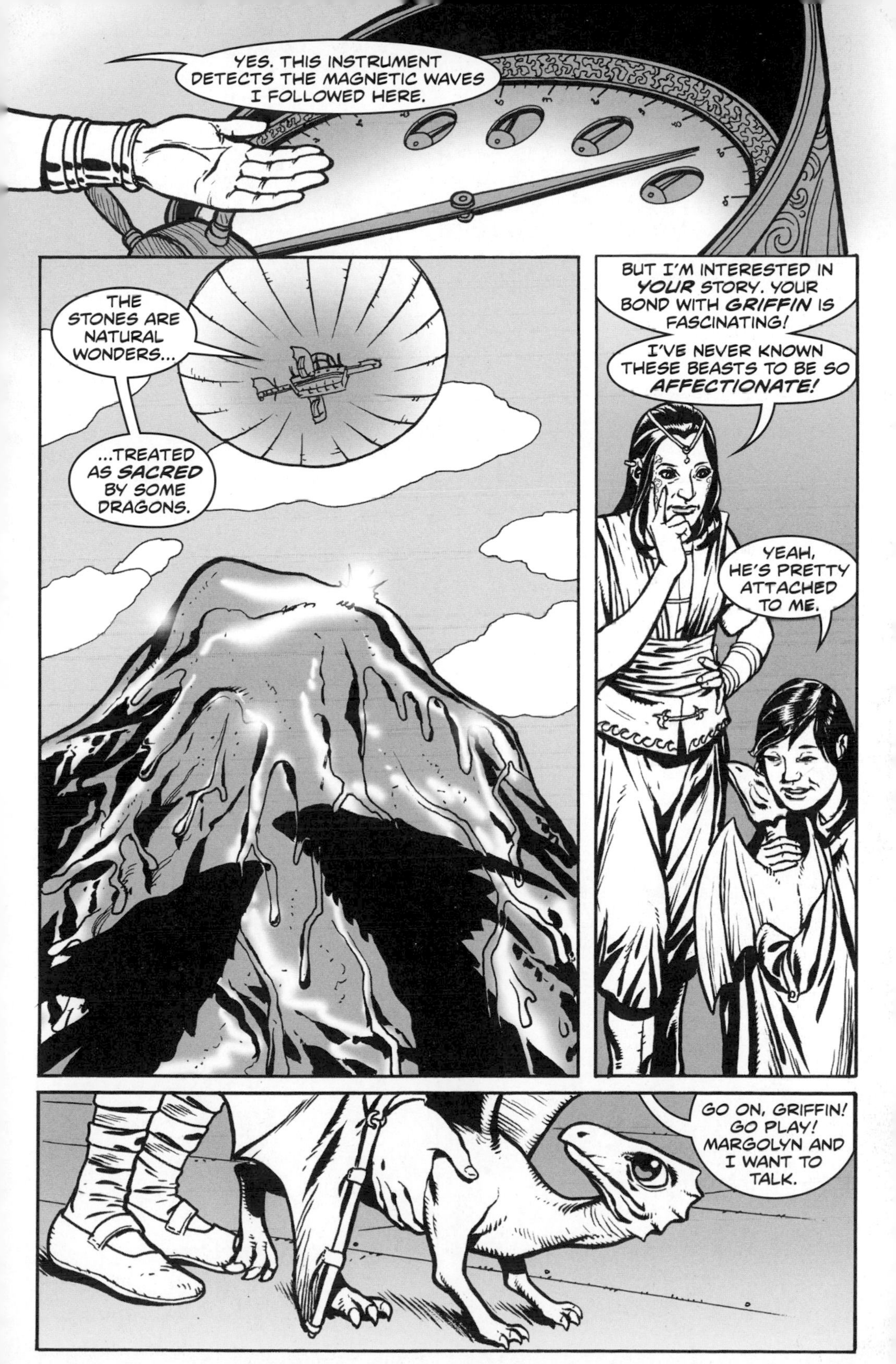
YES. THIS INSTRUMENT DETECTS THE MAGNETIC WAVES I FOLLOWED HERE.
THE STONES ARE NATURAL WONDERS...
...TREATED AS SACRED BY SOME DRAGONS.
BUT I'M INTERESTED IN YOUR STORY. YOUR BOND WITH GRIFFIN IS FASCINATING!
I'VE NEVER KNOWN THESE BEASTS TO BE SO AFFECTIONATE!
YEAH, HE'S PRETTY ATTACHED TO ME.
GO ON, GRIFFIN! GO PLAY! MARGOLYN AND I WANT TO TALK.

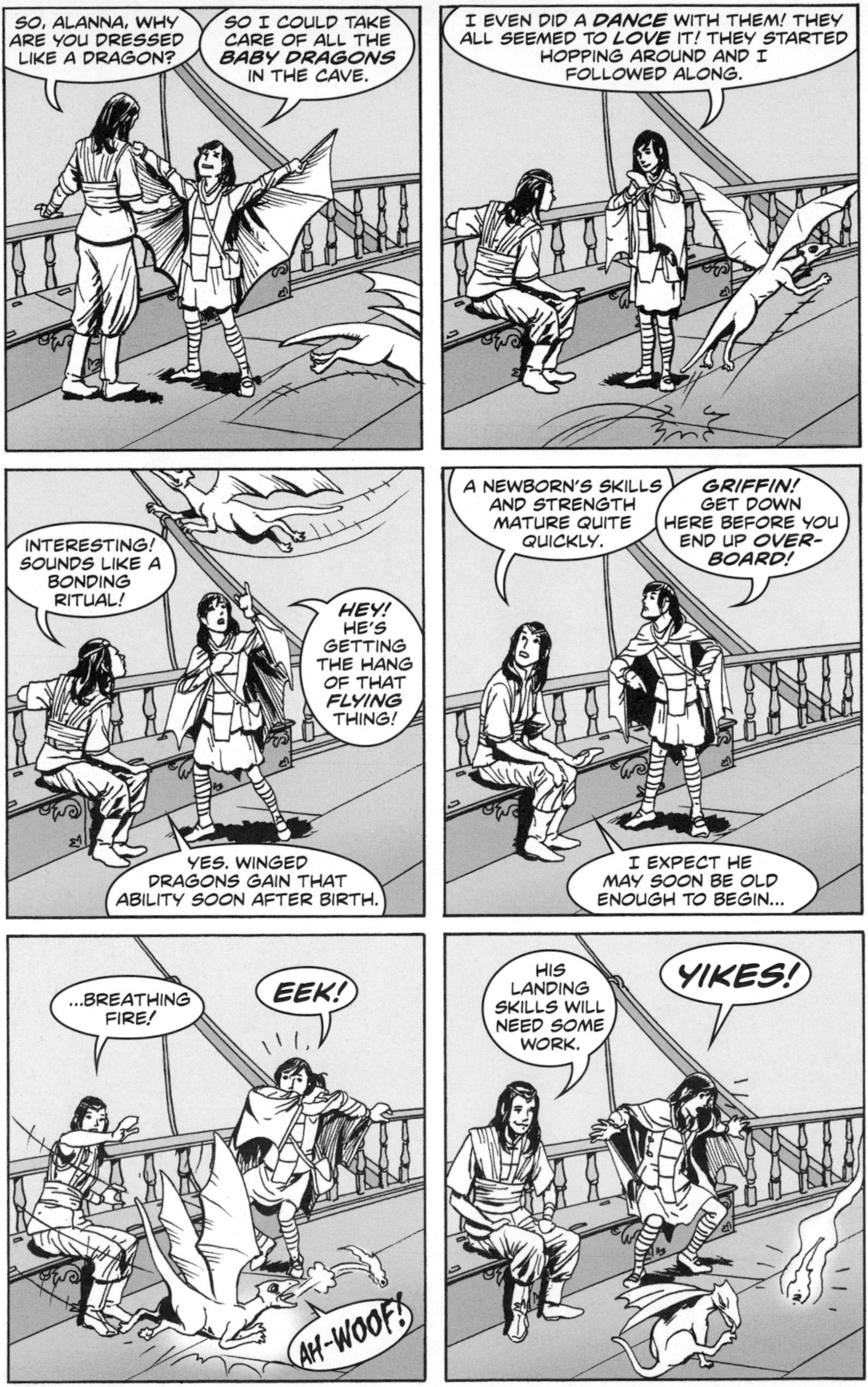
SO, ALANNA, WHY ARE YOU DRESSED LIKE A DRAGON?
SO I COULD TAKE CARE OF ALL THE BABY DRAGONS IN THE CAVE.
I EVEN DID A DANCE WITH THEM! THEY ALL SEEMED TO LOVE IT! THEY STARTED HOPPING AROUND AND I FOLLOWED ALONG.
INTERESTING! SOUNDS LIKE A BONDING RITUAL!
HEY! HE'S GETTING THE HANG OF THAT FLYING THING!
YES. WINGED DRAGONS GAIN THAT ABILITY SOON AFTER BIRTH.
A NEWBORN'S SKILLS AND STRENGTH MATURE QUITE QUICKLY.
GRIFFIN! GET DOWN HERE BEFORE YOU END UP OVER-BOARD!
I EXPECT HE MAY SOON BE OLD ENOUGH TO BEGIN...
...BREATHING FIRE!
EEK!
AH-WOOF!
HIS LANDING SKILLS WILL NEED SOME WORK.
YIKES!

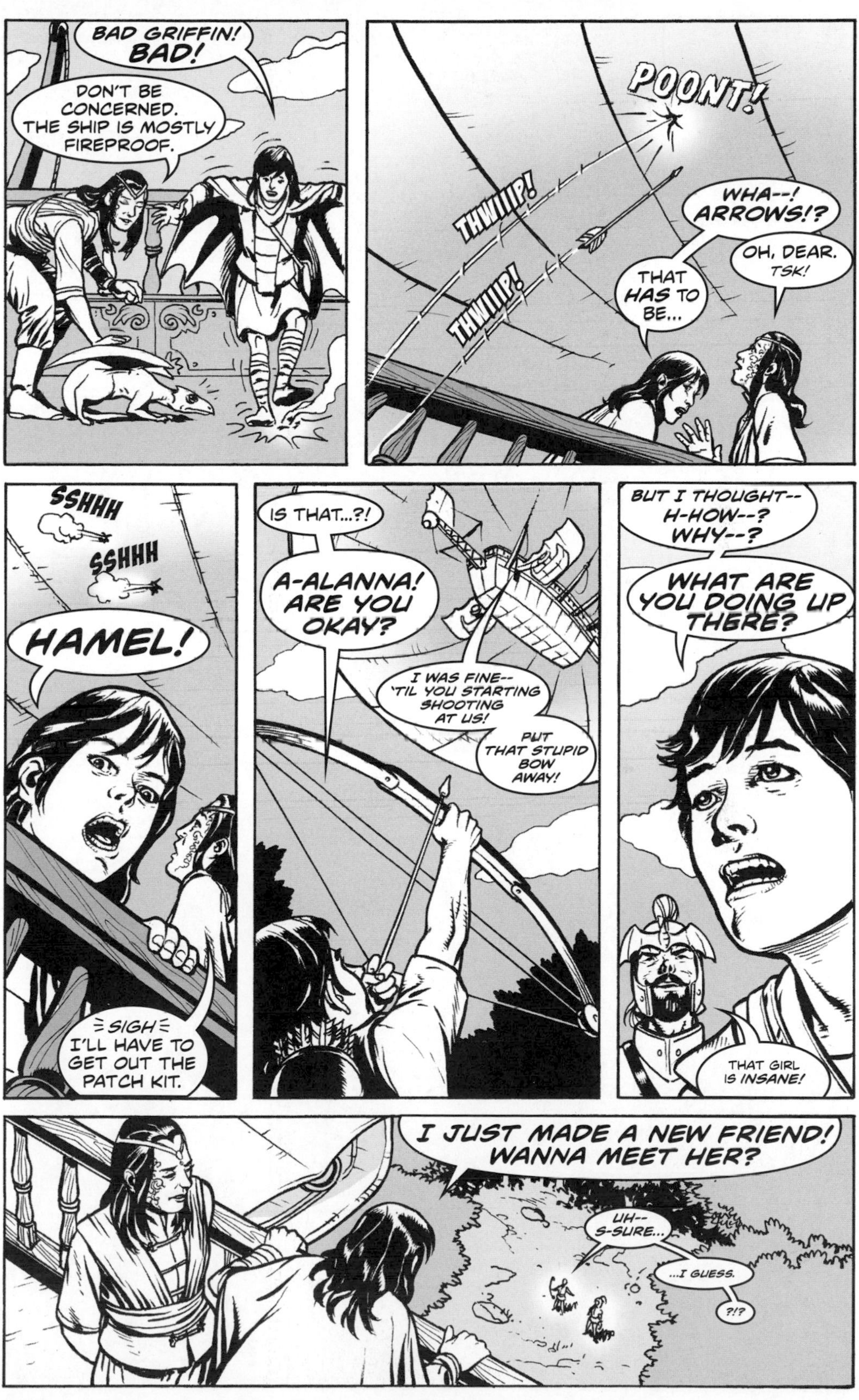

BAD GRIFFIN! BAD!
DON'T BE CONCERNED. THE SHIP IS MOSTLY FIREPROOF.
POONT!
THWIIIP!
THWIIIP!
WHA--! ARROWS!?
THAT HAS TO BE...
OH, DEAR. TSK!
SSHHH
SSHHH
HAMEL!
SIGH
I'LL HAVE TO GET OUT THE PATCH KIT.
IS THAT...?!
A-ALANNA! ARE YOU OKAY?
I WAS FINE-- 'TIL YOU STARTING SHOOTING AT US!
PUT THAT STUPID BOW AWAY!
BUT I THOUGHT-- H-HOW--? WHY--?
WHAT ARE YOU DOING UP THERE?
THAT GIRL IS INSANE!
I JUST MADE A NEW FRIEND! WANNA MEET HER?
UH-- S-SURE...
...I GUESS.
?!?

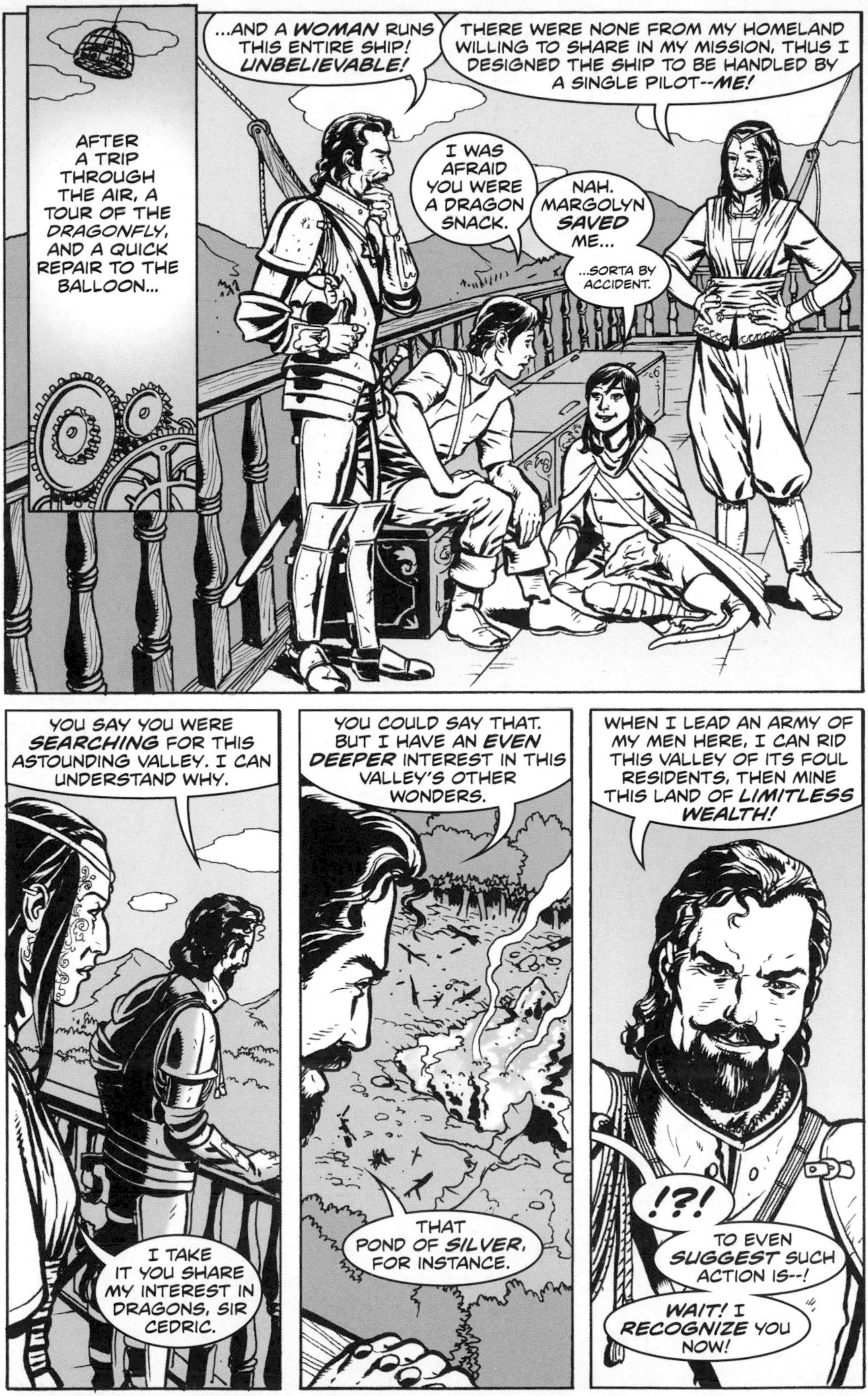
AFTER A TRIP THROUGH THE AIR, A TOUR OF THE *DRAGONFLY*, AND A QUICK REPAIR TO THE BALLOON...
...AND A **WOMAN** RUNS THIS ENTIRE SHIP! **UNBELIEVABLE!**
THERE WERE NONE FROM MY HOMELAND WILLING TO SHARE IN MY MISSION, THUS I DESIGNED THE SHIP TO BE HANDLED BY A SINGLE PILOT--**ME!**
I WAS AFRAID YOU WERE A DRAGON SNACK.
NAH. MARGOLYN **SAVED** ME...
...SORTA BY ACCIDENT.
YOU SAY YOU WERE **SEARCHING** FOR THIS ASTOUNDING VALLEY. I CAN UNDERSTAND WHY.
I TAKE IT YOU SHARE MY INTEREST IN DRAGONS, SIR CEDRIC.
YOU COULD SAY THAT. BUT I HAVE AN **EVEN DEEPER** INTEREST IN THIS VALLEY'S OTHER WONDERS.
THAT POND OF **SILVER**, FOR INSTANCE.
WHEN I LEAD AN ARMY OF MY MEN HERE, I CAN RID THIS VALLEY OF ITS FOUL RESIDENTS, THEN MINE THIS LAND OF **LIMITLESS WEALTH!**
!?!
TO EVEN **SUGGEST** SUCH ACTION IS--!
WAIT! I **RECOGNIZE** YOU NOW!

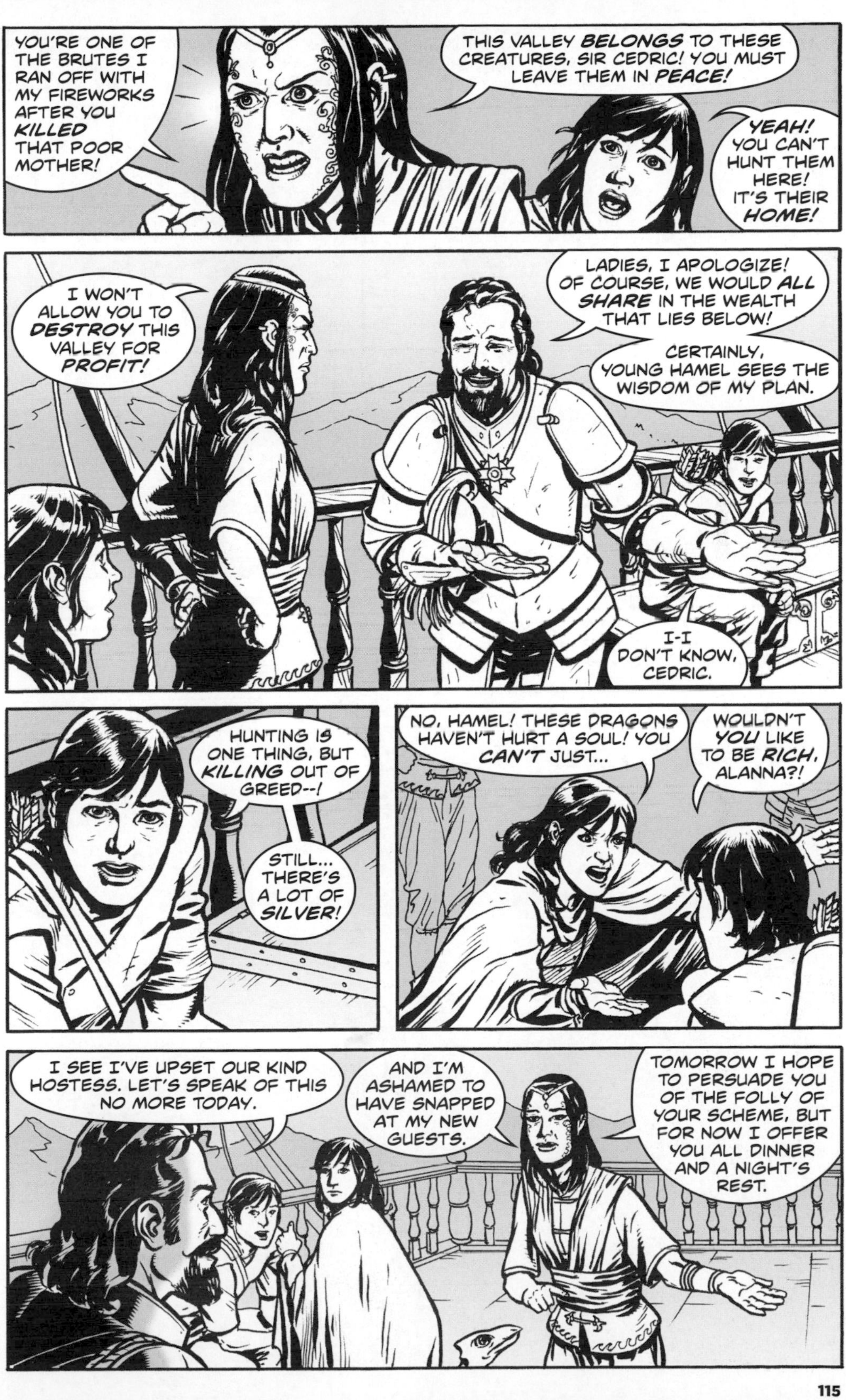
YOU'RE ONE OF THE BRUTES I RAN OFF WITH MY FIREWORKS AFTER YOU KILLED THAT POOR MOTHER!
THIS VALLEY BELONGS TO THESE CREATURES, SIR CEDRIC! YOU MUST LEAVE THEM IN PEACE!
YEAH! YOU CAN'T HUNT THEM HERE! IT'S THEIR HOME!
I WON'T ALLOW YOU TO DESTROY THIS VALLEY FOR PROFIT!
LADIES, I APOLOGIZE! OF COURSE, WE WOULD ALL SHARE IN THE WEALTH THAT LIES BELOW!
CERTAINLY, YOUNG HAMEL SEES THE WISDOM OF MY PLAN.
I-I DON'T KNOW, CEDRIC.
HUNTING IS ONE THING, BUT KILLING OUT OF GREED--!
STILL... THERE'S A LOT OF SILVER!
NO, HAMEL! THESE DRAGONS HAVEN'T HURT A SOUL! YOU CAN'T JUST...
WOULDN'T YOU LIKE TO BE RICH, ALANNA?!
I SEE I'VE UPSET OUR KIND HOSTESS. LET'S SPEAK OF THIS NO MORE TODAY.
AND I'M ASHAMED TO HAVE SNAPPED AT MY NEW GUESTS.
TOMORROW I HOPE TO PERSUADE YOU OF THE FOLLY OF YOUR SCHEME, BUT FOR NOW I OFFER YOU ALL DINNER AND A NIGHT'S REST.

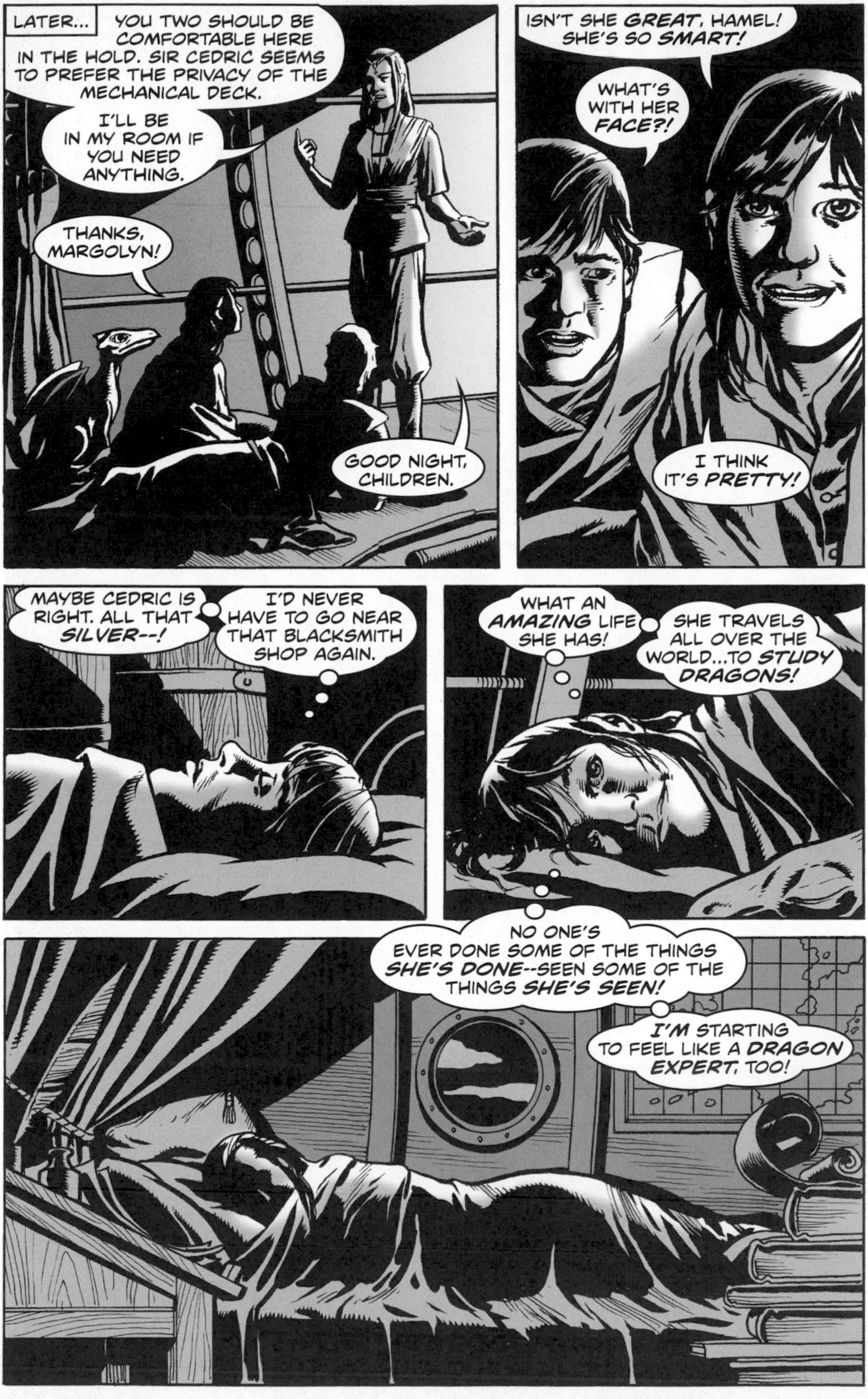
LATER...
YOU TWO SHOULD BE COMFORTABLE HERE IN THE HOLD. SIR CEDRIC SEEMS TO PREFER THE PRIVACY OF THE MECHANICAL DECK.
I'LL BE IN MY ROOM IF YOU NEED ANYTHING.
THANKS, MARGOLYN!
GOOD NIGHT, CHILDREN.
ISN'T SHE GREAT, HAMEL! SHE'S SO SMART!
WHAT'S WITH HER FACE?!
I THINK IT'S PRETTY!
MAYBE CEDRIC IS RIGHT. ALL THAT SILVER--!
I'D NEVER HAVE TO GO NEAR THAT BLACKSMITH SHOP AGAIN.
WHAT AN AMAZING LIFE SHE HAS!
SHE TRAVELS ALL OVER THE WORLD...TO STUDY DRAGONS!
NO ONE'S EVER DONE SOME OF THE THINGS SHE'S DONE--SEEN SOME OF THE THINGS SHE'S SEEN!
I'M STARTING TO FEEL LIKE A DRAGON EXPERT, TOO!

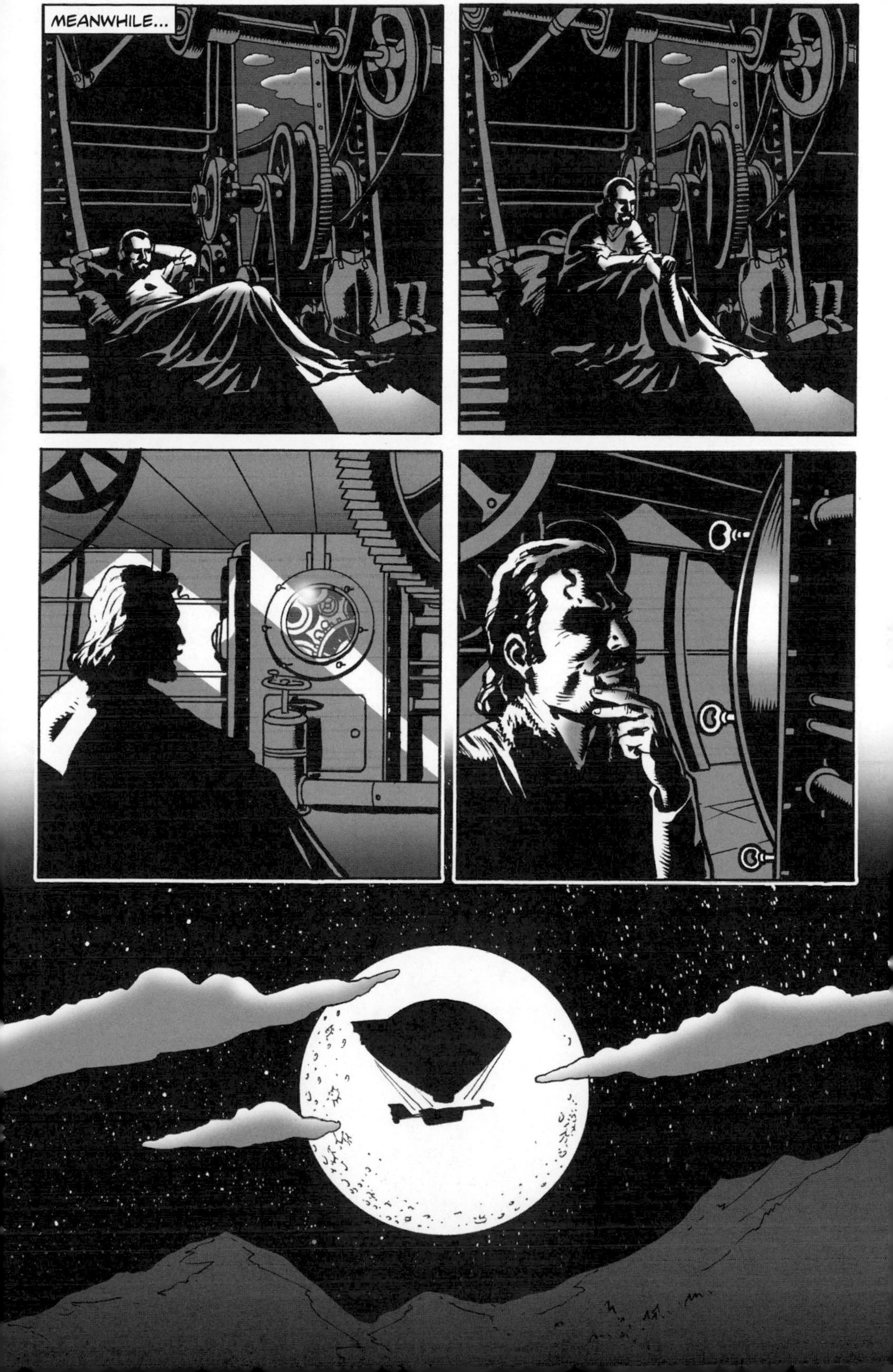
MEANWHILE...

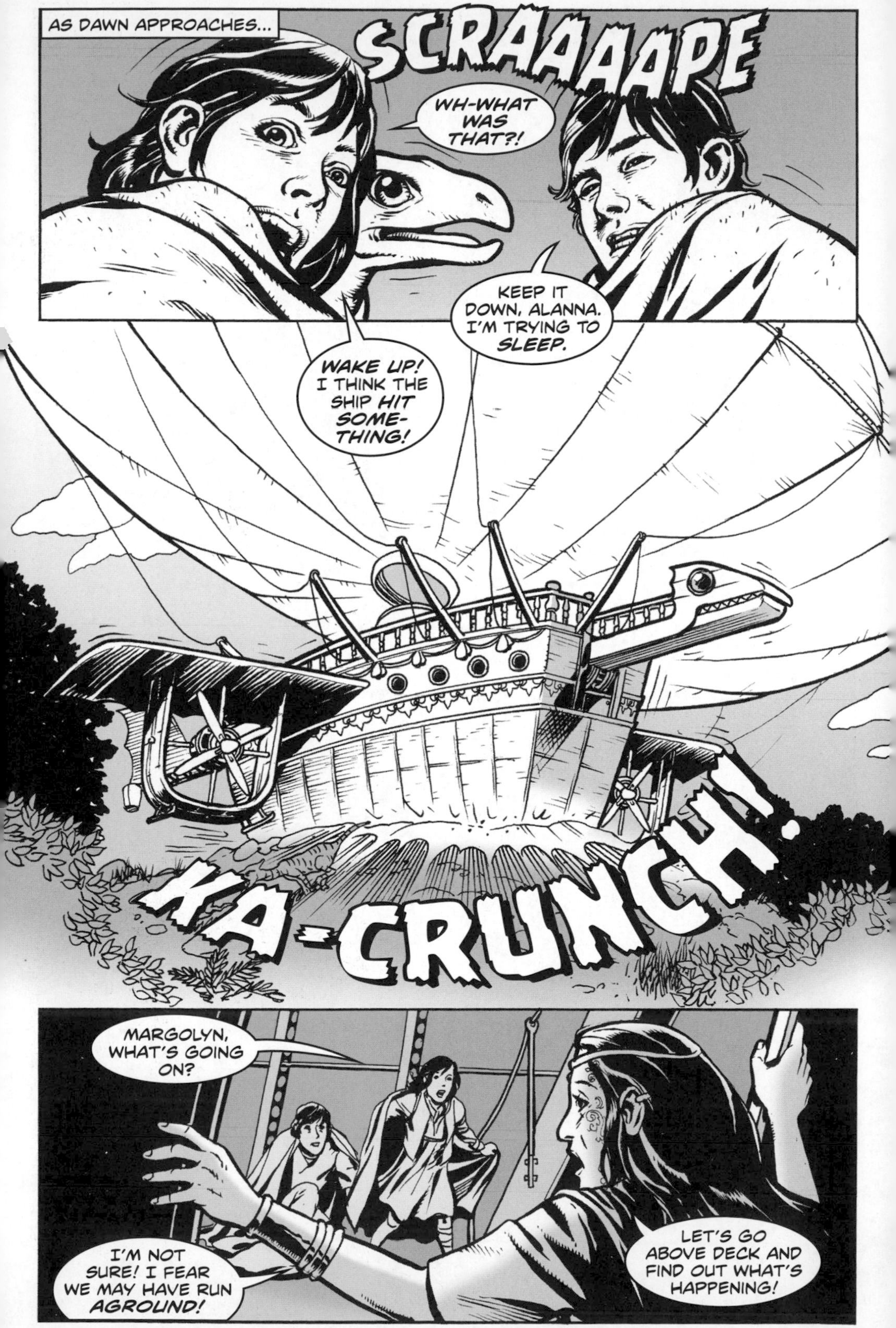
AS DAWN APPROACHES...
SCRAAAAPE
WH-WHAT WAS THAT?!
KEEP IT DOWN, ALANNA. I'M TRYING TO SLEEP.
WAKE UP! I THINK THE SHIP HIT SOME-THING!
KA-CRUNCH!
MARGOLYN, WHAT'S GOING ON?
I'M NOT SURE! I FEAR WE MAY HAVE RUN AGROUND!
LET'S GO ABOVE DECK AND FIND OUT WHAT'S HAPPENING!

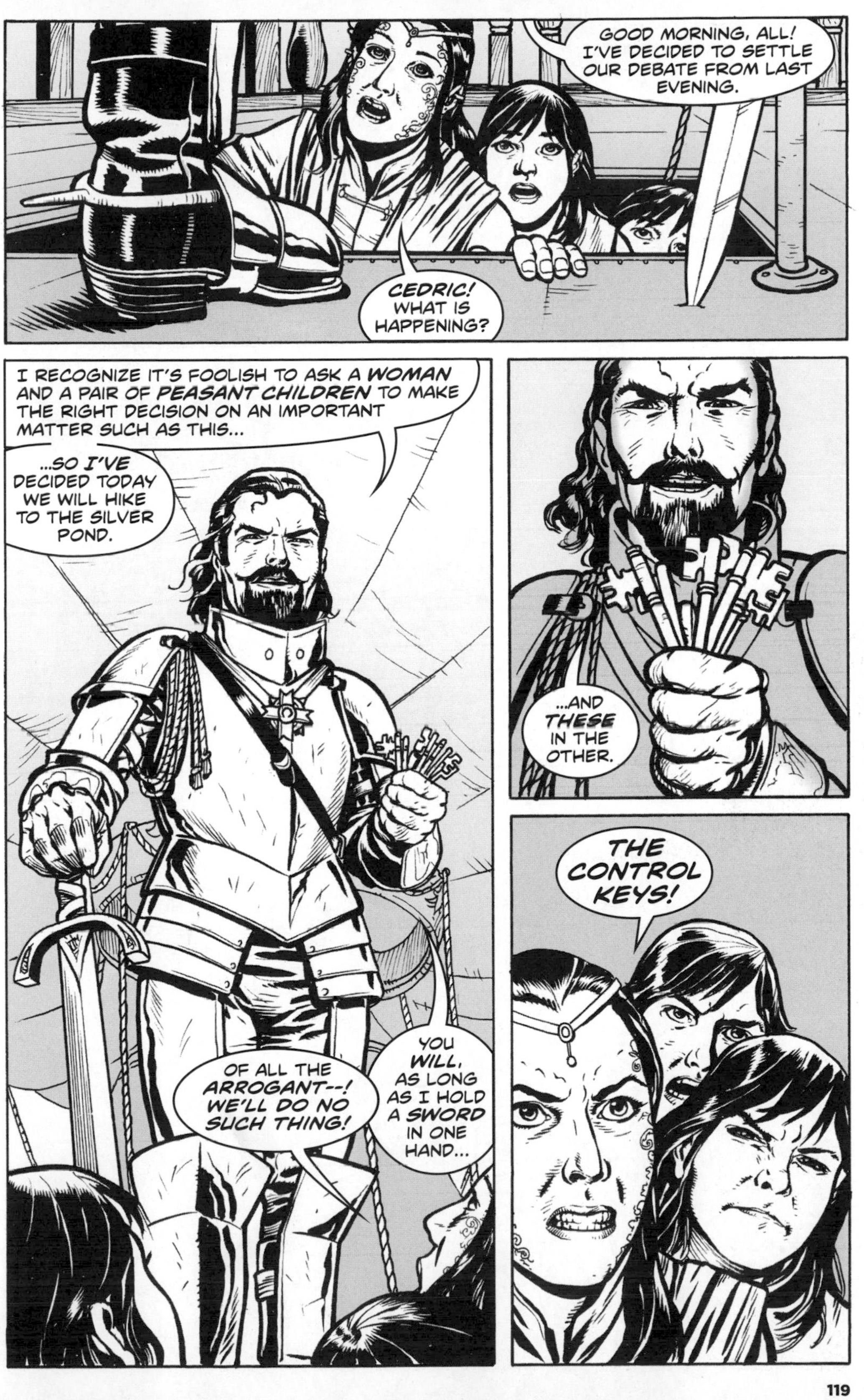
GOOD MORNING, ALL! I'VE DECIDED TO SETTLE OUR DEBATE FROM LAST EVENING.
CEDRIC! WHAT IS HAPPENING?
I RECOGNIZE IT'S FOOLISH TO ASK A WOMAN AND A PAIR OF PEASANT CHILDREN TO MAKE THE RIGHT DECISION ON AN IMPORTANT MATTER SUCH AS THIS...
...SO I'VE DECIDED TODAY WE WILL HIKE TO THE SILVER POND.
OF ALL THE ARROGANT--! WE'LL DO NO SUCH THING!
YOU WILL, AS LONG AS I HOLD A SWORD IN ONE HAND...
...AND THESE IN THE OTHER.
THE CONTROL KEYS!

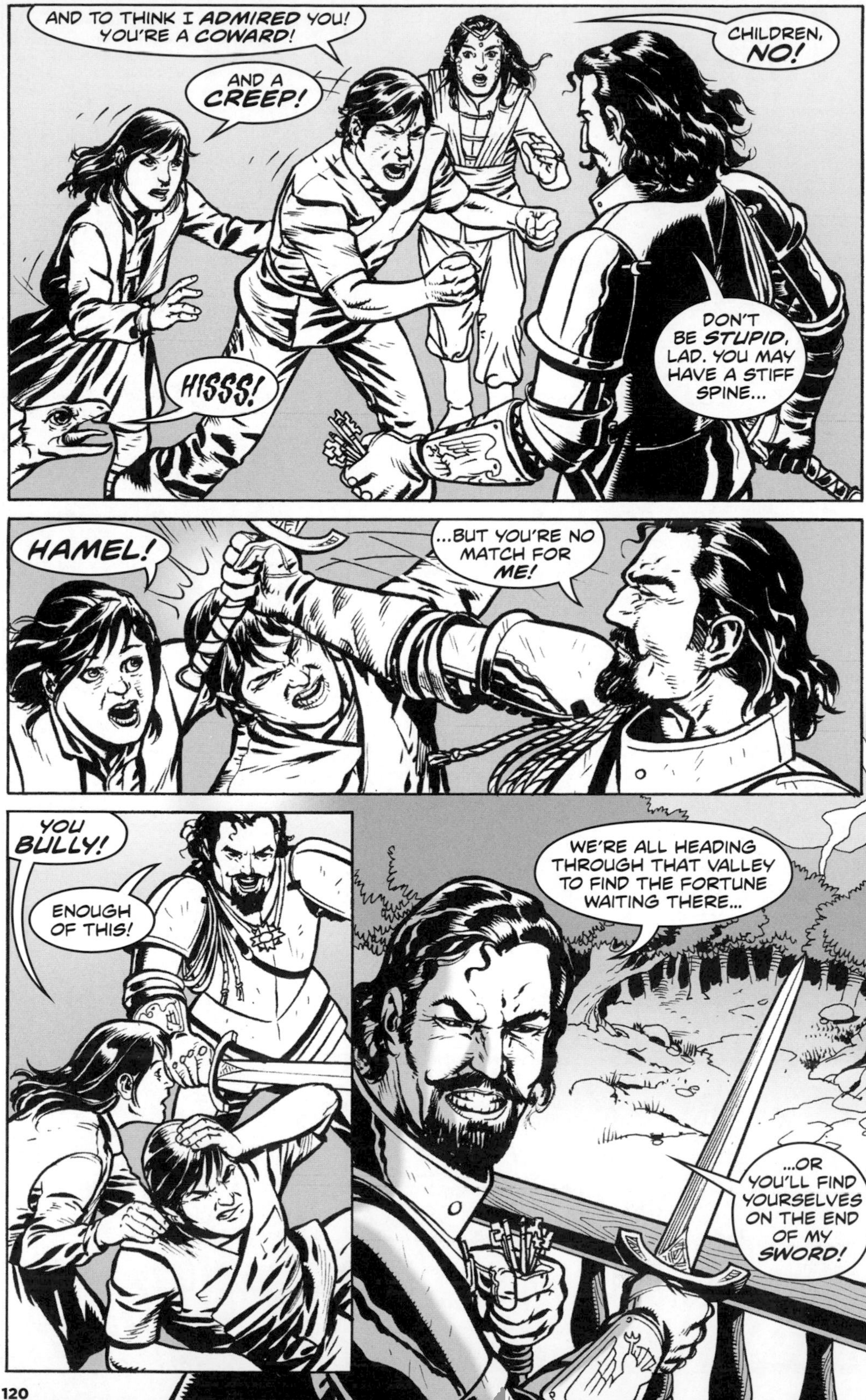
AND TO THINK I ADMIRED YOU! YOU'RE A COWARD!
AND A CREEP!
CHILDREN, NO!
HISSS!
DON'T BE STUPID, LAD. YOU MAY HAVE A STIFF SPINE...
HAMEL!
...BUT YOU'RE NO MATCH FOR ME!
YOU BULLY!
ENOUGH OF THIS!
WE'RE ALL HEADING THROUGH THAT VALLEY TO FIND THE FORTUNE WAITING THERE...
...OR YOU'LL FIND YOURSELVES ON THE END OF MY SWORD!

CHAPTER SEVEN

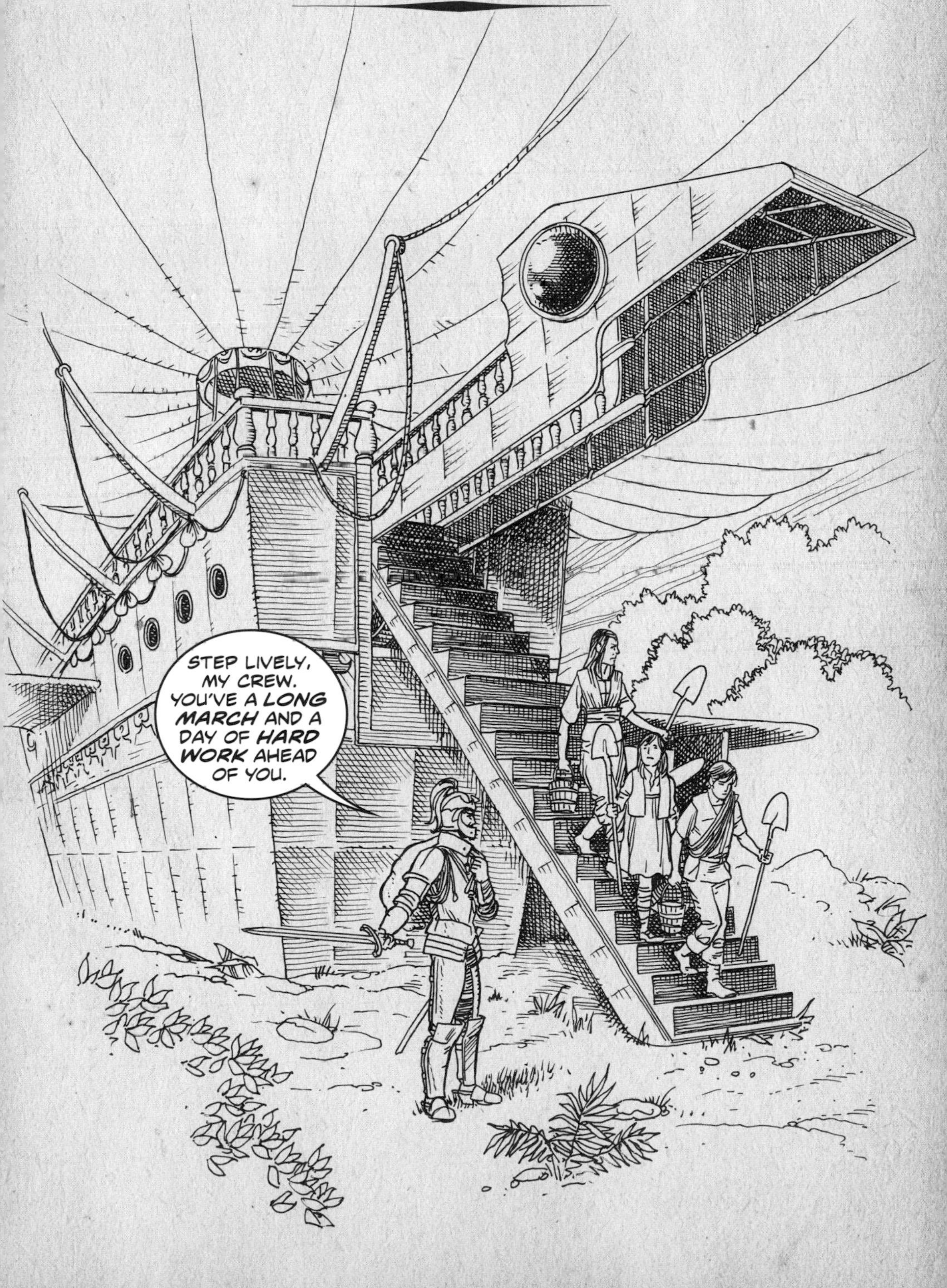
STEP LIVELY, MY CREW. YOU'VE A LONG MARCH AND A DAY OF HARD WORK AHEAD OF YOU.

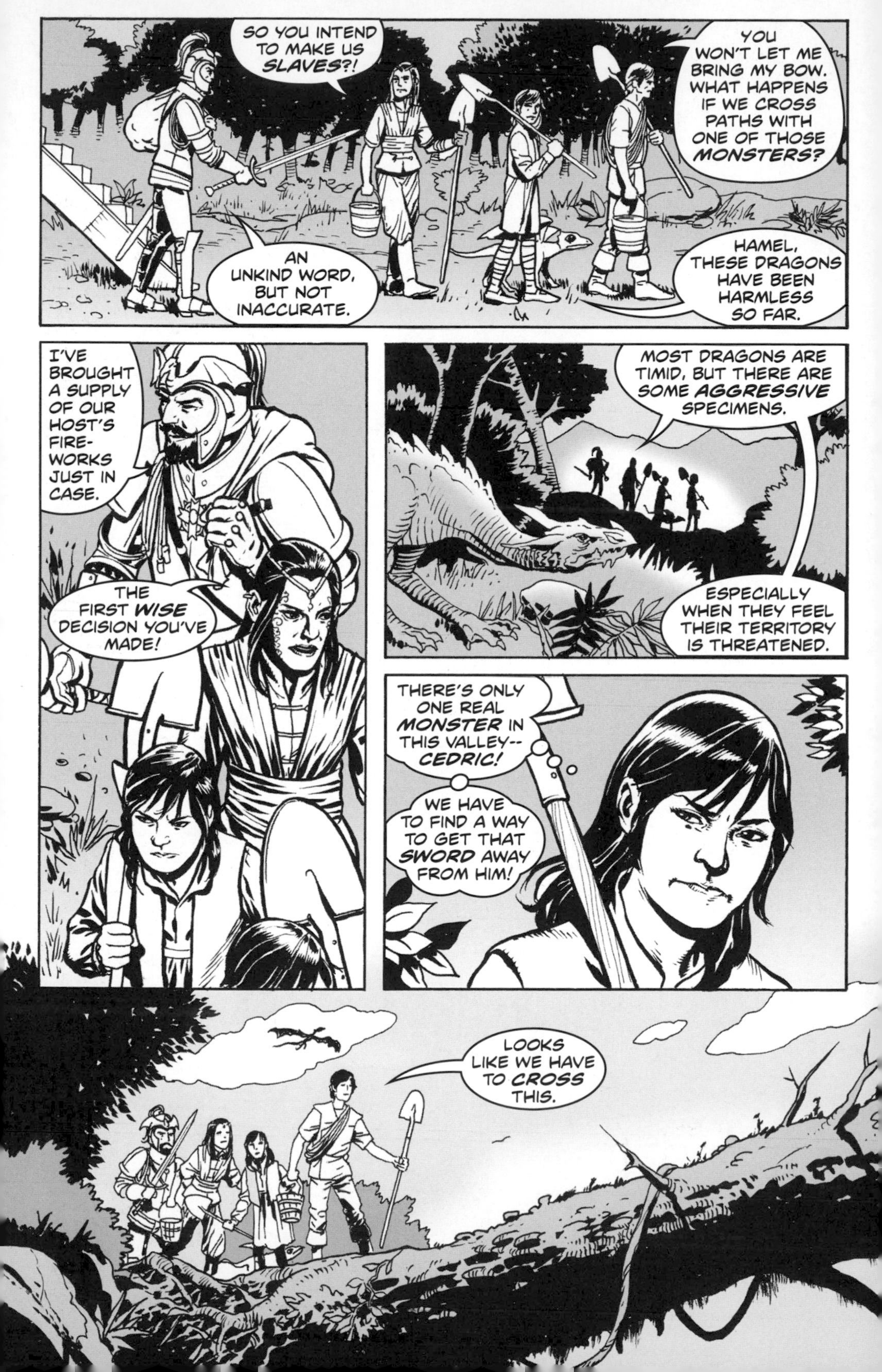
SO YOU INTEND TO MAKE US SLAVES?!
AN UNKIND WORD, BUT NOT INACCURATE.
YOU WON'T LET ME BRING MY BOW. WHAT HAPPENS IF WE CROSS PATHS WITH ONE OF THOSE MONSTERS?
HAMEL, THESE DRAGONS HAVE BEEN HARMLESS SO FAR.
I'VE BROUGHT A SUPPLY OF OUR HOST'S FIRE-WORKS JUST IN CASE.
THE FIRST WISE DECISION YOU'VE MADE!
MOST DRAGONS ARE TIMID, BUT THERE ARE SOME AGGRESSIVE SPECIMENS.
ESPECIALLY WHEN THEY FEEL THEIR TERRITORY IS THREATENED.
THERE'S ONLY ONE REAL MONSTER IN THIS VALLEY-- CEDRIC!
WE HAVE TO FIND A WAY TO GET THAT SWORD AWAY FROM HIM!
LOOKS LIKE WE HAVE TO CROSS THIS.

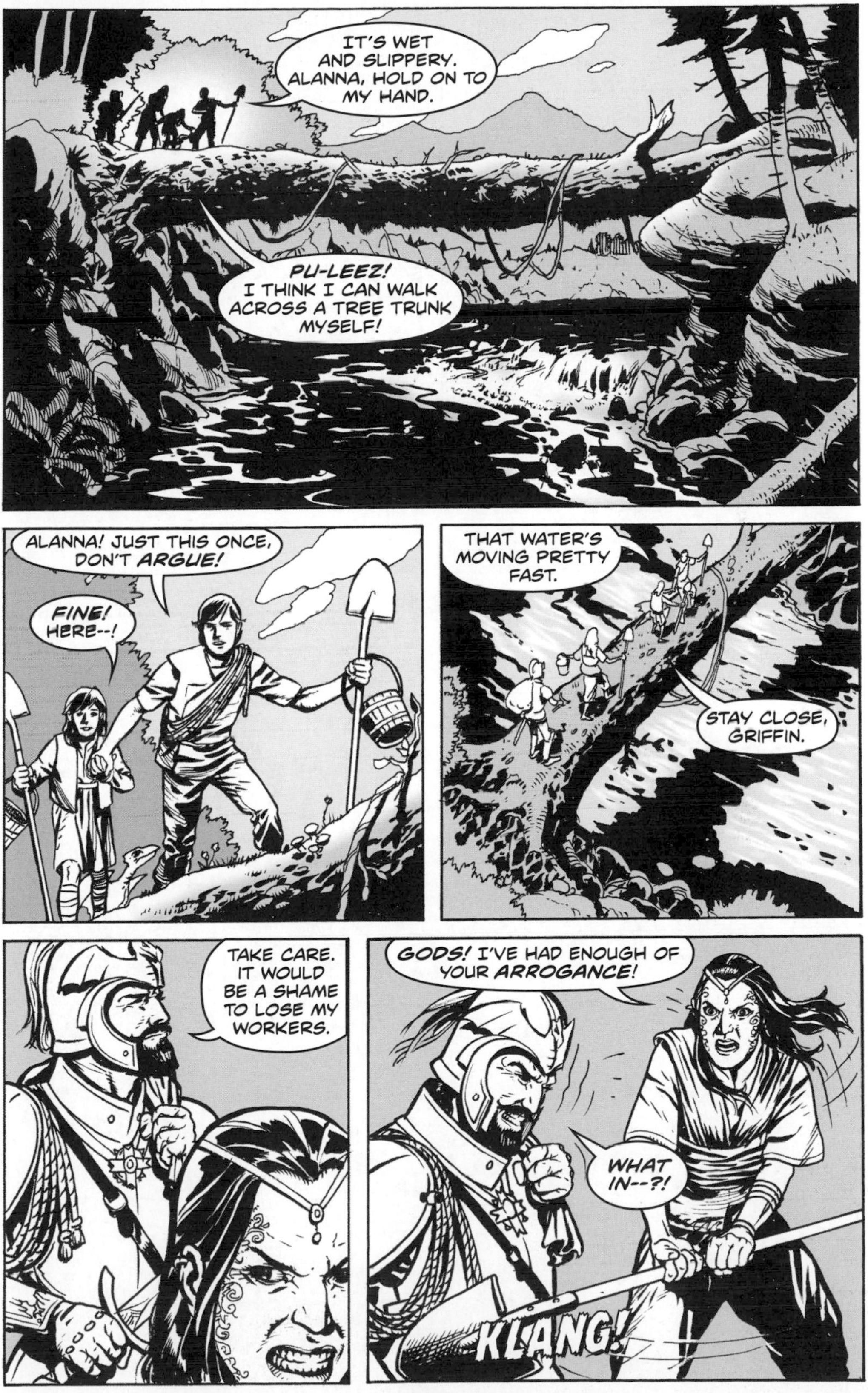
IT'S WET AND SLIPPERY. ALANNA, HOLD ON TO MY HAND.
PU-LEEZ! I THINK I CAN WALK ACROSS A TREE TRUNK MYSELF!
ALANNA! JUST THIS ONCE, DON'T ARGUE!
FINE! HERE--!
THAT WATER'S MOVING PRETTY FAST.
STAY CLOSE, GRIFFIN.
TAKE CARE. IT WOULD BE A SHAME TO LOSE MY WORKERS.
GODS! I'VE HAD ENOUGH OF YOUR ARROGANCE!
WHAT IN--?!
KLANG!

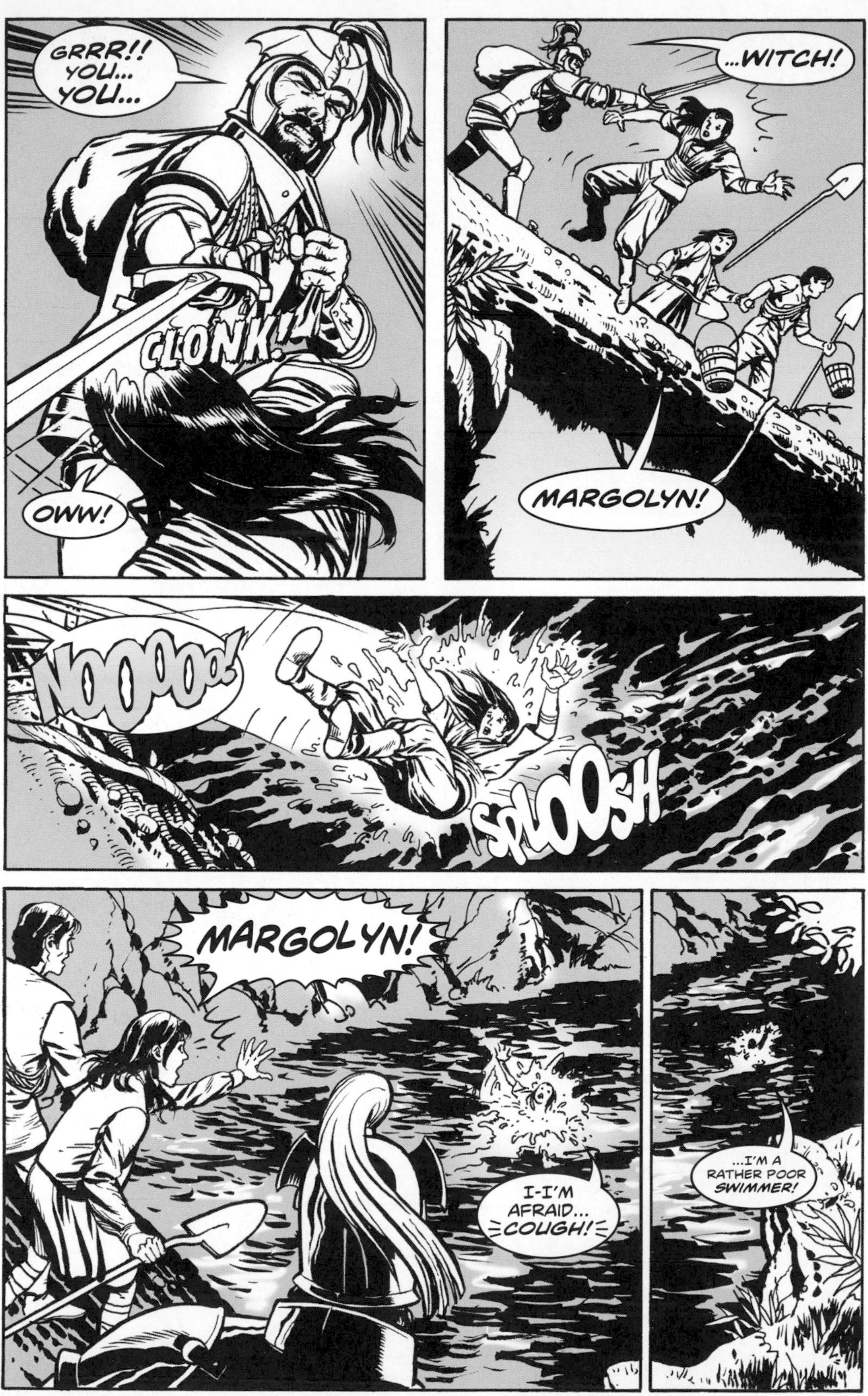
GRRR!! YOU... YOU...
CLONK!
OWW!
...WITCH!
MARGOLYN!
NOOOOO!
SPLOOSH
MARGOLYN!
I-I'M AFRAID... COUGH!
...I'M A RATHER POOR SWIMMER!

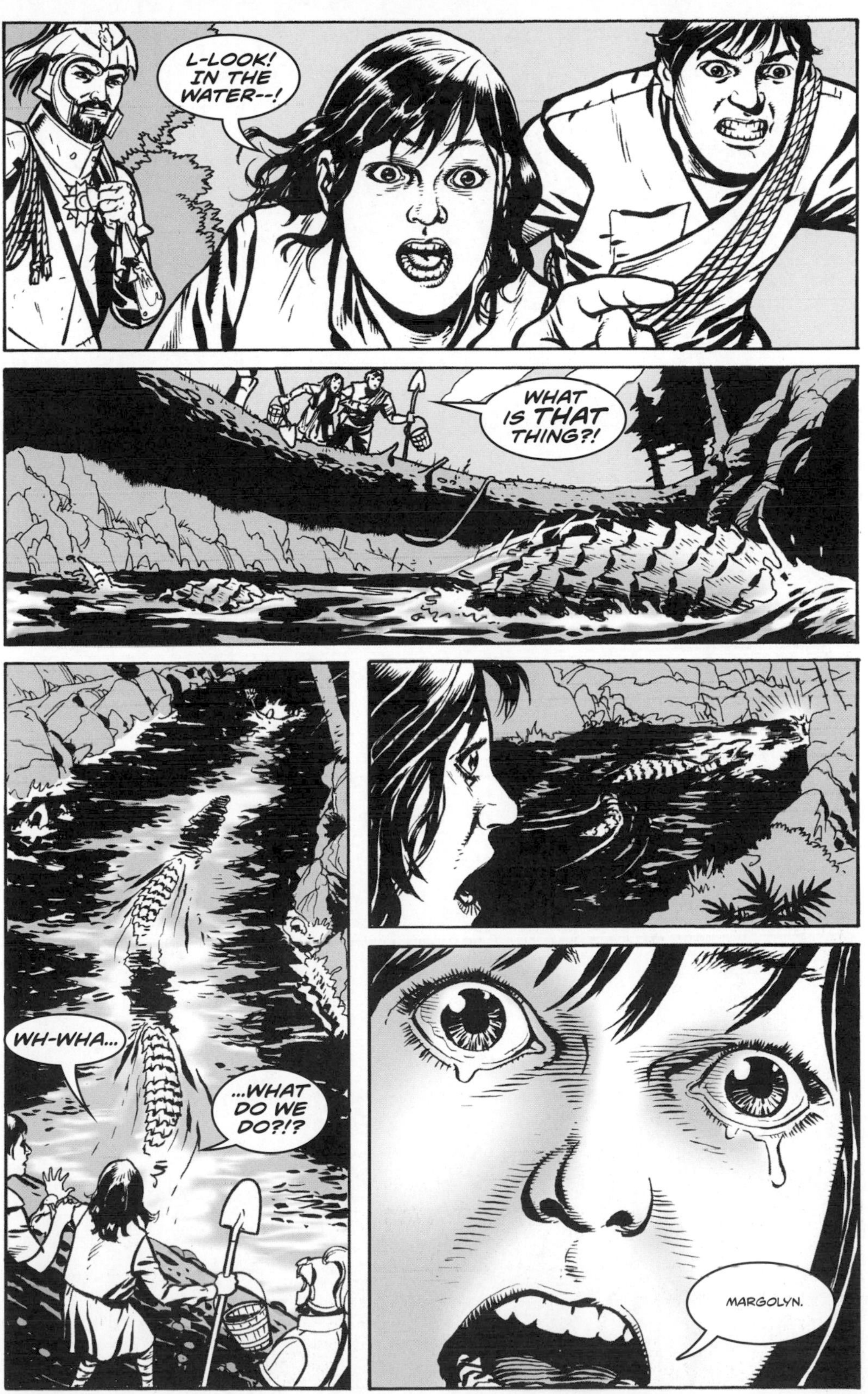
L-LOOK! IN THE WATER--!
WHAT IS THAT THING?!
WH-WHA...
...WHAT DO WE DO?!?
MARGOLYN.

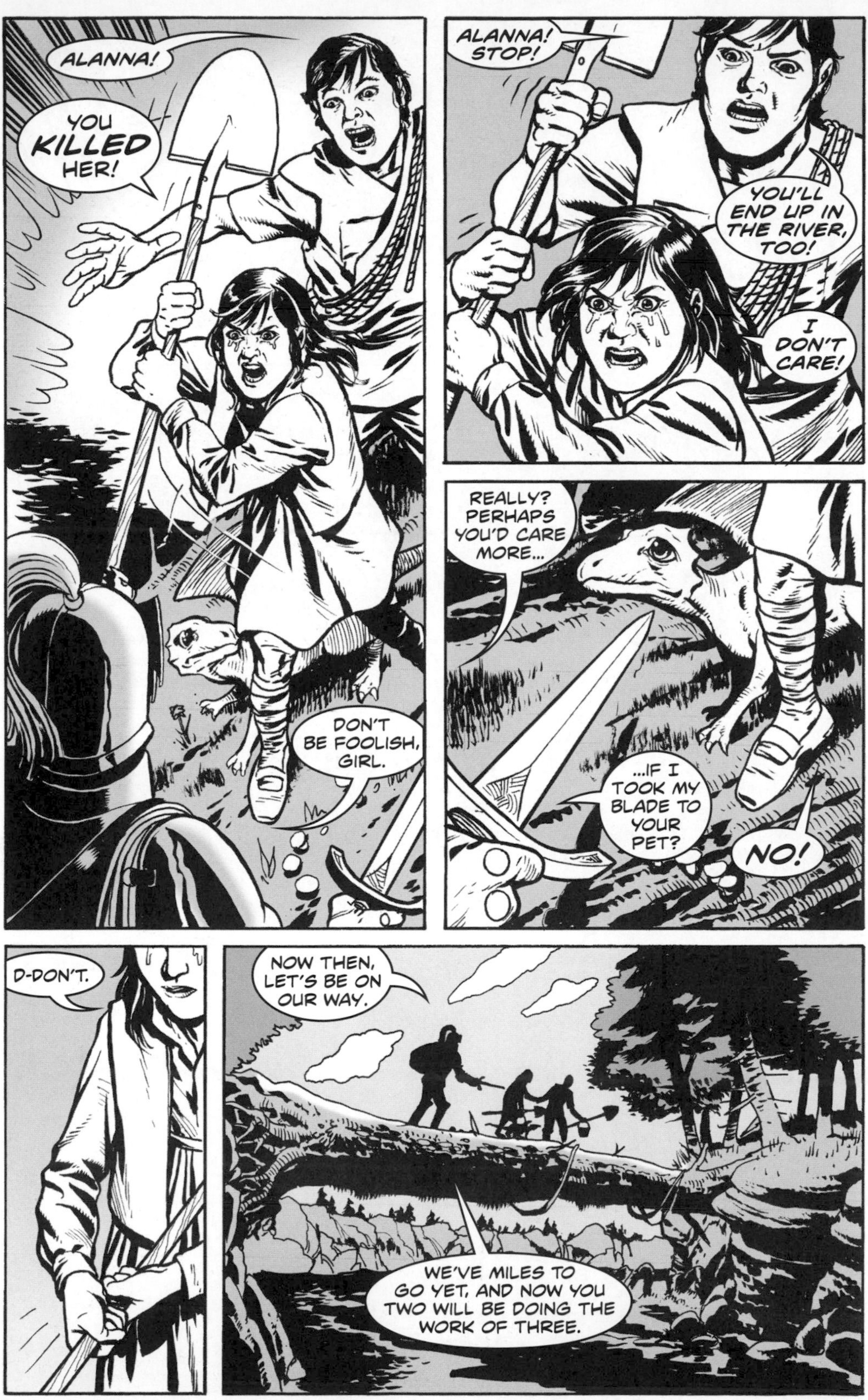
ALANNA!
YOU KILLED HER!
ALANNA! STOP!
YOU'LL END UP IN THE RIVER, TOO!
I DON'T CARE!
DON'T BE FOOLISH, GIRL.
REALLY? PERHAPS YOU'D CARE MORE...
...IF I TOOK MY BLADE TO YOUR PET?
NO!
D-DON'T.
NOW THEN, LET'S BE ON OUR WAY.
WE'VE MILES TO GO YET, AND NOW YOU TWO WILL BE DOING THE WORK OF THREE.

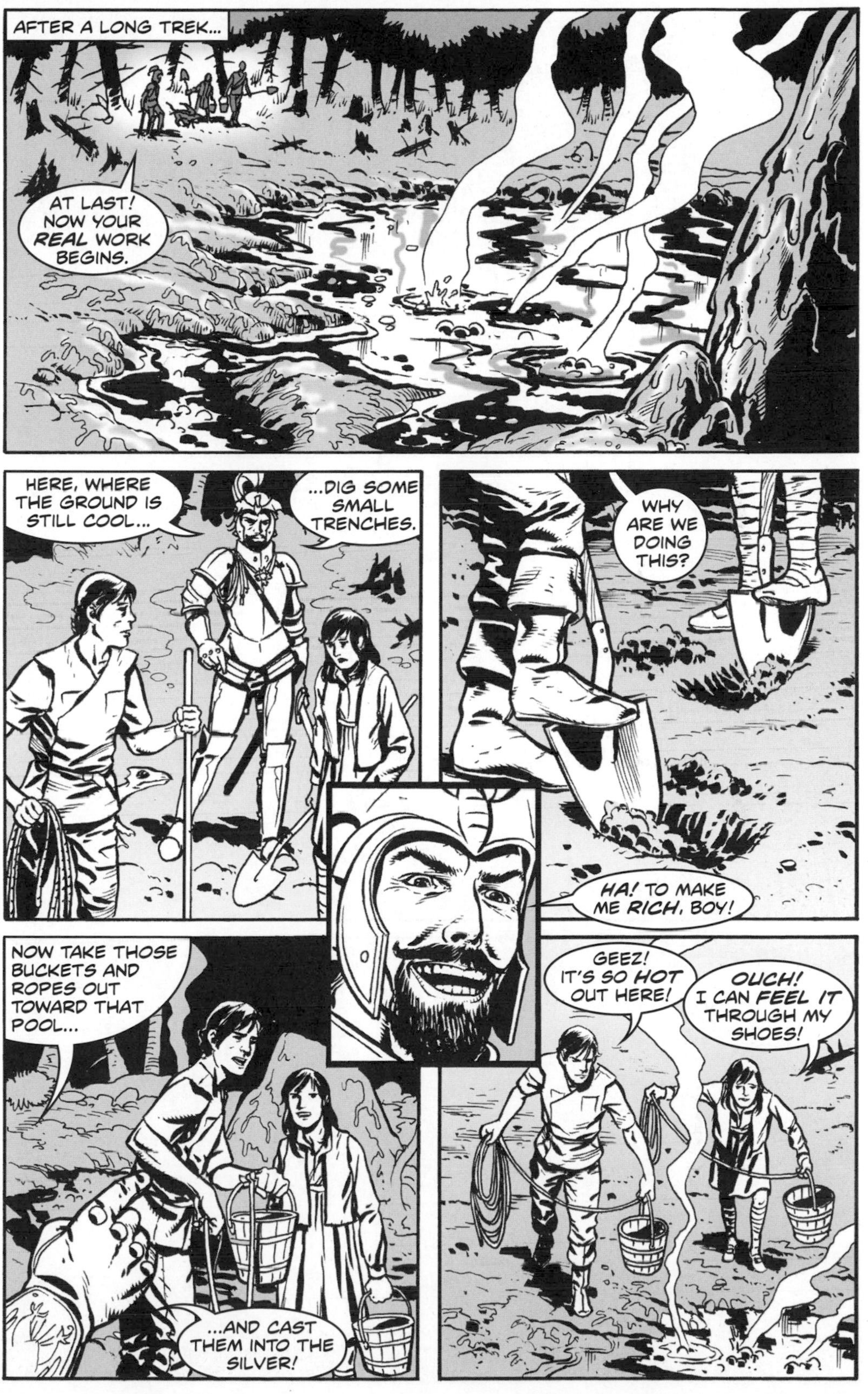

AFTER A LONG TREK...
AT LAST! NOW YOUR REAL WORK BEGINS.
HERE, WHERE THE GROUND IS STILL COOL...
...DIG SOME SMALL TRENCHES.
WHY ARE WE DOING THIS?
HA! TO MAKE ME RICH, BOY!
NOW TAKE THOSE BUCKETS AND ROPES OUT TOWARD THAT POOL...
...AND CAST THEM INTO THE SILVER!
GEEZ! IT'S SO HOT OUT HERE!
OUCH! I CAN FEEL IT THROUGH MY SHOES!

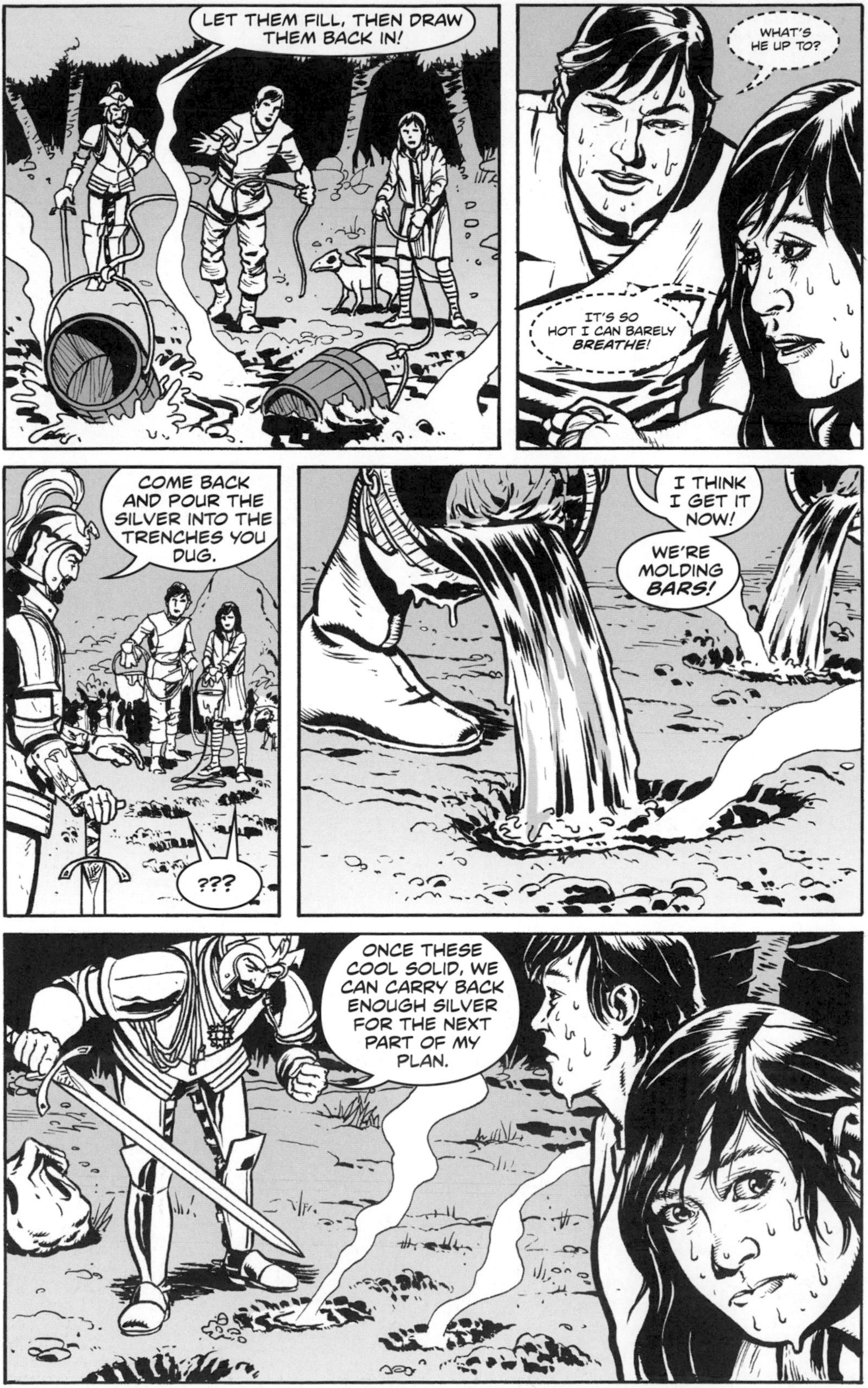
LET THEM FILL, THEN DRAW THEM BACK IN!
WHAT'S HE UP TO?
IT'S SO HOT I CAN BARELY BREATHE!
COME BACK AND POUR THE SILVER INTO THE TRENCHES YOU DUG.
???
I THINK I GET IT NOW!
WE'RE MOLDING BARS!
ONCE THESE COOL SOLID, WE CAN CARRY BACK ENOUGH SILVER FOR THE NEXT PART OF MY PLAN.

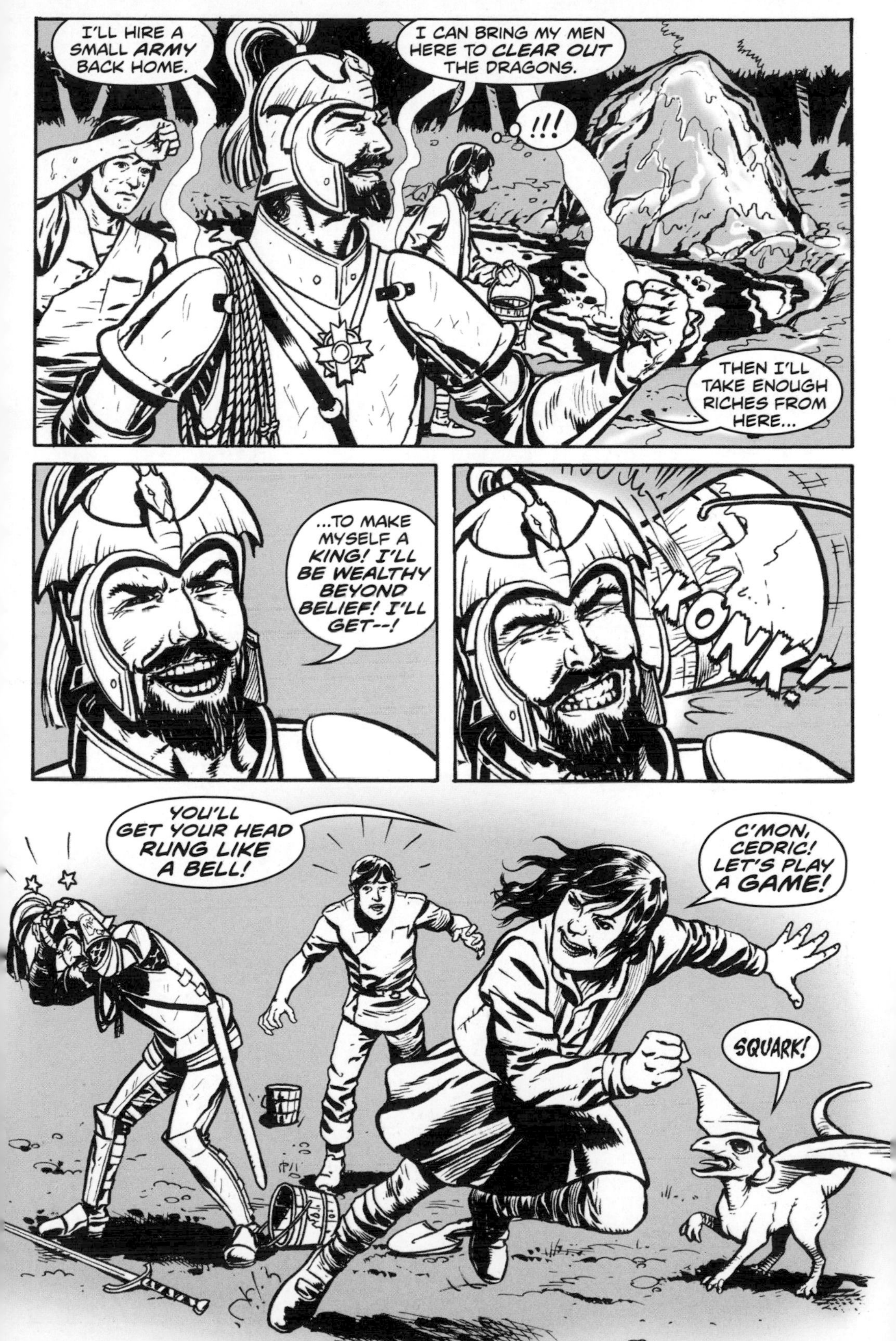
I'LL HIRE A SMALL ARMY BACK HOME.
I CAN BRING MY MEN HERE TO CLEAR OUT THE DRAGONS.
!!!
THEN I'LL TAKE ENOUGH RICHES FROM HERE...
...TO MAKE MYSELF A KING! I'LL BE WEALTHY BEYOND BELIEF! I'LL GET--!
KONK!
YOU'LL GET YOUR HEAD RUNG LIKE A BELL!
C'MON, CEDRIC! LET'S PLAY A GAME!
SQUARK!

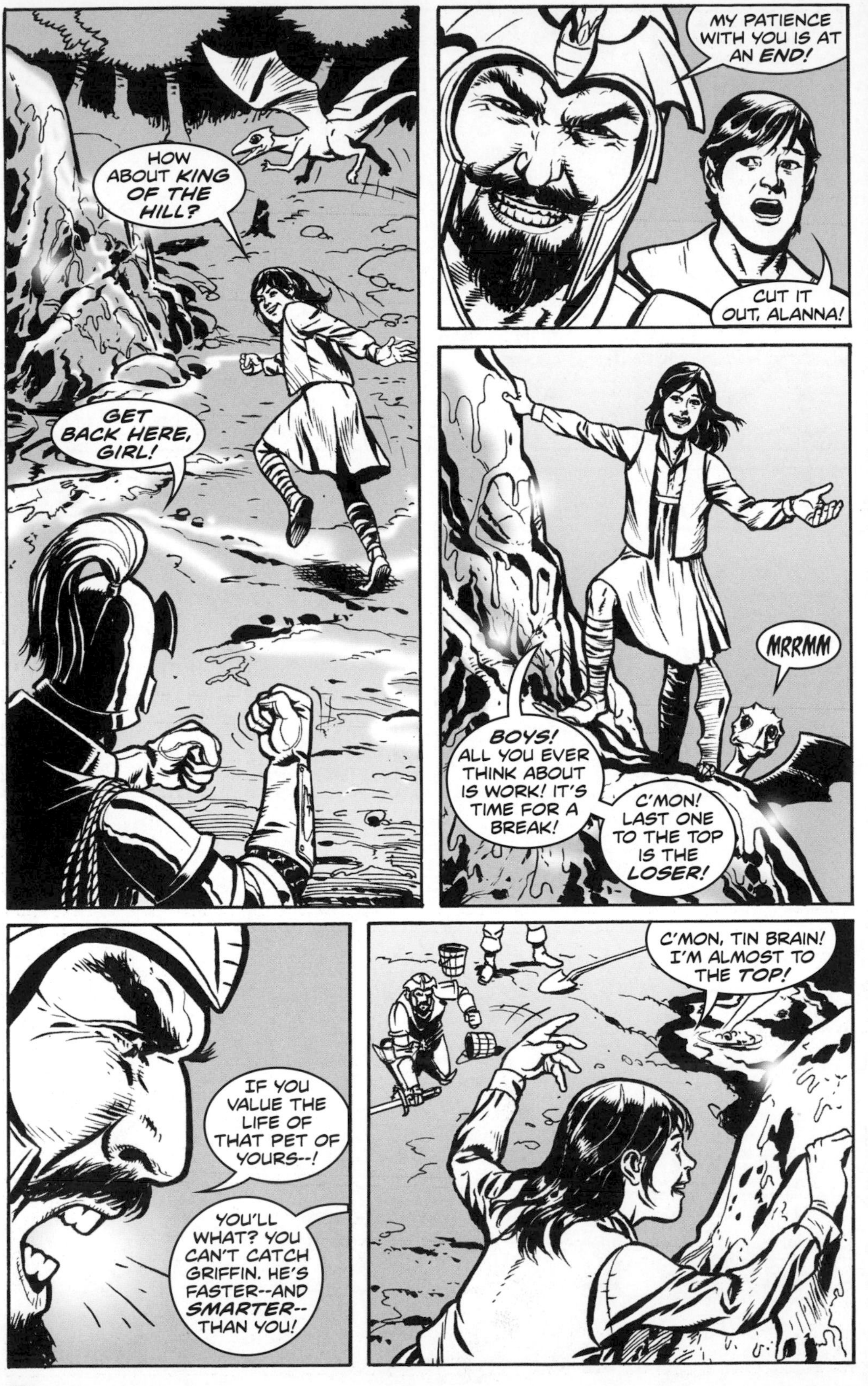
HOW ABOUT *KING OF THE HILL?*
GET BACK HERE, GIRL!
MY PATIENCE WITH YOU IS AT AN *END!*
CUT IT OUT, ALANNA!
MRRMM
BOYS! ALL YOU EVER THINK ABOUT IS WORK! IT'S TIME FOR A BREAK!
C'MON! LAST ONE TO THE TOP IS THE *LOSER!*
IF YOU VALUE THE LIFE OF THAT PET OF YOURS--!
YOU'LL WHAT? YOU CAN'T CATCH GRIFFIN. HE'S FASTER--AND *SMARTER*--THAN YOU!
C'MON, TIN BRAIN! I'M ALMOST TO THE *TOP!*

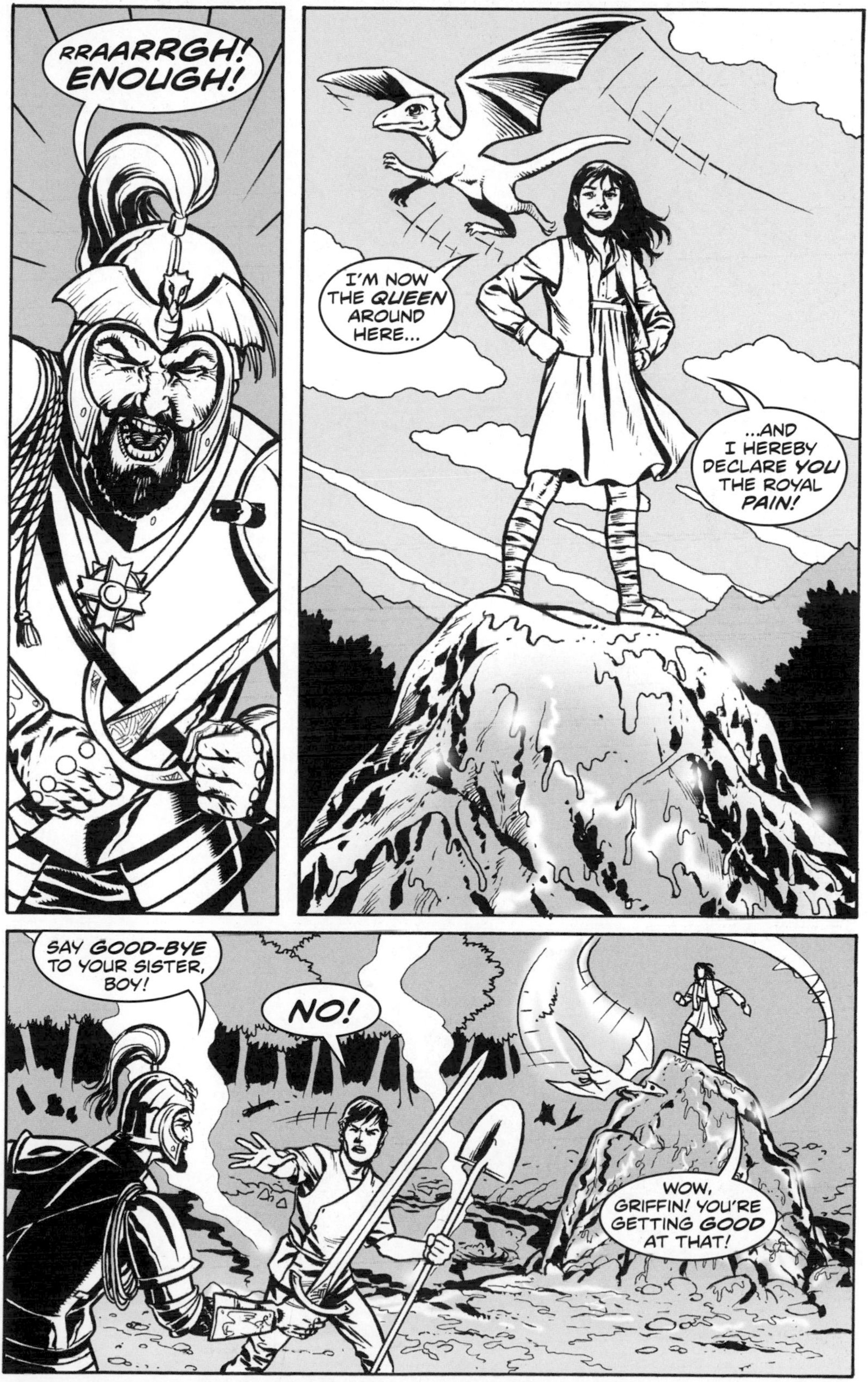
RRAARRGH! ENOUGH!
I'M NOW THE QUEEN AROUND HERE...
...AND I HEREBY DECLARE YOU THE ROYAL PAIN!
SAY GOOD-BYE TO YOUR SISTER, BOY!
NO!
WOW, GRIFFIN! YOU'RE GETTING GOOD AT THAT!

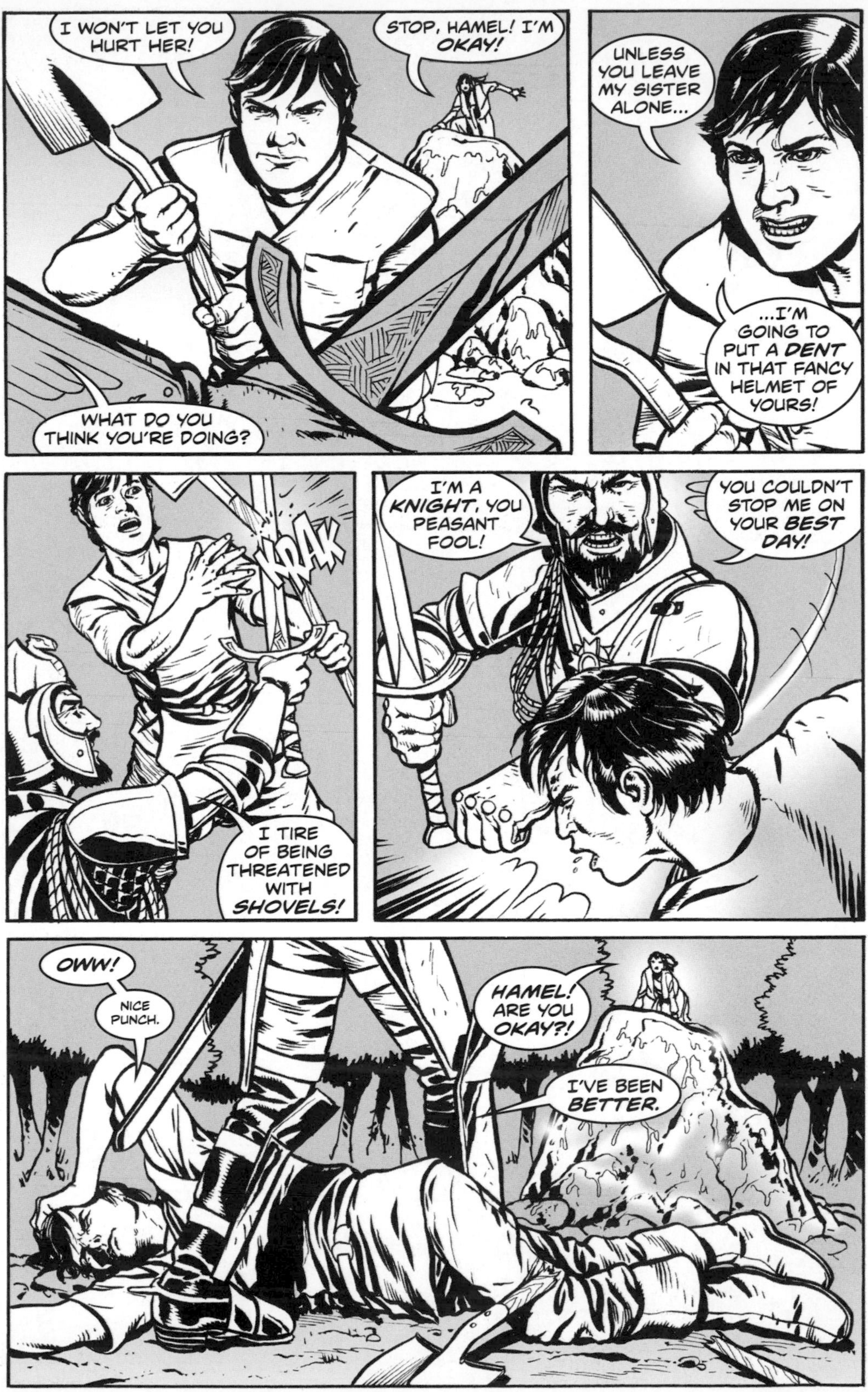
I WON'T LET YOU HURT HER!
STOP, HAMEL! I'M OKAY!
WHAT DO YOU THINK YOU'RE DOING?
UNLESS YOU LEAVE MY SISTER ALONE...
...I'M GOING TO PUT A DENT IN THAT FANCY HELMET OF YOURS!
KRAK
I TIRE OF BEING THREATENED WITH SHOVELS!
I'M A KNIGHT, YOU PEASANT FOOL!
YOU COULDN'T STOP ME ON YOUR BEST DAY!
OWW!
NICE PUNCH.
HAMEL! ARE YOU OKAY?!
I'VE BEEN BETTER.

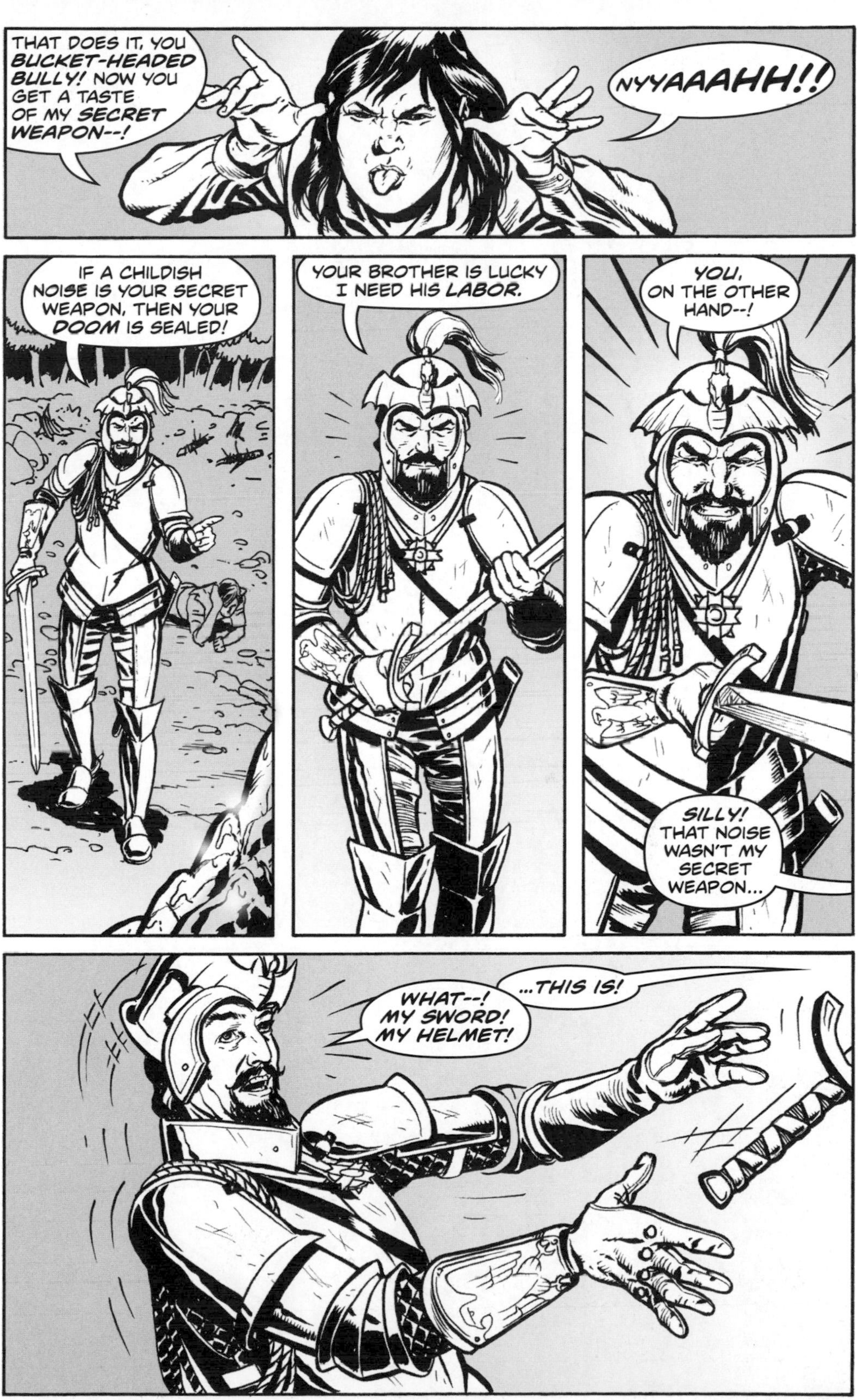
THAT DOES IT, YOU BUCKET-HEADED BULLY! NOW YOU GET A TASTE OF MY SECRET WEAPON--!
NYYAAAHH!!
IF A CHILDISH NOISE IS YOUR SECRET WEAPON, THEN YOUR DOOM IS SEALED!
YOUR BROTHER IS LUCKY I NEED HIS LABOR.
YOU, ON THE OTHER HAND--!
SILLY! THAT NOISE WASN'T MY SECRET WEAPON...
...THIS IS!
WHAT--! MY SWORD! MY HELMET!

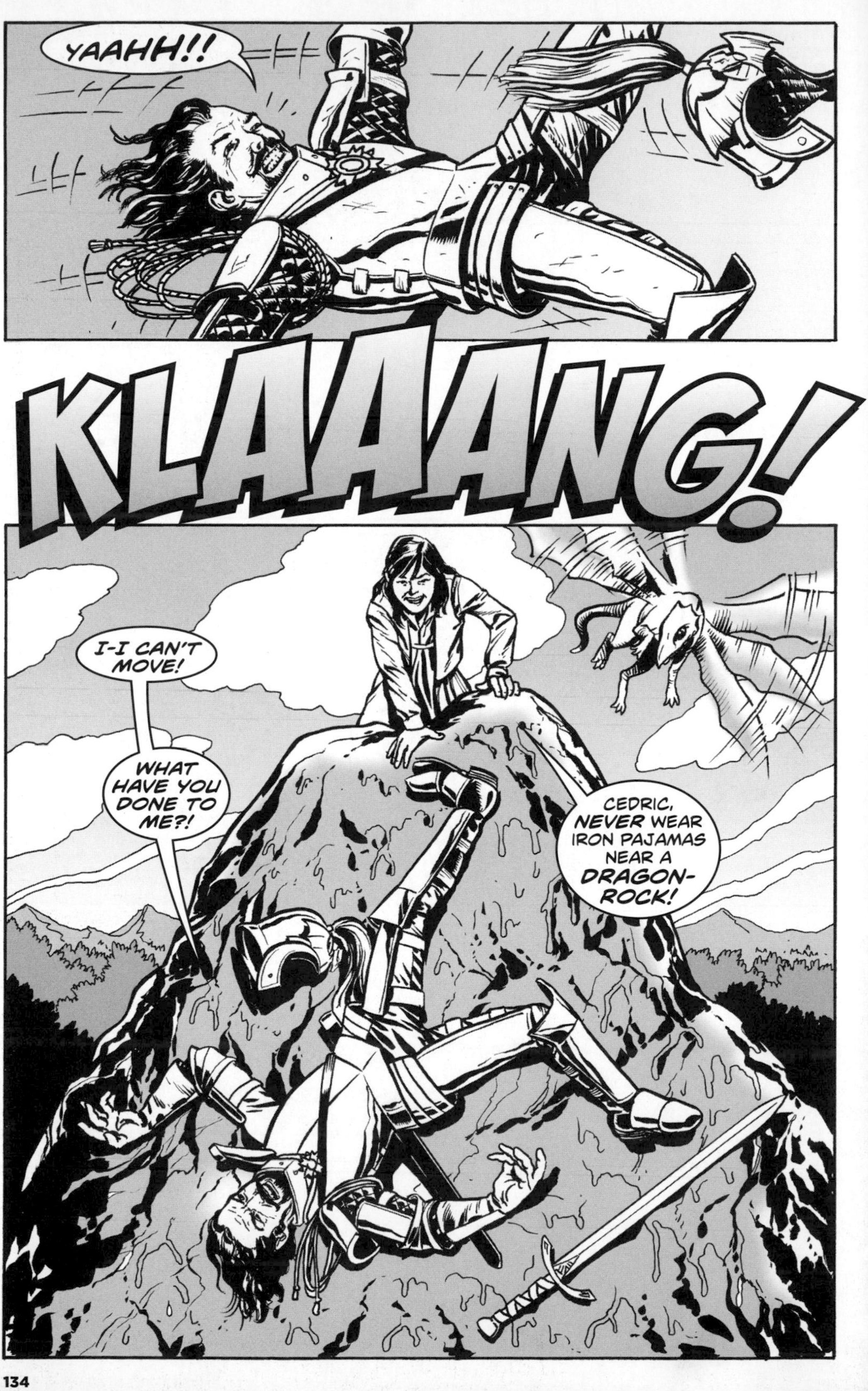
YAAHH!!
KLAAANG!
I-I CAN'T MOVE!
WHAT HAVE YOU DONE TO ME?!
CEDRIC, NEVER WEAR IRON PAJAMAS NEAR A DRAGON-ROCK!

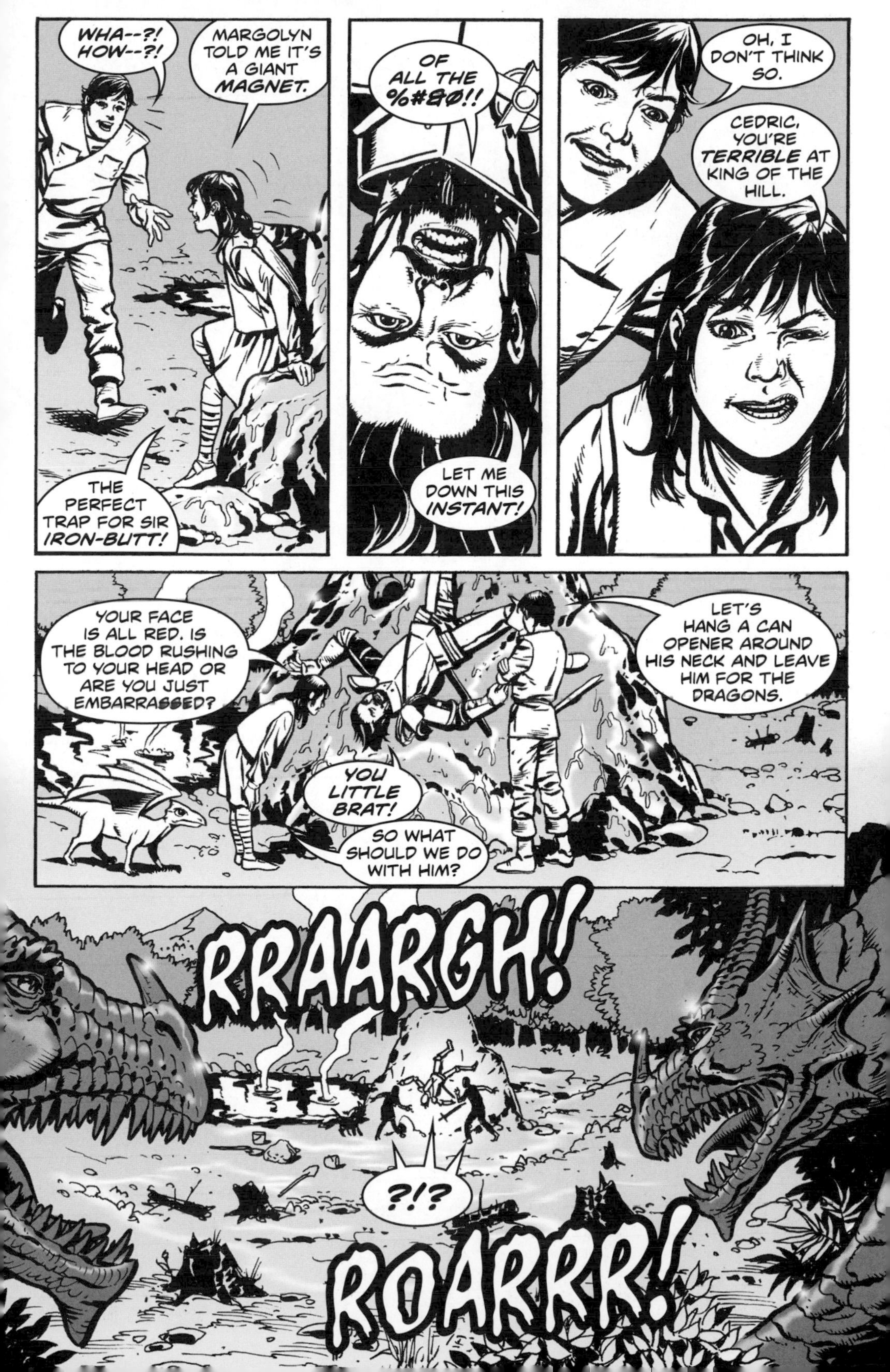
WHA--?! HOW--?!
MARGOLYN TOLD ME IT'S A GIANT MAGNET.
THE PERFECT TRAP FOR SIR IRON-BUTT!
OF ALL THE %#&Ø!!
LET ME DOWN THIS INSTANT!
OH, I DON'T THINK SO.
CEDRIC, YOU'RE TERRIBLE AT KING OF THE HILL.
YOUR FACE IS ALL RED. IS THE BLOOD RUSHING TO YOUR HEAD OR ARE YOU JUST EMBARRASSED?
YOU LITTLE BRAT!
SO WHAT SHOULD WE DO WITH HIM?
LET'S HANG A CAN OPENER AROUND HIS NECK AND LEAVE HIM FOR THE DRAGONS.
RRAARGH!
?!?
ROARRR!

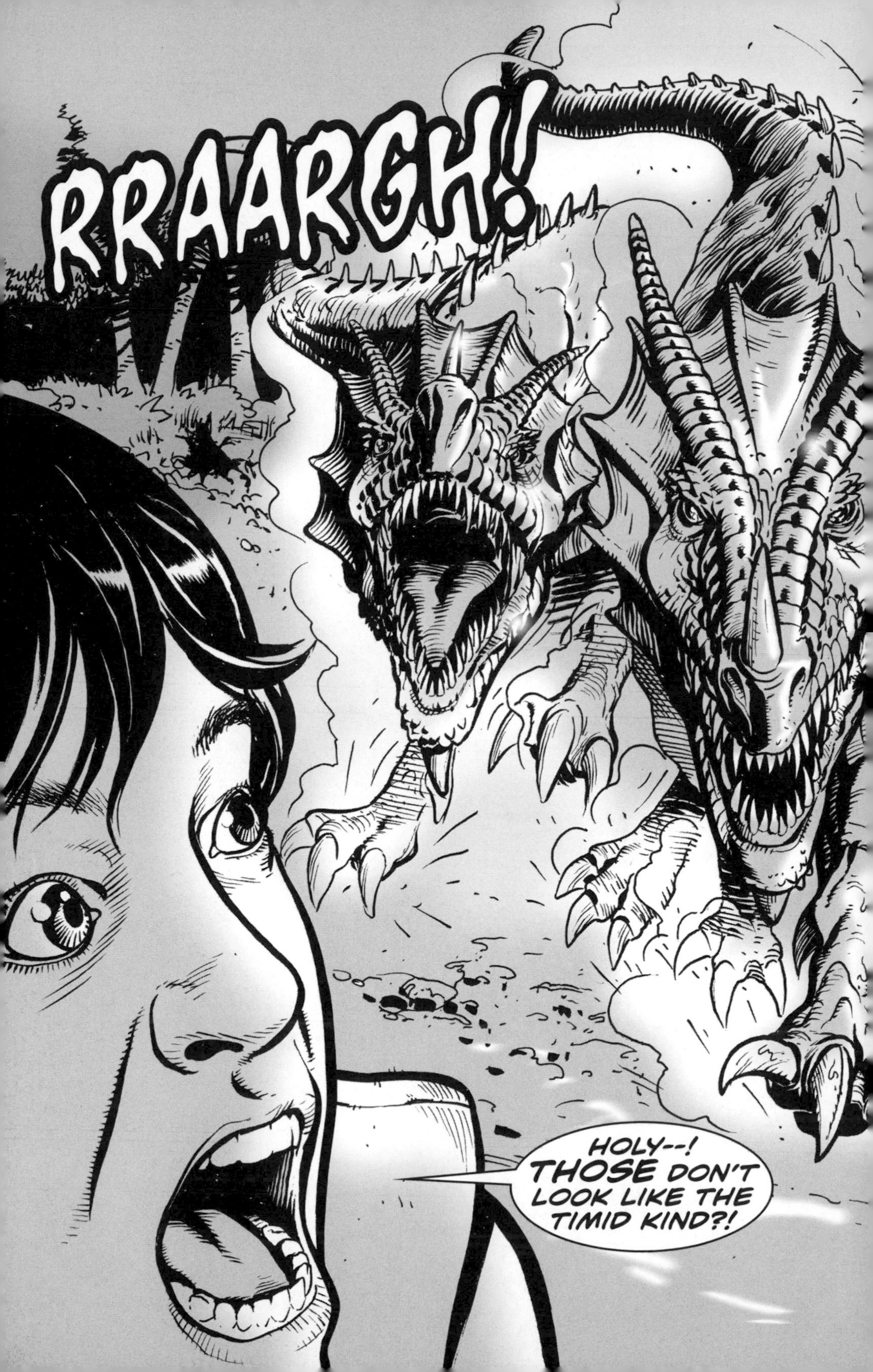
RRAARGH!
HOLY--! THOSE DON'T LOOK LIKE THE TIMID KIND?!

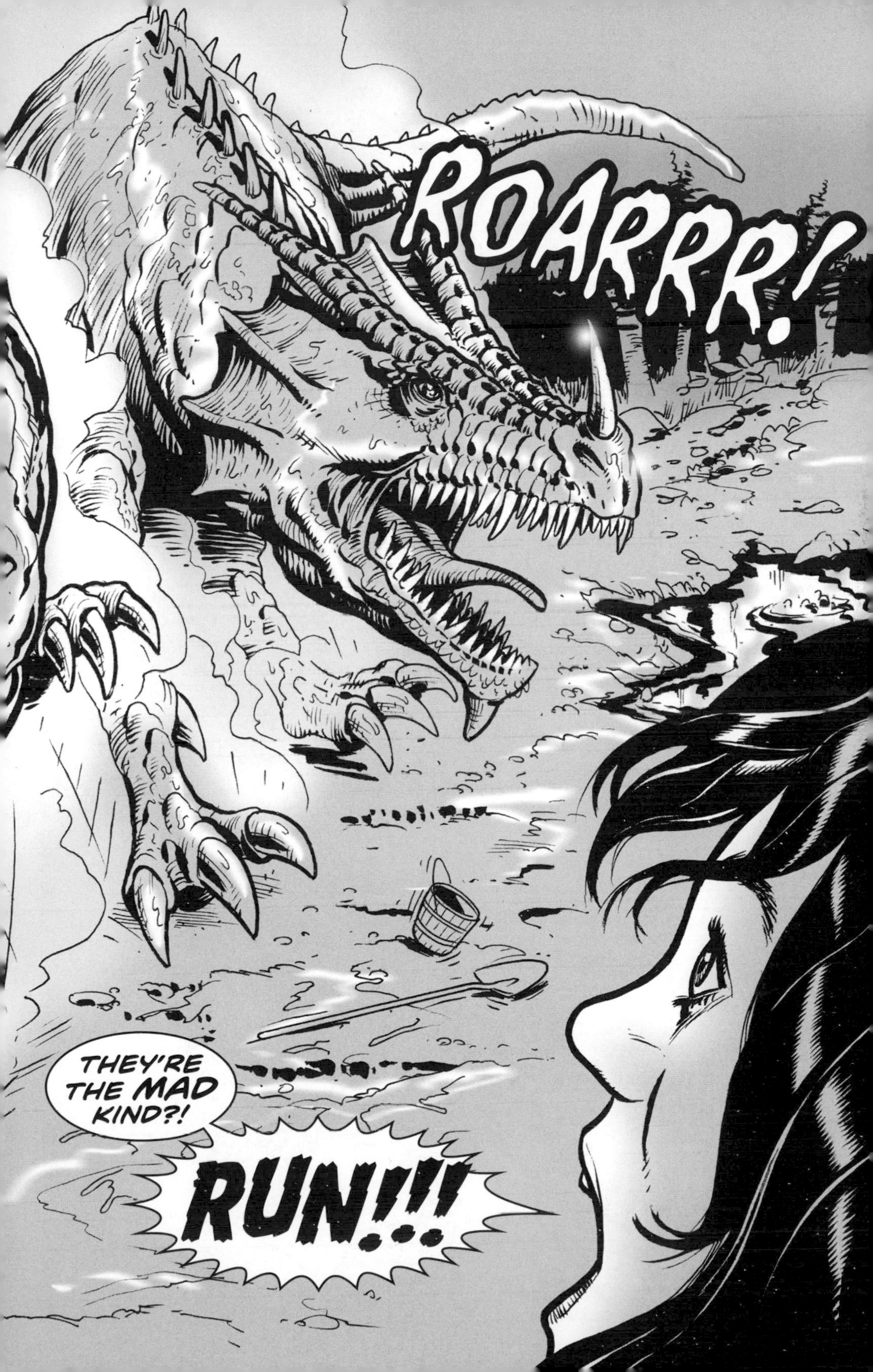
ROARRR!
THEY'RE THE MAD KIND?!
RUN!!!

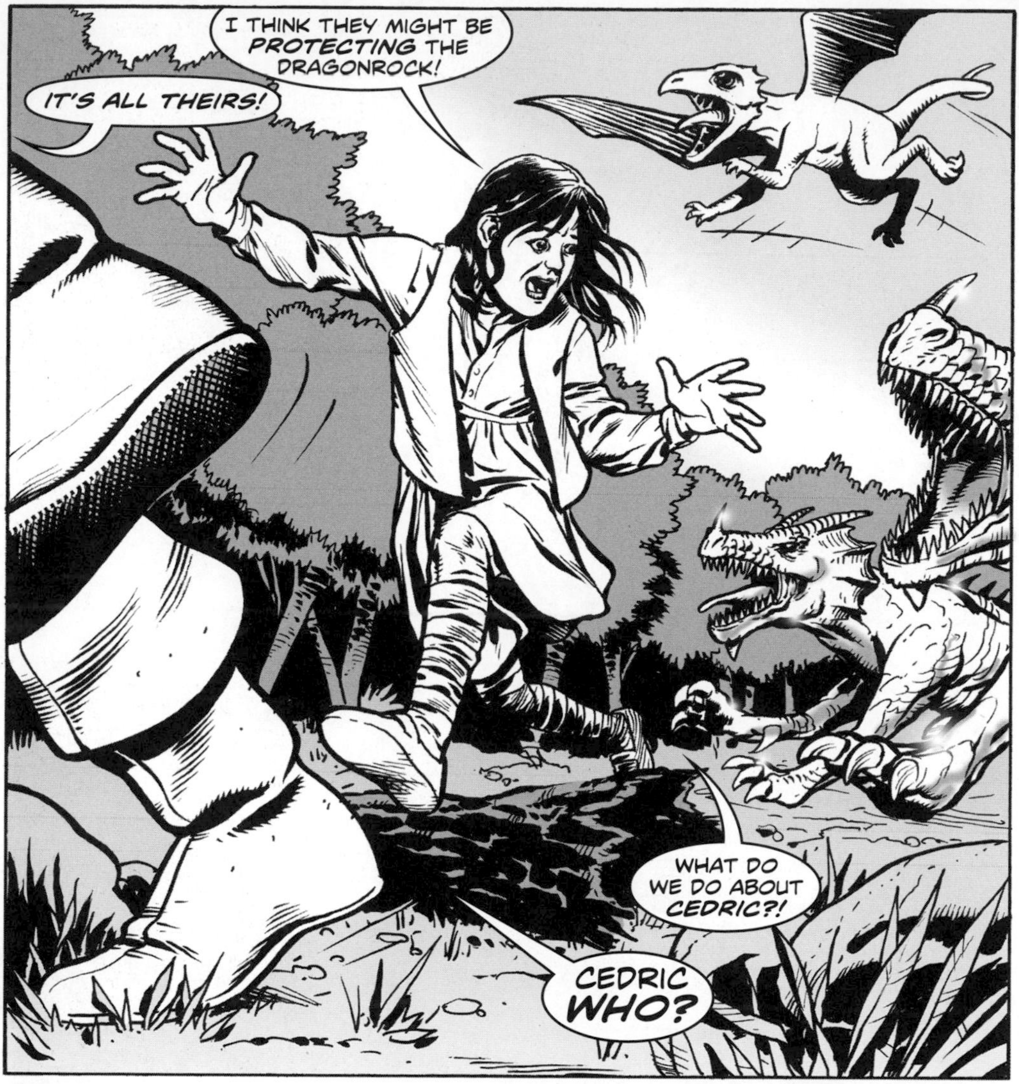
I THINK THEY MIGHT BE PROTECTING THE DRAGONROCK!
IT'S ALL THEIRS!
WHAT DO WE DO ABOUT CEDRIC?!
CEDRIC WHO?

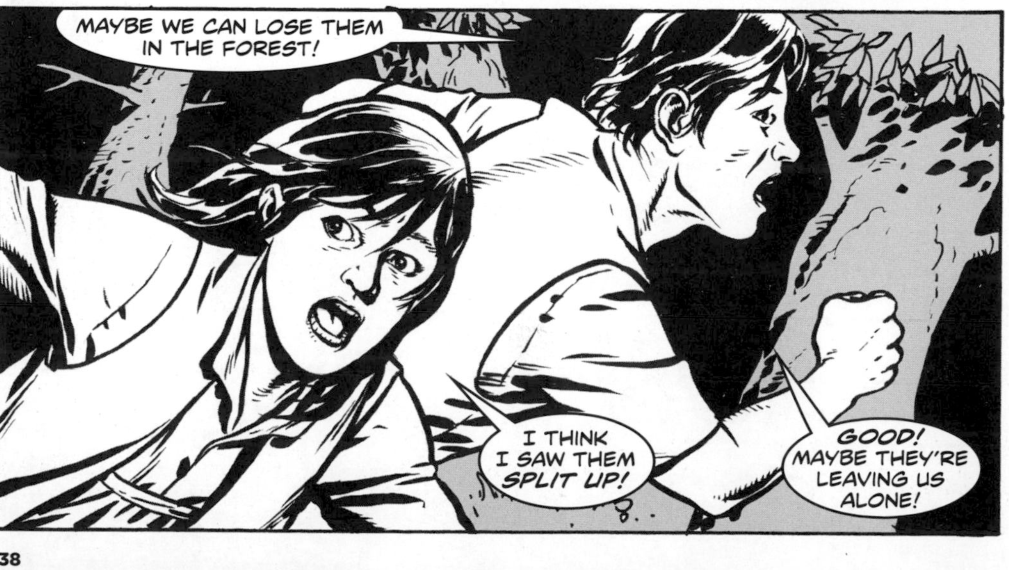
MAYBE WE CAN LOSE THEM IN THE FOREST!
I THINK I SAW THEM SPLIT UP!
GOOD! MAYBE THEY'RE LEAVING US ALONE!

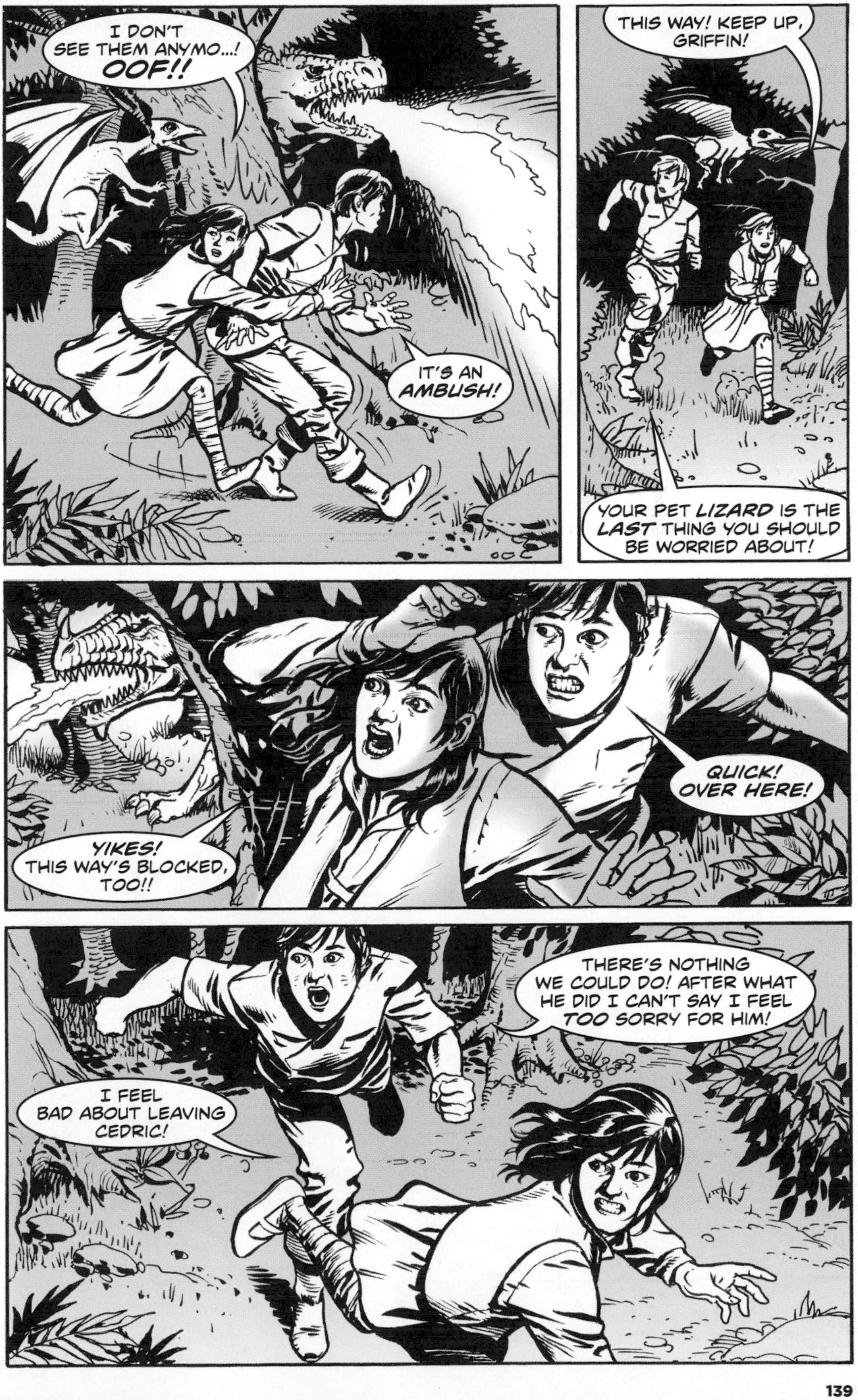
I DON'T SEE THEM ANYMO...! OOF!!
IT'S AN AMBUSH!
THIS WAY! KEEP UP, GRIFFIN!
YOUR PET LIZARD IS THE LAST THING YOU SHOULD BE WORRIED ABOUT!
QUICK! OVER HERE!
YIKES! THIS WAY'S BLOCKED, TOO!!
I FEEL BAD ABOUT LEAVING CEDRIC!
THERE'S NOTHING WE COULD DO! AFTER WHAT HE DID I CAN'T SAY I FEEL TOO SORRY FOR HIM!

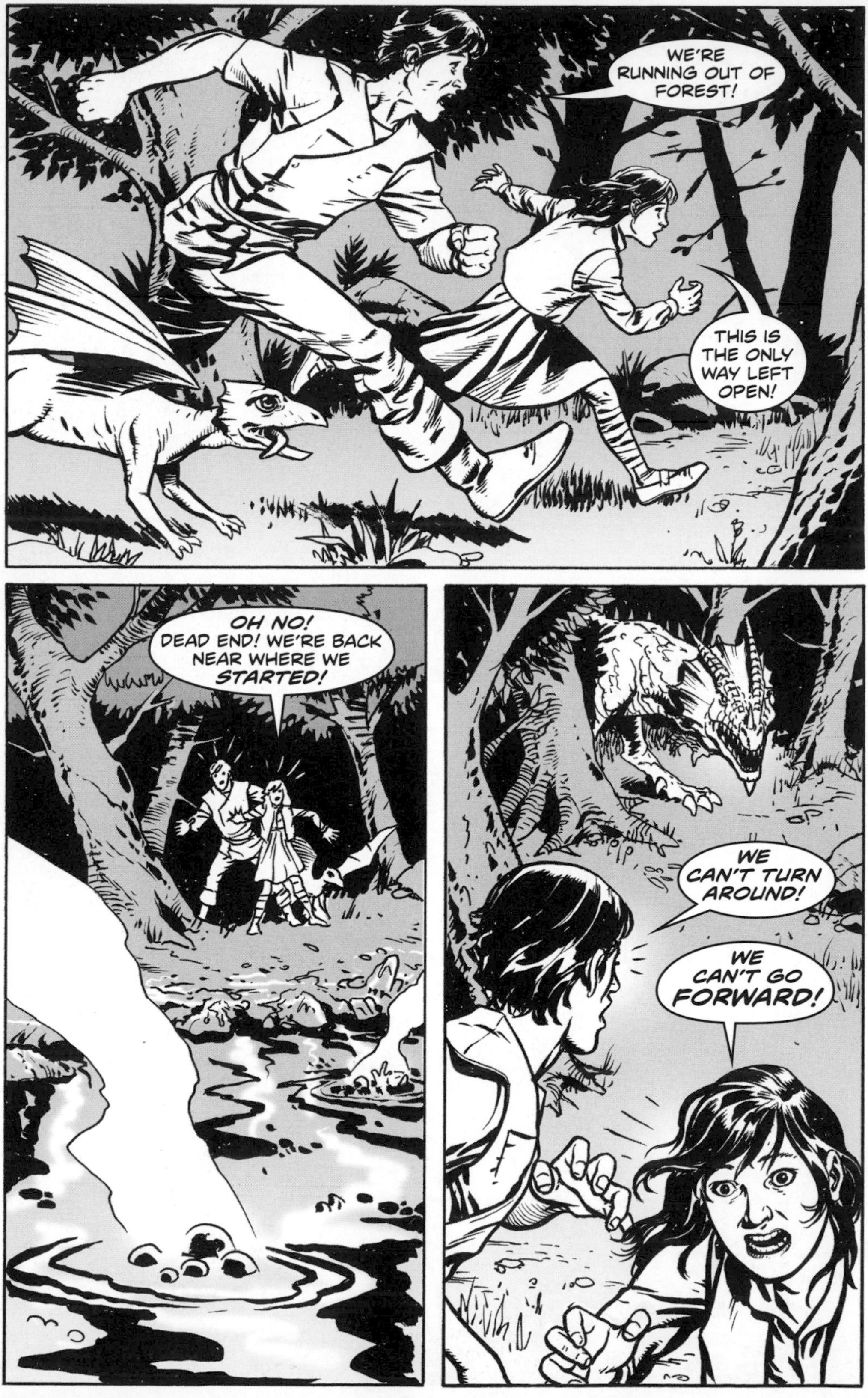
WE'RE RUNNING OUT OF FOREST!
THIS IS THE ONLY WAY LEFT OPEN!
OH NO! DEAD END! WE'RE BACK NEAR WHERE WE STARTED!
WE CAN'T TURN AROUND!
WE CAN'T GO FORWARD!

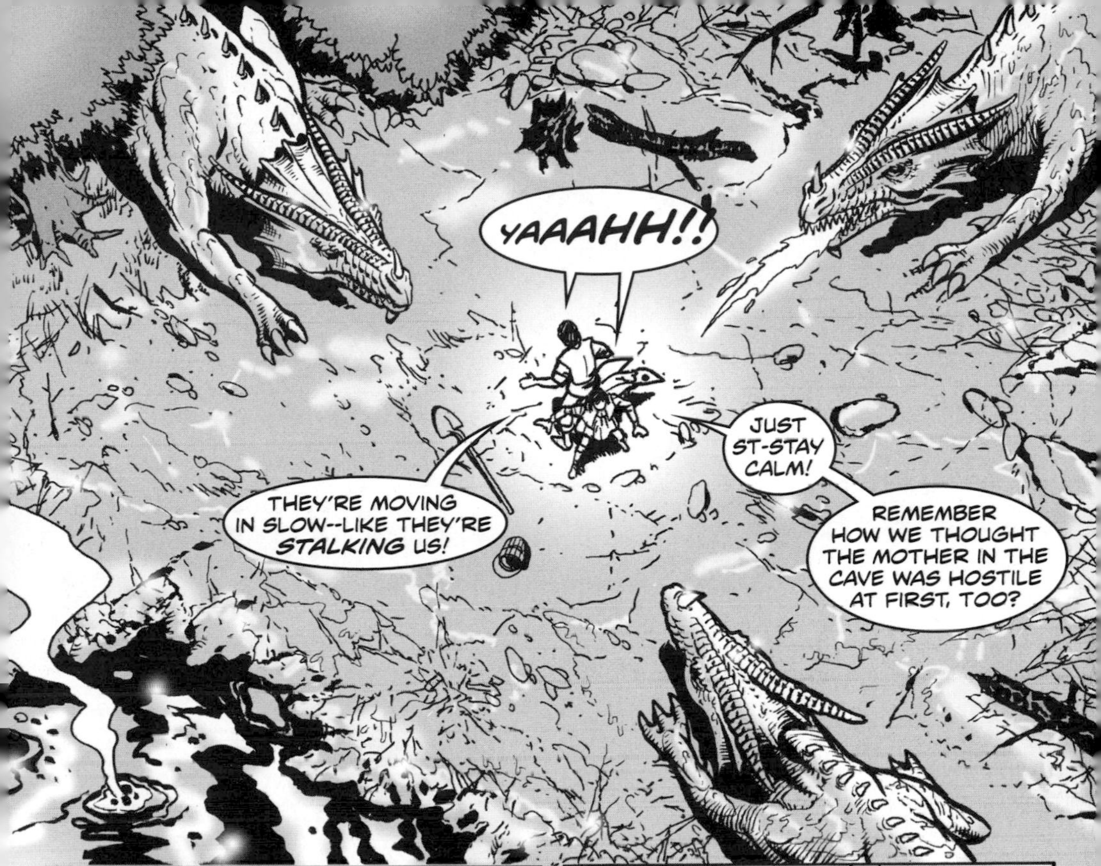
YAAAHH!!
THEY'RE MOVING IN SLOW--LIKE THEY'RE STALKING US!
JUST ST-STAY CALM!
REMEMBER HOW WE THOUGHT THE MOTHER IN THE CAVE WAS HOSTILE AT FIRST, TOO?

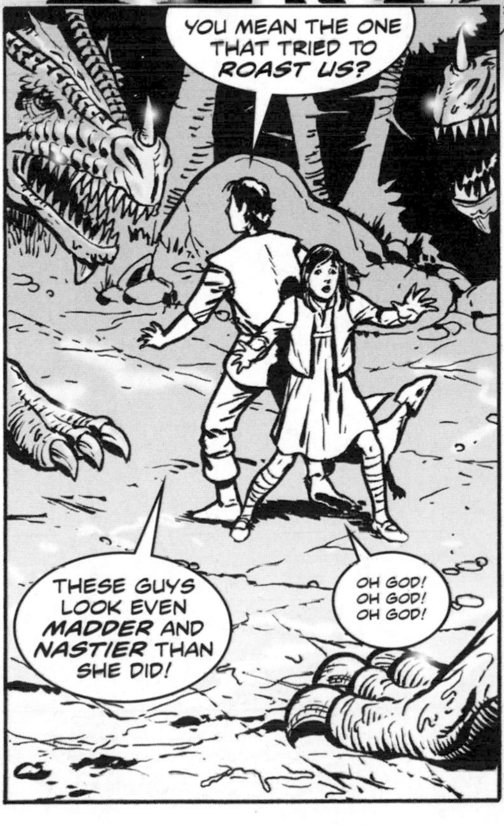
YOU MEAN THE ONE THAT TRIED TO ROAST US?
THESE GUYS LOOK EVEN MADDER AND NASTIER THAN SHE DID!
OH GOD! OH GOD! OH GOD!

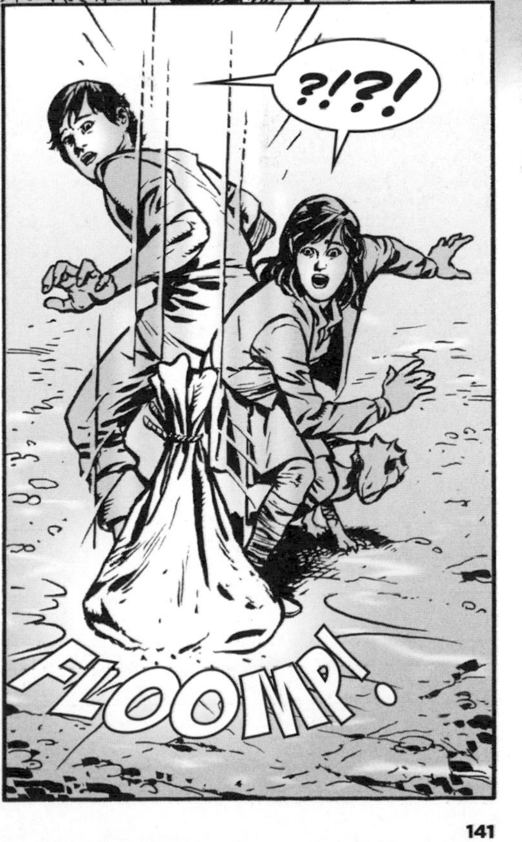
?!?!
FLOOMP!

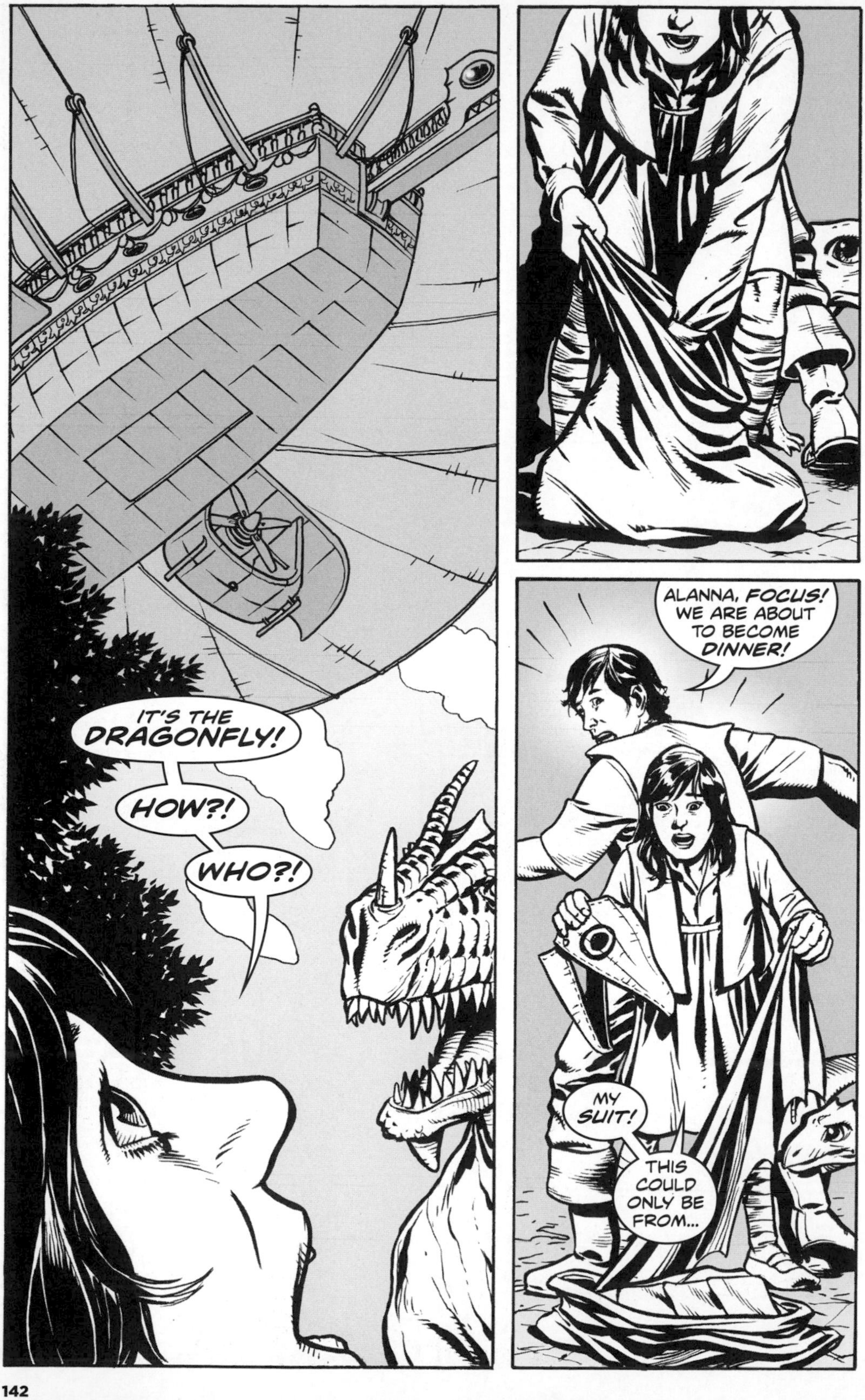
IT'S THE DRAGONFLY!
HOW?!
WHO?!
ALANNA, FOCUS! WE ARE ABOUT TO BECOME DINNER!
MY SUIT!
THIS COULD ONLY BE FROM...

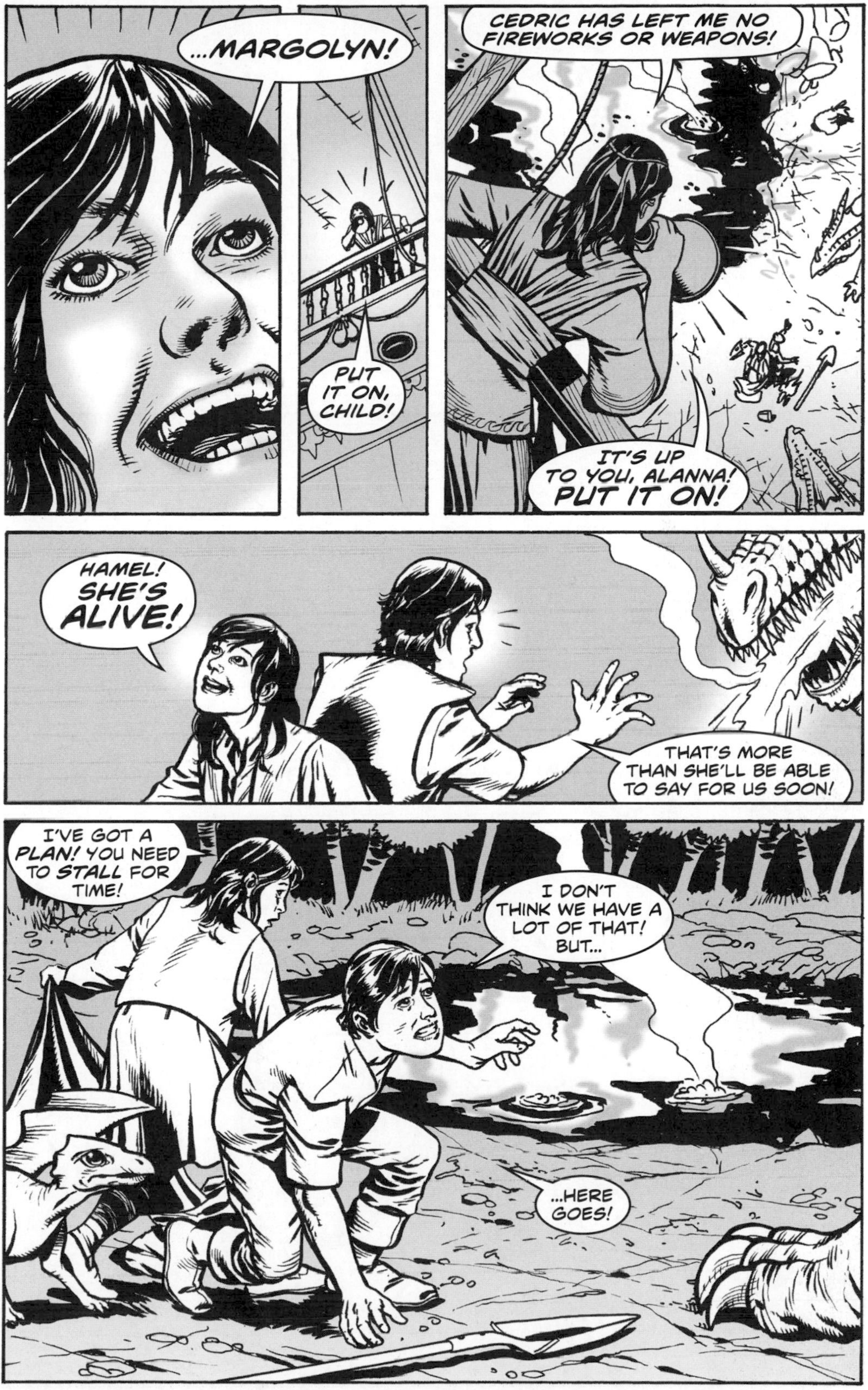
...MARGOLYN!
PUT IT ON, CHILD!
CEDRIC HAS LEFT ME NO FIREWORKS OR WEAPONS!
IT'S UP TO YOU, ALANNA! PUT IT ON!
HAMEL! SHE'S ALIVE!
THAT'S MORE THAN SHE'LL BE ABLE TO SAY FOR US SOON!
I'VE GOT A PLAN! YOU NEED TO STALL FOR TIME!
I DON'T THINK WE HAVE A LOT OF THAT! BUT...
...HERE GOES!

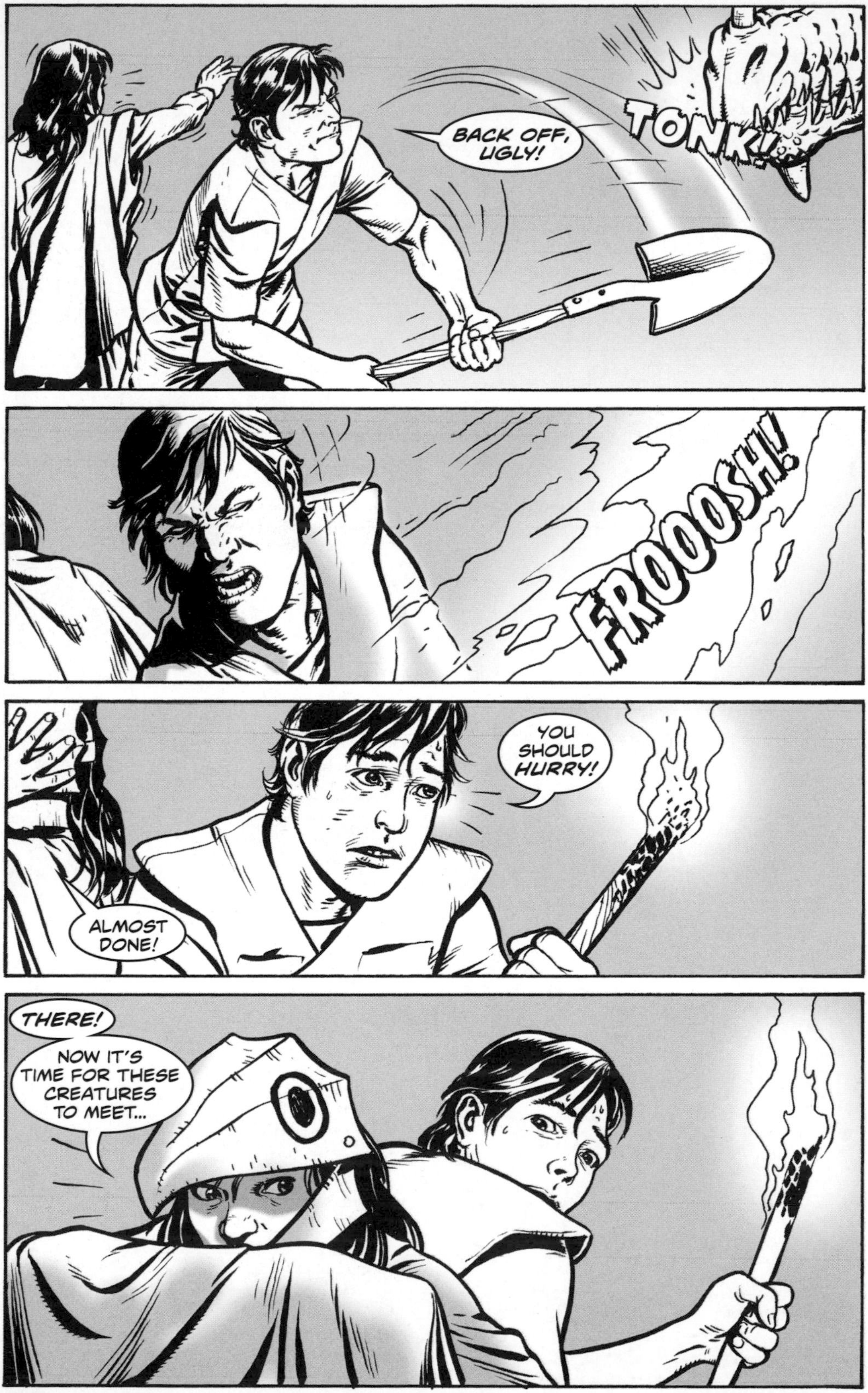
BACK OFF, UGLY!
TONK!
FROOOSH!
YOU SHOULD HURRY!
ALMOST DONE!
THERE!
NOW IT'S TIME FOR THESE CREATURES TO MEET...

CHAPTER EIGHT

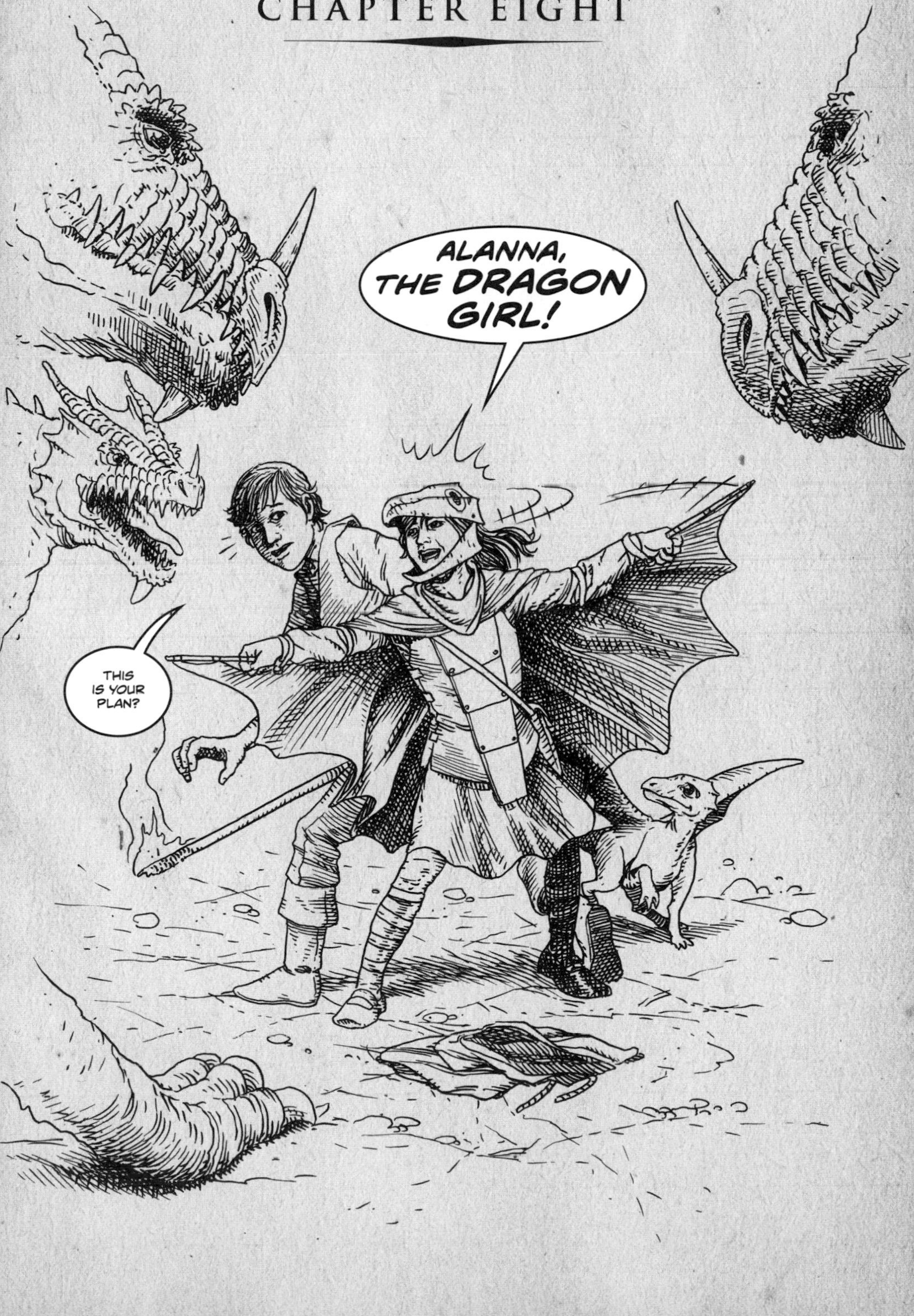
ALANNA, THE DRAGON GIRL!
THIS IS YOUR PLAN?

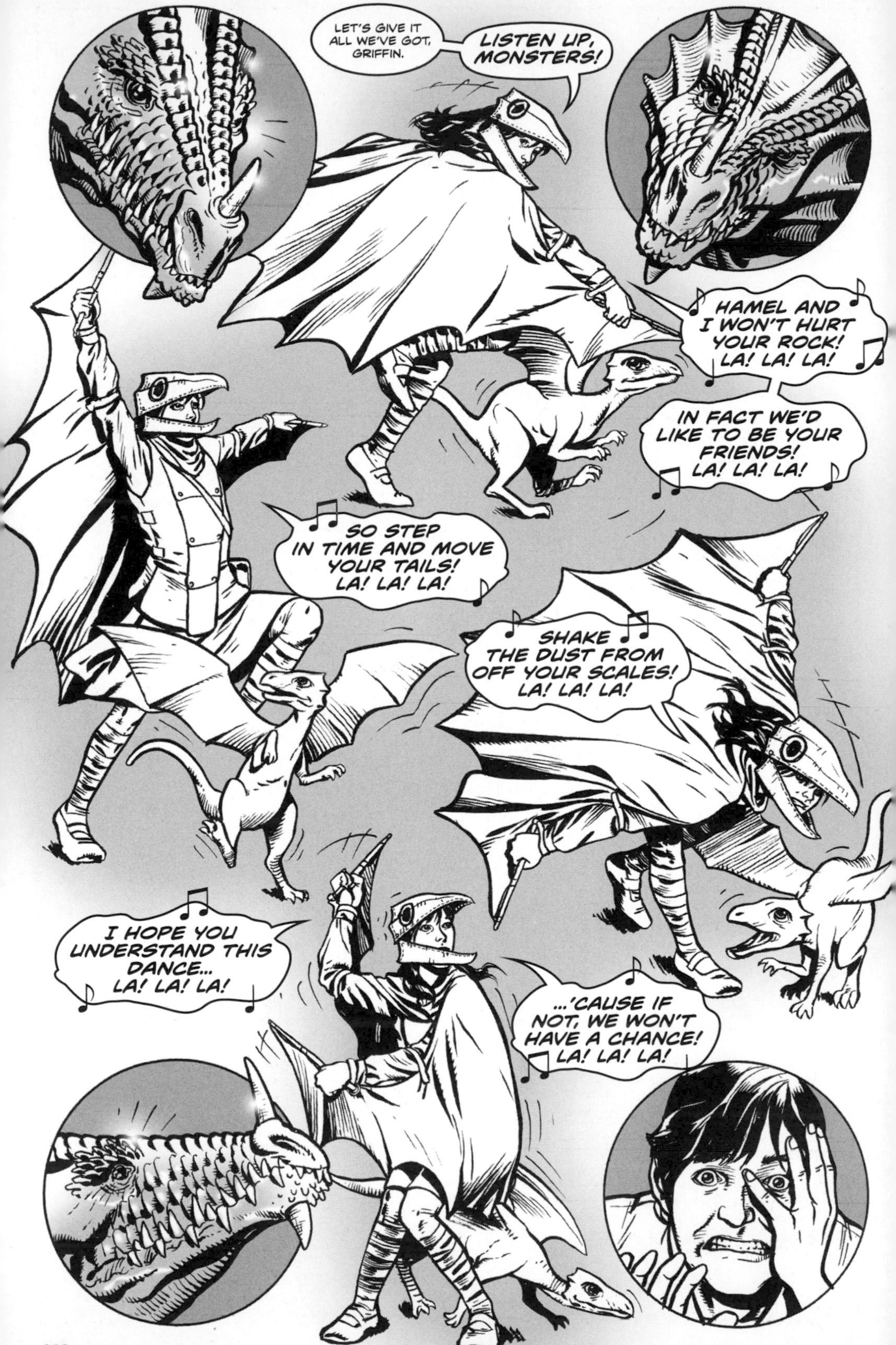

LET'S GIVE IT ALL WE'VE GOT, GRIFFIN.
LISTEN UP, MONSTERS!
HAMEL AND I WON'T HURT YOUR ROCK! LA! LA! LA!
IN FACT WE'D LIKE TO BE YOUR FRIENDS! LA! LA! LA!
SO STEP IN TIME AND MOVE YOUR TAILS! LA! LA! LA!
SHAKE THE DUST FROM OFF YOUR SCALES! LA! LA! LA!
I HOPE YOU UNDERSTAND THIS DANCE... LA! LA! LA!
...'CAUSE IF NOT, WE WON'T HAVE A CHANCE! LA! LA! LA!

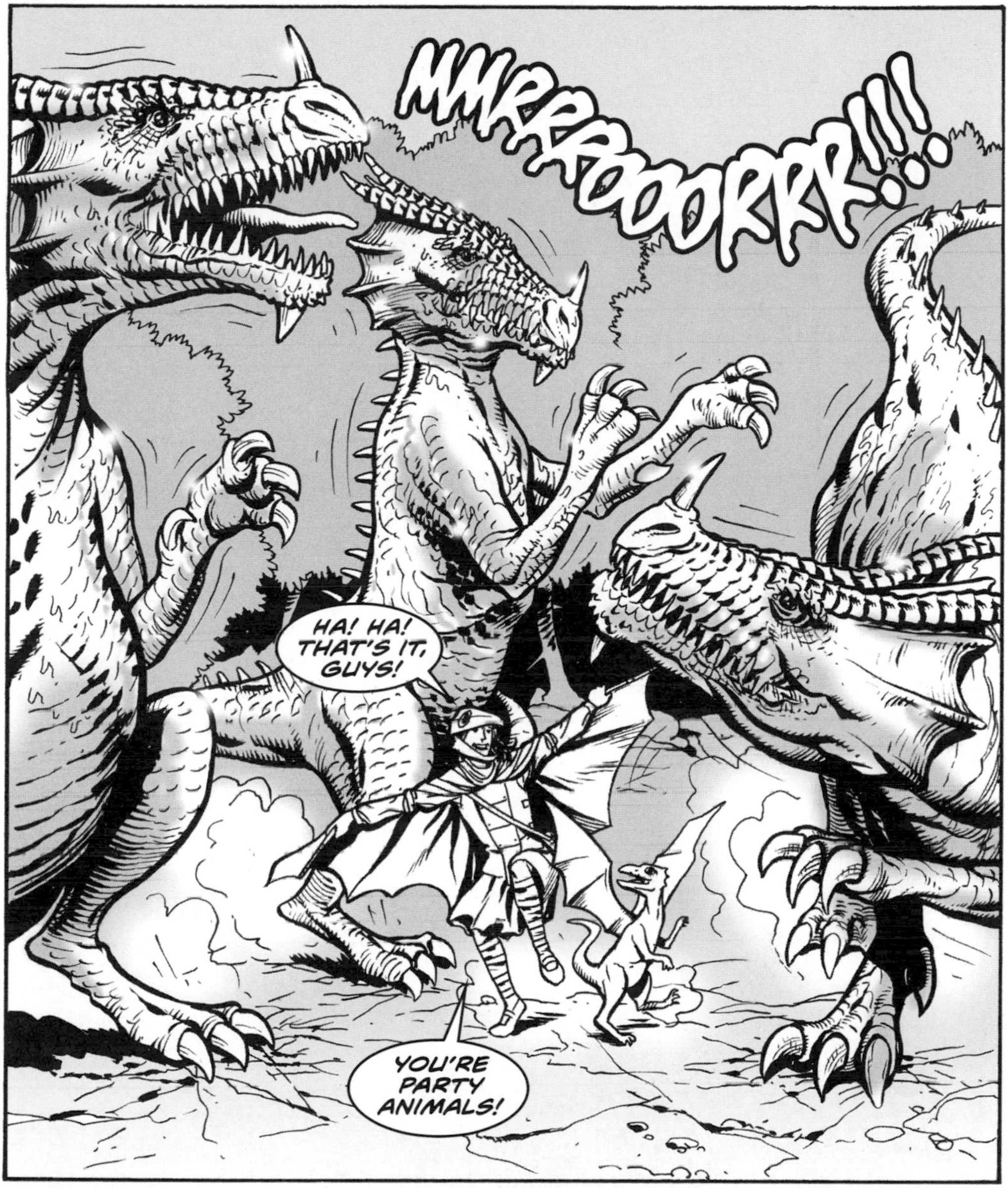
MMRRROOOORRR!!!!
HA! HA! THAT'S IT, GUYS!
YOU'RE PARTY ANIMALS!

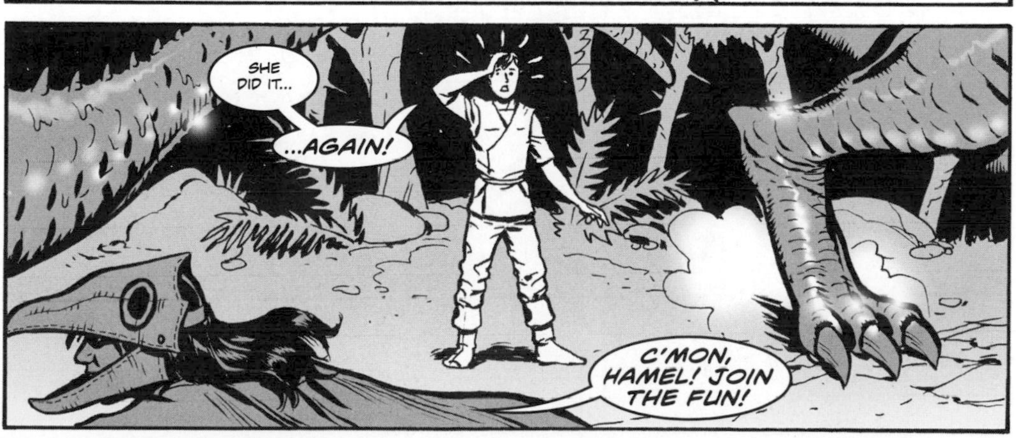
SHE DID IT...
...AGAIN!
C'MON, HAMEL! JOIN THE FUN!

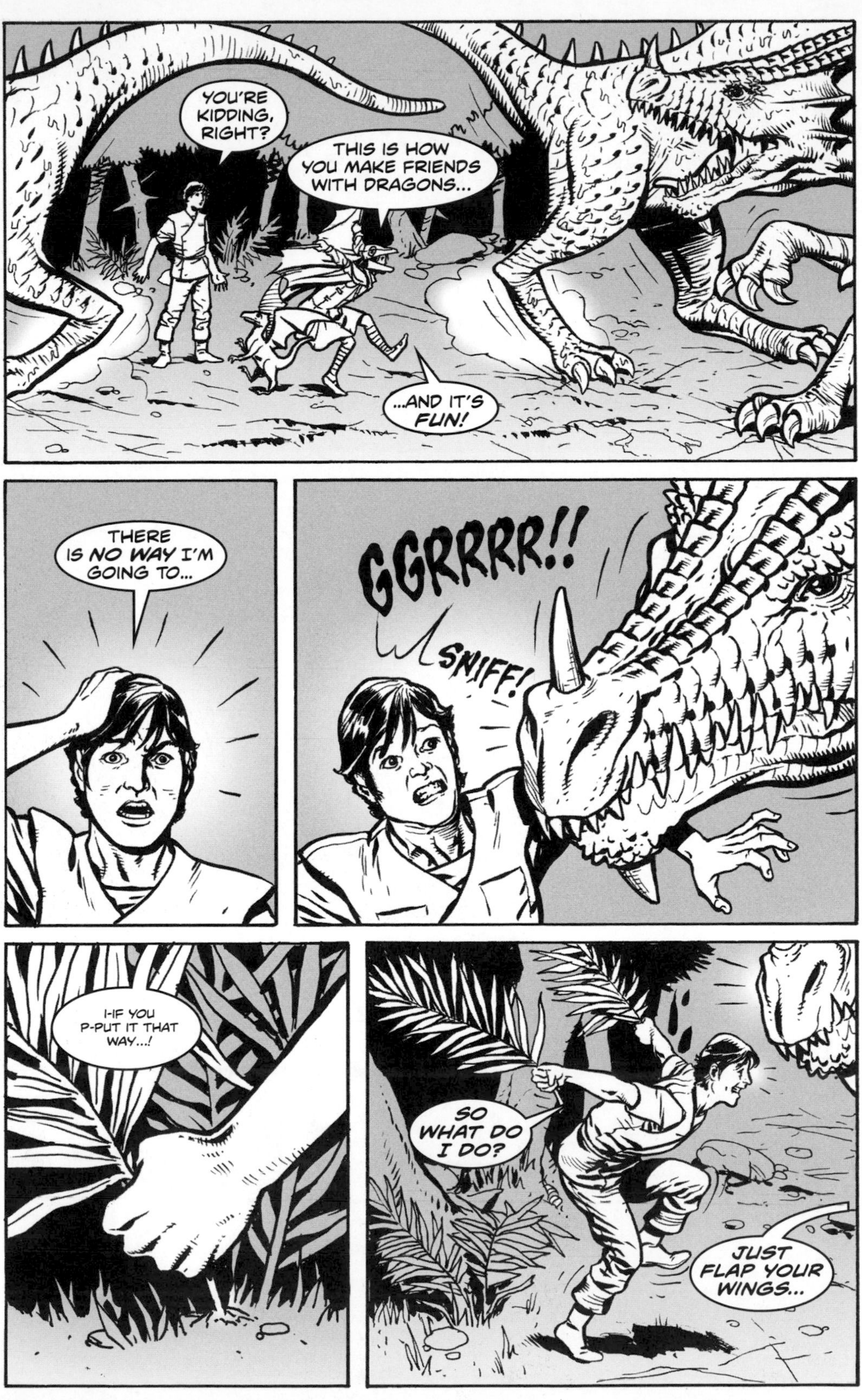
YOU'RE KIDDING, RIGHT?
THIS IS HOW YOU MAKE FRIENDS WITH DRAGONS...
...AND IT'S FUN!
THERE IS NO WAY I'M GOING TO...
GGRRRR!!
SNIFF!
I-IF YOU P-PUT IT THAT WAY...!
SO WHAT DO I DO?
JUST FLAP YOUR WINGS...

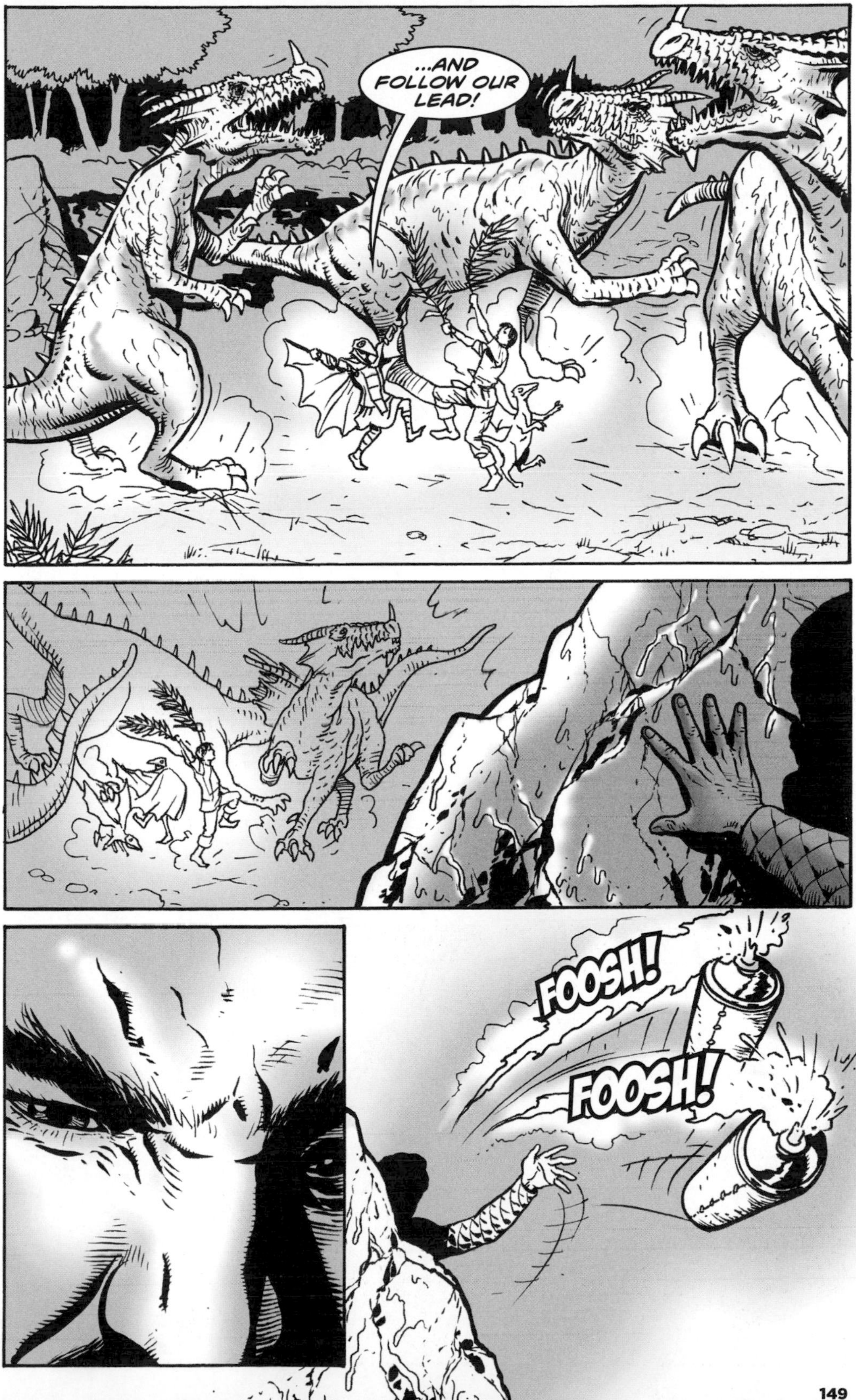
...AND FOLLOW OUR LEAD!
FOOSH!
FOOSH!

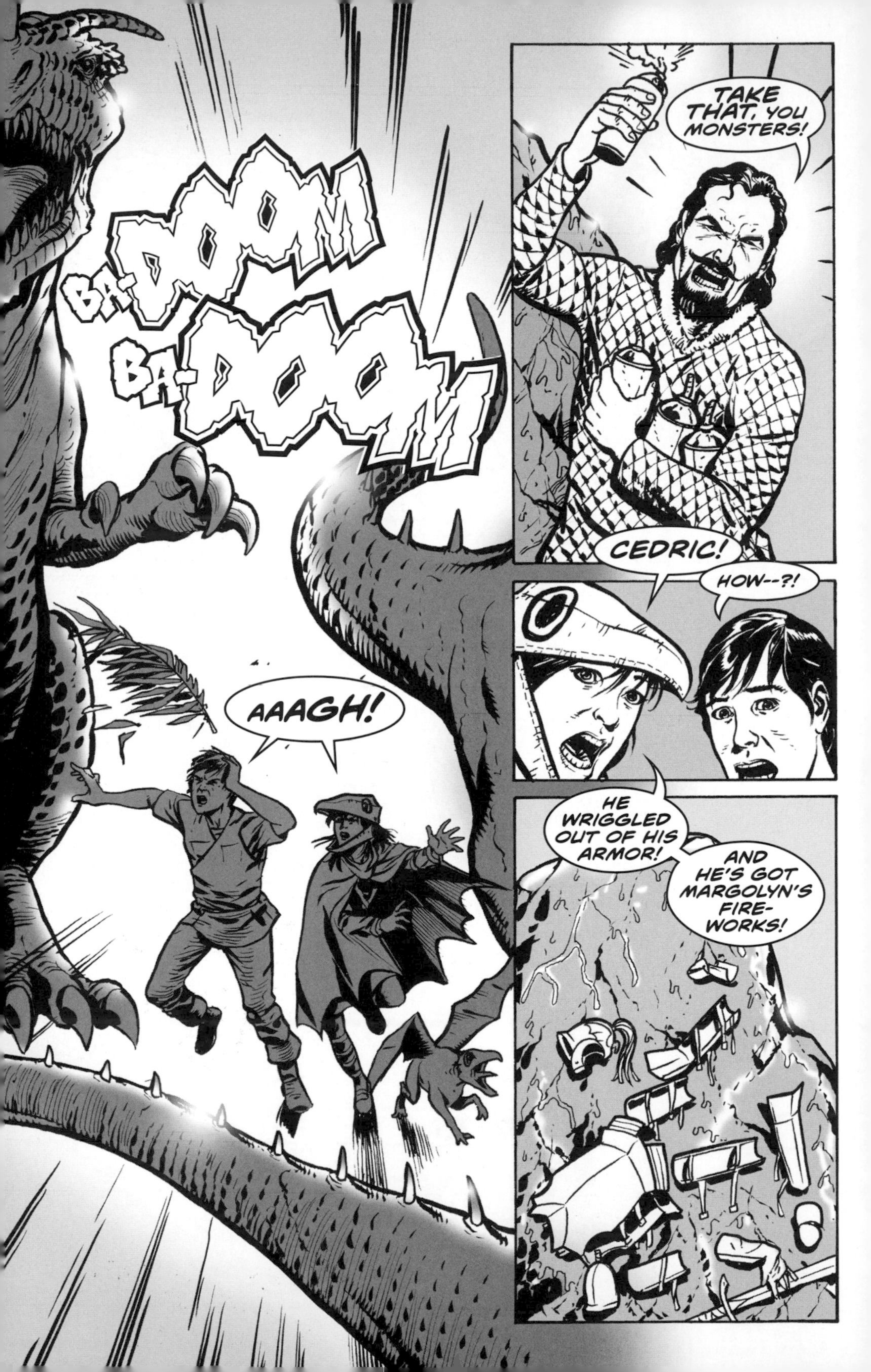
BA-DOOM
BA-DOOM
AAAGH!
TAKE THAT, YOU MONSTERS!
CEDRIC!
HOW--?!
HE WRIGGLED OUT OF HIS ARMOR!
AND HE'S GOT MARGOLYN'S FIRE-WORKS!

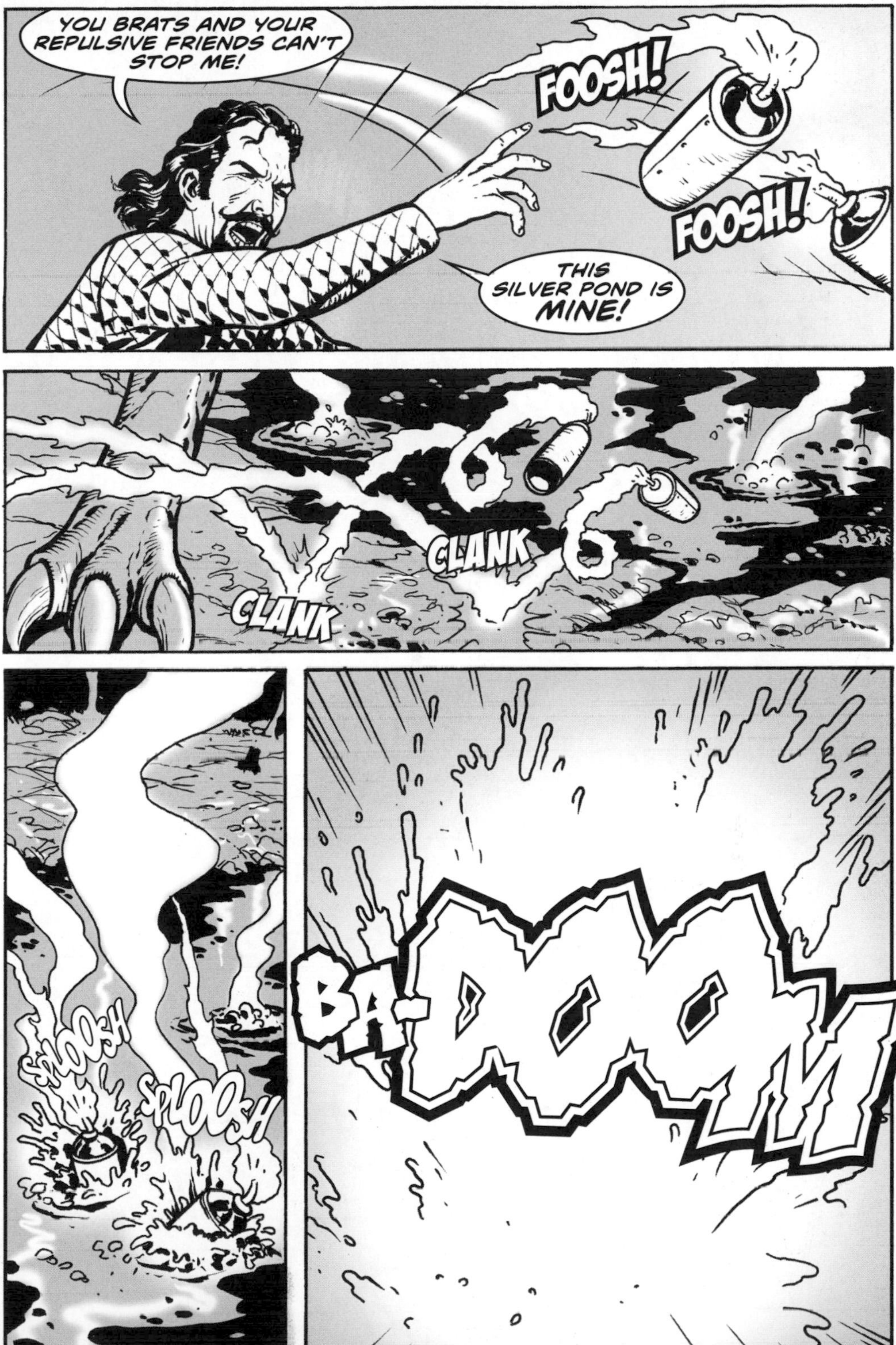
YOU BRATS AND YOUR REPULSIVE FRIENDS CAN'T STOP ME!
FOOSH!
FOOSH!
THIS SILVER POND IS MINE!
CLANK
CLANK
SPLOOSH
SPLOOSH
BA-DOOM

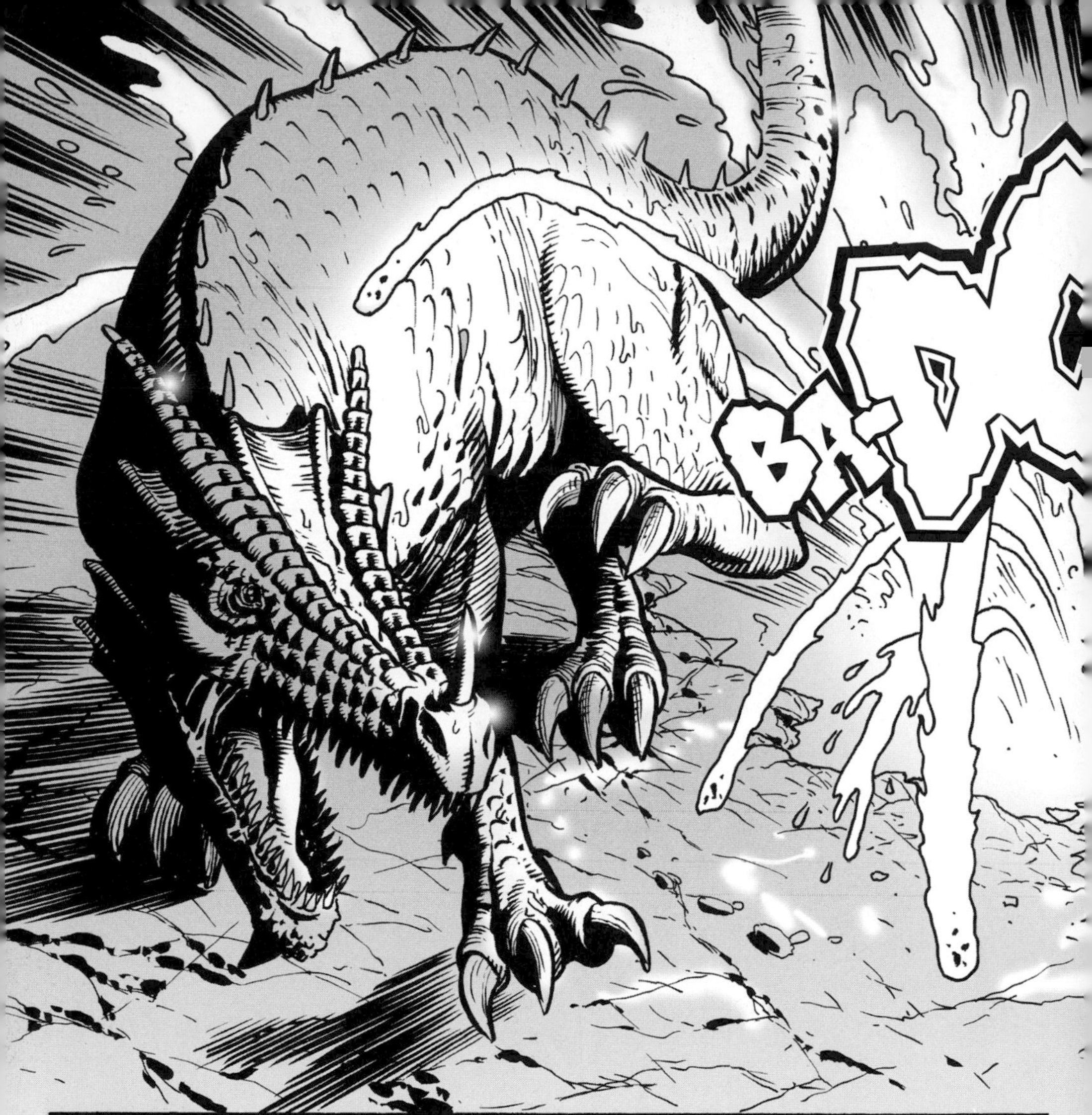

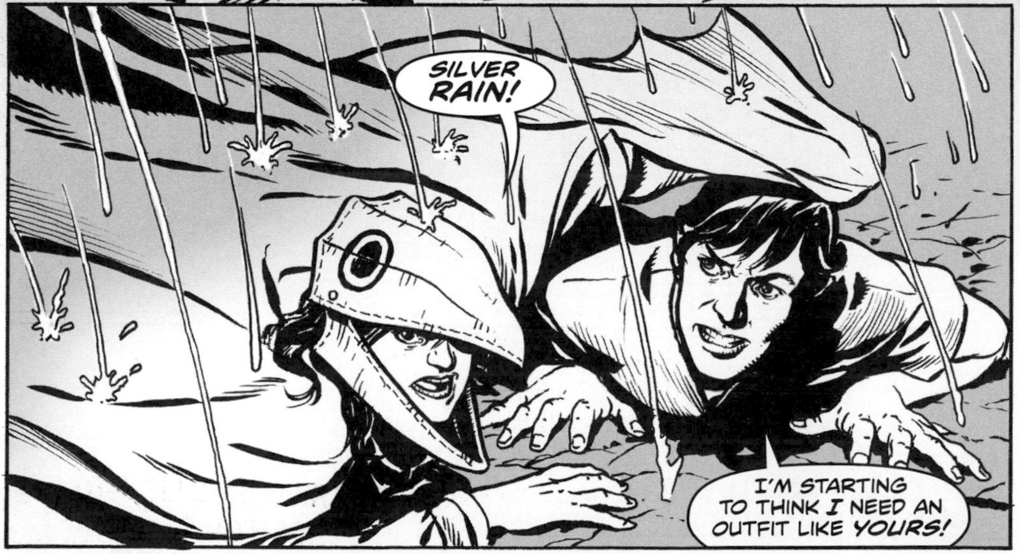
SILVER RAIN!
I'M STARTING TO THINK I NEED AN OUTFIT LIKE YOURS!

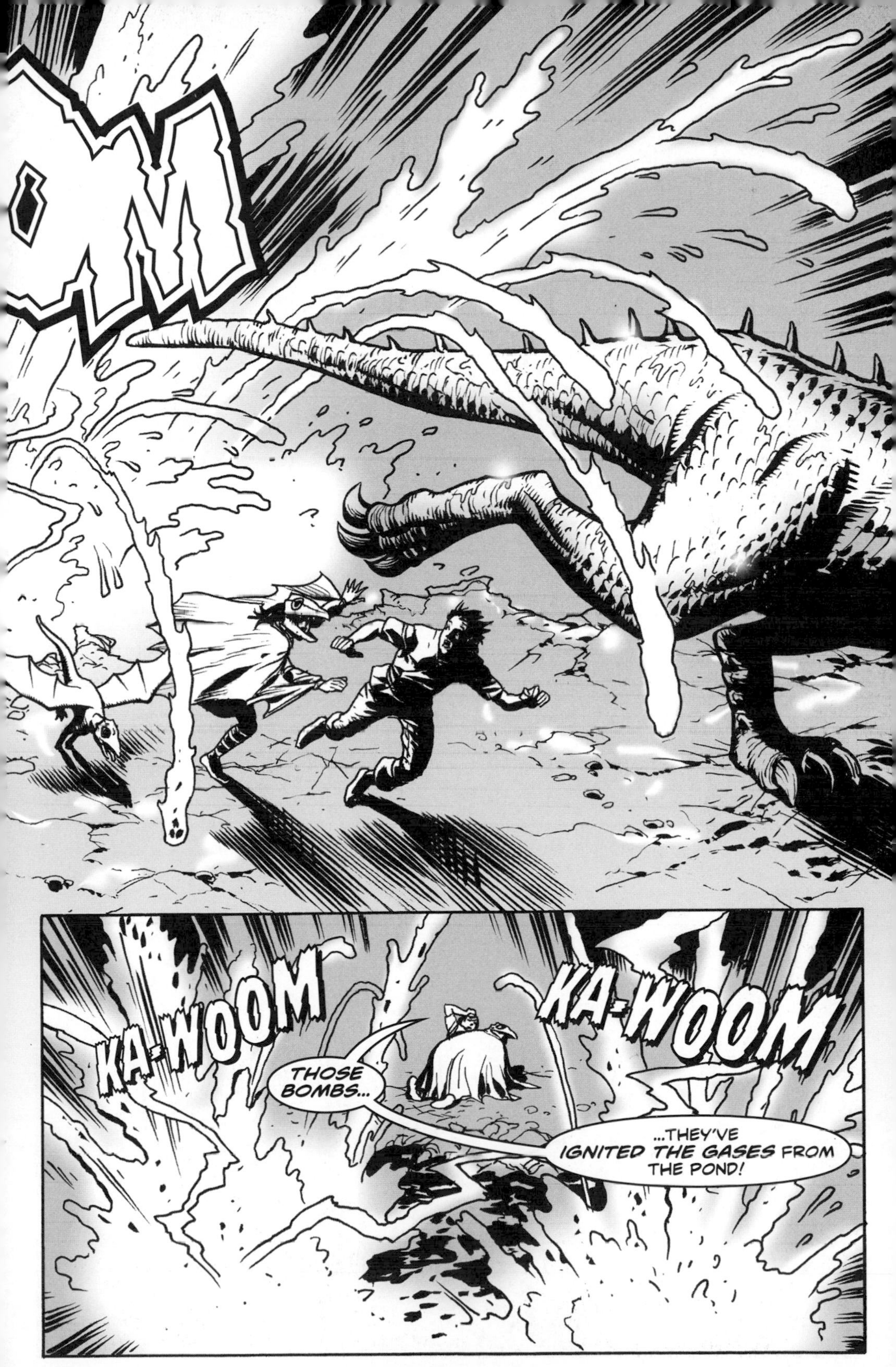
OM
KA-WOOM
THOSE BOMBS...
KA-WOOM
...THEY'VE IGNITED THE GASES FROM THE POND!

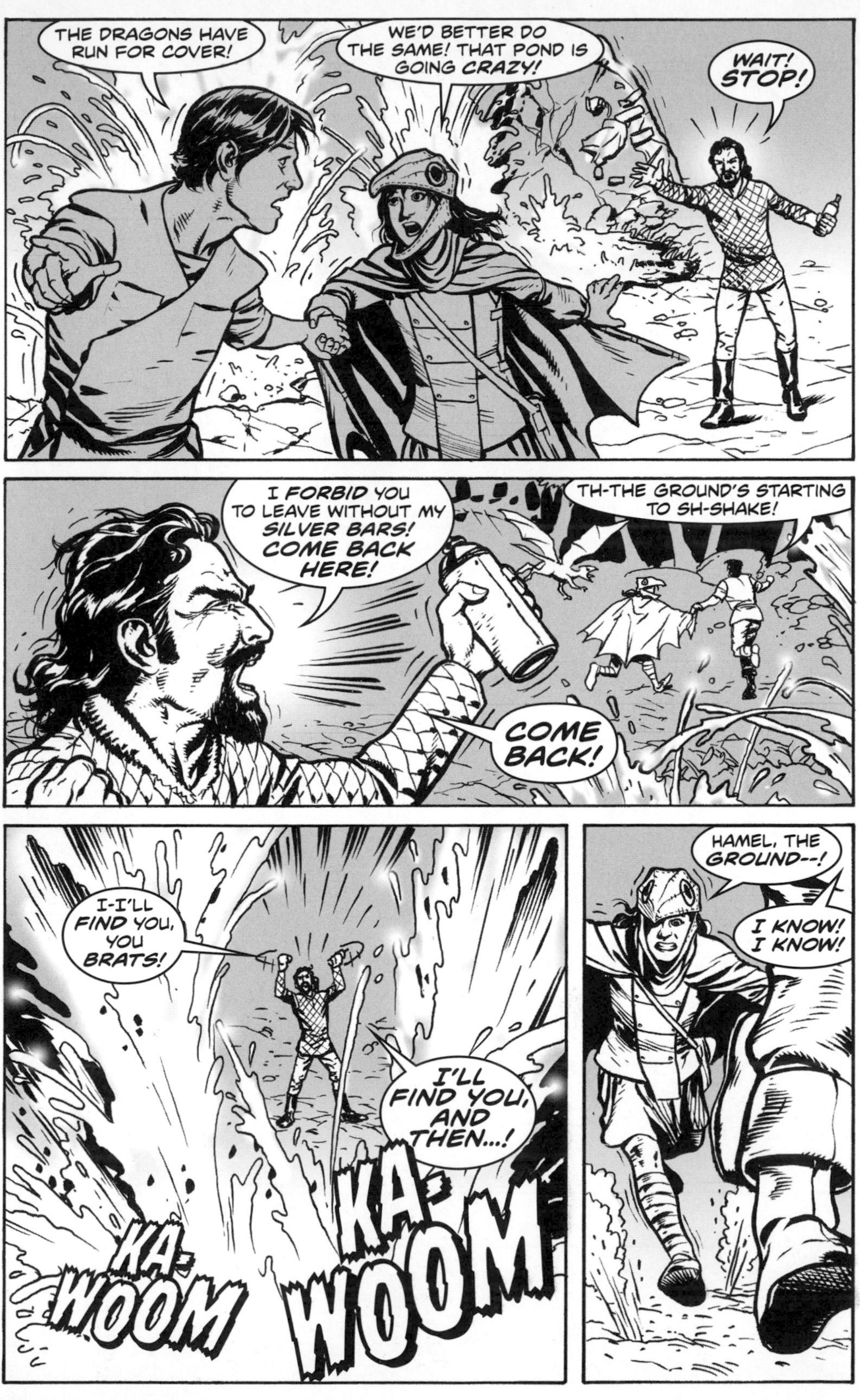
THE DRAGONS HAVE RUN FOR COVER!
WE'D BETTER DO THE SAME! THAT POND IS GOING CRAZY!
WAIT! STOP!
I FORBID YOU TO LEAVE WITHOUT MY SILVER BARS! COME BACK HERE!
TH-THE GROUND'S STARTING TO SH-SHAKE!
COME BACK!
I-I'LL FIND YOU, YOU BRATS!
I'LL FIND YOU, AND THEN...!
KA-WOOM
KA-WOOM
HAMEL, THE GROUND--!
I KNOW! I KNOW!

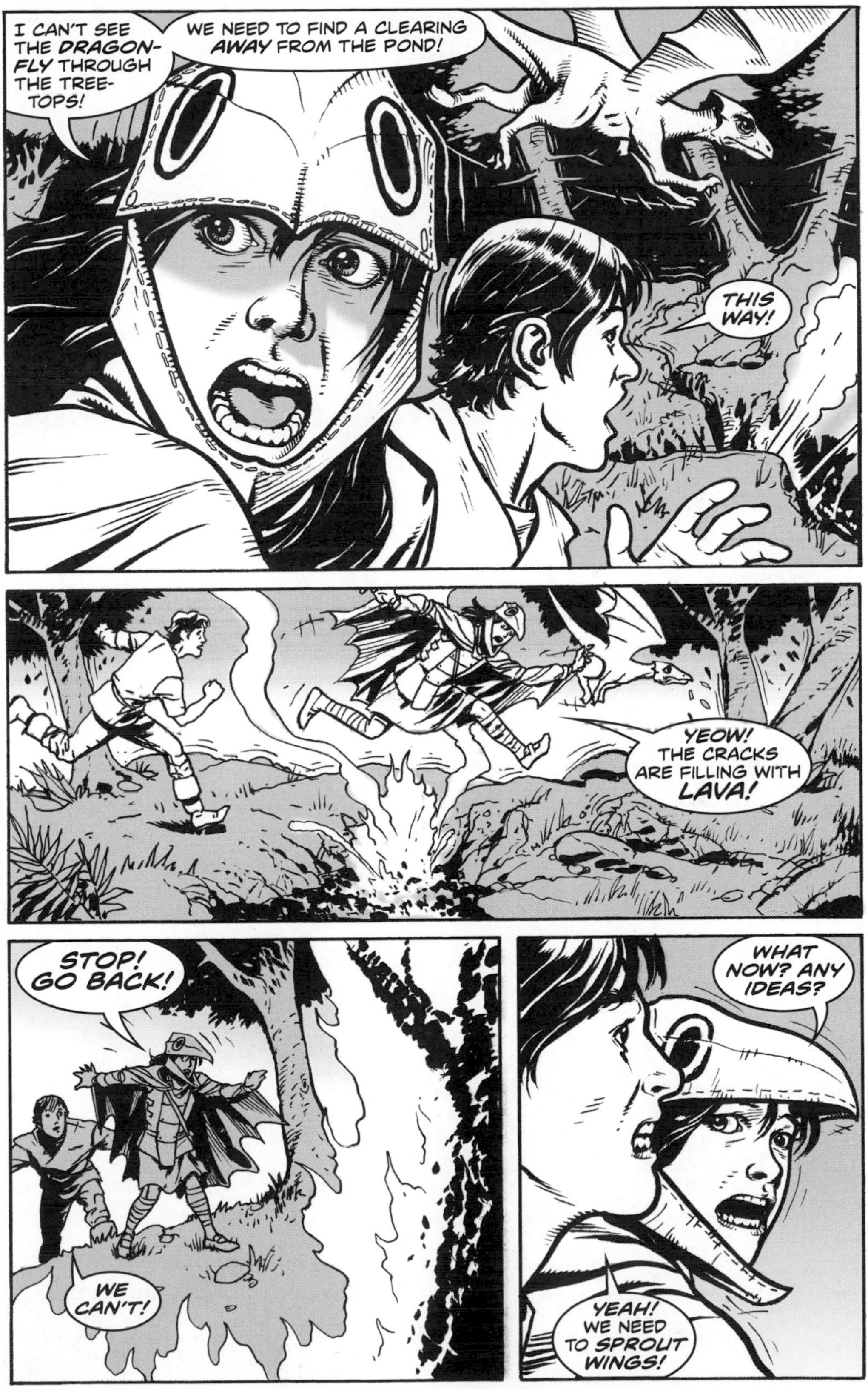
I CAN'T SEE THE DRAGON-FLY THROUGH THE TREE-TOPS!
WE NEED TO FIND A CLEARING AWAY FROM THE POND!
THIS WAY!
YEOW! THE CRACKS ARE FILLING WITH LAVA!
STOP! GO BACK!
WE CAN'T!
WHAT NOW? ANY IDEAS?
YEAH! WE NEED TO SPROUT WINGS!

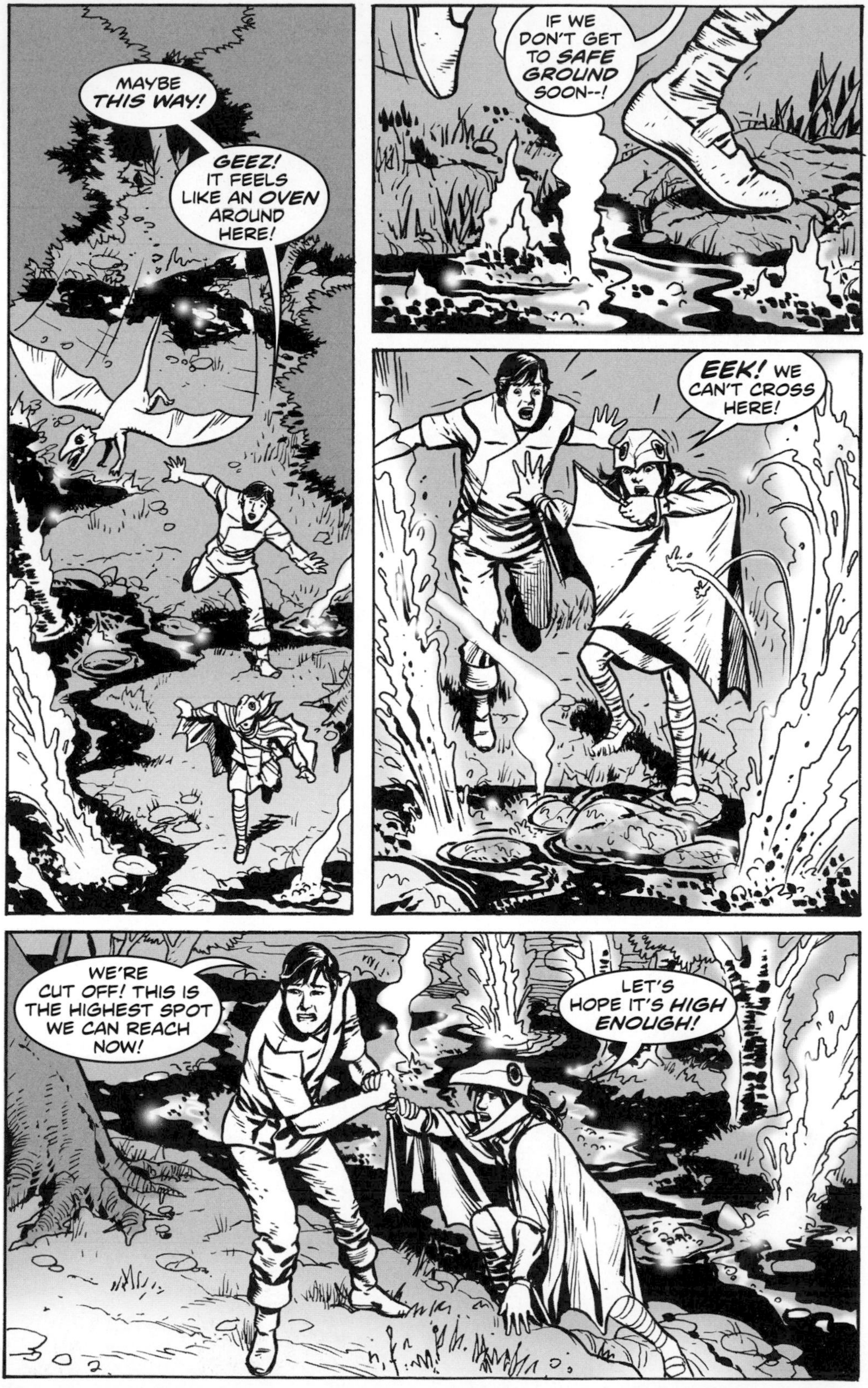
MAYBE THIS WAY!
GEEZ! IT FEELS LIKE AN OVEN AROUND HERE!
IF WE DON'T GET TO SAFE GROUND SOON--!
EEK! WE CAN'T CROSS HERE!
WE'RE CUT OFF! THIS IS THE HIGHEST SPOT WE CAN REACH NOW!
LET'S HOPE IT'S HIGH ENOUGH!

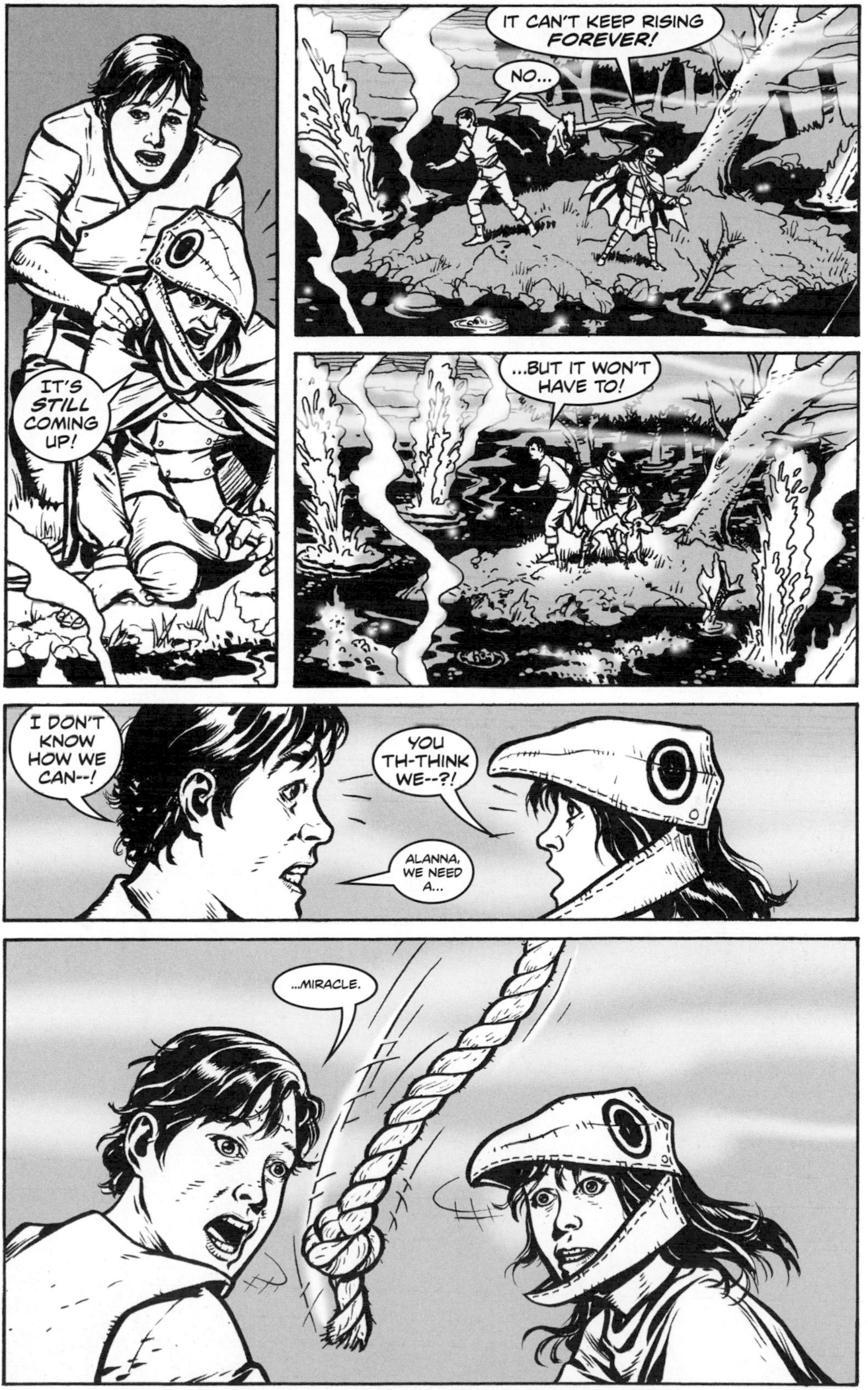
IT'S STILL COMING UP!
IT CAN'T KEEP RISING FOREVER!
NO...
...BUT IT WON'T HAVE TO!
I DON'T KNOW HOW WE CAN--!
YOU TH-THINK WE--?!
ALANNA, WE NEED A...
...MIRACLE.

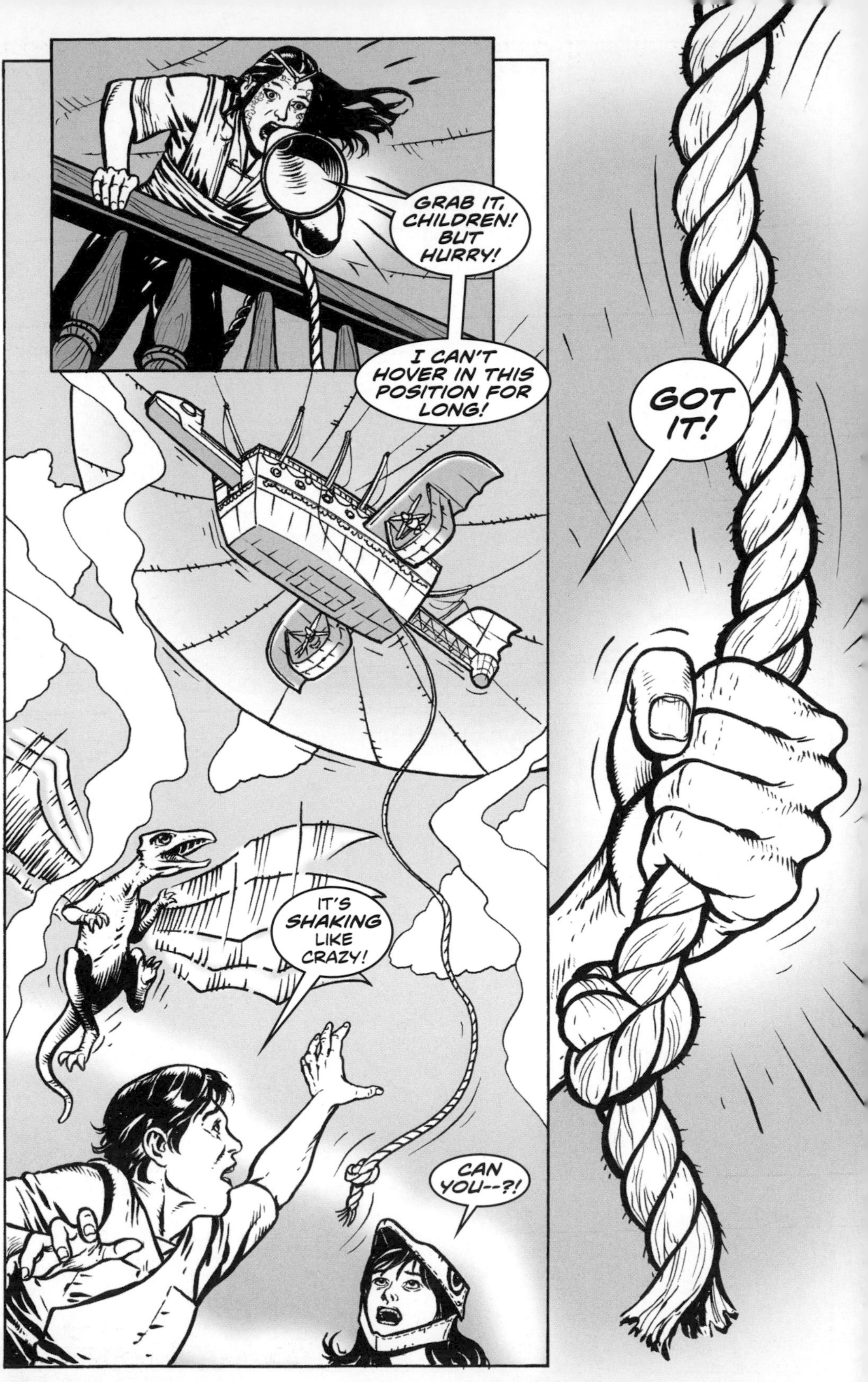
GRAB IT, CHILDREN! BUT HURRY!
I CAN'T HOVER IN THIS POSITION FOR LONG!
IT'S SHAKING LIKE CRAZY!
CAN YOU--?!
GOT IT!

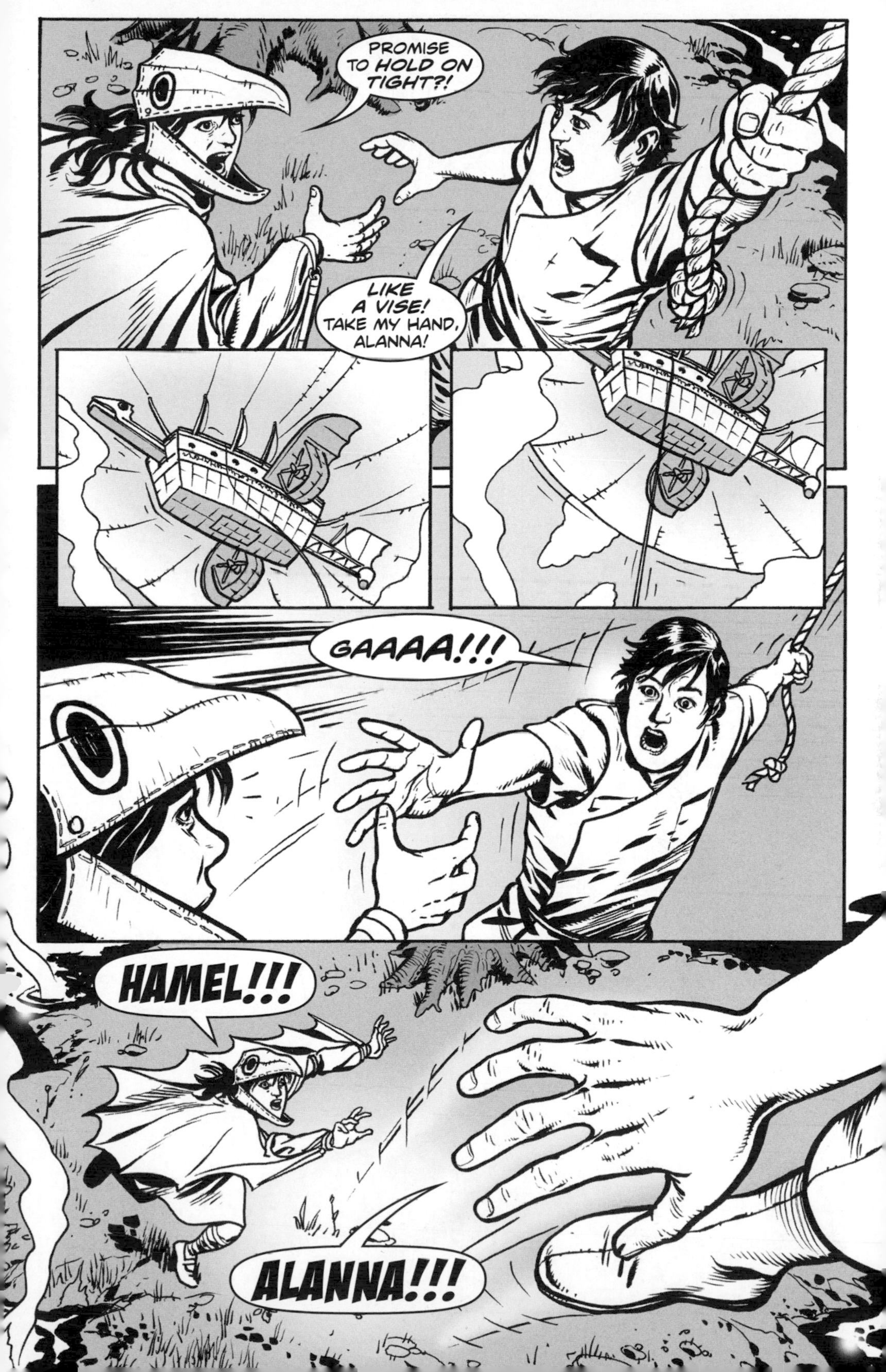
PROMISE TO HOLD ON TIGHT?!
LIKE A VISE! TAKE MY HAND, ALANNA!
GAAAA!!!
HAMEL!!!
ALANNA!!!

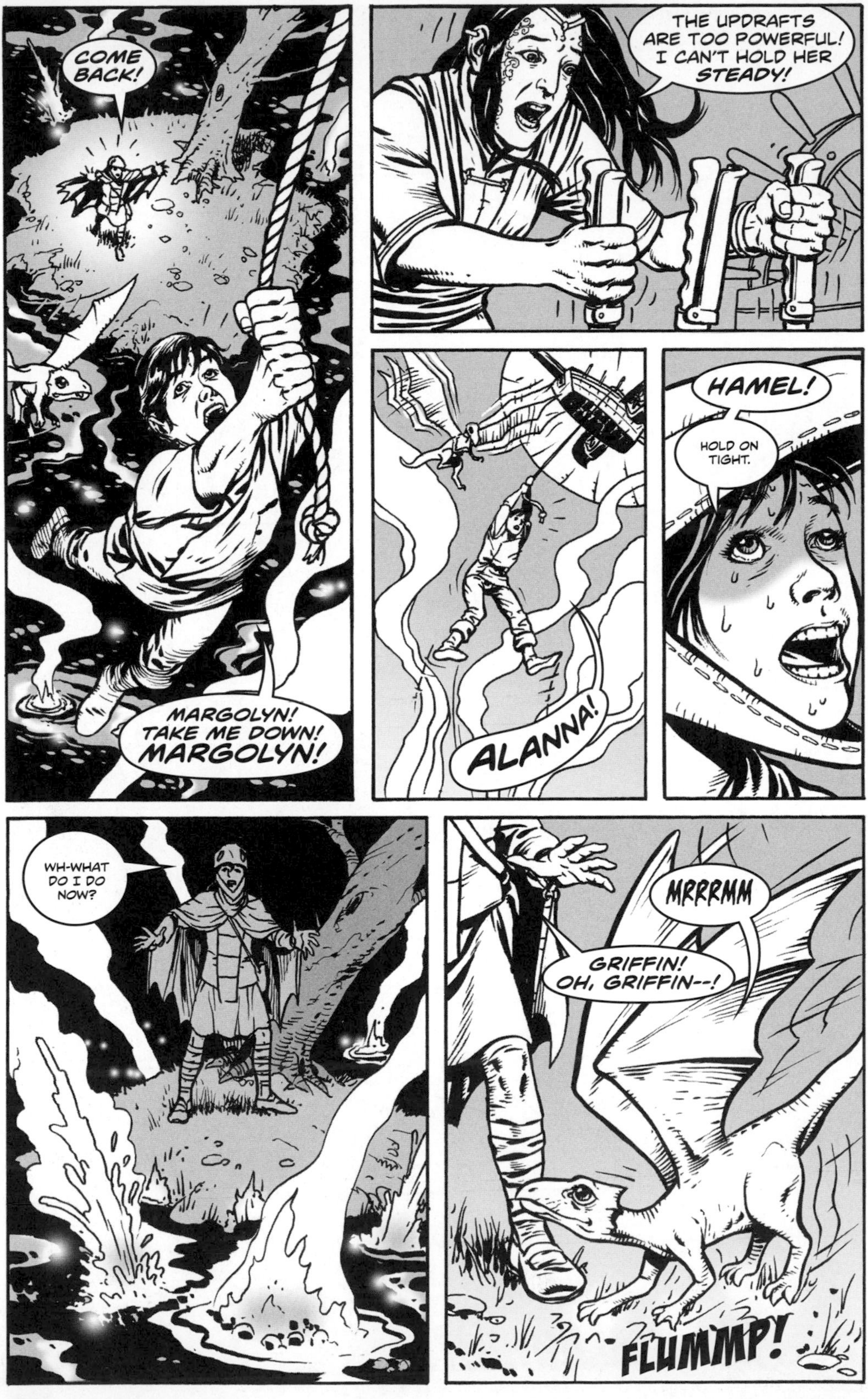
COME BACK!
MARGOLYN! TAKE ME DOWN! MARGOLYN!
THE UPDRAFTS ARE TOO POWERFUL! I CAN'T HOLD HER STEADY!
ALANNA!
HAMEL!
HOLD ON TIGHT.
WH-WHAT DO I DO NOW?
MRRRMM
GRIFFIN! OH, GRIFFIN--!
FLUMMP!

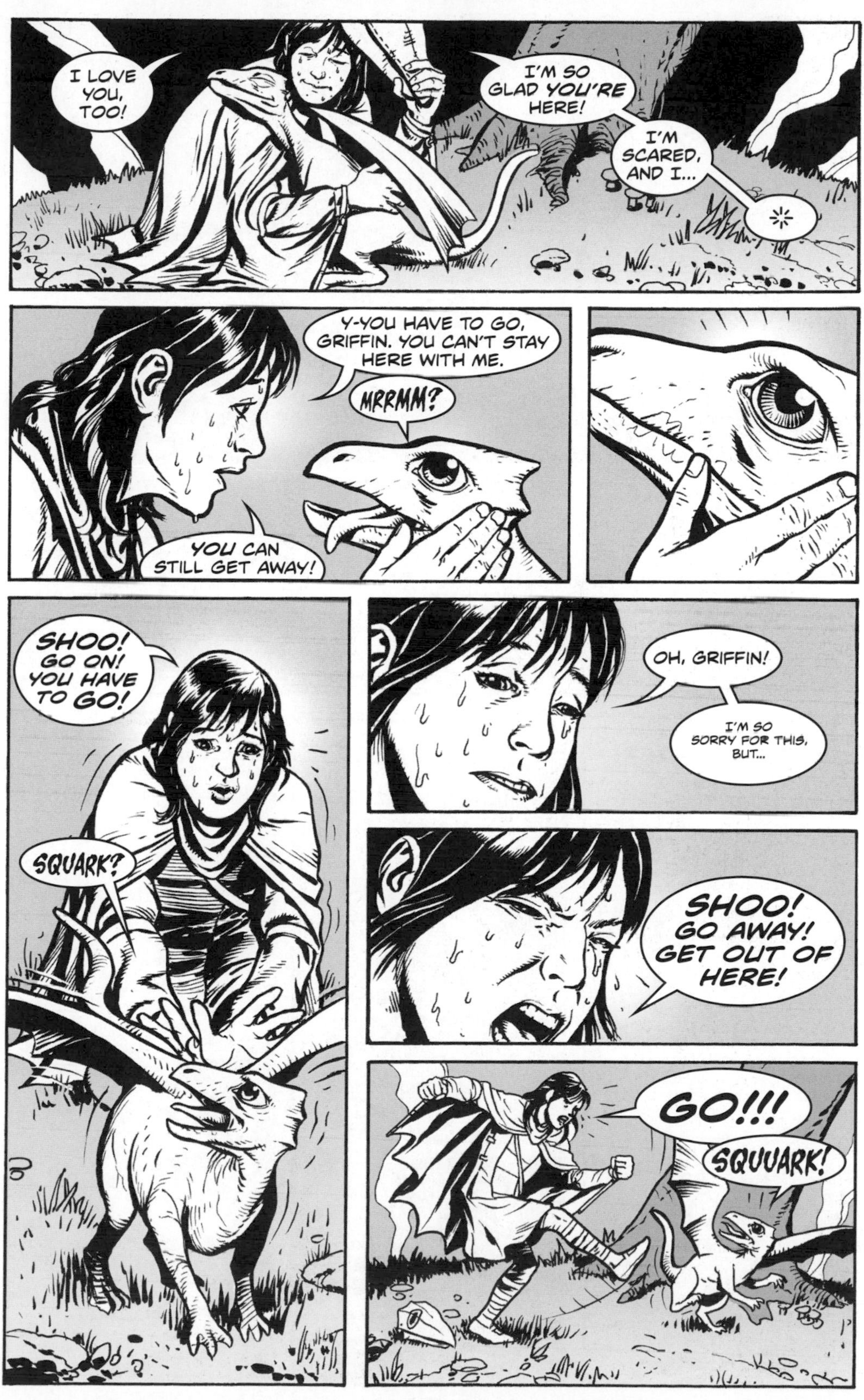
I LOVE YOU, TOO!
I'M SO GLAD YOU'RE HERE!
I'M SCARED, AND I...
Y-YOU HAVE TO GO, GRIFFIN. YOU CAN'T STAY HERE WITH ME.
MRRMM?
YOU CAN STILL GET AWAY!
SHOO! GO ON! YOU HAVE TO GO!
SQUARK?
OH, GRIFFIN!
I'M SO SORRY FOR THIS, BUT...
SHOO! GO AWAY! GET OUT OF HERE!
GO!!!
SQUUARK!

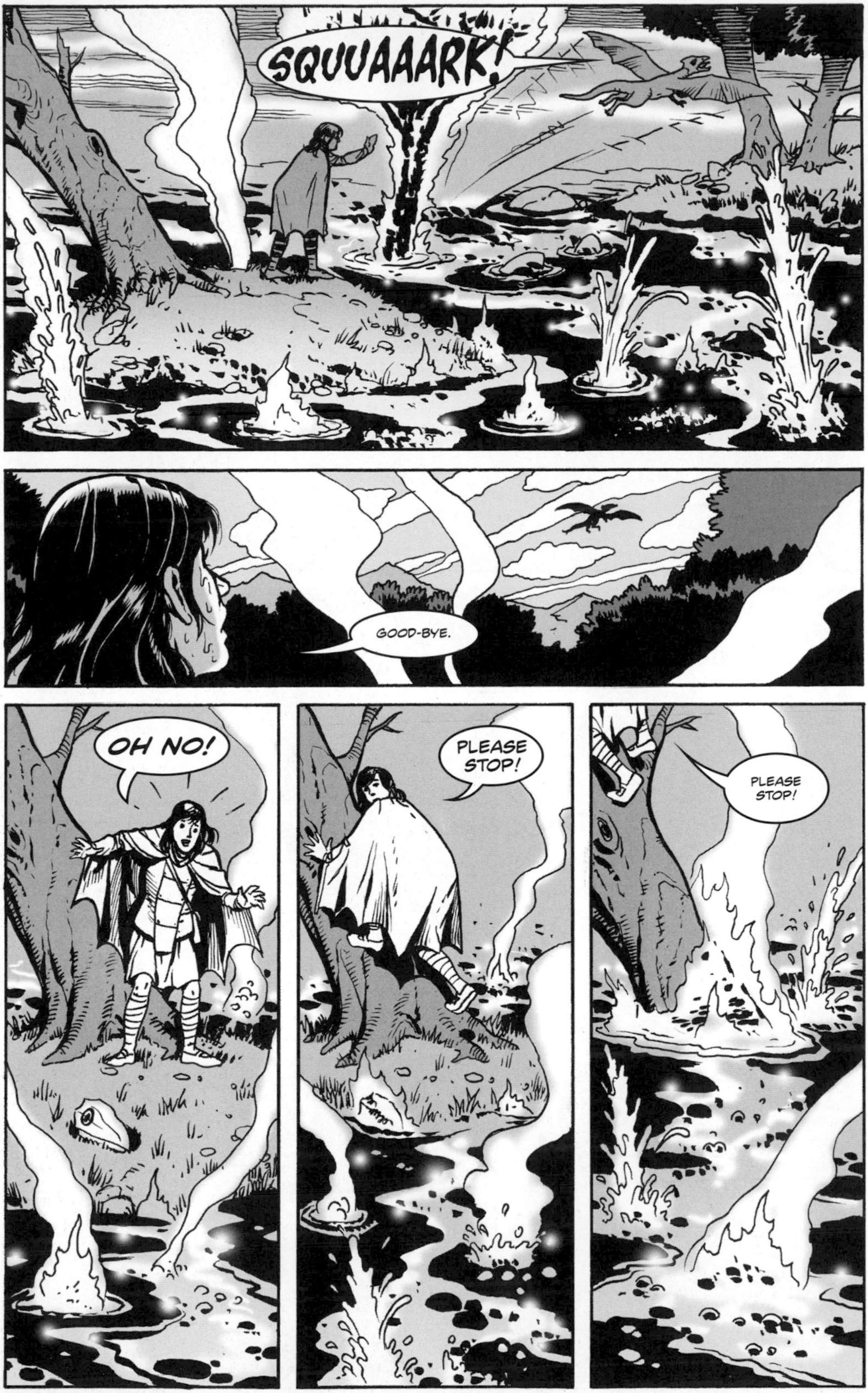
SQUUAAARK!
GOOD-BYE.
OH NO!
PLEASE STOP!
PLEASE STOP!

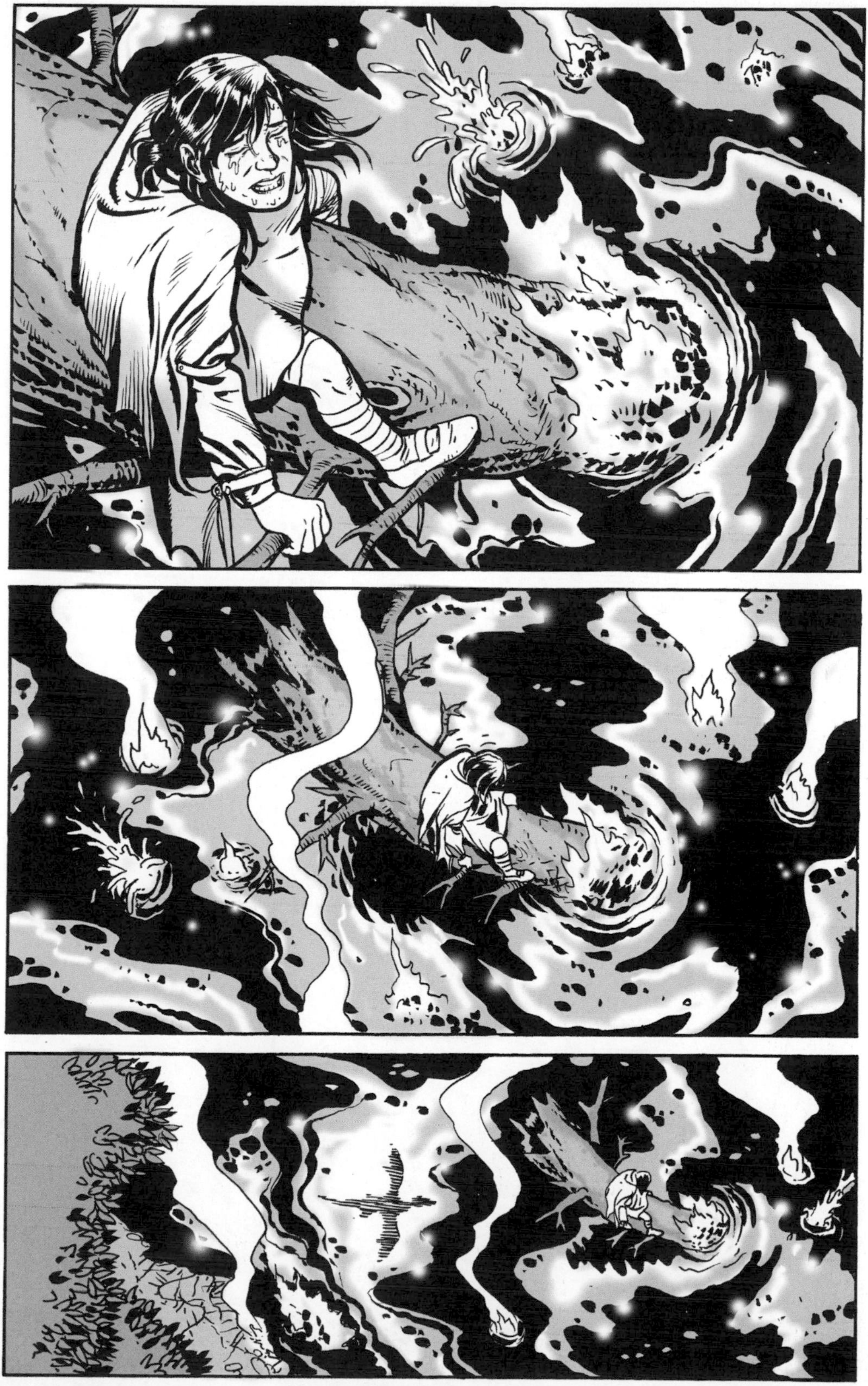

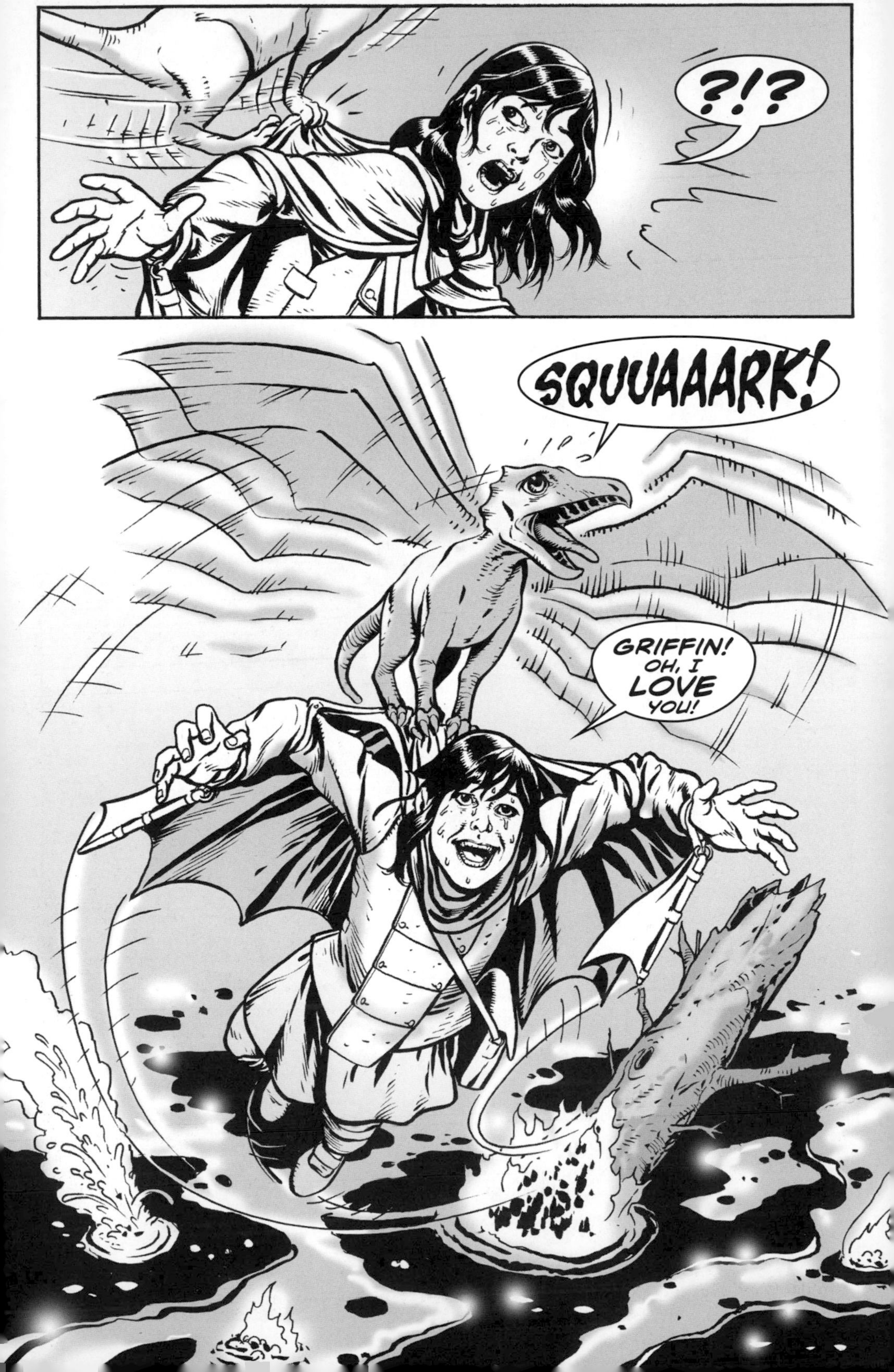
?!?
SQUUAAARK!
GRIFFIN! OH, I LOVE YOU!

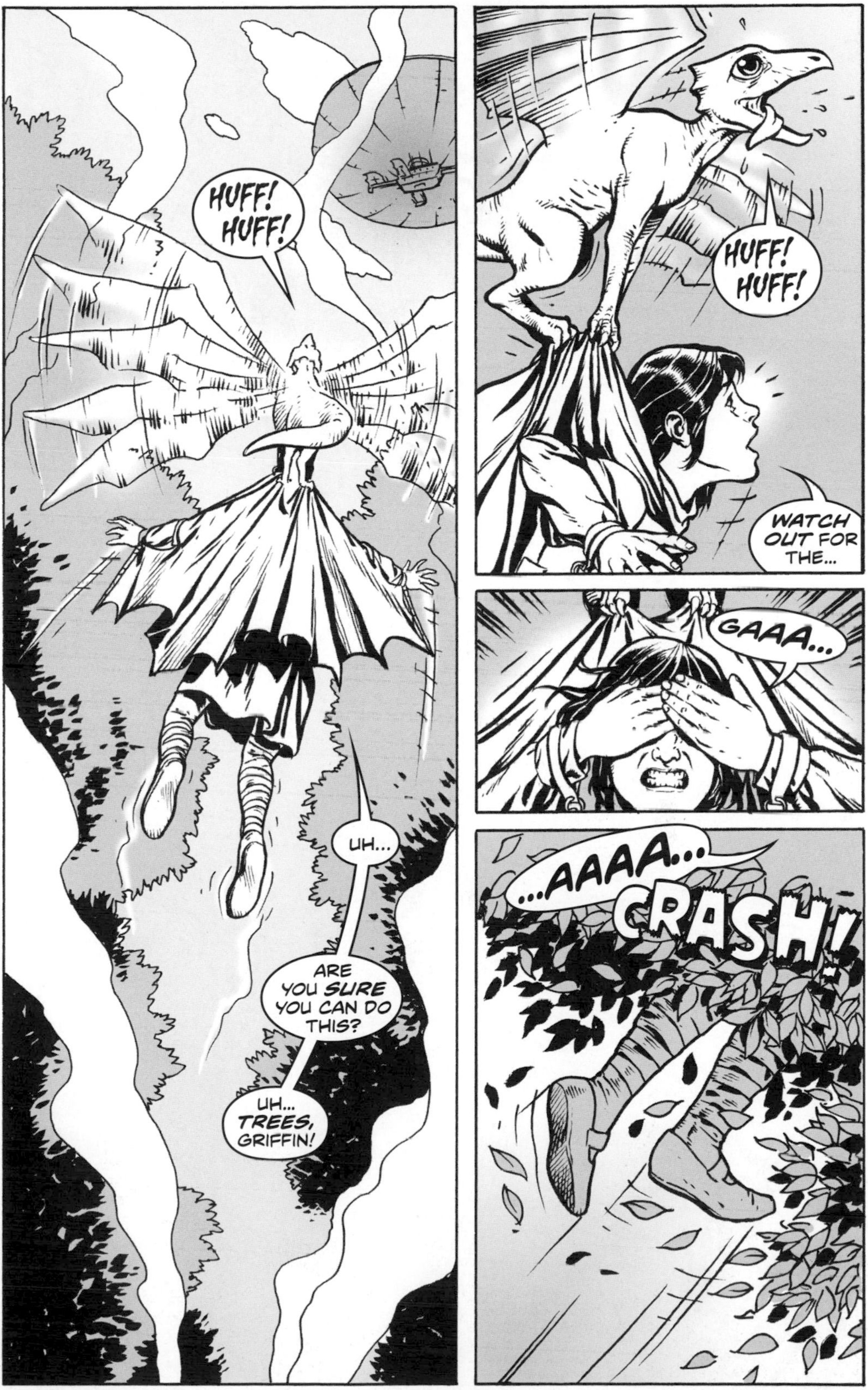
HUFF! HUFF!
UH...
ARE YOU SURE YOU CAN DO THIS?
UH... TREES, GRIFFIN!
HUFF! HUFF!
WATCH OUT FOR THE...
GAAA...
...AAAA...
CRASH!

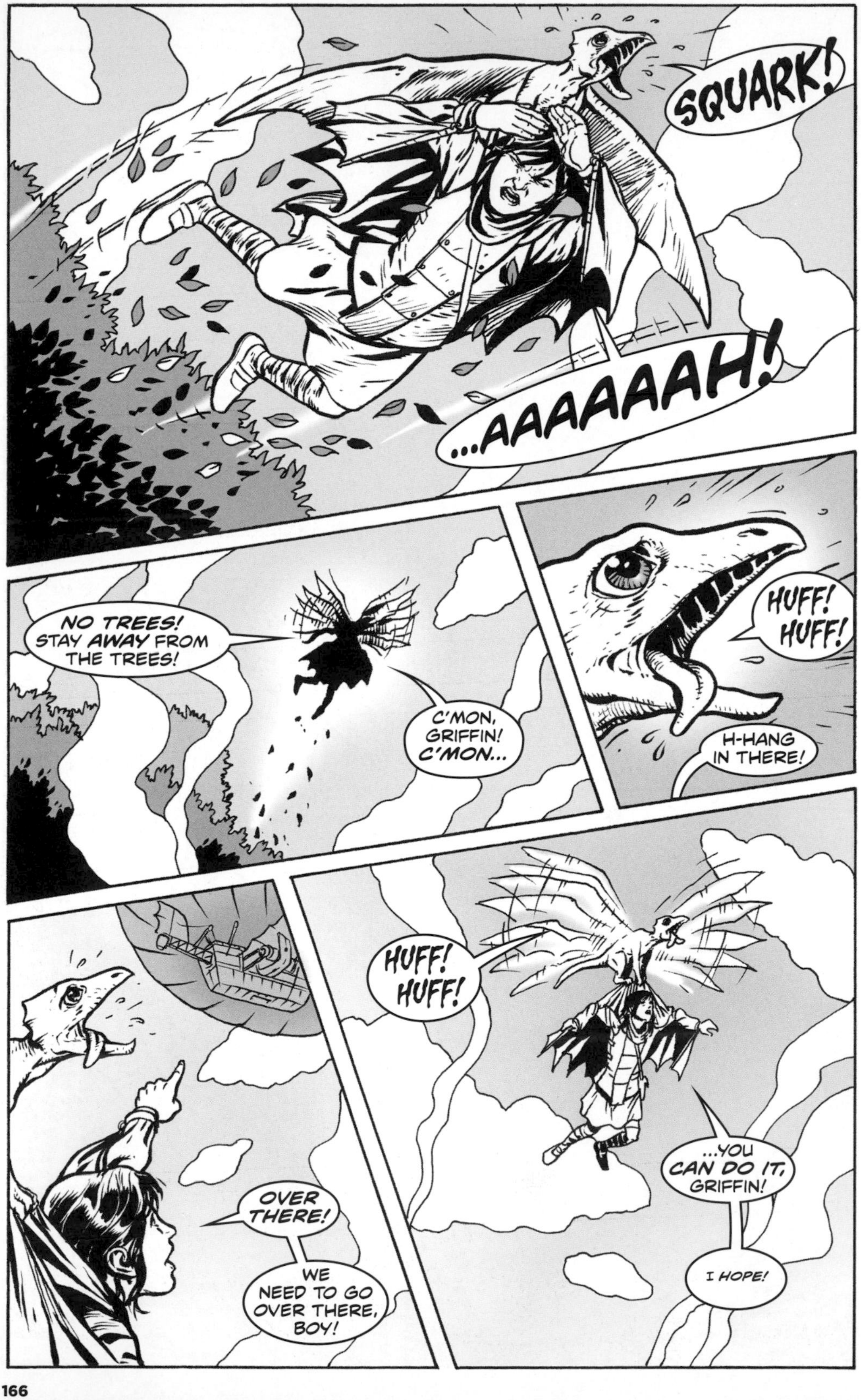
SQUARK!
...AAAAAAH!
NO TREES! STAY AWAY FROM THE TREES!
C'MON, GRIFFIN! C'MON...
HUFF! HUFF!
H-HANG IN THERE!
OVER THERE!
WE NEED TO GO OVER THERE, BOY!
HUFF! HUFF!
...YOU CAN DO IT, GRIFFIN!
I HOPE!

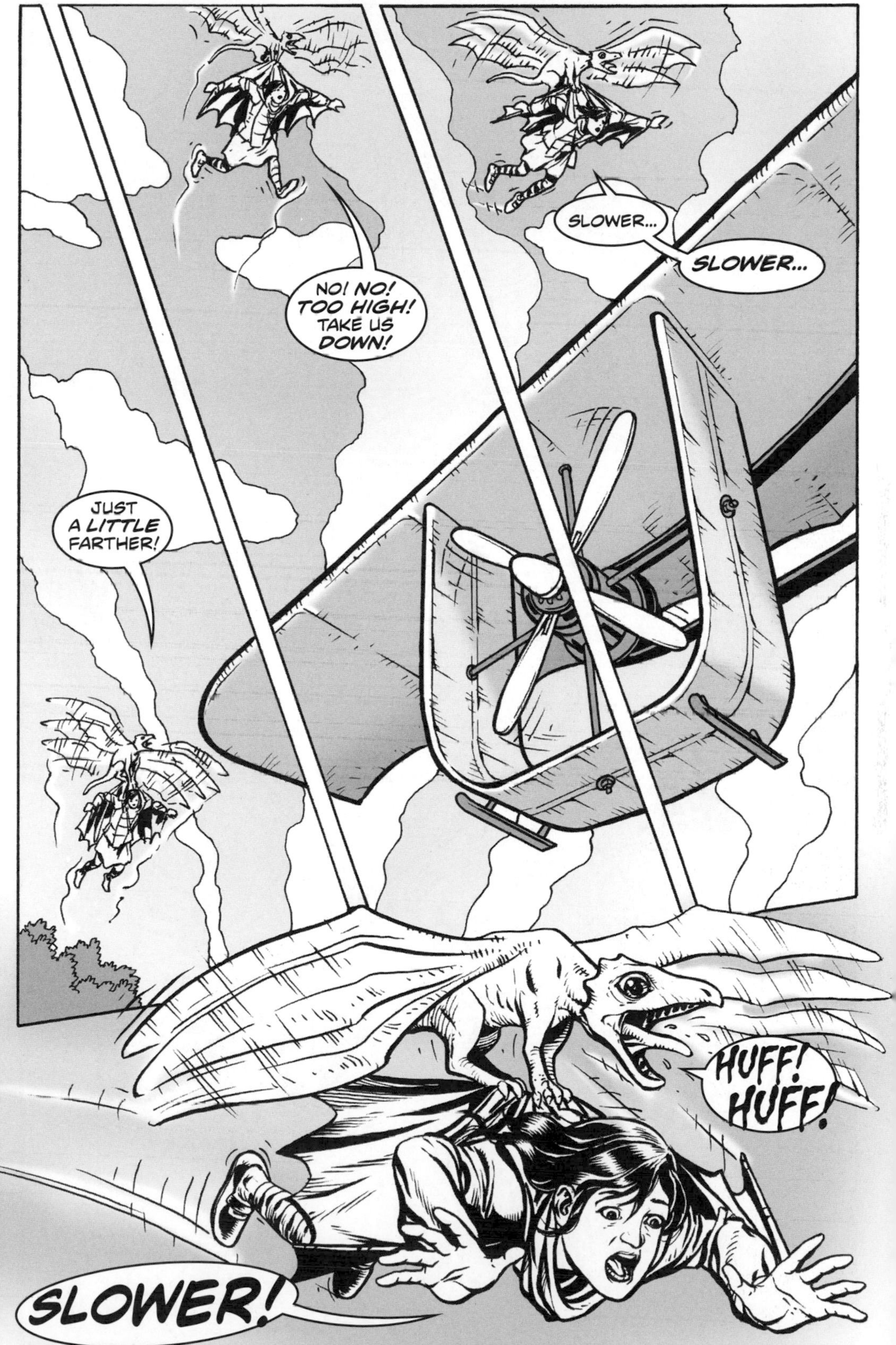
NO! NO! TOO HIGH! TAKE US DOWN!
SLOWER...
SLOWER...
JUST A LITTLE FARTHER!
HUFF! HUFF!
SLOWER!

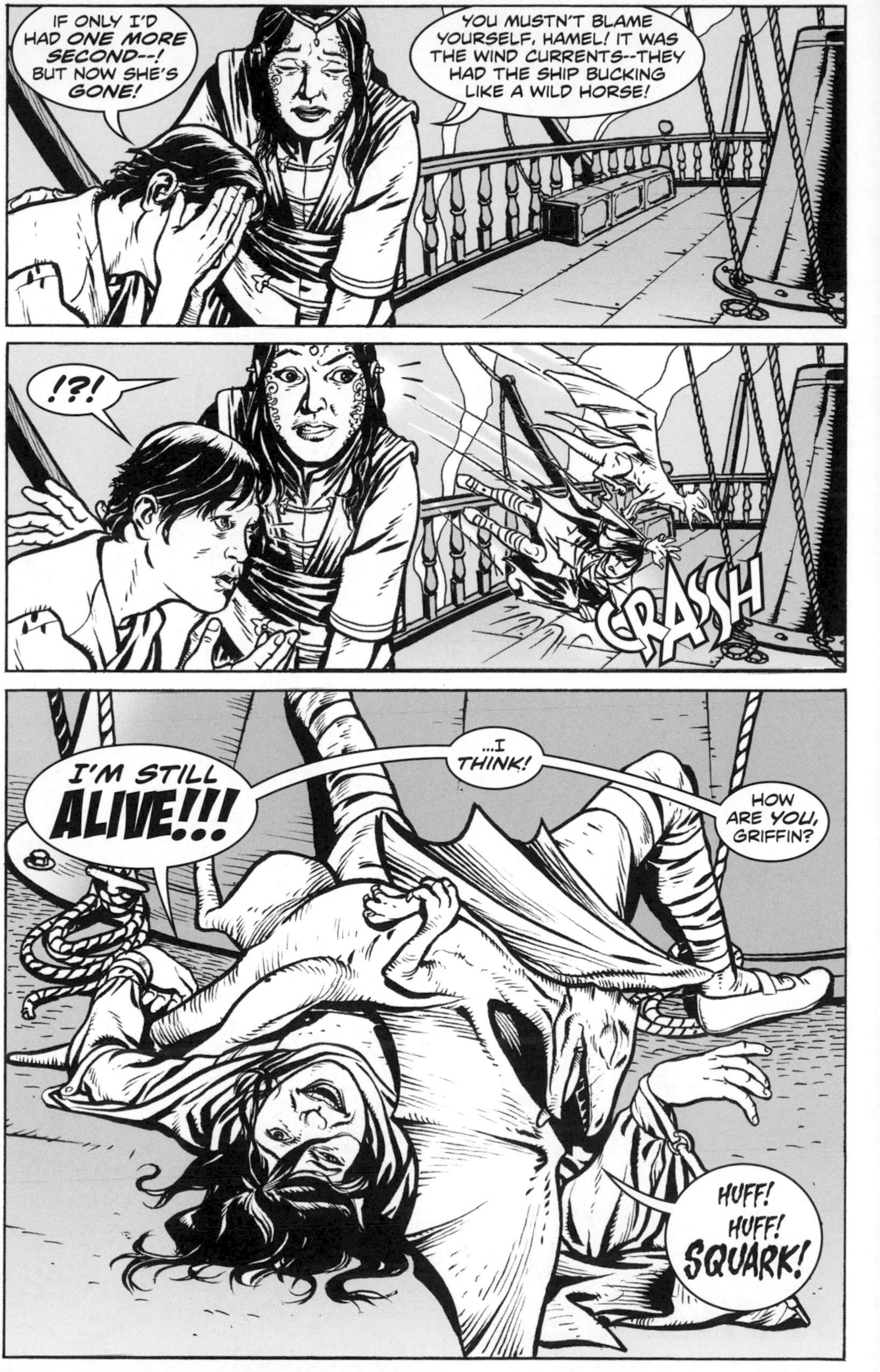
IF ONLY I'D HAD ONE MORE SECOND--! BUT NOW SHE'S GONE!
YOU MUSTN'T BLAME YOURSELF, HAMEL! IT WAS THE WIND CURRENTS--THEY HAD THE SHIP BUCKING LIKE A WILD HORSE!
!?!
CRASH
I'M STILL ALIVE!!!
...I THINK!
HOW ARE YOU, GRIFFIN?
HUFF! HUFF! SQUARK!

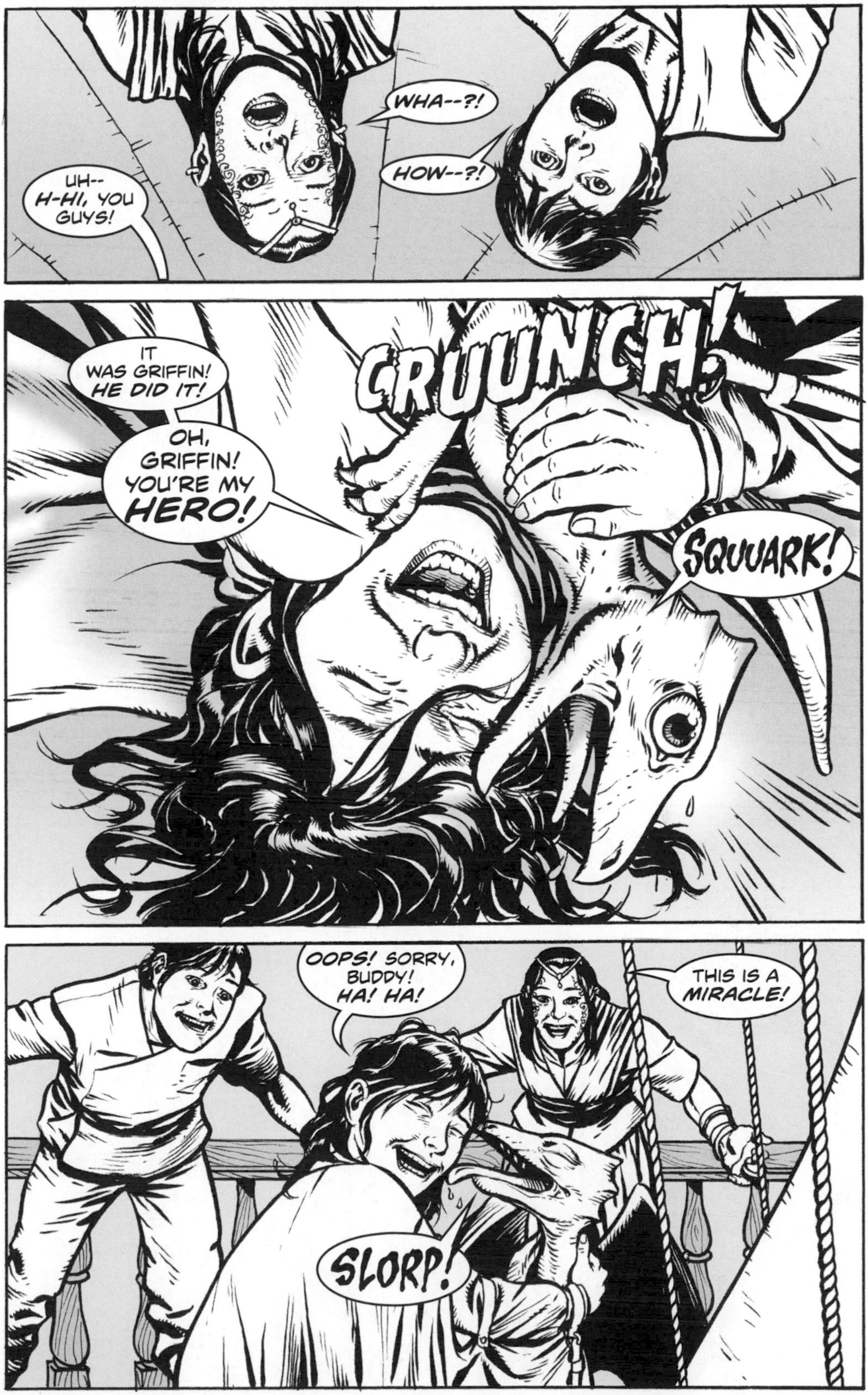
UH-- H-HI, YOU GUYS!
WHA--?!
HOW--?!
CRUUNCH!
IT WAS GRIFFIN! HE DID IT!
OH, GRIFFIN! YOU'RE MY HERO!
SQUUARK!
OOPS! SORRY, BUDDY! HA! HA!
THIS IS A MIRACLE!
SLORP!

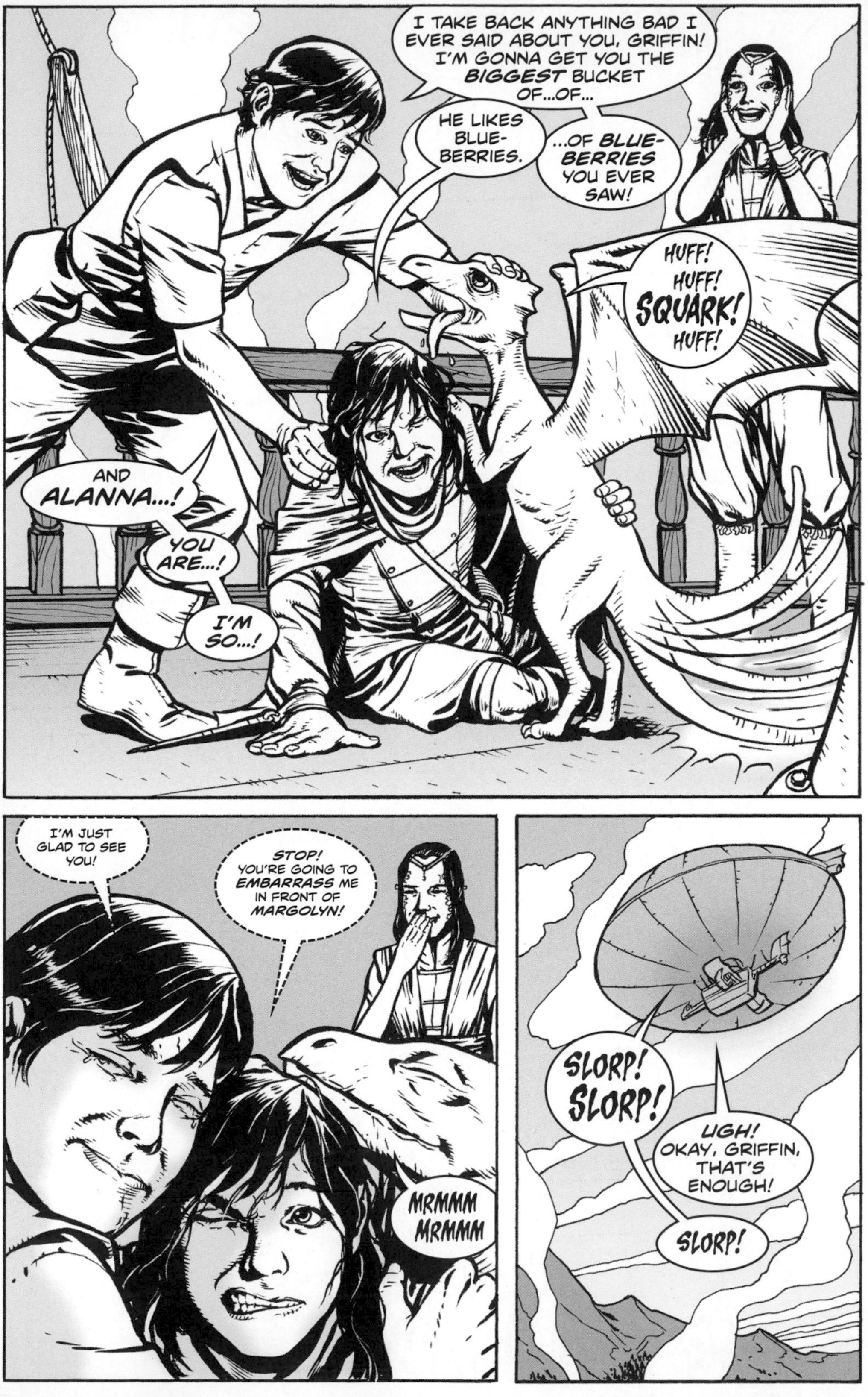
I TAKE BACK ANYTHING BAD I EVER SAID ABOUT YOU, GRIFFIN! I'M GONNA GET YOU THE BIGGEST BUCKET OF...OF...
HE LIKES BLUE-BERRIES.
...OF BLUE-BERRIES YOU EVER SAW!
HUFF! HUFF! SQUARK! HUFF!
AND ALANNA...!
YOU ARE...!
I'M SO...!
I'M JUST GLAD TO SEE YOU!
STOP! YOU'RE GOING TO EMBARRASS ME IN FRONT OF MARGOLYN!
MRMMM MRMMM
SLORP! SLORP!
UGH! OKAY, GRIFFIN, THAT'S ENOUGH!
SLORP!

CHAPTER NINE

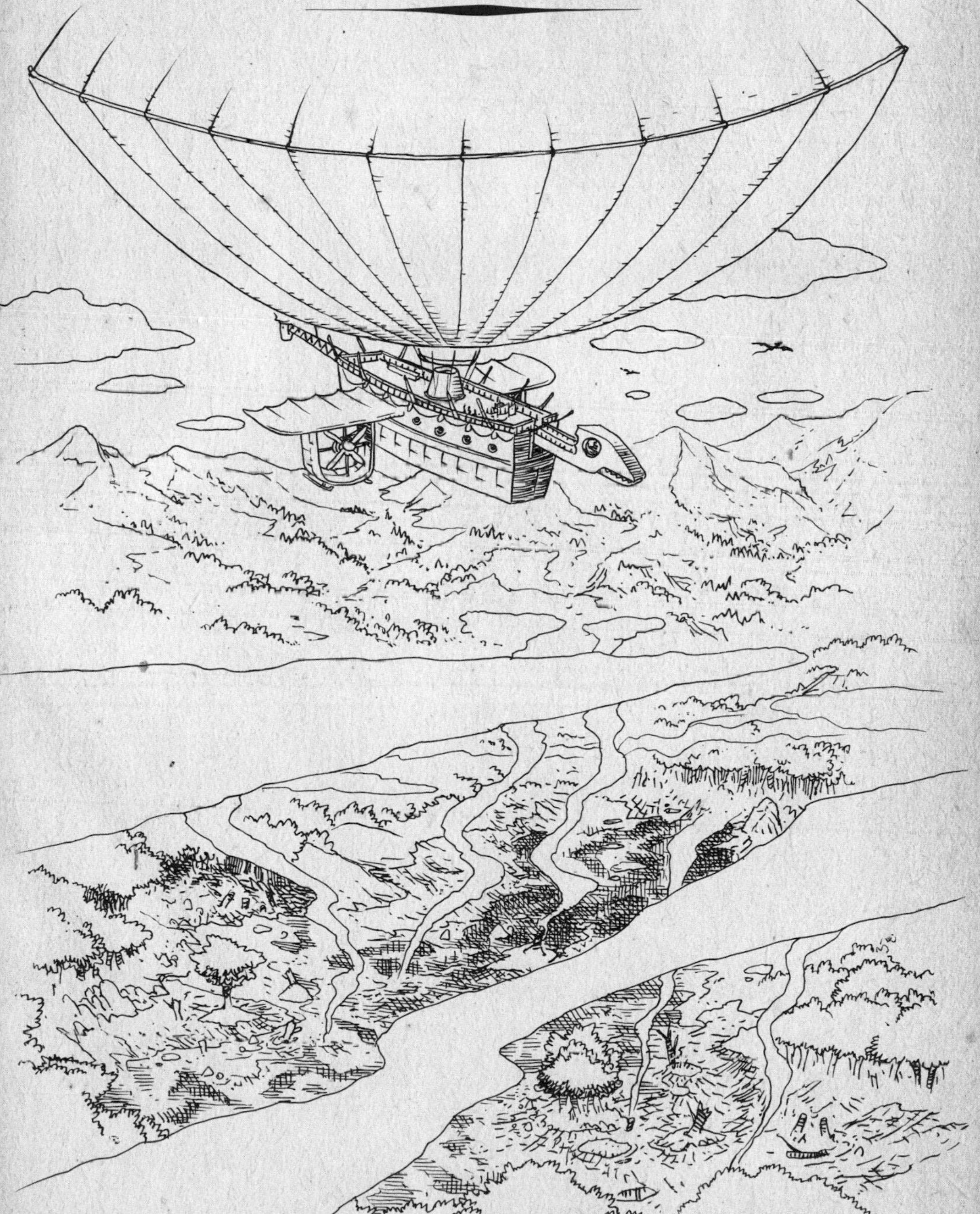

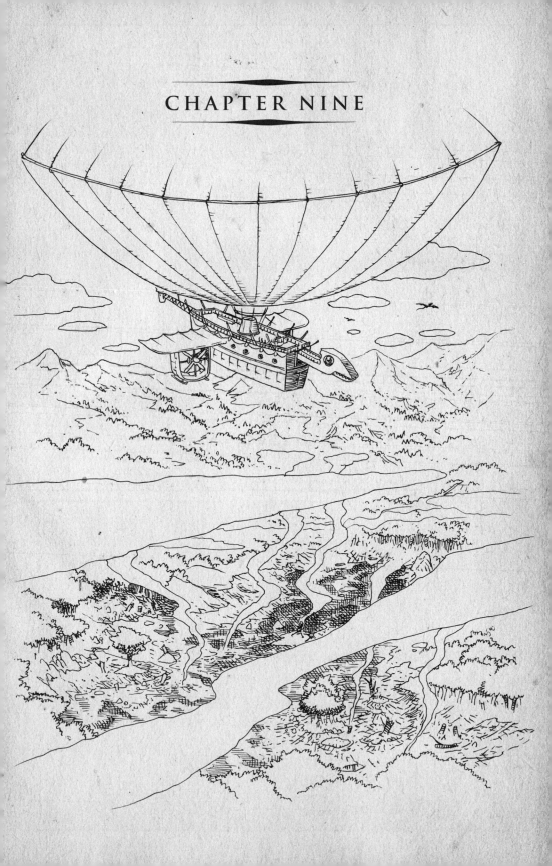

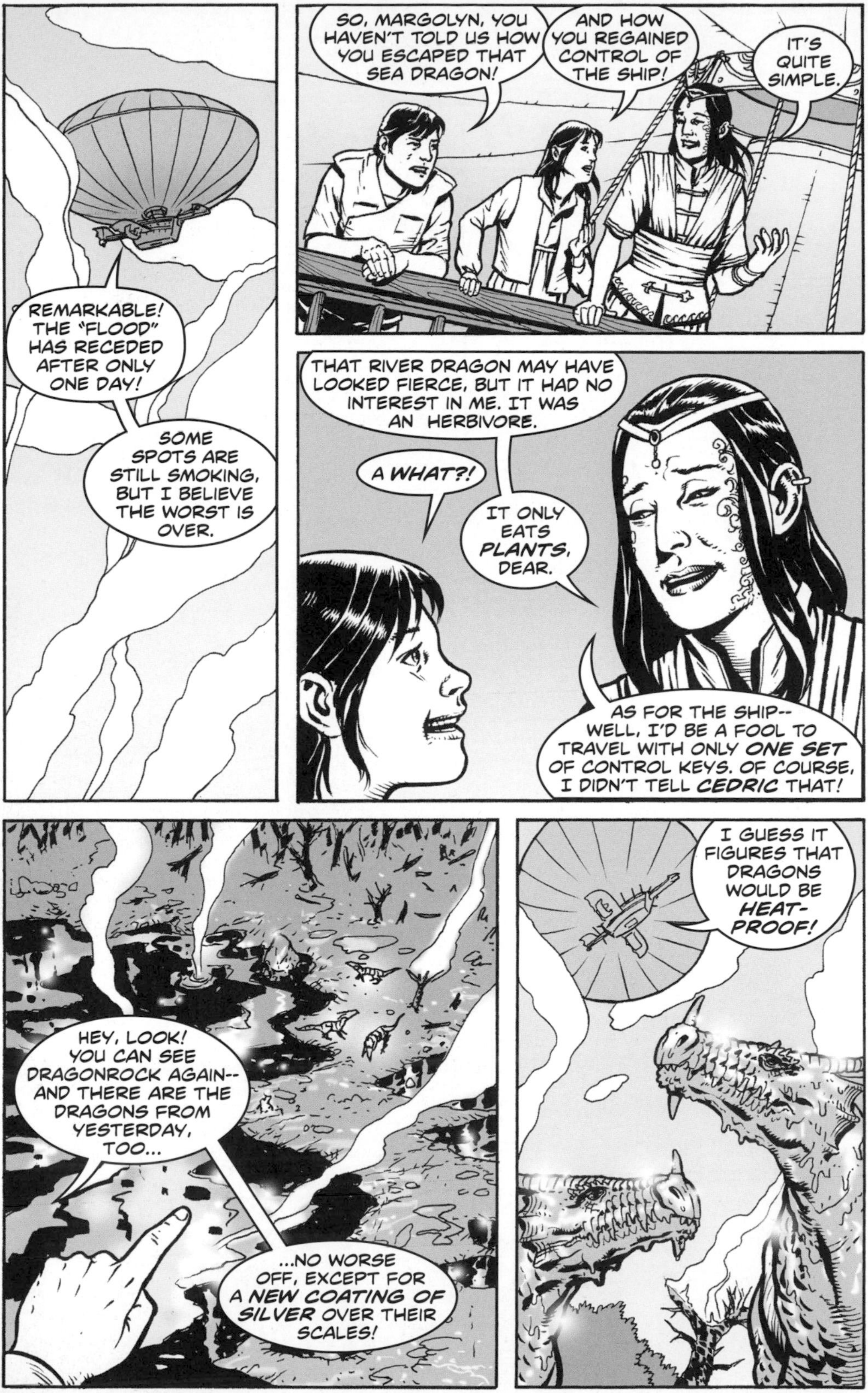
REMARKABLE! THE "FLOOD" HAS RECEDED AFTER ONLY ONE DAY!
SOME SPOTS ARE STILL SMOKING, BUT I BELIEVE THE WORST IS OVER.
SO, MARGOLYN, YOU HAVEN'T TOLD US HOW YOU ESCAPED THAT SEA DRAGON!
AND HOW YOU REGAINED CONTROL OF THE SHIP!
IT'S QUITE SIMPLE.
THAT RIVER DRAGON MAY HAVE LOOKED FIERCE, BUT IT HAD NO INTEREST IN ME. IT WAS AN HERBIVORE.
A WHAT?!
IT ONLY EATS PLANTS, DEAR.
AS FOR THE SHIP-- WELL, I'D BE A FOOL TO TRAVEL WITH ONLY ONE SET OF CONTROL KEYS. OF COURSE, I DIDN'T TELL CEDRIC THAT!
HEY, LOOK! YOU CAN SEE DRAGONROCK AGAIN-- AND THERE ARE THE DRAGONS FROM YESTERDAY, TOO...
...NO WORSE OFF, EXCEPT FOR A NEW COATING OF SILVER OVER THEIR SCALES!
I GUESS IT FIGURES THAT DRAGONS WOULD BE HEAT-PROOF!

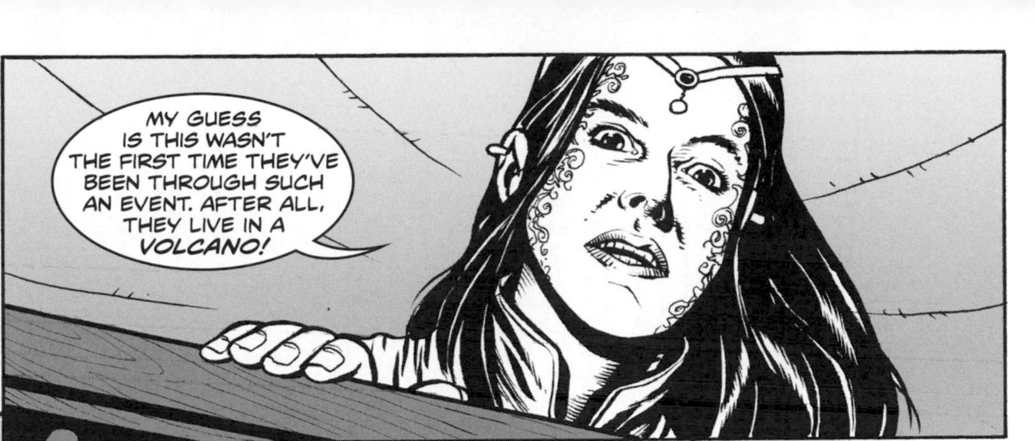
MY GUESS IS THIS WASN'T THE FIRST TIME THEY'VE BEEN THROUGH SUCH AN EVENT. AFTER ALL, THEY LIVE IN A *VOLCANO!*

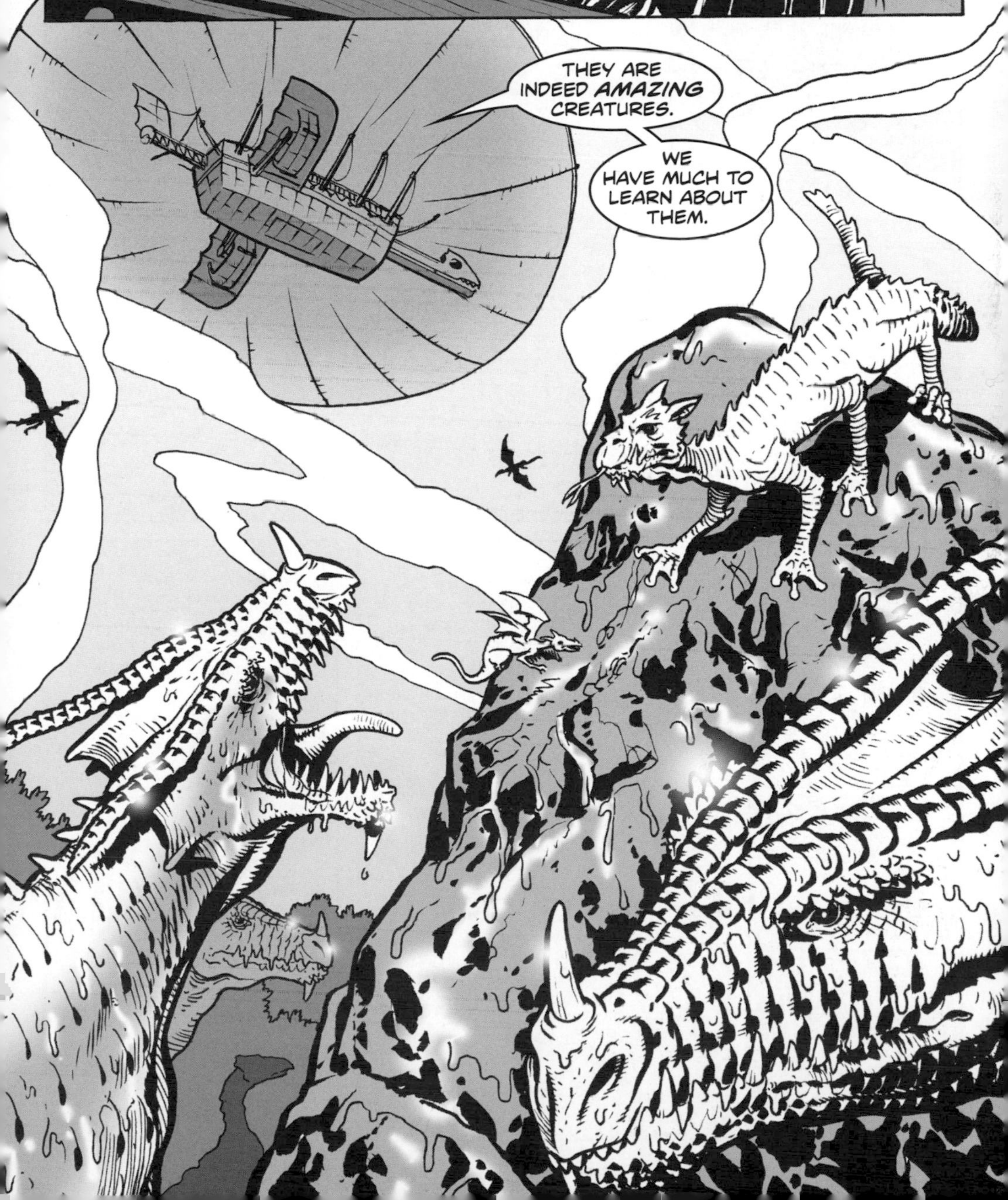
THEY ARE INDEED *AMAZING* CREATURES.
WE HAVE MUCH TO LEARN ABOUT THEM.

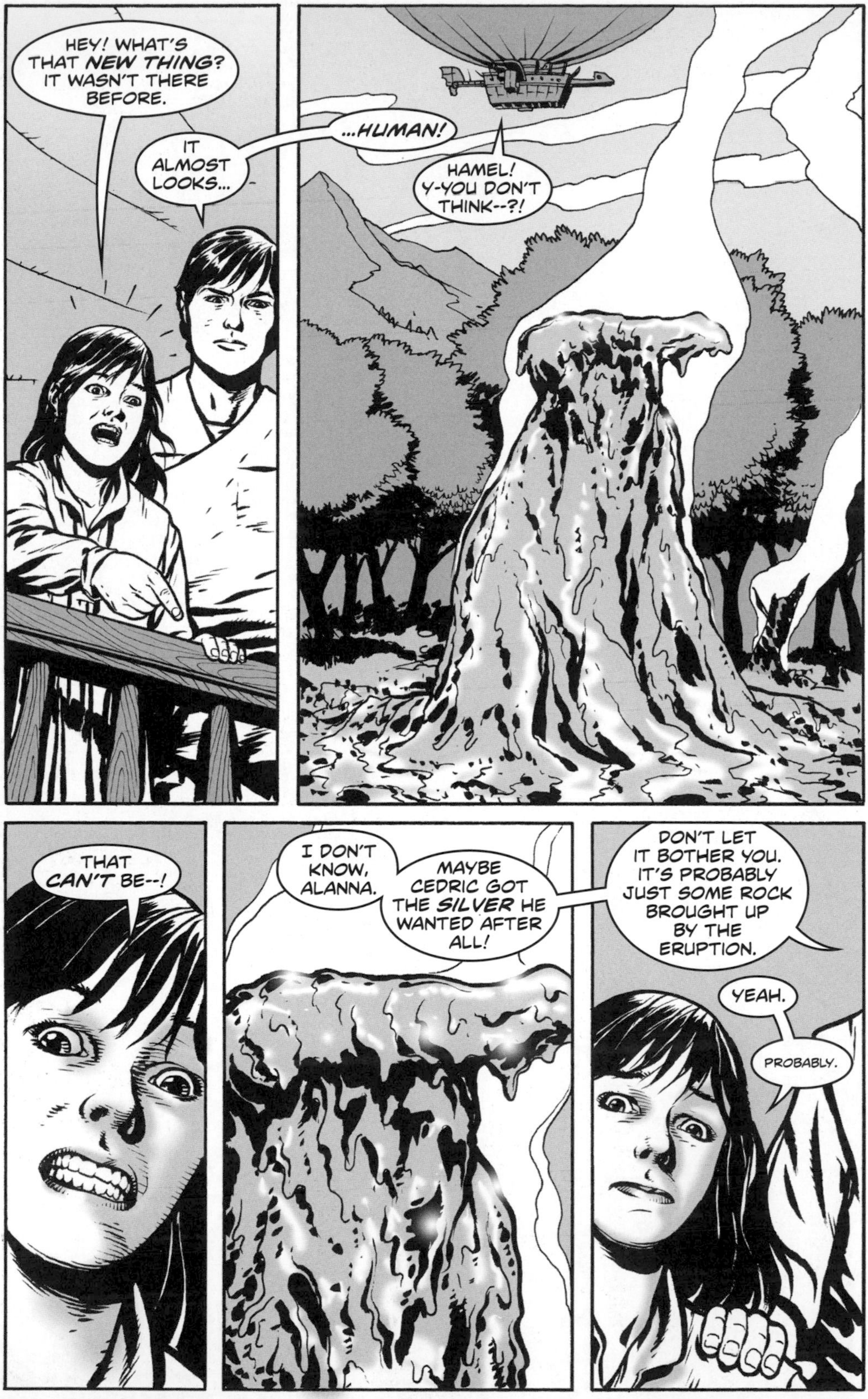
HEY! WHAT'S THAT NEW THING? IT WASN'T THERE BEFORE.
IT ALMOST LOOKS...
...HUMAN!
HAMEL! Y-YOU DON'T THINK--?!
THAT CAN'T BE--!
I DON'T KNOW, ALANNA.
MAYBE CEDRIC GOT THE SILVER HE WANTED AFTER ALL!
DON'T LET IT BOTHER YOU. IT'S PROBABLY JUST SOME ROCK BROUGHT UP BY THE ERUPTION.
YEAH.
PROBABLY.

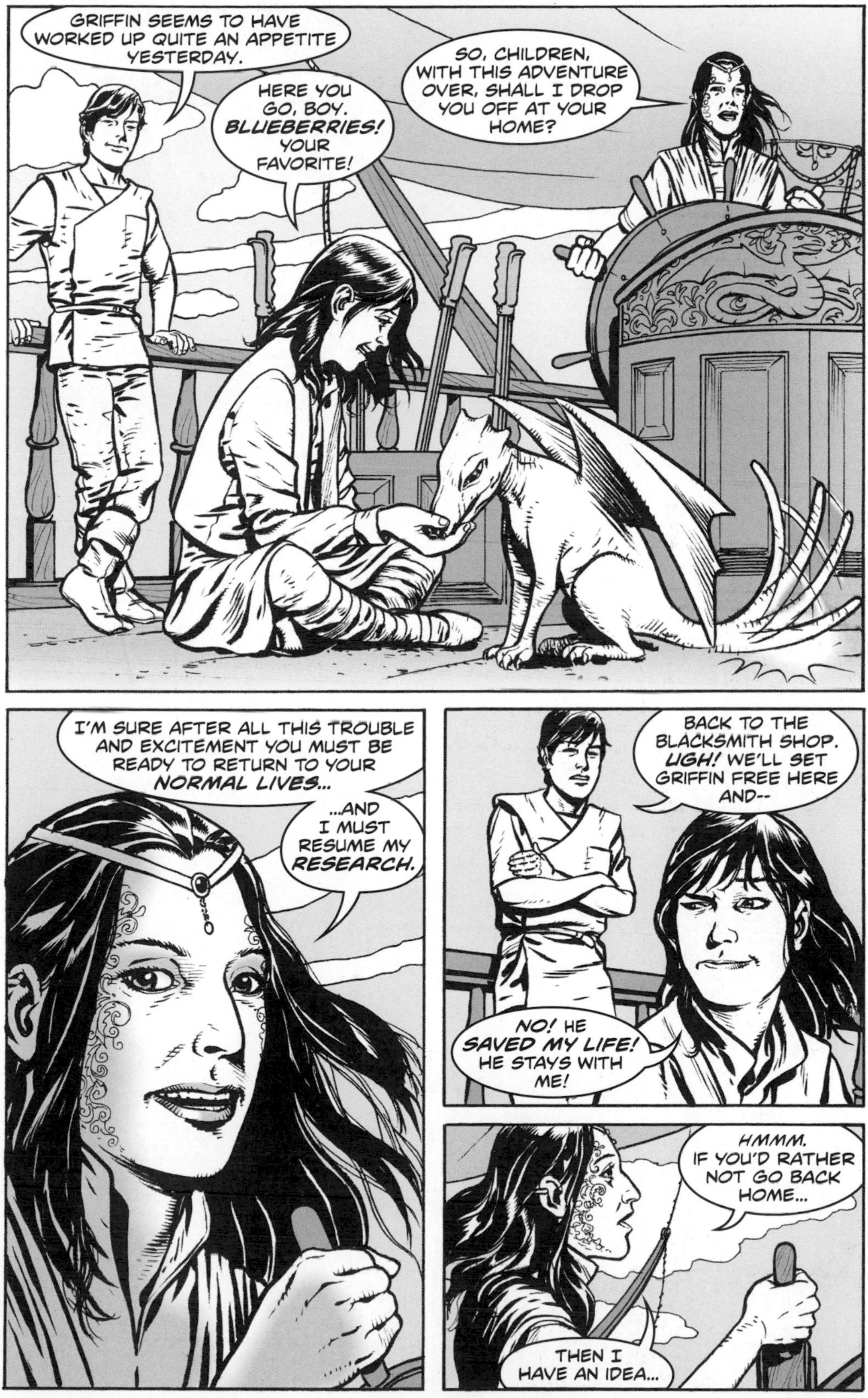
GRIFFIN SEEMS TO HAVE WORKED UP QUITE AN APPETITE YESTERDAY.
HERE YOU GO, BOY. BLUEBERRIES! YOUR FAVORITE!
SO, CHILDREN, WITH THIS ADVENTURE OVER, SHALL I DROP YOU OFF AT YOUR HOME?
I'M SURE AFTER ALL THIS TROUBLE AND EXCITEMENT YOU MUST BE READY TO RETURN TO YOUR NORMAL LIVES...
...AND I MUST RESUME MY RESEARCH.
BACK TO THE BLACKSMITH SHOP. UGH! WE'LL SET GRIFFIN FREE HERE AND--
NO! HE SAVED MY LIFE! HE STAYS WITH ME!
HMMM. IF YOU'D RATHER NOT GO BACK HOME...
THEN I HAVE AN IDEA...

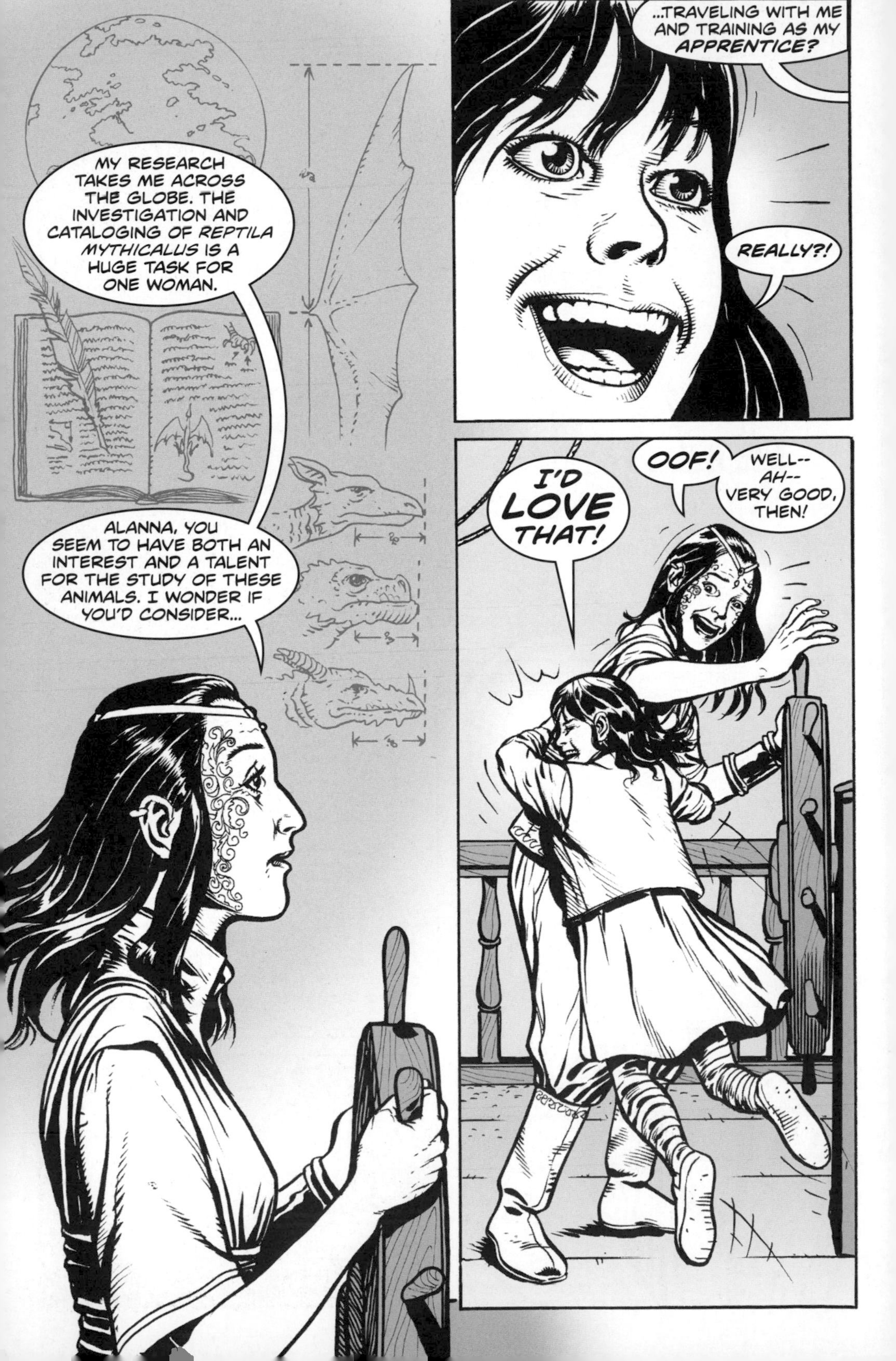

MY RESEARCH TAKES ME ACROSS THE GLOBE. THE INVESTIGATION AND CATALOGING OF *REPTILA MYTHICALUS* IS A HUGE TASK FOR ONE WOMAN.
ALANNA, YOU SEEM TO HAVE BOTH AN INTEREST AND A TALENT FOR THE STUDY OF THESE ANIMALS. I WONDER IF YOU'D CONSIDER...
...TRAVELING WITH ME AND TRAINING AS MY *APPRENTICE*?
REALLY?!
I'D **LOVE** THAT!
OOF!
WELL-- *AH*-- VERY GOOD, THEN!

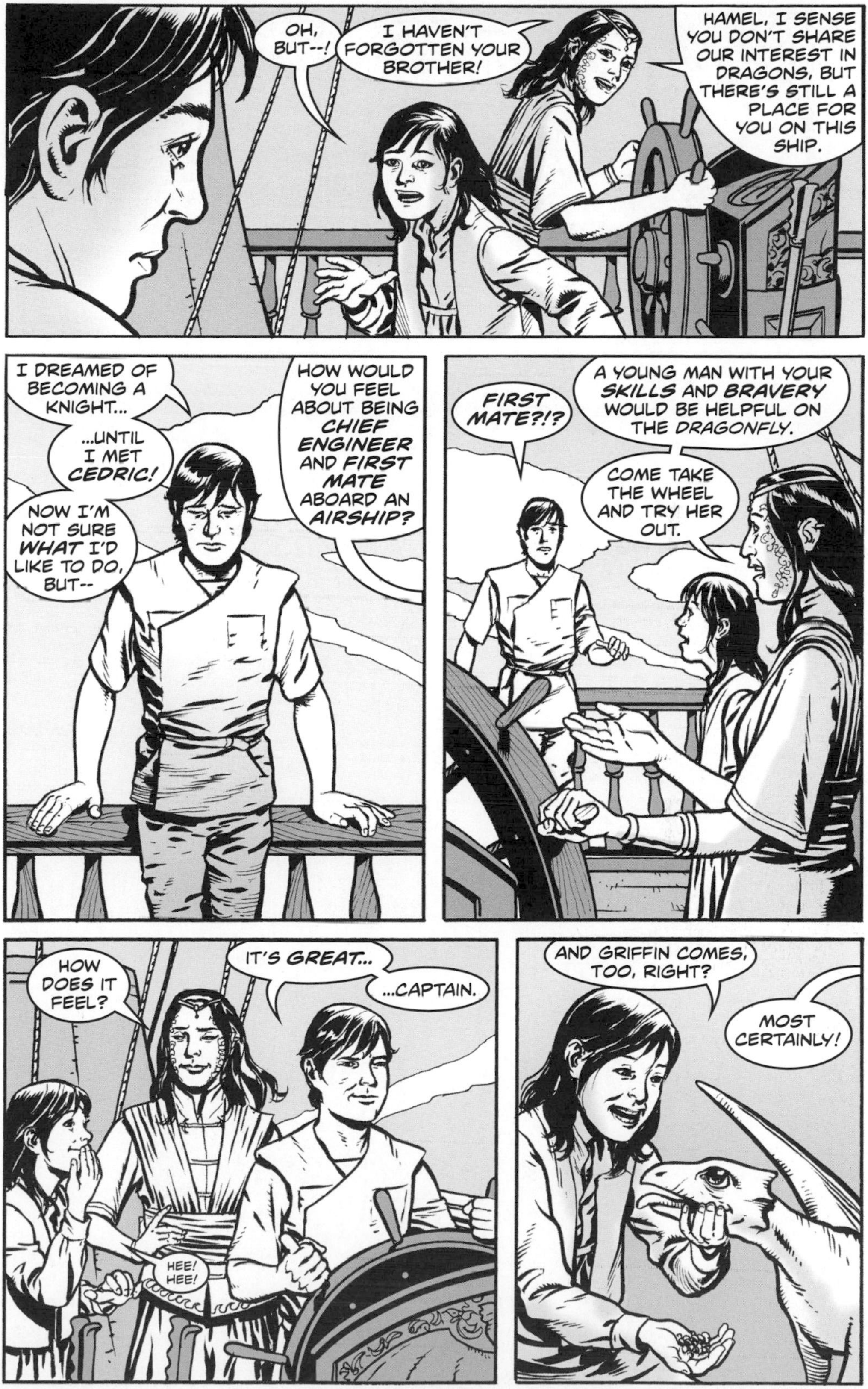
OH, BUT--!
I HAVEN'T FORGOTTEN YOUR BROTHER!
HAMEL, I SENSE YOU DON'T SHARE OUR INTEREST IN DRAGONS, BUT THERE'S STILL A PLACE FOR YOU ON THIS SHIP.
I DREAMED OF BECOMING A KNIGHT...
...UNTIL I MET CEDRIC!
NOW I'M NOT SURE WHAT I'D LIKE TO DO, BUT--
HOW WOULD YOU FEEL ABOUT BEING CHIEF ENGINEER AND FIRST MATE ABOARD AN AIRSHIP?
FIRST MATE?!?
A YOUNG MAN WITH YOUR SKILLS AND BRAVERY WOULD BE HELPFUL ON THE DRAGONFLY.
COME TAKE THE WHEEL AND TRY HER OUT.
HOW DOES IT FEEL?
IT'S GREAT...
...CAPTAIN.
HEE! HEE!
AND GRIFFIN COMES, TOO, RIGHT?
MOST CERTAINLY!

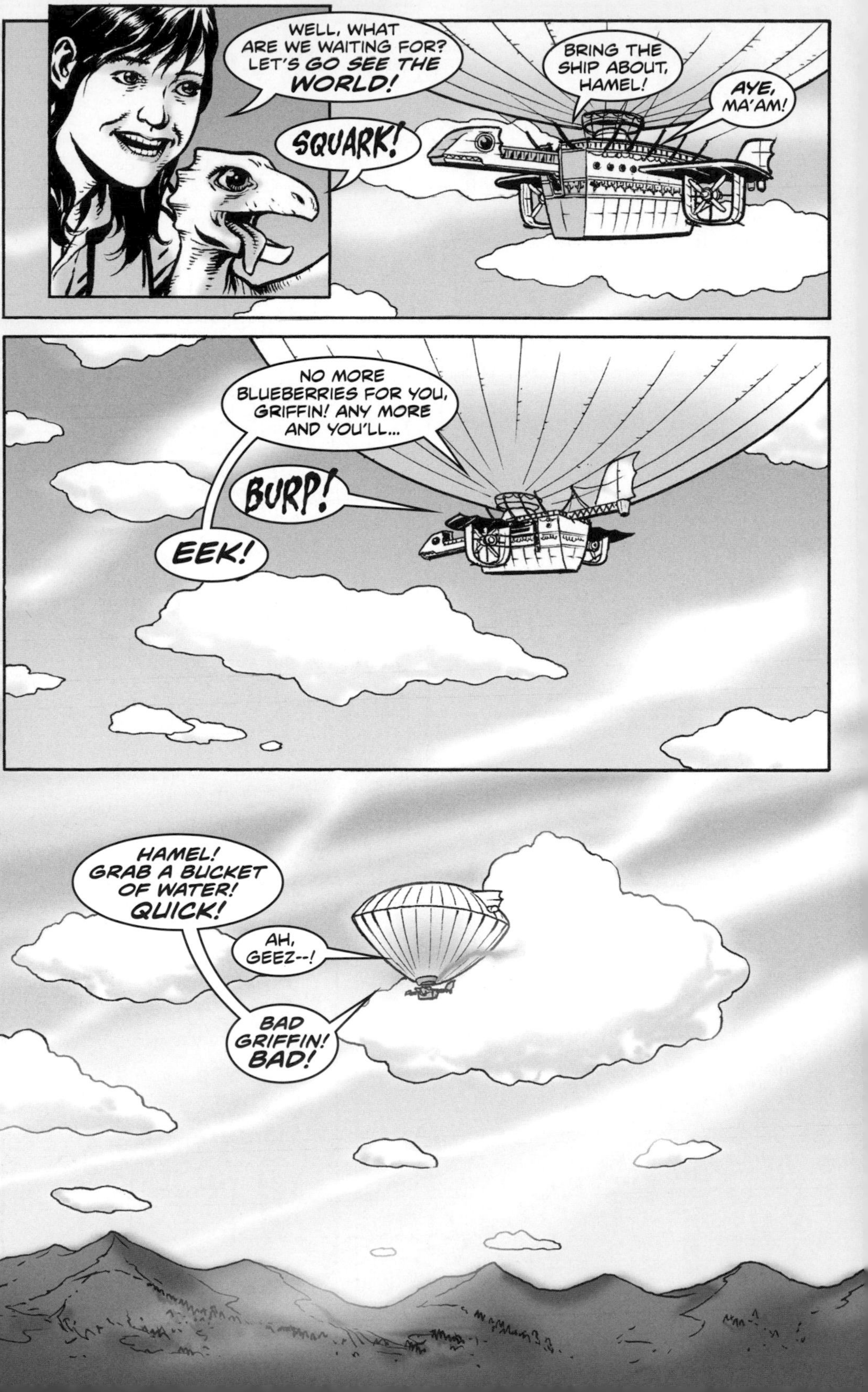

WELL, WHAT ARE WE WAITING FOR? LET'S GO SEE THE WORLD!
SQUARK!
BRING THE SHIP ABOUT, HAMEL!
AYE, MA'AM!
NO MORE BLUEBERRIES FOR YOU, GRIFFIN! ANY MORE AND YOU'LL...
BURP!
EEK!
HAMEL! GRAB A BUCKET OF WATER! QUICK!
AH, GEEZ--!
BAD GRIFFIN! BAD!

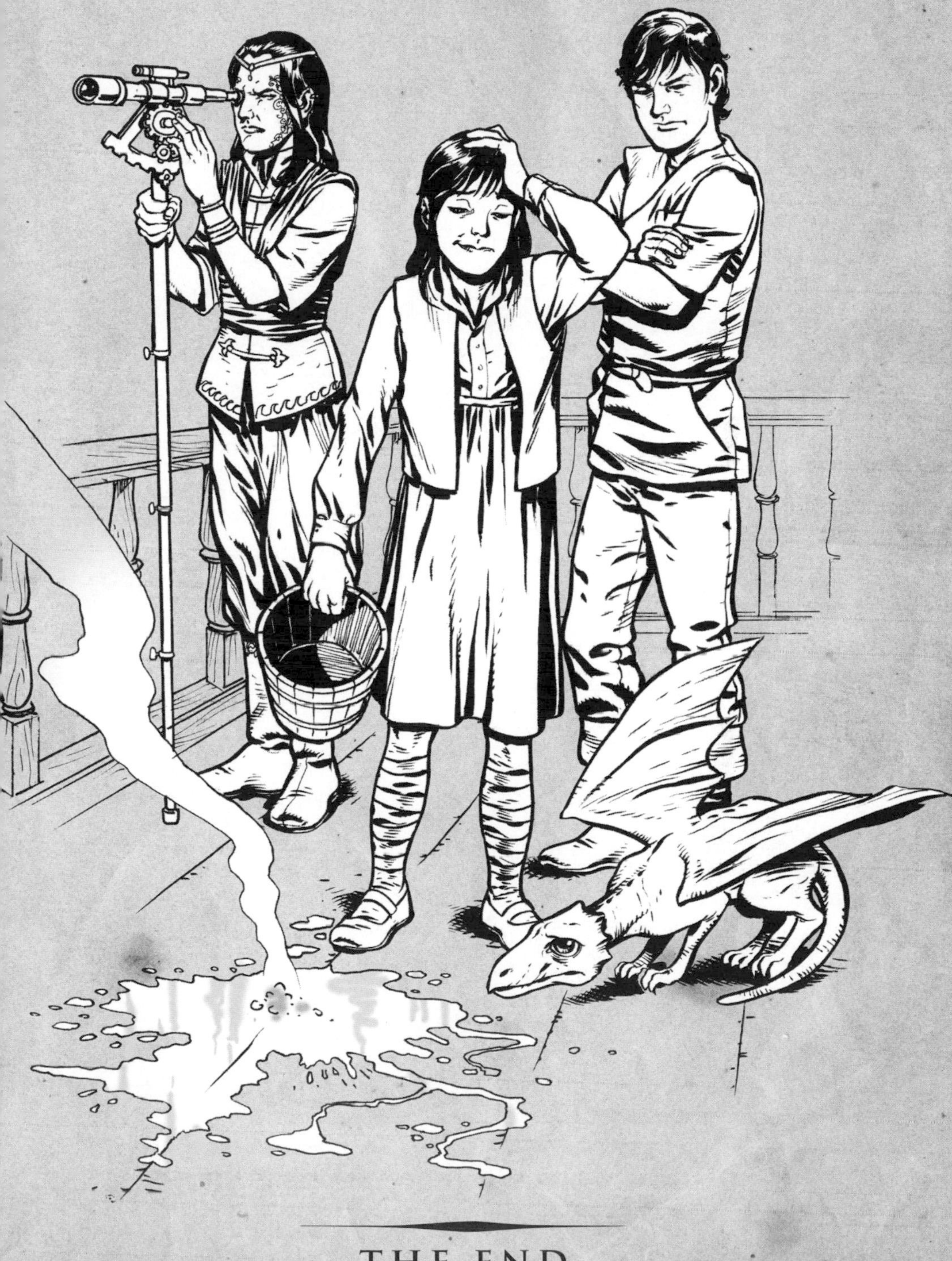

THE END

MORE TO EXPLORE!

Excerpts from the pages of Margolyn's field journals on *Reptila Mythicalus*

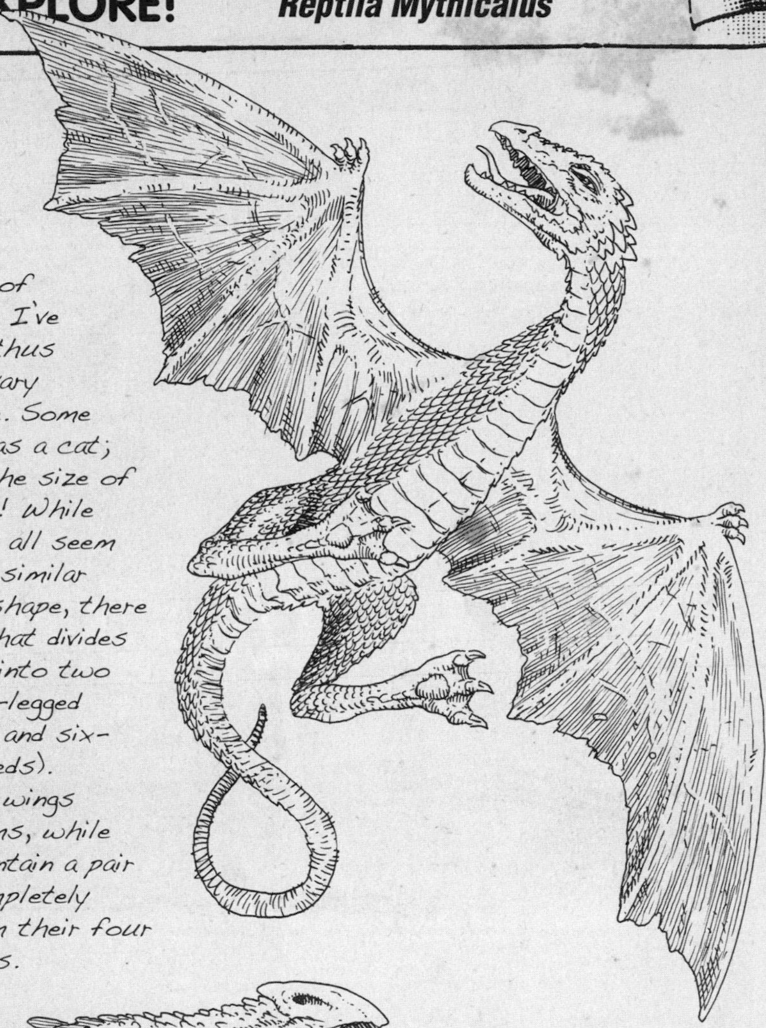

Flying Dragons

The varieties of flying dragons I've encountered thus far seem to vary greatly in size. Some are as small as a cat; others rival the size of the Dragonfly! While flying dragons all seem to maintain a similar aerodynamic shape, there is one trait that divides the category into two groups: four-legged (quadrupeds) and six-legged (hexapeds). Quadrapedes' wings double as arms, while hexapeds maintain a pair of wings completely separate from their four standard limbs.

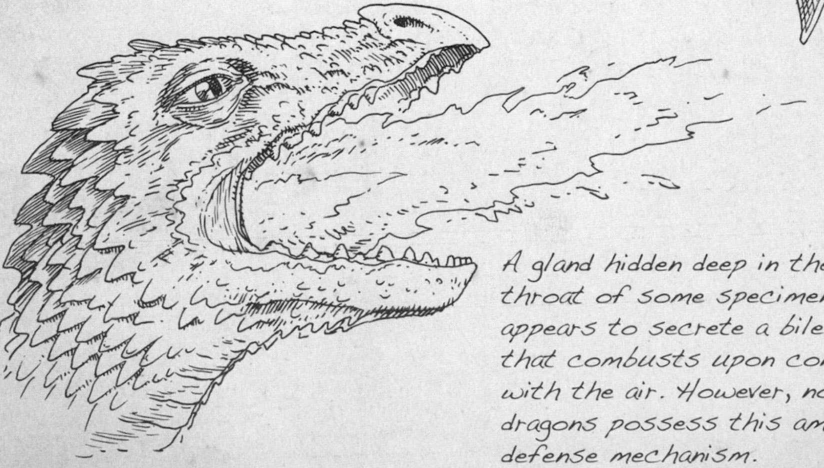

A gland hidden deep in the throat of some specimens appears to secrete a bile that combusts upon contact with the air. However, not all dragons possess this amazing defense mechanism.

Long tails provide balance for walking and flying. The creatures are so masterful with this appendage that it is practically an extra arm to them!

The hides of winged dragons (indeed, ALL dragons!) range widely—from smooth and leather-like, to flexible plates, to intricate scales. Despite this variety, their wings all have a similar light, leathery construction.

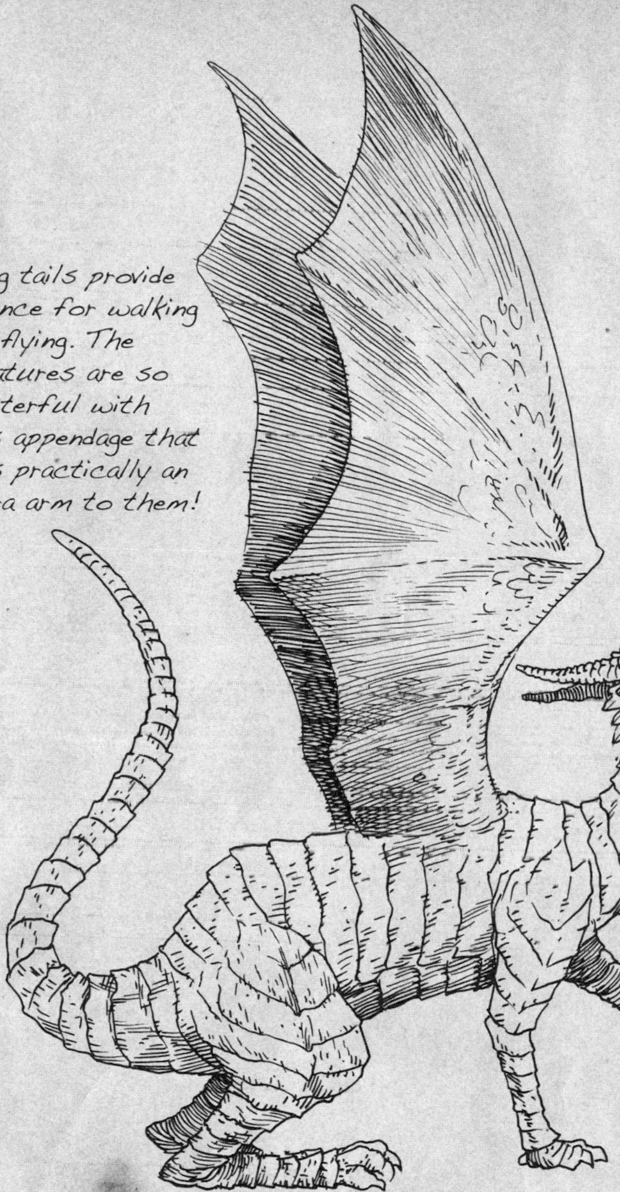

The huge wings required to provide lift for these beasts can fold remarkably small and close to the body!

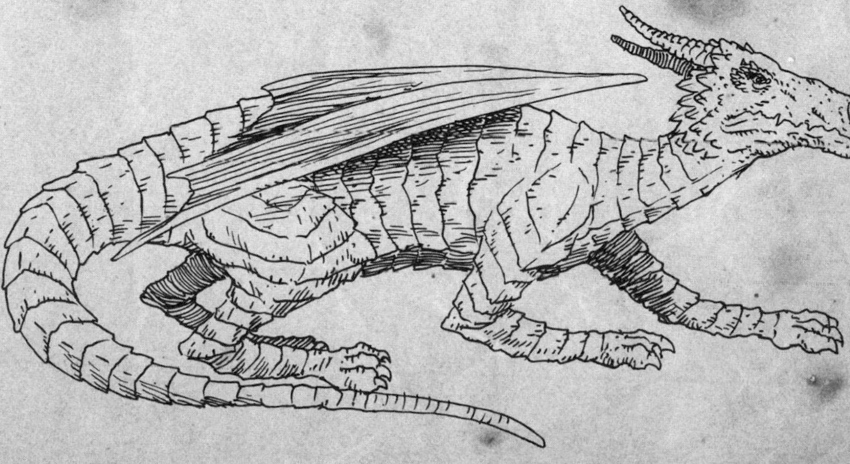

Land Dragons

The shape, size, and variety of
land dragons is truly astounding!
Cataloging these ground-dwellers
will be a daunting task, and
documenting their individual
habits and traits may
take more than
a lifetime.

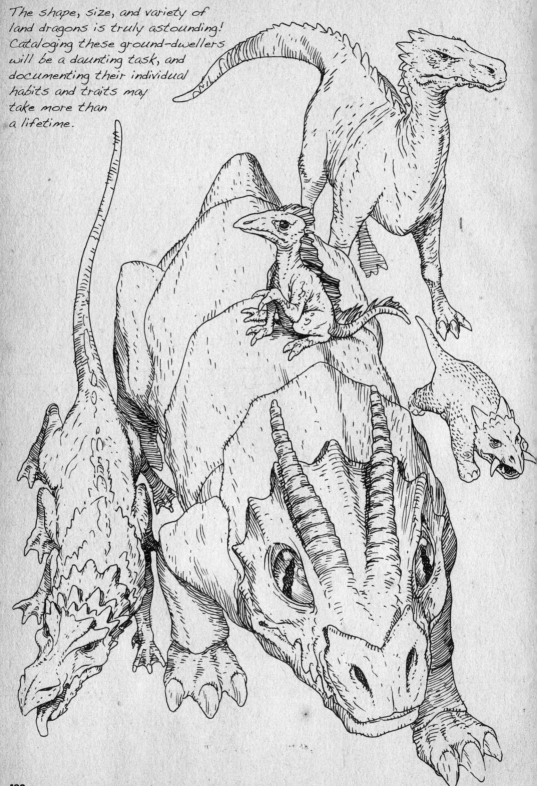

Gentle herbivores are most common among the land dragons, but there are carnivores whose territorial instincts make them aggressive and dangerous.

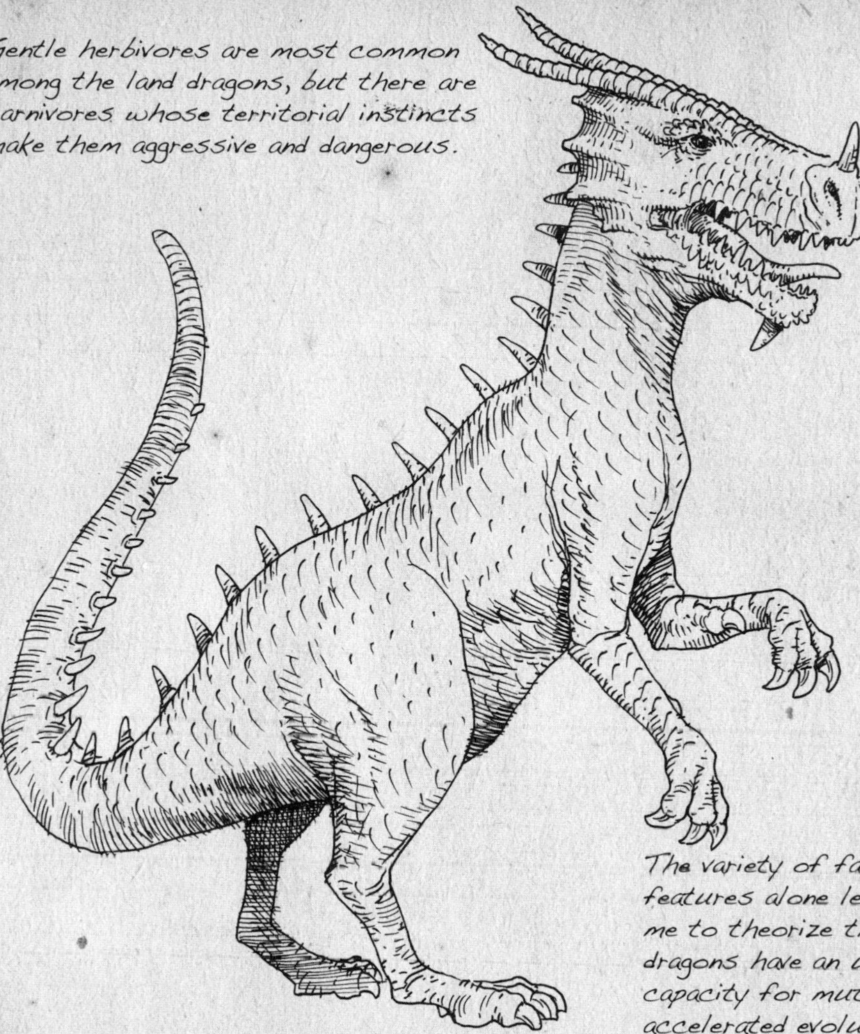

The variety of facial features alone leads me to theorize that dragons have an uncanny capacity for mutation and accelerated evolution.

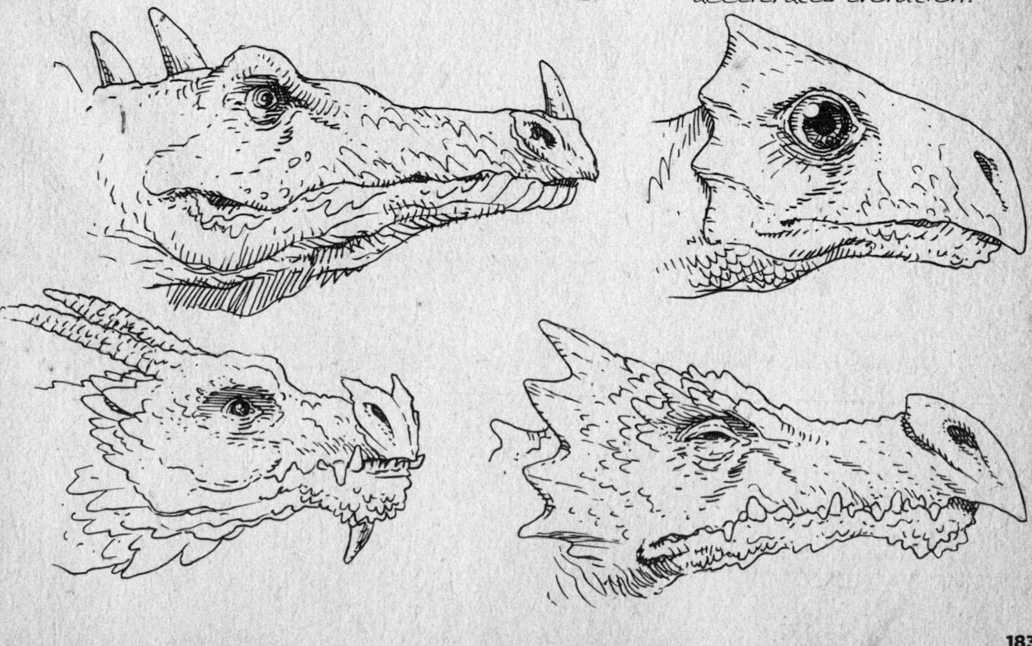

Sea Dragons

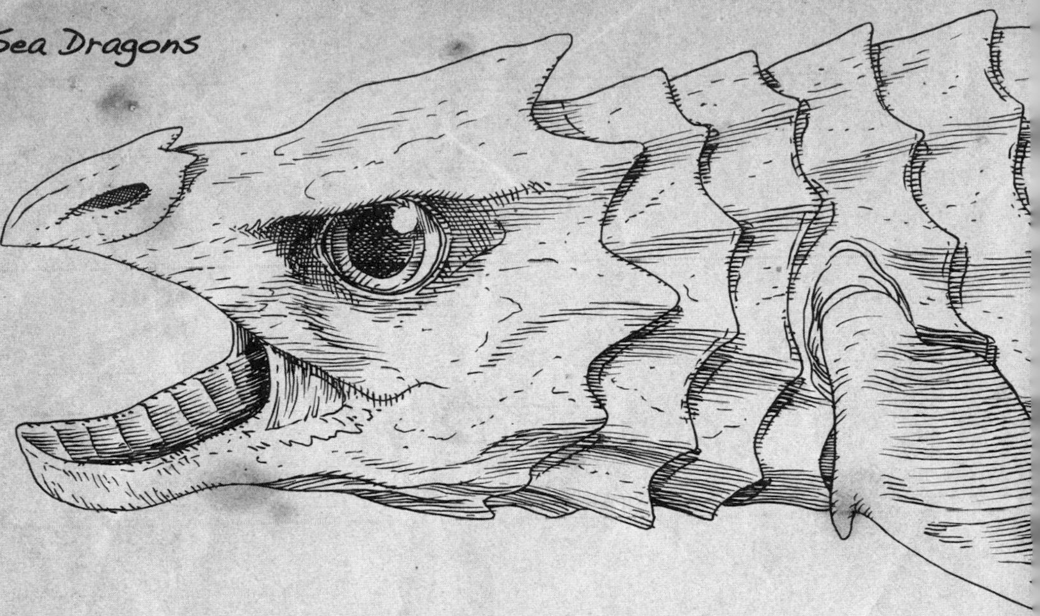

Sea dragons are the most mysterious members of the REPTILA MTYTHICALUS family. Their habitat makes them hard to observe and study, making reliable information about them difficult to come by. They can dwell in either freshwater lakes and rivers or salty open seas. Reports from terror-stricken sailors across the globe seem to indicate that some varieties of sea dragons are the largest beasts in the world. Seafaring folk refer to these giants as "leviathans."

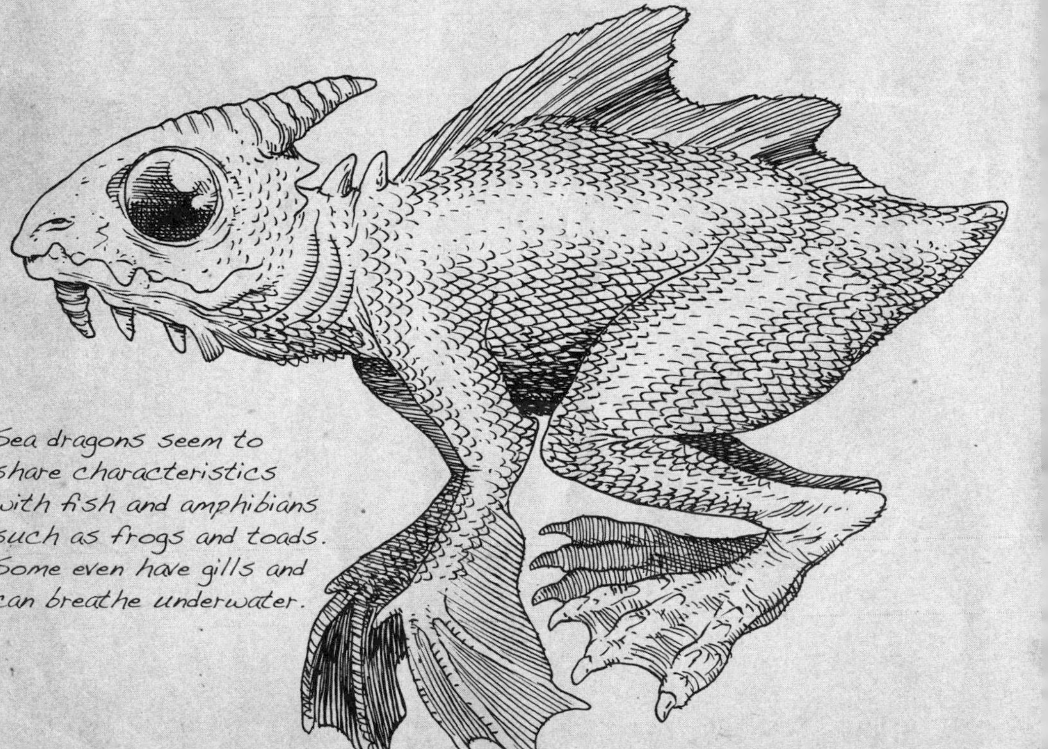

Sea dragons seem to share characteristics with fish and amphibians such as frogs and toads. Some even have gills and can breathe underwater.

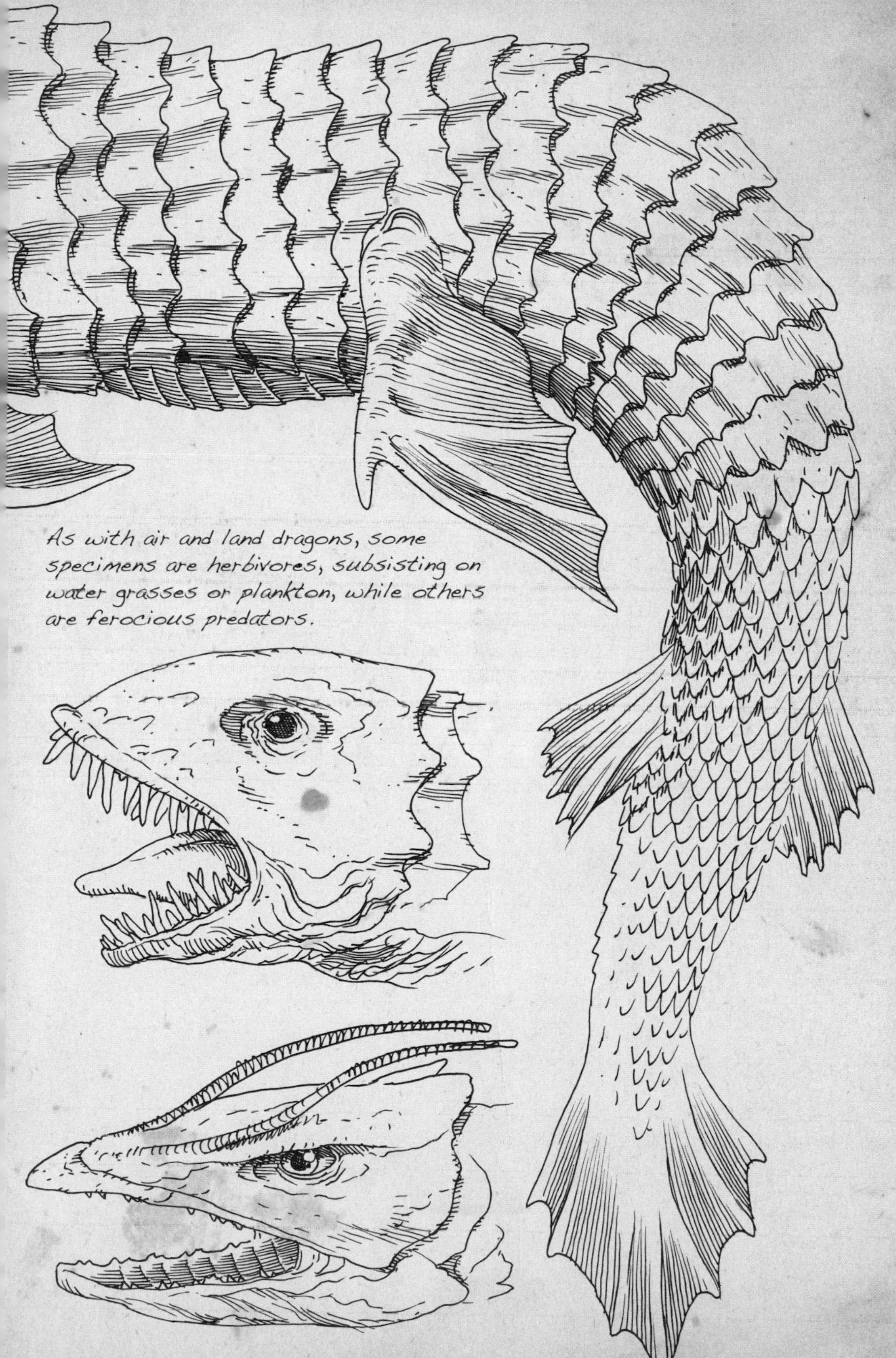

As with air and land dragons, some specimens are herbivores, subsisting on water grasses or plankton, while others are ferocious predators.

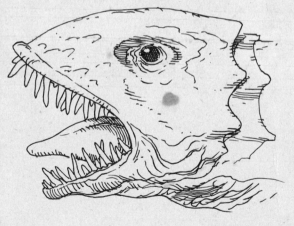

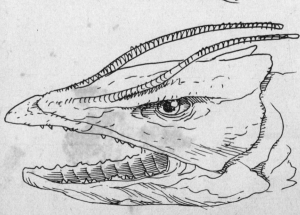

Top deck:
1. Rudder service platform
2. Balloon mooring arms
3. Benches/deck storage
4. Hot air cowling
5. Ship controls
6. Observation platform

Middle deck:
7. Galley/food storage
8. Engine room
9. Master control housing
10. Study/laboratory

Lower deck (Hold):
11. Armory
12. Cargo storage
13. Crane
14. Sleeping quarters
15. Retractable gangplank

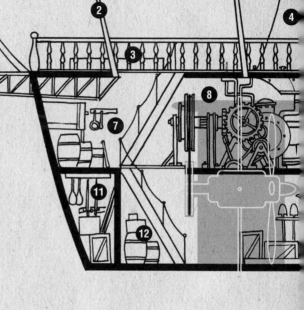

The Dragonfly is powered by an ingenious system of weighted ropes, mainsprings, belts, and gears that run its propellers, rudders, and other mechanisms. Since its weight must be kept to a minimum, it's constructed primarily of wooden framing covered in canvas and wicker. It is slow, as you would expect from a balloon-craft, but it has some maneuverability and propulsion capabilities thanks to its rudders and propellers.

Normally the hot air of the balloon is replenished by a heat pump system that circulates and heats air through coils in the sun-warmed wings and the friction-heated propeller mechanisms of the ship. Air is heated by a burner only when necessary, as the weight of carrying more than a small amount of combustible fuel is prohibitive.

Front view

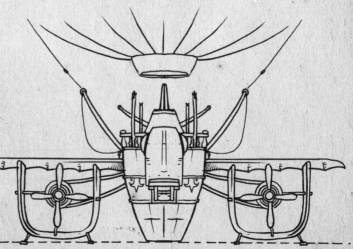

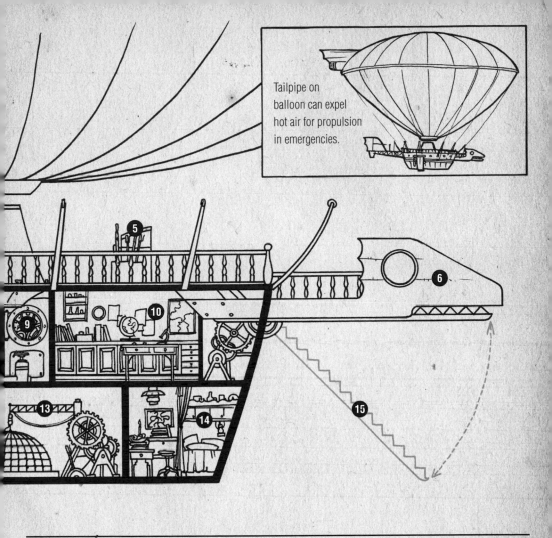

Tailpipe on balloon can expel hot air for propulsion in emergencies.

Top view

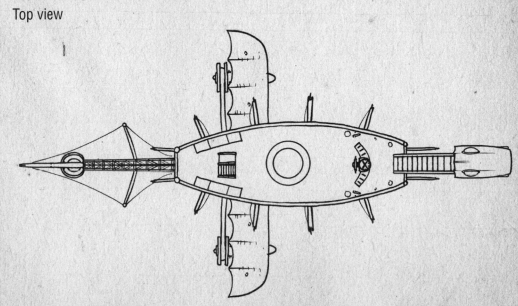

Early character sketches of the characters of *Dragon Girl*

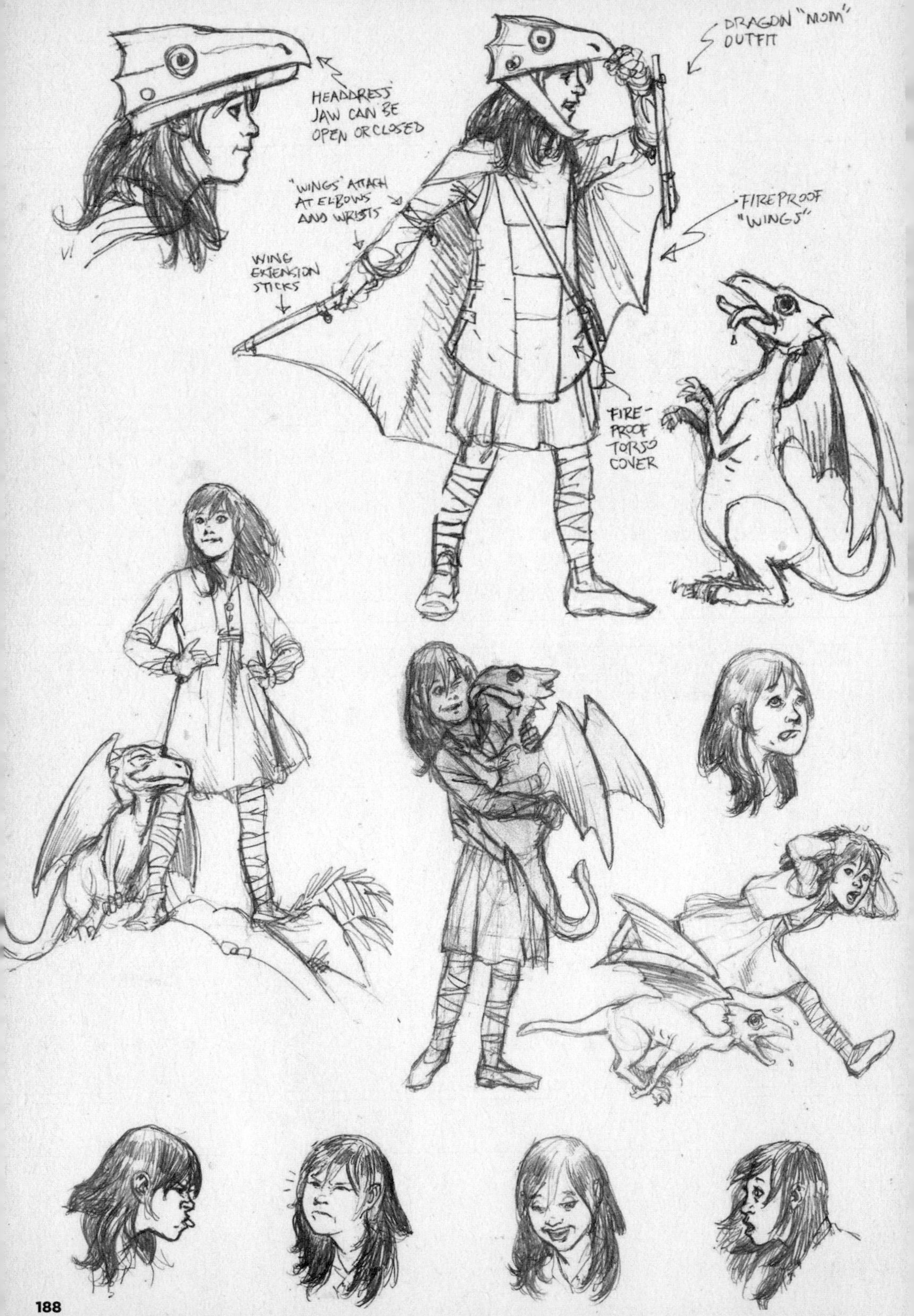
HEADDRESS JAW CAN BE OPEN OR CLOSED
DRAGON "MOM" OUTFIT
"WINGS" ATTACH AT ELBOWS AND WRISTS
WING EXTENSION STICKS
FIREPROOF "WINGS"
FIRE-PROOF TORSO COVER